M000158309

WITH FIRE AND SWORD

A TALE OF THE PAST

BY

HENRYK SIENKIEWICZ

TRANSLATED FROM THE POLISH
FIFTH AND REVISED EDITION

BY

DR. SAMUEL A. BINION

AUTHOR OF "ANCIENT EGYPT," ETC, AND TRANSLATOR OF "QUO VADIS,"
"PAN MICHAEL," ETC , ETC

WITH ILLUSTRATIONS BY
M. DE LIPMAN

VOLUME TWO

Fredonia Books
Amsterdam, The Netherlands

With Fire and Sword:
A Tale of the Past (Volume Two)

by
Henryk Sienkiewicz

ISBN: 1-4101-0058-8

Copyright © 2002 by Fredonia Books

Reprinted from the 1898 edition

Fredonia Books
Amsterdam, The Netherlands
http://www.fredoniabooks.com

All rights reserved, including the right to reproduce
this book, or portions thereof, in any form.

In order to make original editions of historical works
available to scholars at an economical price, this
facsimile of the original edition of 1898 is
reproduced from the best available copy and has
been digitally enhanced to improve legibility, but the
text remains unaltered to retain historical
authenticity.

INTRODUCTION.

Above the Marienkirche, in Cracow, rises two towers of unequal height, and crowned with strange cupolas like Oriental turbans.

Before the cathedral opens the old-world market place with its arches. If you stand in the market-place in the morning, or when the evening sunlight reddens the citadel of the Wawel, strange music suddenly breaks out overhead, sad, silvery; the clarion call of a by gone age. It re echoes away up in the blue, coming from one sees not where, and flows in waves of ringing, pathetic melody over the old capital of the Poles. Then the music suddenly ceases, and there is a stillness, a stillness even more mysterious than the sudden outburst of sound.

That music is a voice from the past. When the hosts were gathered against fair Cracow a minstrel in the highest tower of the cathedral cheered the hearts of the besieged with the martial strains of his clarion, that resounded with warlike challenge over the city, while the battle raged around the walls. A bullet from the enemy cut short his signal and his life; and ever after, morning and evening, the same melody rings out over the city for a memorial, but now in piercing sadness, like a dirge, and stops suddenly at the point where the minstrel fell, breaking off in the middle of a bar.

The life of the Polish nation might well take that broken music as its symbol: it, too, ended in the middle of a bar, cut off from among the nations. High up in the citadel, on its rocky eminence above the town are the crowns and robes and scepters of the kings of Poland, and all the royal finery of jewels and gold. The trappings of kings, but no kings to wear them. For the kings of Poland lie there, in their cold shrines of stone, in the vaults of the fortress:

and every morning and evening they hear the clarion dirge of the nation suddenly broken off. And the rest is silence.

In his great epic of Poland, Sienkiewicz has shown us the nation at the summit of its power—a kingdom—a commonwealth as strong as any in Europe, which had beaten the Tartars and Swedes, and before which even the grand dukes of Moscow had more than once retreated vanquished. Poland stretched from the Black Sea to the Baltic, across all Europe, and from the Dnieper to the Oder. The Polish arms had a thousand splendid achievements on their roll of honor, and were yet destined for signal victories over the Turks, which should leave all Christendom their debtors.

But the novelist also shows the seeds of the nation's ruin, ready to grow rank and luxuriant, even at the noontide of glory.

The Slavonic world was divided into three parts: the despotism of Moscow, beginning a new life under the young dynasty of the Romanoffs; the kingdom of Poland, really an association of powerful oligarchs, in which the mass of the people had no voice nor freedom; and the wild hordes of the Cossacks, where every man was his own lord among the great rivers that flow into the Black Sea.

To-day the despotism stands alone. It has overshadowed the free hordes of the Cossacks; it has overshadowed the kings of Poland, and driven back the Tartars to the uttermost verge of the ocean. It has, indeed, overshadowed much more—a sixth part of the whole world.

Sienkiewicz has shown the elements of disintegration at work among the Cossack hordes. He has also shown clearly the causes that ruined Poland: the kinglets rising up around the elective king with almost royal might, and with ambition too great even for kings. Then round the magnates Pototskis, Kalinovskis, Vishnyovyetskis, were the lesser nobles, withstanding them in their turn, as the magnates withstood the king. Then, beneath all, the people, dumb serfs, down trodden, with no voice in their destinies, and not even the name of freedom. A kingdom divided against itself and fated to fall. The vaulting ambition of the nobles caused their ruin and the ruin of their country. Foes from without had been powerless in face of a united land.

CHARLES JOHNSTON.

BOOK III

CHAPTER I.

It was a bright, clear night as a small troop of horsemen moved forward on the right bank of Valadynka, in the direction of the Dniester.

They moved forward very slowly, almost step by step. At their head, a little in advance of the rest, rode two of them as an advance guard. But there was, apparently, no reason to be watchful, and, instead of looking round them, they conversed the whole time; and, as they continually pulled up their horses, they would look back at those who were following them and call out:

"Slowly there, slowly!"

And the horsemen moved still more slowly. They hardly appeared to advance.

At length, as they rounded a hill which had shaded them, they came out into an open space which was flooded with moonlight, and one could now understand better why they moved so slowly. In the middle of the caravan, the horses carried between them a litter, fastened to their saddles, in which lay a human form.

The silver moonbeams lighted up the pale face and closed eyes.

Ten men rode behind the litter. By their lances without pennants, one knew they were Cossacks. Some of them were leading pack-horses, others rode untrammeled.

But little as the foremost horsemen appeared to be watching the neighborhood, so much the more uneasily and anxiously did the rest look round them on all sides.

And yet the region appeared to be a perfect desert.

The silence was broken only by the sound of horse's hoofs and the cry of one or two of the foremost riders, who, from time to time repeated the warning:

"Slowly, carefully!"

Presently he turned to his companion.

"Is it far, Horpyna," he asked. His companion, whom he

had called "Horpyna," a gigantic young woman dressed like a Cossack, looked up at the starry sky and answered:

"Not much farther; we shall be there before midnight. We are now goin along Uoroshchi Pass, then we come to the Tartar plains; and then we shall get at once into the Czortowy Jar (Devil's Hollow). Oh, it would be dangerous to ride through there after midnight before the cock crows! I might do it, but it would be hard with you, very hard!"

The foremost horseman shrugged his shoulders.

"I know," he said, "that you are allied with the Devil, but there are remedies even against him."

"Devil or no devil, there is no remedy," answered Horpyna. "If you, Falcon, should look the whole world through for a hiding-place for your young princess, you could not find a better one. Here, no one comes through after midnight, except with me; and no foot of man has ever trodden the Devils' Hollow. If anyone wishes his fortune told, they stand at the entrance to the Hollow and wait till I come out. Fear nothing! No one gets in there; neither Poles, Tartars, nor anyone else. The Devil's Hollow is gruesome. You will see it."

"Let it be as gruesome as it likes, I tell you I will come, and come there, as often as I have a mind to."

"Will you do it in the daytime?"

"Whenever it pleases me; and if the Devil himself stood across the entrance, I would take him by the horns."

"Ah, Bohun; Bohun!"

"Ah, Dontsovna, Dontsovna! Do not be worried about me. If the Devil gets me or not, it won't be your fault; but I will tell you one thing. Do what you like with your Devil; but if any harm happens to the princess, there is no devil or vampire who will be able to save you from my hands."

"They tried to drown me once when I was living with my brother on the Don; another time, the executioner in Yampol had already shorn my head, and still nothing happened to me. But that is another matter. I will watch over her for you. Not a hair shall fall from her head on account of the ghosts; and in my cave, she is safe from human beings. She will not vanish from you."

"Oh, you owl! If you say this, why did you prophecy to me that it would go hard with me? Why did you shout into my ear 'a Pole stands by her! a Pole stands by her?'"

"I did not say that; it was the spirits. But perhaps things

have changed now. To-morrow, I will tell your fortune above the water by the millwheel. You can see everything clearly in the water, but you have to look into it for a long time. You yourself shall see it; but you are a mad dog. If one tells you the truth, you fly into a rage and seize your axe."

The conversation ceased. Again, one heard only the sound of hoofs on the stones and other sounds which came from the river, like the chirping of crickets. Bohun paid no attention to these sounds, which might have aroused attention at that time of night. He turned his face up towards the moon, and became plunged in deep thought.

"Horpyna," he said, after a pause.

"What do you want?"

"You sorceress; you must know if it is true that there is an herb which, if brewed, will cause the one who drinks it to fall in love. Love-wort or whatever it is called."

"Lubystka. But no lubystka will help your misery. If the princess did not love anyone else, one might give it to her to drink; but, if she loves another—do you know what will happen?"

"What?"

"Why, she will love the other all the more intensely."

"Go to destruction, together with your lubystka. You can only prophecy evil, but you cannot advise me."

"Listen, then; I know another herb that grows in the ground. Whoever drinks of this herb will lie two days and two nights like a log and will not know what happens to him. I will give her some of this herb—and then . . ."

The Cossack raised himself in his saddle and looked the witch through and through with his gleaming eyes.

"What are you croaking?" he asked.

"Tayhodi," cried the witch, and burst into a frightful laugh; like the neighing of a mare.

The laughter echoed ominously in the sides of the ravine.

"Bitch!" said the Cossack leader.

And the fire left his eyes and he sank once more into deep thought.

At length he said, as if talking to himself:

"No! No! When we took Bar, I was the first who penetrated into the convent in order to shelter her from the drunken fellows and to beat in the brains of anyone who dared to touch her; and she, herself, plunged a knife into her breast—now she lies there unconscious. If I should touch her, only with my hand, she would stab herself again or jump into the river. I! unhappy one, could not prevent it."

"You are at heart a Pole and no Cossack; if you will not take possession of the maiden, Cossack fashion."

"Oh, if I were a Pole! if I were a Pole!" cried Bohun. "If I were a Pole!"

He seized his cap with both hands, for he was overcome with wild sorrow.

"She must have bewitched you, this young Pole," murmured Horpyna.

"She must, indeed," he answered sadly. "Oh, if the first bullet had only killed me, or that I had ended my dog's life on the stake. . . . I desire only one being in the world, and this one will not have me."

"Fool!" cried Horpyna, angrily, "why, you have her!"

"Shut your jaw," answered the Cossack furiously.

"And, if she kills herself, what then?"

"Then I would tear you to pieces; tear myself to pieces; dash my head on the stones and bite everyone like a dog. I would give my soul for her, the honor of a Cossack; and would fly to Yahorlik, and farther away, to the end of the world; if I could fly with her, if I could live with her, could die with her!"

"Nothing will happen to her; she will not die."

"If she should die, I would nail you to the door!"

"You have no authority over her."

"I have none, none at all. I would that she might stab me with her knife; that she might kill me; it would be better."

"The foolish little Pole. If she would only give herself to you of her own free will. Could she find a better one than you?"

"If you can manage that, I will send you a pot full of ducats and another full of pearls. We got good booty in Bar, and before that, too."

"You are rich as Prince Yeremy—and loaded with fame. They say that even Kshyvonos fears you."

The Cossack waved his hand.

"What good does that all do me, when my heart aches?"

And again, there was a silence. The river bank became more wild, more desolate. The pale moonlight gave fantastic shapes to the trees and rocks. Presently Horpyna spoke.

"Here is the Uoroshchi Pass. We must ride together."

"Why?"

"It is uncanny here."

They reined in their horses and, in a few minutes, were joined by those that were riding behind them. Bohun rose in his stirrups, and looked into the litter.

"Is she asleep?" he asked.

"She is sleeping as sweetly as a child," answered the old Cossack.

"I gave her a sleeping draught," said the fortune teller.

"Slowly, carefully," said Bohun, almost devouring the sleeping form with his eyes. Do not waken her. The moon is shining straight in her face, my darling."

"Quiet; do not wake her," whispered one of the Cossacks.

And the cavalcade proceeded on its way. They soon reached the Uoroshchi Pass. This was a low, barren hill, that lay close by the river; like a round disk on the ground. The moon streamed down on it and lighted up the white stones that were spread over its whole surface. In places, these formed heaps and looked like the remains of ruined churches and castles. In some places, there were flat stones that stood on end and looked like gravestones in a church-yard. The whole hill looked like a great heap of ruins. Possibly, at one time, long ago, in the time of the Yagyello, men had lived here. Now, the hill and the whole region, as far as Rashkov, was a desolate wilderness in which only wild animals dwelt and where at night, lost souls carried on their orgies.

The cavalcade had hardly ascended the hills halfway, when the light wind which had been blowing changed to a regular storm, which blew around the hill with a peculiar melancholy and ominous whistling sound and it seemed to the Cossacks as though, from among these ruins heavy sighs and groans issued as though forced from some human breast, and then changed into laughing and crying voices of children. The whole hill seemed alive and began to resound with various voices. Behind the stones, tall dark forms seemed to look forth; strange shadows glided forth among the pebbles; in the semi-darkness weird lights gleamed in the distance, like the glittering of wolves eyes. Finally, from the farther end of the hill, between the heaps of stones and ruins there came a howling as from the depths of the earth, which was also accompanied by the former sounds.

"Are those siromakhs?" whispered a young Cossack to the leader.

"No, those are vampires!" answered another, softly.

"Oh God, have mercy on us!" cried others, as they took off their caps and crossed themselves devoutly.

The horses pricked up their ears and snorted. Horpyna, who rode at the head of the cavalcade, growled, half to herself, and half aloud, some unintelligible words like a Satanic pater.

When they arrived at the end of the pass, she turned and said:

"It is all right now. I had to restrain them with a charm for they were very hungry."

Every breast uttered a sigh of relief. Bohun and Horpyna again rode on in front; but the Cossacks who shortly before had held their breath began to whisper and talk to one another. Each one remembered some former adventures with spirits and ghosts.

"If Horpyna were not here, we should never get through," said one of the men.

"She is a great sorceress."

"And our Ataman is not afraid of 'didkas.' He saw nothing, he heard nothing; he was only looking round at the young lady."

"If what happened to me had happened to him, he would not feel so safe," answered the sergeant.

"And what happened to you, Father Ovsivuy?"

"I was riding once from Reimentarovki to Hulaypol. It was at night and I was passing by a graveyard. Suddenly, I saw something spring from one of the grave-mounds to my saddle-cloth. I looked round. It was a deathly pale child. The Tartars had probably taken it from its mother to sell it as a slave and it died on the way unbaptized. The eyes shone like two candles; it moaned and moaned. It sprang from the saddle-cloth to my neck and I felt that it was biting me behind the ear. Oh, God! A vampire! . . . But I had served long in Wallachia, and, there, there are more vampires than people; but there is a protection against them. I sprang from my horse and stuck the blade of my sword into the earth. Perish! I cried. The Vampire moaned, seized the blade, and glided down it under the ground. I traced a cross on the earth with my sword and rode away."

"Then there are a great many vampires in Wallachia, father?"

"Every other Wallach changes into a vampire after his

death, and the Wallachian vampires are the worst of all. They call them there Brukolaks."

"And which is stronger, father, a 'didka' or a vampire?"

"A didka is stronger, but a vampire is more tenacious. If you know how to manage a didka, it will serve you, but the vampire is good for nothing; it only scents blood. But a didka is its ataman."

"And Horpyna rules the didkas."

"It must be so. As long as she lives, she will rule them Why, if she had no power over them, the Ataman would not give his darling up to her; for the vampires thirst for maiden's blood above all."

"I have heard that they cannot do anything to the souls of the innocent."

"Not to the soul but to the body."

"It would be too bad for the beauty! She is like milk and blood. Our little father knew right well what to capture in Bar!"

Ovsivuy clacked his tongue.

"I cannot blame him. The golden Polish girl."

"I am sorry for her, father," said the young Cossack. "When we laid her in the litter, she folded her little white hands and prayed and prayed, 'kill me,' she entreated! 'Do not ruin me; wretched one!'"

"No evil will happen to her!"

Further conversation was interrupted by the approach of Horpyna.

"Hey, Cossacks," said the seeress, "this is the Tartar plain, but do not be afraid. Only once a year, do they have a bad night here; and the Devils' Glen and my abode are close at hand."

Presently, the sound of dogs barking was heard. The cavalcade stepped into the entrance of the glen, which lead down almost perpendicularly from the banks of the river and was so narrow that four riders abreast could hardly pass along it. At the bottom of the glen was a spring, which gleamed in the moonlight as it hurried to meet the river. As the cavalcade advanced, they found that the walls of the cave widened out and enclosed a roomy, level space which was shut in on all sides by rocks. Here and there were trees. No breath of wind stirred their leaves. Long, black shadows from the trees fell on the ground. In the spaces lighted by the moon, gleamed white, round or longish objects, which the horrified

28

Cossacks recognized as human ribs and skulls. They looked round mistrustfully, crossing themselves from time to time on breast and brow. A light suddenly flashed in the distance between the trees and, at the same moment, two large, ugly black dogs approached, howling and barking at the sight of the men and horses. On hearing Horpyna's shouts, they were soon pacified and walked round the horsemen growling.

"These are not dogs," whispered the Cossacks. "These are not dogs," grunted old Ovsivuy, in a tone which evinced his conviction.

Behind the trees, a shanty, and behind it a stable, and then a dark building appeared. The shanty looked outwardly neat and roomy. The windows were lighted.

"That is my dwelling," said Horpyna to Bohun. Yonder is the mill which grinds no wheat but our own; but I am a prophet, and prophesy from the water above the wheel. I will also prophesy for you. The young lady must go into the stranger's room but, if you wish to make it pretty, we must take her over to the other side first. Stop here, and dismount."

The cavalcade came to a standstill. Horpyna began to call:

"Cheremis! Huku! Cheremis! Huku!"

A form, holding a bundle of pitch-pine shavings in his hand, stepped before the house and, raising this flaming wood in his hand, silently observed those present. It was an old, ugly, gray-haired man; almost a dwarf in stature; with a flat, square face and slanting eyes.

"What kind of a devil are you?" asked Bohun.

"You must not ask him," said the giantess, "His tongue is cut out."

"Come nearer."

"Listen," said the woman, "perhaps we can take the young girl into the mill, the Cossack will be trimming up the guest-room and hammering nails into the walls and that will wake her up."

The Cossacks had dismounted and were carefully unfastening the litter. Bohun, himself, watched everything with the greatest anxiety and himself bore the end of the litter towards the head, as they carried her into the mill. Karzel went on ahead holding the pitch-pine torch. The princess, who was still sleeping from the effect of the draught which Horpyna had prepared for her from soporific herbs, did not

awake; though her eyelids twitched from the glare of the
torches which lighted up her face with a rosy glow. Perhaps
she was being soothed by wonderful dreams, for she smiled
sweetly whilst they carried the litter, though it resembled a
funeral procession. Bohun gazed at her. He felt as though
his heart would burst his ribs. "My darling, my darling,"
he whispered softly and the stern, though handsome, face of
the chief became gentle, and glowed in the reflection of the
great love which had taken him captive, and which forged his
fetters ever more firmly; as the wild steppes are gradually
overspread by flames from the embers which the traveller
has forgotten to extinguish.

Horpyna, who was walking beside him, said:

"When she awakes from this sleep she will be well."

"God be praised! God be praised!" answered the chieftain.

Meanwhile, the Cossacks had begun to take the packs off
the six horses before the door of the cabin, and to unpack the
pieces of furniture, rugs, and other treasures that they had
plundered in Bar. A good fire had been made in the guest-
room and while some of the men continued to bring fresh
rugs and draperies, the others fastened these on the wooden
walls. Bohun had not only thought of a safe cage for his
bird, but also determined to adorn it, so that the bird should
not find captivity too unbearable. He soon came back from
the mill and, himself, superintended the work. The night
was passing; the moon was withdrawing her pale light from
the summits of the rocks; and the muffled sounds of the ham-
mers was still to be heard. The simple peasant room was
transformed more and more into a habitable chamber. At
length, when the walls had been completely covered, and
everything put in order, the sleeping princess was brought
back and laid upon soft cushions. Then, all was quiet. Only
in the stables were heard, for a time, through the silence,
loud bursts of laughter, resembling the neighing of a horse.
This was the young sorceress, who was joking before the fire
with the Cossacks and distributing blows and kisses among
them.

CHAPTER II.

The sun was already high in the heavens when the princess awoke and opened her eyes. Her glances fell first on the ceiling of the room and from thence wandered around the room. Her awakening consciousness struggled with the remains of her sleep and her dreams. Astonishment and uneasiness were visible in her face. "Where was she? How had she got here? In whose power was she? Was she dreaming or was she awake? What meant this luxury that surrounded her? What had happened to her up to this time?" At this moment, the dreadful scene of the taking of Bar suddenly came vividly before her vision. She remembered everything. The slaughter of the thousands; people, nobles, citizens, priests, the religious people and children—the blood-stained heads of the "blacks," the heads and necks round which were twined reeking entrails, the noise of the drunken people; the day of judgment of the completely-destroyed town—and then, Bohun's appearance and her abduction. She remembered also that, in a moment of despair, she had stabbed herself with her own hand; and a cold perspiration broke out on her forehead. Perhaps the knife had glided aside, for she felt only a slight pain; and, at the same time, she felt that she was alive, that health and strength were returning; and, lastly, she remembered that they had carried her a long, long distance in a litter. "Where was she now? Was she in a castle? Rescued, freed, in safety?" and here, her looks wandered around the room. The windows were like those in a peasant's cabin, small and square. One could not see through them for they were made of thin skin instead of glass. Was this truly a peasant's cabin. But that could not be, for the splendor of its furniture contradicted such a supposition. Instead of a ceiling, the girl saw above her a canopy of crimson silk, embroidered with gold stars and moons. The walls, that were not any too large, were covered entirely with draperies. On the floor, lay a rug, woven in various colors; as though it were strewn with fresh flowers.

436

The mantelpiece was covered with Persian taffeta. Everywhere was gold fringe, silk, velvet; from the ceiling and the walls to the very cushions on which her head rested. The bright daylight which penetrated the covering of skin in the litlte windows gave some light, but was lost in the crimson, the purple, and the sapphire of the velvet, and seemed to make a rainbow-like twilight. The princess was bewildered; she could not trust her eyes. "Is this magic? Or have the hosts of Prince Yeremy rescued her from the Cossacks and placed her in a princely castle?"

The girl folded her hands.

"Holy Virgin, grant that the first face which appears at the door may be that of a protector and a friend."

Just then, through the heavy gold embroidered portière, there came to her ears, as from a distance, the sound of a lute and, to its accompaniment, a voice sang a song that she knew well:

> " Love for Thee is worse than sickness;
> Sickness is a passing ill;
> And life may yield fresh joy and hope,
> But Love's wound Time ne'er can heal."

The princess raised herself on her couch, but, the more she listened, the wider did her eyes open with terror—finally she gave a frightful scream and threw herself back into the cushions, as if she were dead.

She had recognized Bohun's voice.

But her scream had, at any rate, pierced the walls of the guest room; for, presently, the heavy curtain was moved aside and the chieftain himself appeared on the threshold. Helena covered her eyes with her hands and her pallid lips repeated, as in a fever:

"Jesus Maria! Jesus Maria!"

And yet, the sight that terrified her so, would have rejoiced the eyes of many a girl; for a radiance fairly streamed from the face and apparel of this young Cossack. The diamond buttons of his doublet glistened like the stars in the sky; his dagger and sabre flashed with jewels. His coat, made of silver lace, and the red Kontush, with the slashed sleeves, heightened the beauty of his tawny face. He stood thus before her, slender, black eyed, magnificent; the handsomest of all the young men of the Ukraine.

But his eyes were sad, like stars that are veiled by clouds, and he looked almost humbly at her; and, as she saw that the expression of fear did not leave her face, he began to speak, in a low, sad voice:

"Fear nothing, Princess!"

"Where am I, where am I?" she asked, looking at him through her fingers.

"In a safe place, far from the war. Fear nothing, thou, my beloved soul! I brought thee here from Bar that neither the people nor the war might do thee any injury. The Cossacks left no one alive; you, alone, came away alive."

"What am I doing here? Why do you pursue me?"

"I pursue you! My God!" And the chieftain folded his hands and shook his head, like a man who has suffered a great wrong.

"I am dreadfully afraid of you."

"Why do you fear me? If you command me, I will not move from the door. I am your slave. It is enough for me to remain here, on the threshold, and look into your eyes. I am not going to do you any harm. Why do you hate me? Oh, gracious God! At sight of me, you stabbed yourself with a dagger, although you had known me a long time and knew that I came to rescue you. I am not a stranger to you, but a dear friend; and, yet, you stabbed yourself with a knife, Princess!"

The pale cheeks of the girl became suddenly crimson.

"Because I preferred death to disgrace," she said. "And I swear, that, if you do not respect me, I will kill myself; even if I should lose my soul's salvation!"

The eyes of the girl flashed fire. The chieftain saw that there was no trifling with this princely Kurtsevich blood, which, in its excitement, would carry out whatever it threatened; and he knew that the girl would aim the dagger more surely the second time than the first.

So he answered nothing, but walked forward two or three steps to the window, and sat down on a bench covered with gold embroidery, and hung his head.

There was silence for a while.

"You can rest in peace," he said, "as long as I am sober, as long as the gorzalka does not mount to my head; so long, you will be to me as a statue of a saint in the churches. And, from the time I found you in Bar, I left off drinking. Before that, I drank, drank to drown my sorrow in gorzalka. What could I do? But now, neither sweet wine nor gorzalka passes my lips."

The princess was silent.

"I will look at you;" he continued, "gladden my eyes with the sight of your rosy cheeks, and, then, I will go."

"Give me back my freedom," said the girl.

"But you are not a prisoner? You are mistress here. And whither would you go? The Kurtseviches are dead; the villages and settlements are destroyed by fire; the prince is not in Lubni. He is marching against Khmyelnitski and Khmyelnitski against him. Everywhere is war, shedding of blood, everywhere are Cossacks, hordes and soldiers. Who will protect you? Who take care of you, if not I?"

The princess raised her eyes. Then it occurred to her, that there was still someone in the world who would take her to himself and defend her; but she would not name him, for fear of awaking the terrible lion. At the same time, a deep sorrow filled her heart. Was he still alive whom her soul longed for? As long as she remained in Bar, she knew that he was alive; for, immediately after Zagloba's departure, the name of Skshetuski came to her ears, together with the news of the victories of the terrible Prince. But how many days and nights had pasesd since that time! How many fights, how many dangers might have overtaken him! She could now only get news of him through Bohun, whom she dared not and would not ask.

She buried her head in her pillow.

"Then I must remain here a prisoner?" she asked moaning. "What have I done to you that you should pursue me like misfortune?"

The Cossack raised his head and began to speak, so softly that one could hardly understand him.

"What thou hast done to me—I do not know; but I do know that if I am thy fate, thou art also mine. If I did not love thee I should be as free as the wind of the fields, with a heart free from care, with a free soul and famous as Konashevich Sahaydachny himself. Thy cheeks are my fate, thine eyes are my fate; neither free will nor Cossack honor are any longer dear to me. What did I care for beauty until you grew from a child to a maiden! Once, I took a galley, on board of which were the most beautiful girls, destined for the Sultan; and not one of them won my heart! The Cossack-brothers played with them, and then I had a stone tied round the neck of each one and had her thrown into the water. I feared no one; no one dared attack me. I went to

the war against the heathen, took booty; and, as the prince
is in his palace, so was I on the steppes; and to-day—here I
sit, a slave, entreating for a kind word from you; and I may
not have it, and have never had it—not even then, when
girl, if you treated me differently, if you had ever treated
me differently, all this would not have happened that has
happened. I would not have killed your relations; I would
not have joined the disaffected peasants; but, through thy
unkindness I have lost my reason. Thou mightest have led
me whither thou would'st. I gave thee my blood, my soul;
now, I am stained with the blood of the nobility. Formerly,
I killed only Tartars, and brought home booty for thee that
thou might's walk in gold and jewels, like God's cherubim.
Why did'st thou not love me then? Oh heavy, heavy does re-
pentance weigh on my heart. I may not live with thee; and,
without thee, I canot live! Not at a distance, not near, not
on the mountains, not in the valleys—thou, my beloved, my
little dove! But pardon me, that I came for thee to Rozloga
in the Cossack fashion with sword and fire. But I was drunk
with anger towards the princes, and, on the road, I drank
gorzalka—I, unhappy murderer, and then, when thou fleddest
from me, I howled like a dog, and my wounds pained—I
would not eat, and I called my mother, Death, to take me
away—and thou would'st that I should now give thee up to
lose thee again, my darling my little dove!"

Bohun interrupted himself; his voice was choking and he
was almost sobbing; and Helena's face grew first white, then
red. The more intense the love that spoke in Bohun's words,
the greater was the abyss that opened before the girl, a bottomless abyss without hope of escape.

When the Cossack had paused awhile, he collected himself
and then continued:

"Demand what thou wilt! See how this room is adorned!
This is all mine, this is booty from Bar. I brought it here
for thee from Bar, on six horses. Ask what thou wilt—
yellow gold, rich dresses, bright jewels, humble slaves! I am
rich, I have enough property. Khmyelnitski will not grudge
it nor will Kshyvonos. Thou shalt live like the Princess
Vishniovyetski. I will conquer palaces for thee; will give
thee half of the Ukraine for, even if I am a Cossack, not a
nobleman, I am an bunchuk ataman. Ten thousand soldiers
are under me, more than under Prince Yeremy. Ask what
thou wilt if thou wilt only not leave me, darling, and learn
to love me!"

THE PRINCESS RAISED HERSELF ON THE COUCH.

The princess raised herself, pale as death, from her cushion; but her sweet, beautiful face bore the impress of such an unyielding will, of so much pride and power, that, at this moment, this dove resembled a young eagle.

"If you are waiting for my answer," she said, "know, that should I be forced to pass my whole life moaning in captivity, I would never love you, so help me God!"

Bohun underwent a struggle with himself.

"Do not say such things to me," he said in a hoarse voice.

"And do not speak to me of your love, for I am ashamed of it; it insults and angers me! I am not for you."

The chieftain rose from his seat.

"And for whom then, Princess Kurtsevich? To whom would you belong in Bar, if I had not been there."

"He who saved my life to disgrace and imprison me is my enemy and not my friend."

"And do you remember that the peasants would have killed you? It is frightful to think of it. . . . "

"The dagger would have killed me. You snatched it from me."

"And I will not give it back to you, for you must be mine!" said the Cossack exploding.

"Never, I prefer death!"

"You must and you shall!"

"Never!"

"Well, if you were not wounded, after what you said to me to-day, I would this very day send some soldiers to Rashkov and have a monk brought hither by the hair of his head; and, to-morrow, I would be your husband. What then? Is it not a sin not to love one's husband? Ha! Gracious lady, so, the Cossack's love insults you and makes you angry? Who are you then that I should be to you as a peasant? Where are your palaces, your Boyars, your soldiers? Why are you insulted? Why are you angry? I took you in war, you slave! Oh, if I were a peasant, I would teach you wisdom with a whip upon your white back, and satisfy myself with your beauty without the assistance of any priest. If I were a peasant, and not a knight!"

"Heavenly angels, save me!" whispered the princess.

Meanwhile, rage became more and more apparent in the face of the Cossack. Anger seized him by the hair.

"I know why it insults you, why I am distasteful to you! You are saving your maiden honor for another; but nothing will come of it, as true as I live, as true as I am a Cossack. For that mangy nobleman, that miserable Pole; death and destruction to him! He hardly looked at you, had hardly turned you round once in the dance, when you were completely infatuated with him! And thou, Cossack, suffer and break thy head! But I will catch him and I will flay him alive and nail him up. Know, that Khmyelnitski is marching against the Poles, and I am going with him; and I will find your dove, even if he were under the earth. And when I come back, I will at once throw his head on the highway under foot."

Helena had not heard the last words of the ataman. Pain, anger, her wound, excitement, fear, had robbed her of her strength, and intense weakness took possession of her limbs. Her sight failed and her thoughts became confused. She fainted.

Bohun stod there, awhile, pale with anger, foam on his lips, when, suddenly, noticing this lifeless, powerless form, with her head hanging helplessly, an unearthly cry escaped his lips.

"It is all over with her, Horpyna! Horpyna! Horpyna!"

And he fell to the ground. The giantess came hurrying to the guest room.

"What is the matter with you?"

"Save her! Save her!" cried Bohun, "I have killed her— my soul, my light!"

"Are you crazy?"

"I have killed her, killed her!" groaned the warrior, wringing his hands.

But Horpyna, approaching the princess, soon saw that she was not dead, but in a dead faint; and as soon as she got Bohun got out of the room, she began to restore her.

After a while, the princess opened her eyes.

"Well dearie, there is nothing the matter," said the witch, "one can see that you were frightened at him and lost consciousness; but the fainting-fit is over and your health will come back. You are as sound as a nut and will live a long time and enjoy happiness."

"Who are you?" asked the princess in a weak voice.

"I? Your servant, for so he commanded."

"Where am I?"

"In the Devil's Hollow. It is an absolute wilderness. You will see no one here but him."

"Do you live here too?"

"This is our farm. I am Dontsovna; my brother commands a squadron under Bohun; he has good Cossacks. And I stay here, and will keep you in this golden room. The cabin is turned into an enchanted castle. It fairly glitters. He brought all this here for you."

Helena looked sharply into the bright face of the girl. She appeared to be perfectly sincere.

"And will you be good to me?"

The white teeth of the witch gleamed as she laughed.

"I will, indeed! Why should I not," she said. "But you must be good to the ataman. He is a falcon, a famous young soldier. He will. . . . "

Here the witch leaned over and whispered something into Helena's ear, and then broke into a loud laugh.

"Away!" screamed the princess.

CHAPTER III.

Two days later, in the morning, Dontsovna sat with Bohun beneath a willow near the mill-wheel and looked at the foaming water.

"You will watch her, will protect her, will not let her out of your sight, so that she shall never leave the Hollow!" said Bohun.

"Towards the side of the river, the ravine has a narrow opening, but here it is roomy. Let the entrance be filled with stones and we will stay here as if we were at the bottom of a well. If necessary I can find a way out."

"What do you live on here?"

"Cheremis plants corn behind the rocks. He also plants grape-vines and catches birds in nets. With all that and what you have brought we have no lack of anything except bird's milk. Do not fear, she will not escape from the ravine and no one will find out that she is here unless some of your people gossip it."

"I have sworn them. They are all faithful Cossacks. They will not talk, although one should flay them. But you said yourself that people often come here for you to tell their fortunes."

"Sometimes they come from Rashkov; sometimes, when they know about me, from God knows where; but they stay by the river. You saw those bones. There were some who tried to come in. There lie their bones."

"You killed them?"

"Who killed them, killed them. Whoever wishes to have his fortune told, must wait outside the hollow; and I go to the mill-wheel. Whatever I see in the water I go and tell him. I will look for you in a minute, but I do not know if I shall see anything; for one cannot always see."

"As long as you do not see anything evil."

"If it is something evil you will not ride away from here. It would be better if you did not leave."

"I must. Khmyelnitski sent me a letter to Bar to tell me

444

to come back and he gave Kshyvonos the same orders. Now that the Poles are marching toward us with a large force we must keep our forces together."

"And when will you come back?"

"I do not know. There will be a great battle; greater than any we have had. Either we shall die, or the Poles. If they beat us, I will hide myself here; but if we beat them, I will come for my little bird and drive with her to Kiev."

"And if you fall?"

"That is why I've come to you to tell my fortune. I want to find out."

"And if you fall?"

"Our mother has borne us but once."

"Bah! bah! And what shall I then do with the girl? Shall I wring her neck, or what?"

"If you lay a hand on her I will have you impaled by oxen." The officer reflected gloomily.

"If I fall, tell her to think of me."

"Oh, the ungrateful little Pole! To think that she should not love you in return for so much love. If it were I, I would not be so contrary. Ha! Ha!"

With these words, Horpyna punched him twice in the side with her fist and showed him all her teeth as she smiled.

"Go to the devil!" said the Cossack.

"Now, now! I know that you are not for me."

Bohun stared into the foaming water above the wheel as if he himself could read his own future.

"Horpyna," he said presently.

"What?"

"Will she fret for me when I am gone?"

"If you will not make her your own Cossack fashion perhaps it is better that you should go away."

"I will not; I cannot; I dare not. I know she would die.'

"Then it is better for you to go. As long as she sees you, she cannot bear you; but, when she has stayed here with me and Cheremis for one or two months, she will begin to like you better."

"If she were well, I know what I would do. I would let a priest come from Rashkov and I would marry her; but now I am afraid that, if she should be frightened, she would die. You saw that yourself."

"Let be. What good would the Priest and the marriage do you? No, you are no true Cossack. No! I will not have any priest or any other minister here. In Rashkov the Tartars from Dobrudja are stationed. They would attack us and, if they should come, you would never see the princess again. What have you got into your head? Go away, and come back again."

"And you, look into the water and tell me what you see. Tell me the truth and do not lie, even though you should see me dead."

Dontsovna approached the trough and raised the second sluice that shut off the water from the mill-wheel. The flood poured with double force over the wheel which went round faster and faster, until it was completely enveloped in spray. Curdling foam gathered beneath the wheel, as from boiling water.

The fortune-teller fixed her dark eyes on that foaming water and, seizing her long braids that hung down behind her ears, she began to cry out:

"Huku! huku! Show thyself! In the oak wheel, in the white foam, in the bright spray, good, or bad, show thyself."

Bohun approached and sat down beside her. His face betrayed anxiety and feverish curiosity.

"I see," screamed the witch.

"What dost thou see?"

"The death of my brother; two oxen are dragging Dontsa to the stake."

"To the devil with your brother!" growled Bohun, who wanted to find out something else.

For a time one heard only the rattle of the wheel, which was turning madly.

"My brother's head is blue, quite blue. The ravens are pecking him," said the witch.

"What else do you see?"

"Nothing! Oh, how blue he is! Huku! huku! Show thyself! In the oak wheel, in the white foam, in the bright spray! I see. . . . "

"And what?"

"A battle. The Poles are fleeing before our soldiers."

"And I? Am I pursuing them?"

"I see you, too. You are fighting with a small knight. Hur! hur! hur! Beware of that little knight."

"And the princess?"

"She is not there. I see you again. Some one is with you who has betrayed you. Your false friend."

Bohun devoured with his eyes, first the foaming water, then Horpyna; and racked his brain to explain the prophecy.

"What friend."

"I do not see. I do not know if he is old or young."

"Old; quite old!"

"Perhaps he is old."

"Then I know who he is. He has already betrayed me once; an old nobleman with a grey beard and a white eye. Death and destruction to him! He is not my friend."

"He is spying on you. I see him again. Wait! The princess is there, too, with a coronet on her head, in a white dress; and, above her, is a hawk.'

"That is I."

"Perhaps it is you. . . . A hawk. . . Or a falcon? . . . It is a hawk!"

"It is?"

"Wait. There is nothing more to be seen. In the oak wheel, in the white foam. . . Oh! Oh! a crowd of soldiers, numerous as the trees in the forest, numerous as the thistles in the steppes and you, above them all; and they are carrying three bunchuks before you."

"And is the princess with me?"

"No, she is not there. You are in the camp."

Again, they were silent for a few minutes. The wheel whirled round so that the whole mill trembled.

"Ha! What is all this blood? So much blood! So many corpses, wolves and ravens among them. A pestilence comes from them. Nothing but corpses! Nothing but corpses! Far away in the blue distance, one sees nothing but corpses, nothing but blood."

Suddenly, a gust of wind blowing across the wheel swept away the cloud of spray and, at the same time, above them in the mill, the ugly Cheremis appeared, with a bundle of wood on his back.

"Cheremis, put down the sluice," cried the girl.

And then she went to wash her hands and face in the brook. The dwarf meanwhile put down the sluice and stemmed the water.

Bohun sat still in thought, and only the approach of Horpyna roused him.

"You saw nothing else?" he asked.

"I told you whatever appeared and could see nothing more."

"And were you not lying?"

"By my brother's head, I spoke the truth. They were going to impale him. With his feet tied to oxen, they will have him dragged to the stake. I am sorry for him! But he is not the only one who is doomed to death. How many bodies I saw! I have never seen so many. There is going to be a great war on the earth!"

"And so you saw me with a hawk over my head?"

"Yes, I did."

"And she had on a coronet?"

"A coronet and a white dress."

"And how do you know that I am this hawk? I told you about the young Pole, the nobleman, perhaps it is he?"

The girl frowned and reflected.

"No," after a while she said, shaking her head. "If it were a Pole, there would be an eagle."

"Thank God! Thank God! I am now going to the servants to tell them to get the horses ready and we will set out this night."

"Yes, it is necessary that you should go."

"Khmyelnitski has commanded it and Kshyvonos has commanded it. You saw rightly that there is going to be a great war, for I saw that in Bar, and also in Khmyelnitski's letter."

Bohun really could not read, but he was ashamed to acknowledge it, for he did not wish to appear uneducated.

"Well then, go," said the witch. "You are fortunate, for you will become a hetman. I saw above you three bunchuks, as clearly as I see these fingers."

"I shall be a hetman and marry a princess! It would not be suitable for me to marry a peasant girl."

"You might speak differently to a peasant girl, but you are ashamed of yourself before this one. You ought to be a Pole."

"I am not inferior to a Pole."

Then Bohun went into the stable, to the servants; and Horpyna began to cook the dinner.

By evening, the horses were ready for the journey; but the chieftain was not in a hurry. He sat in the guest room upon a pile of rugs, with a lute in his hand, and looked at the princess who had already left her couch, but had taken refuge in the other corner of the room and was telling her beads softly. She paid no more attention to Bohun than if he were not there. He, on the contrary, followed her every movement with his eyes, caught, with his ears, her every sigh—and knew not how he could bear it. He constantly opened his lips to begin a conversation, but his throat seemed choked. The pale, quiet face, with a certain expression of sternness around the mouth and brow, robbed him of courage. He had formerly never remarked this expression in her face. Involuntarily, the remembrance of similar evenings in Rozloga came to his mind, and a vivid picture of the Kurtseviches and himself, sitting round the oak table. The old princess was pulling the leaves off the summer roses; the princes were throwing dice, and he was watching the beautiful princess, just as he was now watching her. But, then, he was happy; then, she would listen to his stories of military expeditions with a zither in her hand, her black eyes resting on his face and her parted cherry lips showing with what interest she listened.

Now, she did not even look up. Formerly, when he played the lute, she would listen and look up at him, till his very heart melted. And yet, wonder of wonders, now, he was her master; he had taken her by force. She was his booty, his slave, he could command her—and nevertheless, he was formerly far nearer to her and felt himself far more her equal. The Kurtseviches were like brothers to him and she, their sister, was for him not only the beloved of his heart, the falcon, the dearest black-eyed girl; but, also, almost a relation. And, now, she sat there before him, a proud, gloomy, silent and merciless mistress. Anger took possession of him. He would show her what it meant to despise a Cossack! But he loved this merciless mistress; he would pour out his blood for her and, whenever fury possessed him, it seemed to him as though an unseen hand seized him by the forelock, as though a voice called into his ear, "Halt!" Presently, he broke into a violent fury, and then he dashed his head against the floor. The reason was this: The Cossack was filled with anguish; he felt that he was a burden to her in this room. If she would only smile on him once, say one kind word to him, he would fall at her feet—and then ride to the devil; to drown his sorrow, his anger and his feeling of humiliation in the blood of the Poles. But, here, he felt as though he were the slave of this princess. If he had not known her formerly, and known that she was a Polish lady of one of the first noble families, he would have had more courage—but she was the Princess Helena, whose hand he had sued for from the Kurtsevichi; for whom he would give Rozloga and all that he possessed. And the greater his shame before her at being a peasant the less is his daring.

29

Time pressed. From outside came the buzz of conversation from the servants, who were probably sitting in their saddles, awaiting the ataman who was suffering such tortures. The bright flame from the pitch-pine lighted up his face, his rich mantle, his lute—and the princess. If she would only cast one glance in his direction; The ataman felt bitterness, anger, oppression; he also felt foolish. He wished to take a touching farewell and feared that the parting would not be what he so longed for; he feared that he must leave her in bitterness, anger and pain.

Oh, if it were not the Princess Helena, who had wounded herself with the dagger; who would like now to kill herself; who was so dear to him, so dear to him, and all the dearer, the prouder and more cruel she showed herself!

A horse neighed outside the window. The chieftain gained courage.

"Princess," he said, "it is time for me to leave."

Helena was silent.

"And you do not bid me God speed."

"God speed," she said earnestly.

The Cossack's heart throbbed. She had said what he wanted, but he would have liked to hear it said in a different tone.

"Now I know," he said, "that you are angry with me; that you despise me. But I can tell you one thing; that another would have treated you worse than I have done. I brought you here because I could not do otherwise, but what harm have I done you? Have I not treated you as was becoming? Like a king's daughter? Say yourself! am I such a villain that you cannot give me one kind word? And yet, you are in my power."

"I am in God's power," she said, as earnestly as before; "but, as you have restrained yourself in my presence, I am grateful to you."

"Well, then, I will go with only this word of farewell. Perhaps you may repent; perhaps a longing will come over you."

Helena was silent.

"I am sorry to leave you here alone," said Bohun, "sorry, also, that I must go away; but it must be. It would be easier for me if you should give me a blessing on my journey. What can I do to conciliate you?"

"Give me back my freedom, and God will forgive you everything, and I will also bless you."

"Well, perhaps that may happen yet," answered the Cossack. "Perhaps you may yet regret that you have treated me so cruelly."

Bohun wanted to buy a leave-taking, even if with a half promise, which he had no intention to fulfil and gain his end, for a ray of hope beamed in Helena's eyes and the expression of sternness melted from her face. She folded her hands on her breast and looked at him with a cheerful face.

"Would you? . . . . "

"I do not know," said the Cossack softly, for shame and compassion were striving for the mastery. "I cannot now, I cannot. Hordes are encamped in the wild fields; divisions of the army are marching in every direction. The Dobrudja Tartars are marching here from Rashkov. It cannot be, now, for I am afraid—but when I come back. . . . I am a little child in your presence. You do what you will with me. . . . I do not know, I do not know." . . . .

"May God and the Holy Virgin protect you. God be with you."

She stretched out her hand to him. Bohun sprang towards her and pressed her hand to his lips. Then, suddenly raising his hand, an earnest look came into his face, and he let fall her hand. Going towards the door, he bowed himself repeatedly in the Cossack manner, and disappeared behind the portiere. Presently, a louder hum was heard outside. The clatter of weapons and then the words of a song sung by several voices.

" I shall be the bravest of all the brave,
Among the Cossacks, among my friends,
Through long, long years until the end of the world."

The voices and the sound of hoofs were presently lost in the distance.

CHAPTER IV.

"God has already worked a manifest miracle in her behalf," said Zagloba to Volodiyovski and Podbipyenta, in Skshetuski's chamber. "A manifest miracle, I say, when he helped me to rescue her from the hands of those dogs, and protected her along the whole journey. Let us trust that he will once again have compassion on her and on us. If she is only alive! But something whispers to me that he has stolen her again, for mark, gentlemen, as the informer told us, he has been made the second in command, next to Pulyan, under Kshyvonos. May the Devil take him! Therefore he must have been at the taking of Bar."

"Perhaps he did not find her among the crowd of unfortunate ones. There were twenty thousand killed there," said Volodiyovski.

"You don't know him. I would swear that he knew she was in Bar. I am convinced that he saved her from the slaughter and has taken her away somewhere."

"You do not give us much comfort or hope; for, in Skshetuski's place, I would rather see her dead than let her remain in those vile hands."

"And that is no comfort for, even if she be dead, she has been wronged."

"It is enough to make one desperate," said Volodiyovski.

"Yes, to make one desperate," repeated Longin.

Zagloba twirled his moustache and his beard and then he burst forth:

"Ah! May they get the scabs, the whole of this dog's brood. May the heathen make ropes of their guts! God has made all kinds of men, but they were made by the devil—such sons, Sodomites. May they be devoured by wild beasts."

"I did not know this sweet maiden," said Pan Michael sadly, "but I would rather that misfortune should pursue me than her."

"I have seen her only once in my life; but when I think of her I am so sad that I do not care to live," said Pan Longin.

452

"If that's how you feel," cried Zagloba, "how do you suppose I feel, who loves her as my own daughter and have brought her safely through so many dangers—how do you suppose I feel!"

"And how does Pan Skshetuski feel?" asked Volodiyovski.

Thus despairing, the knights presently became silent.

Zagloba was heard first:

"Can no one advise anything?" he asked.

"If nothing can be done, it is our duty to avenge her," answered Volodiyovski.

"God grant that we may have a battle," sighed Pan Longin.

"They say that the Tartars have already crossed the river and have struck camp in the Wild Lands."

"It must not be," said Zagloba. "We cannot forsake the poor girl without doing something to help her. I have dragged my old bones far enough in this world. It would be better for me if I could find rest somewhere, could stretch myself out in some bakery, to get warm; but, for the sake of this poor thing, I would travel far, even to Stambul, though I had to put on a peasant's jerkin and carry a lute; a lute, which I cannot look at without abomination."

"You are so clever. Can you not think out a plan how we can help her," said Podbipyenta.

"I have already thought of several plans. If only half of Prince Dominik's men were as devoted as I am, Khmyelnitski would long ago have been disemboweled and hung up by his feet on the gallows. I have already spoken to Skshetuski about it, but just now one can do nothing with him. Sorrow has completely unmanned him, and is wasting him more than an illness. Watch him, that he may not lose his reason. It often happens that a great sorrow will make the mind ferment like wine, until it finally becomes sour."

"It often happens, often happens," said Longin.

Pan Volodiyovski moved back and forth uneasily and said:

"What remedy are you thinking of?"

"My remedy! Well, first we must try and find out if the poor girl, the beautiful creature—may the holy Angels keep her from harm—is still alive; and we can do that in two ways. We may find among our Cossacks true and safe men, who will undertake to go over to the Cossacks, in appearance only, but in reality to mingle among Bohun's soldiers and try to find out something from them."

"I have Russian dragoons," interrupted Volodiyovski. "I can find such men among them."

"Wait a minute! . . Or we will take prisoner some of the rascals who took Bar and see if they do not know anything. They all look to Bohun as to a rainbow, so impressed are they with his devillish spirit. They sing songs about him—may their throats rust—and one relates to another what he has done, or what he has not done. If he has taken our poor child prisoner they will not hide it.

"We can send men to make inquiries and take a prisoner as well," remarked Pan Podbipyenta.

"You've struck it. The chief thing is for us to find out if she is alive. Then, as soon as you gentlemen desire to help Pan Skshetuski with a true heart, place yourselves under my command; for I have the most experience. We will disguise ourselves as peasants and try to find out where he has hidden her. Once we know that, I will lay my head we shall get her. Skshetuski and I have the most at stake, for Bohun knows us both; and, should he recognize us—our own mother would not know us again. But he has not seen either of you."

"He has seen me," said Podbipyenta, "but that makes no difference."

"Perhaps God will deliver him into our hands," said Pan Volodiyovski.

"I do not want to see him at all," continued Zagloba. "May the hangman delight in his countenance! We must go to work carefully, if we do not wish to spoil everything. It is impossible that he should be the only one who knows of her hiding-place, and it is safer to ask some one else about it."

"Perhaps our men whom we send out will find out for us. If the prince will only allow me, I will choose the most reliable and will send them out to-morrow."

"The prince will allow it, sure enough; but I doubt whether they will find out anything. Listen, gentlemen, something has just occurred to me. How would it be if, instead of sending out men we should dress ourselves as peasants and undertake the journey ourselves."

"Oh, no, that will not do," cried Pan Volodiyovski.

"Why will it not do?"

"You cannot understand military service. When the regiments, without exception, stand ready for battle, it is a sacred thing. Though father and mother should be on their deathbed, no soldier would demand leave of absence; for that would be the most dishonorable thing that a soldier could do, just before a battle. After the battle is fought and the enemy scattered, one may do it, but not beforehand; and remember, Pan Skshetuski, himself, may have the greatest wish to do the same, but he would not stir. He longs to go, the Prince loves him; and yet, he says not a word, because he knows his duty. This, gentlemen, is public duty, the other is private duty. I do not know how it is elsewhere, although I judge that it is the same everywhere. But, with our prince, it was never the custom to ask leave before a battle, not even for the officers. And, though Skshetuski's heart should break, he would not approach the prince with such a proposition."

"He is a Roman and a stickler for form, I know that," said Pan Zagloba, "but if anyone should whisper a word to the prince, he would probably grant him and you leave willingly."

"Such a thing would not occur to him. The prince is responsible for the whole Commonwealth. What are you thinking of? It is a question here of matters of grave importance, which concern the whole nation, and a private consideration would have no weight with him. And, even if he should voluntarily grant leave—which however it quite improbable—as God is in Heaven not one of us would now leave the camp, for we are bound in honor to serve our unhappy country in the first place, and not to think of our own interests."

"I know that also. I know and understand the service from early times; and, therefore, I say to the gentlemen that this idea only came into my mind, but I did not say that it had taken root there. Besides, to tell the truth, we could not do much even that way, as long as the power of those rascals is not defeated; but if they are beaten and pursued, and have to save their own throats, then we can boldly go among them and easily get information from them. If the rest of the army would only join us as soon as possible! Otherwise, we shall grieve ourselves to death near this Cholhanski Kamyen. If our prince only had the chief command we should have gone away long ago. But it is easy to see that Prince Dominik likes to rest quite often as he is not here yet."

"He is expected in three days."

"God grant that it may be as soon as possible. Is it not true that the Cup-Bearer is to come to-day?"

"So it is said."

At this moment the door opened and Pan Skshetuski stepped in. His face appeared to be petrified with sorrow, such a chill and stillness seemed to come from him.

This young face, so stern and earnest, was a strange sight. A smile never lighted it up and it seemed as if death itself would not alter him much. His beard had grown long, half-way down to his waist; his raven black hair showed a few silver threads.

His companions and friends divined his sorrow, though he tried not to let it be perceived; otherwise, he was perfectly conscious, apparently calm; and more zealous than before in his military duties, and quite occupied with the approaching battle.

"We were just speaking of your misfortune, and it is also ours," said Zagloba, "for, God is our witness, that nothing can give us any comfort. But it would be sterile sympathy if we only helped you to shed tears. So we have decided to shed our blood for the sake of the dear one, if she is still on the earth, and to rescue her from prison."

"May God reward you," said Skshetuski.

"We will go with you even into Khmyelnitski's camp," said Pan Volodiyovski, looking anxiously at his friend.

"May God reward you," repeated Pan Yan.

"We know," said Zagloba, "that you have sworn that you will find her, dead or alive; and we are ready, even this very day. . . ."

Skshetuski had seated himself on a bench with his eyes cast to the ground and said nothing. Zagloba was quite annoyed.

Could he intend to give her up? he thought. If he does, may God be with him. I see there is neither gratitude nor remembrance in the world; but there are others who will save her. Let them do it, for I would sooner draw my last breath.

Absolute silence reigned in the room and was only broken by a sigh from Pan Longin. Meanwhile little Volodiyovski approached Skshetuski and shook him by the shoulder.

"Where do you come from," he asked.

"From the prince."

"And what's the news?"

"I am going to-night on an expedition."

"Are you going far?"

"As far as Yarmolints, if the road is clear. Volodiyovski looked across at Zagloba. They understood each other at once.

"That is the way to Bar," growled Zagloba.

"We will go with you."

"You must ask for leave and find out if the prince has laid out any other work for you."

"We will go together. I have something else I wish to ask him."

"And so have we," said Zagloba.

They rose and went out. The prince's quarters were at some distance, at the other end of the camp. They found the front room full of officers from the different regiments; for soldiers came hither from all parts of the country to the Cholhanski Kamyen to offer their services to the prince. Pan Volodiyovski had to wait a long time before he and Pan Longin could appear before the prince, but Yeremy at once gave them permission to set out themselves, and to send out dragoon spies, who should pretend to desert from the camp and go over to Bohun's Cossacks and hear what these had to say about the princess. To Volodiyovski, he said:

"I am thinking up new duties for Skshetuski, for I see that he is buried in his sorrow and that it is consuming him. I am unutterably sorry for him. Has he said nothing to you about her?"

"Very little. At first, he started up and wanted to go blindly into the midst of the Cossacks; but he remembered that the regiments without exception were in readiness for war, and that we were in the service of our country, which must be saved before all else; and that is why he did not come to see your highness. God only knows what is passing in his mind."

"This has hit him hard. Watch him, for I see you are a faithful friend to him."

Pan Volodiyovski bowed low and left the room and, at this moment, the Voyevoda of Kiev with the Starosta of Stobnitski, with Pan Denhof the starosta of Sokalski, and other dignitaries, entered the prince's quarters.

"How goes it?" asked Pan Skshetuski.

"I am going with you, but, before that, I must go to my regiments, for I am to send several men away."

"Let us go together."

They went and, with them, Pan Podbipyenta, Zagloba and old Zatsvilikhovski, who was also going to his regiment. Not far from the tents of Volodiyovski's dragoons they met Pan Lashch who was rolling along, rather than walking, at the head of some nobles; for, like his companions, he was perfectly drunk. Zagloba sighed as he saw him. They had

become acquainted and grown to like each other at Konstantinov, from the fact that they had similar characters and were
alike as two drops of water.   Pan Lashch, although he was
an awe-inspiring knight, feared by the Heathen, as were not
many others, was at the same time a noted drunkard, glutton,
and dice thrower, who, in the intervals of fighting, praying,
duelling and slaughtering, loved nothing better than to be
in the company of such men as Zagloba, to drink for all he
was worth and to listen to anecdotes.   He was a brawler of
the first water, who, of his own self, created so much disturbance and so often transgressed the law that, in any other
country, he would long ago have lost his head.   Many sen-
tences were hanging over him but, even in times of peace, he
did not pay much attention to them and during war he forgot
them completely.   He had joined the prince at Rosolovtsa and
had done him no small service at Konstantinov; but, from
the moment they began to rest in Zbaraj, he became more
and more unendurable from the disturbances that he constantly created.   It may be remarked at the same time, that
no one could have told or have written down how much wine
Zagloba had drunk with him; how much he had talked to
him, how many stories he had told him, to the great joy of
the host, who invited him to come there every day.   But
since the news of the taking of Bar, Zagloba had become earnest; he had lost his humor, his vivacity and no longer visited
the commander.   Pan Lashch had begun to think that this
jolly nobleman had left the army and gone elsewhere, when
he suddenly came across him.   He stretched both hands out
towards him and said:

"Well met, sir, why do you never come to see me?   What
are you doing?"

"I am keeping Pan Skshetuski company," answered the
nobleman in a melancholy tone.

Pan Lashch could not bear Skshetuski because he was so
serious and he called him "The Sedate."   He knew of his
unhappiness, for he had been at that dinner in Zbaraj when
the news of the taking of Bar had been brought; but, as he
was naturally a man of unrestrained feelings and was also
drunk, he did not know how to respect the sorrow of others
and, seizing a button of the lieutenant's coat, he said:

"So you are weeping for your girl.   Was she pretty?
What?"

"Let me alone, good sir," said Skshetuski.

"Wait a minute."

"As I am under orders I cannot stay."

"Wait a minute," said Lashch, with the obstinacy of a drunken man. "You may be under orders, but I am not; no one can command me."

And then he repeated the question in a lower voice:

"Was she pretty? What?"

The lieutenant frowned.

"I must tell you, good sir, that it will be better not to re-open the wound."

"Not to open the wound? Do not be afraid! If she is pretty she is alive."

Skshetuski's face grew deathly pale, but he controlled himself, and said:

"Sir, do not oblige me to forget to whom I am speaking."

Lashch opened his eyes very wide.

"What does that mean? You threaten me? You? Me? On account of a wench?"

"Go your way, Pan Lashch," thundered old Zatsvilikhovski trembling with rage.

"You creatures, you grey-coats, you pack of servants," screamed the commander. "Gentlemen, draw your swords," and, drawing his, he sprang towards Skshetuski. But at that moment it was knocked out of his hand by Pan Yan and flew like a bird into the air, while its owner, who had lost his balance, from the force of the blow, fell over and lay full length on the ground. Skshetuski did nothing further but remained standing still, white as death, as though he were stunned. Meanwhile, a tumult arose. From one direction came the commander's soldiers and from the other direction Volodiyovski's dragoons, like a swarm of bees from a hive. There were loud cries of "Fight! fight!"

Many who came running up did not know what it was all about. Their swords clashed. At any moment, the tumult might have turned into a general fight. Fortunately Lashch's companions had noticed that an increasing number of Visni-ovyetski's soldiers were arriving on the spot. They were becoming sobered by fear, and, seizing the commander they fled with him.

It is certain that if Pan Lashch had been dealing with less well-disciplined soldiers he would have been cut into small pieces. But old Zatsvilikhovski needed only to cry "Stop!" and all swords disappeared in their sheaths.

Nevertheless, the whole camp resounded with the noise; and the echo even reached the ears of the prince, especially as Pan Kushel, who was on duty, dashed into the room in which the prince was having an interview with the Voyevoda of Kiev, the starosta of Stobnik and Pan Denhov, and cried:

"Your Highness, the soldiers are fighting with swords."

At that moment, the commander, pale and almost unconscious with anger, fell like a bomb into the room.

"Your Highness, justice!" he cried. "In this camp, things are going on just as they do with Khmyelnitski. No respect is paid to blood or rank. The officials of the crown are struck with swords. If your Highness will not exercise justice and sentence the guilty ones to be hanged, I must see to it myself."

The prince sprang from his seat at the table.

"What has happened? Who attacked you, good sir?"

"Your officer, Skshetuski."

The greatest astonishment was visible in the countenance of the prince.

"Skshetuski!"

Suddenly the door was opened and in stepped Zatsvilikhovski.

"Your Highness, I was a witness," he said.

"I did not come here to give an account of it but to demand punishment," cried Lashch.

"The prince turned towards him and, looking at him fixedly, said, quietly and impressively:

"Slowly! slowly!"

There was something so awe-inspiring in his eyes and in his quiet voice that Pan Lashch, although noted for his great boldness, was suddenly silent, as though he had lost his speech; and the other gentlemen were almost frightened.

"Speak," said the prince to Zatsvilikhovski.

Zatsvilikhovski related the whole story. That Pan Lashch had ridiculed, in a manner unworthy not only of a dignitary but also of a nobleman, the sorrow of Pan Skshetuski and had then sprung upon him with his sword, and, with remarkable moderation for his years, the lieutenant had merely satisfied himself with knocking the sword out of his opponent's hand. The old man concluded as follows:

"And your Highness well knows that, although I am in my seventieth year, no lie has ever passed my lips and never shall, as long as I live. I could not under oath change one word of my statement."

The prince knew that Zatsvilikhovski's words were as true as gold and he knew Pan Lashch equally well; but he did not answer. He took a pen and began to write. When he had finished, he said, looking at Pan Lashch:

"You shall have justice, gracious sir."

The commander wished to say something, but it seemed as if words were wanting and he put his hands to his sides, bowed and went proudly out of the room.

"Zelinski," said the prince, "give this note to Pan Skshetuski."

Pan Volodiyovski, who had not left the lieutenant's side, was rather uneasy when he saw the prince's boy come into the room. He was certain that they would have to appear before the prince at once, but the boy left the letter without a word and went out. Skshetuski read it and handed it to his friend.

"Read it," he said.

Pan Volodiyovski glanced at it and cried:

"A promotion!"

And, putting him arm round Skshetuski's neck, he kissed him on both cheeks. The colonel's full dignity in a hussar regiment was almost the highest rank. The prince himself was captain in the regiment in which Skshetuski served, and Pan Suffchynski from Siench was nominally colonel; but he was an old man and had long since retired from active service. Skshetuski had for some time performed the duties of both positions, which often occurred in other regiments where the two chief positions were often only by courtesy or honorary positions. The king, himself, was captain of the royal regiment and the primate himself was captain of the primate's regiment. The officers in both regiments, high court officials, also served actually as lieutenants and colonels. Such a lieutenant or rather colonel was Skshetuski, but there was a great difference between the mere exercise of the duties, between the honorary dignity and the real rank. At this instance, however, through this appointment, Skshetuski had become one of the first officers of the Voyevoda of Russia.

But, while his friends were shouting for joy and wishing him happiness on his promotion, Skshetuski's features remained fixed and calm; his face bore the same petrified, stern expression. For there were no dignities nor honors in the world that could now cheer him or give him any happiness. He rose, however, and went to thank the prince, and little

Pan Volodiyovski went to his own quarters, rubbing his hands.

"Well, well," he said, "to be appointed colonel of a hussar regiment; that very seldom happens to such a young man; indeed never!"

"If God would only give him back his happiness," said Zagloba.

"Did you notice that he did not move a muscle?"

"He would willingly resign," said Longin.

"I do not wonder, sir," sighed Zagloba. "I would give my five fingers here for her, although I took a flag with them."

"Yes, indeed, yes!"

"Then Pan Suffchynski must have died," remarked Volodiyovski.

"Probably he is dead."

"Who will then get the lieutenancy? The ensign is so young and only saw his first service at Konstantinov."

This question remained undecided, but Colonel Skshetuski himself brought the answer:

"Sir," he said, turning to Popbipyenta, "the prince has appointed you lieutenant."

"Oh God! Oh God!" groaned Longin, holding his hands as if for prayer.

"He might just as well have appointed his Lithuanian mare." growled Zagloba.

"Well, and the expedition?" asked Pan Volodiyovski.

"We are to start without delay," answered Skshetuski.

"How many men has the prince commanded us to take?"

"A Cossack and a Wallachian squadron, altogether five hundred men."

"Ha! That is a military expedition not a scouting party; but, if that is the case, it is time to set out."

"Let us set out! Let us set out!" repeated Zagloba. "Perhaps God may help us to get some news."

Two hours later, as the sun was setting, the four friends rode away from the Cholhanski towards the South. Almost at the same moment the commander with his men left the camp. A number of officers from the different regiments, came to see these last set out, amid cries and insults. The officers formed a circle round Pan Kushel who was telling them the reason why this man had been sent away and how it had happened.

"I brought him the prince's order," said Pan Kushel, "and,

believe me, honored sirs, it was an important errand; for, when he read it, he began to below like an ox when he is branded. He wanted to spring on me with his battle-axe and I wondered that he did not strike me. But it seems that he saw through the windows Pan Korytski's Germans, who were surrounding his quarters, and my dragoons, with their muskets in their hands, and then he began to shout:

"Well, well; I will go if I am driven out. I will go to Prince Dominik who will receive me kindly. I will not," he continued, "serve among beggars any longer, but I will revenge myself,' he screamed, 'as true as I am Lashch, and I will get satisfaction from that creature!' I thought he would choke with rage and he chopped the table in several places with his axe. And I must tell you, honored sirs, that I am not sure that some evil may not happen to Pan Skshetuski, for one cannot trifle with Pan Lashch. He is a hard, proud man who never let an insult go unpunished, and he is courageous; and, besides that, he is a 'dignitary.' "

"What could happen to Skshetuski while under the protection of the prince?" said one of the officers, "although he might be capable of anything this Pan Lashch, he would certainly respect the prince's mighty hand."

Meanwhile, the lieutenant not dreaming of the designs which Pan Lashch had formed against him, was riding at the head of his division and getting farther and farther away in the direction of Ojygovtsa towards the Bug and Medviedovki. Although September had dyed all the leaves yellow, the night was as clear and warm as in July, as it had been almost for the whole year. For there had been hardly any winter and, in Spring, everything had blossomed out at once where, in other years, deep snow lay on the steppes. After a very wet summer, the early autumn months were dry and mild, with clear days and bright nights. They rode forward therefore, at a good pace; not especially carefully, as they were still too near the camp to fear an attack. They rode fast, the lieutenant at their head with several horses; and, with him Volodiyovski, Zagloba and Longin.

"Look, gentlemen, how the moonlight lies on the hill. One could almost swear it was daylight. There is a saying that it is only in war times that we have such nights, so that the souls that leave their bodies may not strike their heads against the trees in the dark, like sparrows, against the beams in a barn; and may find their way more easily. This is Friday, too, the day of the Lord, on which no poisonous vapors rise from the ground, and no evil spirits can approach men. I feel happier and a ray of hope is dawning in my soul."

"The best of all is, that we finally got away and are trying to do something to rescue her," said Pan Volodiyovski.

"And the worst thing is to remain in one place with your sorrow," said Zagloba, "as soon as one has mounted his horse, despair falls gradually from one's shoulders, until it is finally completely shaken off."

"I do not believe," whispered Volodiyovski, "that one can shake off everything, for example, a feeling which has fastened itself in your heart like a leech."

"If it is sincere," said Longin, "it conquers you, even if you fight with it as you would with a bear."

Longin relieved his pent up feelings by a deep sigh, that resembled a puff from a blacksmith's bellows. Little Volodiyovski, however, raised his eyes to heaven as if he would search the very stars that were also beaming on Princess Barbara.

The horses of the whole company began to snort and the riders answered them with "Sdrov, Sdrov!" (Health! health!) Then all was silent until a melancholy voice in the rear began sing:

> " Thou marchest to war, poor little one
> Thou marchest to war!
> Thy nights in the open sky,
> Thy days sultry."

*   *   *   *   *   *   *

"Old soldiers say that, when horses snort, it is a sign of good luck. My deceased father used to tell me that," said Volodiyovski.

"Something tells me that we are not riding on a fool's errand," answered Zagloba.

"God grant that comfort may come to the colonel's breast," sighed Longin.

Zagloba turned round and nodded his head, like a man who cannot get rid of his thoughts. Presently he said:

"Altogether there is something quite remarkable in my mind and, in any case, I must tell you my thoughts, for I cannot endure them any longer. See here, have you not noticed that for some time, Skshetuski—I do not know, I may be mistaken—but it seems to me as if he thought less than any of us about rescuing that poor girl."

"What are you talking about!" answered Volodiyovski. "That is only his temperament. He will never betray his feelings."

"He was always that way."

"That does not matter now. Do you remember, sir, when we gave him some hope, he only said 'God reward you. Me and you!' as indifferently as though it were a question of anything else in the world. And God knows, it is black ingratitude on his part; for, how the poor thing longed for him, and how she cried on his account, would more than cover an ox-hide with writing. I witnessed it myself."

Pan Volodiyovski shook his head.

"It cannot be that he has given her up," said he, "although it is true that when we first saw him, when that devil had taken her from him in Rozloga, he was so desperate that we feared for his reason. But he is much more rational now. It is better if God has given him strength and peace in his soul. As his true friends we ought to be glad of it."

As he said this, Volodiyovski put spurs to his horse and rode forward to join Skshetuski, while Zagloba remained some time in silence beside Pan Podbipyenta.

"Do you not think with me that if it were not for love, there would be much less wickedness in the world?"

"Whatever God has ordained will come to pass," answered the Lithuanian.

"Oh, you never stick to the point. This is something totally different. Why was Troy taken? Eh? Will not this war be carried on on account of fair tresses? Khmyelnitski longed for Chaplinski's wife, or perhaps Chaplinski wanted Khmyelnitski's wife and, on account of their sinful desires, we twist necks."

"That was a dishonorable love, but there is a nobler kind which, thank God, is the more usual."

"Now you answer more sensibly. Will you soon begin to work in that vineyard. I heard that some one tied a scarf round you when you set out for the war."

"Little brother, little brother!" . . .

"But the three heads are in your way. What?"

"Ah, yes, indeed."

"Well, then, I will tell you what: Make one good stroke and cut off at a blow the heads of Khmyelnitski, the Khan, and Bohun."

"If they would only put themselves in my way," answered

30

Longin, his eyes turned to heaven and his voice trembling with emotion.

Meanwhile, Volodiyovski rode beside Skshetuski and looked at his deathlike face which gazed silently from under his helmet, until he presently pushed his stirrup against Skshetuski's.

"Yan," he said, "it is a pity that you give yourself up to your reflections."

"I am not thinking, I am only praying," answered Skshetuski.

"That is a holy and praiseworthy occupation, but you are not a monk that you should occupy yourself entirely with praying."

Pan Yan slowly turned his martyr face to Volodiyovski and asked, in a dull voice full of lifeless resignation:

"Tell me, dear Michael, what is left for me but to pray?"

"It remains for you to rescue her," answered Volodiyovski.

"I will do it—to my last breath, but, even if I find her alive, will it not be too late? God help me. I could bear anything else, but not that. God save my reason. I desire nothing further than to snatch her from those accursed hands. Then, she may seek refuge where I shall also seek it. It was evidently not the will of God. . . . Let me pray, Michael, and do not reopen my bleeding wounds." . . . .

Volodiyovski's heart was oppressed. He would willingly have comforted him, have whispered hope; but the words would not pass his lips, so they rode on in gloomy silence. Skshetuski's lips moved quickly in prayer, by which means he endeavored to drive away his dreadful thoughts, and the little knight was really frightened when the moonlight shone on that face; for it seemed to him as though it were the very face of a monk, wasted by penance and fasting and mortification.

> " Thou shalt find after the war is over,
> poor little one,
> Thou shalt find after the war is over
> Desolation at home
> And your body full of wounds.

CHAPTER V.

Pan Skshetuski made an effort to advance in such a way that he and his men might rest by day in the woods and ravines carefully stationing numerous sentinels around them, pushing forward at night. Wherever they approached a village, he generally surrounded it so that none could come out. He collected provisions, food for the horses, and, above all, he gathered news of the enemy; then he moved onward without doing the people any harm. After he had left, however, he soon changed his route so that the enemy might not be able to find out in the village in what direction he had gone. The object of the expedition was to learn whether Kshyvonos was besieging Kamenets with his forty thousand men; or, if he had given up the useless seige and gone to help Khmyelnitski, so as to fight a decisive battle; and, also to find out whether the Tartars of the Dobrudja were doing, whether they had already crossed the Dniester and united with Kshyvonos, or if they were still on the other side. This was very important information for the Polish camp, and the Commanders themselves should have striven to gather it. As, however, it never came into their minds, for they were inexperienced, the Voyevoda of Russia took his burden upon himself. Should it turn out that Kshyvonos with the hordes of Byalogrod and Dobrudja had given up besieging the hitherto impregnable Kamenets and have joined Khmyelnitski, it would be necessary to attack the latter as soon as possible, before his power had reached its fullest extent. Meanwhile, the general of the army, Prince Dominik Zaslavski-Ostrogski did not hurry himself and, when Skshetuski set out, he was not expected in the camp for two or three days. He was probably carousing on the way, as was his custom, and was enjoying a good time; and meanwhile, the moment was passing, in which Khmyelnitski's power could be broken. And Prince Yeremy despaired at the thought, that if the war was carried on any longer in this manner, not only Kshyvonos would reach Khmyelnitski with the Tartar hordes from the Dniester, but even the Khan, himself, with all his forces from Perekop, Nohay, and from Azov.

There were even rumors in the camp that the Khan had already crossed the Dnieper and was marching, day and night, with two hundred thousand horse; and still Prince Dominik did not arrive. It became more and more probable that the army that was stationed at the Cholhanski Kamyen would have to encounter a force of five times its size and if the commanders suffered defeat, would no longer be able to hinder the enemy from penetrating into the very heart of the Commonwealth to Cracow and Warsaw.

Kshyvonos was the more dangerous because, in case the commanders should try to make their way into the heart of the Ukraine, he could go directly from Kamenets towards the north, to Konstantinov, and thus cut off their retreat. And they would, in any case, be between two fires. Therefore Pan Skshetuski resolved not to wait for news of Kshyvonos but to check him. Quite carried away by the importance of his task, on the success of which depended the fate of the whole army, the lieutenant joyfully risked his life and that of his soldiers. But this undertaking might be considered the act of a madman if the young knight had intended with his five hundred men to attack Kshyvonos' division which had been strengthened by the addition of the hordes of Byalogrod and Dobrudja.

But Pan Skshetuski was much too experienced a soldier to undertake any such folly. He knew well that, in case of a battle, within an hour a wave of men would be riding over the dead bodies of himself and his companions; so he thought of other plans. First he spread the news among his soldiers, that they were going out as an advance guard of the whole division of the terrible Prince; and his news was told from mouth to mouth in all the country seats, villages, and little towns through which they had passed. It spread with the speed of lightning along the shores of the Zbrucha, Smotrycha, Studzienicy, Uushki, Kalusiku, and, following their course, reached the Dniester and beyond there, as if wafted by the wind, from Kamenets to Yahorlik. It was repeated by the Turkish pashas in Khotsim, by the Zaporojians in Yampol, and by the Tartars in Rashkov; and the well-known cry "Yeremy is coming!" resounded everywhere, and filled with terror the hearts of the rebels, who trembled with horror, and never felt secure by day or night.

And no one doubted the truth of the rumor. It seemed
quite natural that the commanders should attack Khmyelnitski and that Yeremy should attack Kshyvonos; such was
the situation. The latter believed it himself and let his hands
fall inactive at his sides.

What should he do? Go to meet the prince? His forces
were greater at Konstantinov and a different spirit ruled the
"blacks;" and, yet, they were beaten, their ranks broken to
pieces and they hardly escaped with their lives. Kshyvonos
was convinced that his Cossacks would fight like madmen with
any other army of the Commonwealth, under any other leader;
but at the approach of Yeremy's army, they would all fly
asunder like a flock of swans before an eagle, like the thistle-
down of the steppes before a wind.

To wait for the prince at Kamenets was still worse. Kshyvonos resolved to turn towards the East, and go as far as
Bratslav, to dodge his evil genius and to try and reach Khmyelnitski. It was certain that by making this detour he would
not reach Khmyelnitski as soon as he ought, and in time to
fight; but he would hear the results and, besides, have time
to think of his own safety. Meanwhile, the wind bore other
news; that Khmyelnitski had been killed. Skshetuski was
the first to spread the rumor. The unlucky Kshyvonos did
not know at first what he ought to do.

He decided, finally, to turn in the direction of the East and
to penetrate as far as possible into the steppes. Perhaps he
might come across Tartars and take refuge with them. Before
all things, however, he wanted to be certain; so he sought carefully among his officers one who was reliable and fearless
enough for him to send out with a detachment to gain information. The choice was difficult. There were not many who
had any desire for such an enterprise, and for this mission
one needed a man who would not let himself be compelled
through the torture of fire, the fear of the stake or the wheel,
to utter a word regarding Kshyvonos' plans of flight.

Finally Kshyvonos found one.

One night he sent to Bohun and said to him:

"Listen, Yurku, my friend! Yeremy is marching towards
us with a large army and we, unhappy ones, are lost."

"I also heard that he was coming. We spoke of it, little
father, before now; but why should it be all up with us."

"We cannot conquer him, we might another, but not Yeremy. The Cossacks are afraid of him."

"But I am not afraid of him—I conquered one of his regiments, the other side of the Dnieper."

"I know that you do not fear him. Your fame as a Cossack, as a warrior, may well compare with his fame as a prince; but I cannot give him battle, for my people will not. Do you not recollect what they said at the council? How they all wanted to attack me with their swords because I, as they said, wanted to lead them to a butchery?"

"Well, let us go to Khmyelnitski. There we shall get blood and men."

"They say that Khmyelnitski has already been beaten by the commanders."

"I do not believe that, Father Maxim. Khmyelnitski is a fox; without the Tartars he would not dare attack the Poles."

"I agree with you, but we must have certainty. If anyone who was not afraid of Yeremy would set out with some scouts and try and take a prisoner who could give us news I would give him a cup full of red golden crowns."

"I will go, Father Maxim, not for the sake of the red gold, but for the glory of a soldier and of a Cossack."

"You, the second Ataman under me, you will go? You will certainly yet be the first ataman of the Cossacks and have good soldiers under you, for you do not fear Yeremy. Go, you falcon, and then ask what you wish. I will say to you that if you were not going, I should go myself; but I must not."

"You must not, for, if you should go, father, the soldiers would cry out that their commander had fled; and they would scatter themselves all over the world. But, if I go, they will gain fresh courage."

"And what escort shall I give you?"

"I will not take many men. It is easier to hide and to creep about with a small number. But give me five hundred brave, young fellows and I will wager my head on it that I will bring you some prisoners with information, not any chance ones, but soldiers from whom you may learn everything."

"Start at once. In Kamenets they are already firing cannon for joy to welcome the Poles, who will destroy us, innocent ones."

Bohun left and began at once to get ready for his journey. His men were drinking, as was the custom on such occasions, for slaughter in case Mother Death should take them. And he drank with them till he foamed at the mouth and raged and stormed. And then he had a barrel of tar opened and, just as he was fully dressed, he threw himself into it, dived about in it twice so that his head was covered and called out:

"I am black as Mother Night. Poles' eyes will not recognize me."

And then, after he had rolled about in Turkish rugs that he had taken as booty, and rubbed the tar off to some extent, he sprang upon his horse and rode off, followed by his faithful warriors in the shadow of the darkness.

"To honor! To happiness!"

In the meantime Skshetuski had already reached Yarmoliets. There he had met with resistance, had bathed the inhabitants in blood; and, after he had informed them that on the following day Prince Yeremy would arrive, he allowed his weary soldiers and horses to rest. He assembled his comrades for a council and said to them:

"So far God has led us safely. I have remarked also, from the terror which seems to have seized the peasantry, that they take us for the advance-guard of the prince and believe that the whole army is following us, but we must be careful they do not observe that we are only one party going everywhere."

"And how long shall we have to go thus?" said Zagloba.

"Until we find out what Kshyvonos has determined to do."

"Pshaw! Then we shall probably not get back to the camp in time for the battle."

"That is possible," answered Skshetuski.

"I am not at all satisfied, sir," said the nobleman, "our hands got somewhat into practice on the rebels at Konstantinov. We beat a few men there, but that is like a fly for a dog. My fingers itch for more. . . . "

"You may perhaps enjoy more battles, here, than you think," answered Skshetuski earnestly.

"Oh, how's that?" said Zagloba very uneasily.

"Because, any fine day, we may come across the enemy. And, although we are not here in order to get in his way with our weapons, still we shall be obliged to defend ourselves. But, to come to the point. We must cover a wider stretch of the territory, so that they may hear of us in different places at the same time, and we must here and there cut down those that withstand us, in order to spread fear, and to scatter the same rumor abroad. That is why I think we ought to divide our forces."

"I think the same," said Volodiyovski. "We want to make

ourselves seem as many as possible, in order that those who escape may give Kshyvonos news that hundreds of thousands are coming."

"Lieutenant, you are our leader. It is for you to command," said Podbipyenta.

"Well, I will go through Zinkov to Solodkovtsa, and if possible still farther," said Skshetuski. "You, Lieutenant Podbipyenta, will go straight out in the direction of Tatazysk, and you Michael ride to Kupin, and Pan Zagloba will ride to Zbrucha near Satanova."

"I?" said Zagloba.

"I have said it. You are a cunning man and full of good ideas. I thought you would like to undertake this command, but if that is not the case, Sergeant Kosmach may take the fourth division."

"He will take it, but under my command," cried Zagloba, on whom it suddenly dawned that he was to be leader of an especial division. "I merely asked because I was sorry to be separated from you."

"Have you had experience in military affairs?" asked Volodiyovski.

"Have I had experience! No stork had yet thought of bringing you as a present to your father and mother, when I was already leading larger divisions of scouts than these. I have served for an age in the army and would serve yet if it had not happened that a solitary biscuit had remained stationary in my stomach for three years. I was obliged to go on a pilgrimage to Galatz,—but I will tell you about this pilgrimage at some other time, for it is time now to set out."

"Start in at once, gentlemen, and spread the news everywhere that Khmyelnitski has already been beaten and that the prince has passed Roskirov," said Skshetuski. "Do not take any mean prisoner that you may chance to come across, but try and find some scouts from Kametets who can give you news about Kshyvonos, for those that we have taken give contradictory reports."

"If I could only meet Kshyvonos myself. If he would only take it into his head to ride out on a scouting expedition, I would give him pepper and ginger. Fear nothing, gentlemen, I will teach these vagabonds to sing, yes, even to dance."

In three days, we will meet again in Yarmolints, and now, each go your way," said Skshetuski, "and spare your men, gentlemen."

In three days in Yarmolints," repeated Zagloba, Volodiyovski and Podbipyenta.

CHAPTER VI.

As soon as Zagloba found himself alone at the head of his division, he began to feel uneasy, and even sad. He would have given a great deal if Skshetuski, Volodiyovski, or Longin had been at his side; all of whom he admired with his whole heart, with whom he felt perfectly secure and in whose valor and caution he believed blindly.

He rode gloomily, therefore, at the head of his men, looking mistrustfully round him on all sides, reviewing in his mind all the dangers that might happen to him, and growled:

"It would have been much more jolly if one of them had been with me. When God fits a man for anything he provides the work for him to do. The three ought to have been born horse-flies, for they love to be in the midst of blood. They are as happy in war as another would be with the pitcher, or as a fish in water. That is their business. Light bellies, but heavy fists. I have seen Skshetuski at work and know that he is an expert. He handles men as the monks do their prayers. That is his favorite trade. That Lithuanian, who has no head of his own and is looking for three strange heads, has nothing to lose. I am least well acquainted with the little fellow. To judge by what I saw at Konstantinov, and by what Skshetuski has said of him, he must be a hornet. Fortunately, he is not very far from me and I think it will be better for me to join him, for may the ducks tread me if I know which way I have to go."

Zagloba felt very much alone in the world, so much so that he began to pity himself.

"Yes, yes," he grunted, "each one has somebody upon whom they can depend and I—not a companion, no father, no mother; I am an orphan—but enough."

At this moment Sergeant Kosmach approached him.

"Commander, where are we going?"

"Where are we going?" repeated Zagloba, "what?"

Suddenly, he straightened himself in his saddle and twisted his moustache, "To Kamenets if I desire it! Do you understand, sir?"

The sergeant bowed and drew silently back to join his companions, without being able to understand why the commander should have been so angry. Zagloba, however, cast a few more threatening looks around him and then became calm and continued, to himself:

"If I go to Kamenets you may give me a hundred strokes of the bastinado, Turkish fashion. Tut! Tut! If only one of them were with me, I should feel more courage. What can I do with a hundred men. I would rather be alone and then I would trust my own judgment. Now, there are too many of us to be able to use craft, and too few to be of any service in defence. It was an unfortunate thought of Skshetuski's, to divide the patrol. And whither shall I go? I know what lies behind me, but who can tell me what lies before me and who can assure me that the devil has not laid a trap for me somewhere. Kshyvonos and Bohun are a nice pair. May the devil flay them alive! God preserve me from Bohun at least! Skshetuski is anxious to meet him. May the Lord grant his wish! I wish for him whatever he wishes for himself, for I am his friend, Amen. I will go to Zbrucha and come back to Yarmolints and bring him some spies; more than he wishes. There will be no trouble about that."

Kosmach approached him again:

"Commander, behind the rise, we can see some horsemen."

"May they ride to the devil! Where? Where?"

"There, behind the hill; I saw their pennants."

"Soldiers, then?"

"So it seems."

"May the dogs bite them! Are they many?"

"I do not know. They are still at some distance. If we were to hide behind these rocks, we might attack them unawares; as they must pass by here. If there should be many of them, Volodiyovski is not far off and he would hear the shots and come to our assistance."

Zagloba's courage suddenly increased and flew to his head, like wine. Perhaps despair may have given him this impulse for action. Perhaps, also, the hope that Pan Voldiyovski might be near by. In any case, he rolled his eyes frightfully, drew his word, that flashed, and cried:

"Hide behind the rocks! We will attack them unawares. We will show these scoundrels."

The prince's practised soldiers turned toward the rocks and placed themselves in readiness for a sudden attack.

An hour had already passed when the noise of approaching riders was heard. This was accompanied by the echo of joyous songs and, presently, those in hiding heard the sounds of a violin, of bagpipes, and of a little drum. The sergeant approached Pan Zagloba and said:

"Those are not soldiers, Colonel, not Cossacks. It is a wedding."

"A wedding!" said Zagloba, "I will play them a trick; you shall see." As he said this, he put spurs to his horse, the soldiers following him, and placed himself in the middle of the road.

"Follow me!" cried Zagloba. The column moved forward at a trot and then changed into a gallop and, when they came from behind the rocks, they stood still suddenly before the procession, who were frightened and confused at this un-expected sight.

"Halt! Halt!" was heard from both sides.

It was, indeed, a peasant's wedding. The bagpipes, the drummers and the fiddler rode at their head, with two jesters who were already half drunk, and were making jokes. Be-hind them came the bride, a fresh looking girl in a dark dress, with long hair hanging over her shoulders. She was sur-rounded by her bridesmaids, who were singing, and carried wreaths in their hands. All the girls rode astride; they were adorned with wild flowers and, in the distance, looked like a crowd of gaudy Cossacks. Behind them came the bridegroom on a big horse, surrounded by friends carrying wreaths on long sticks like pikes. The procession closed with the bridegroom's parents and the guests. All were on horse-back; and the barrels of gorzalka, mead and beer were drawn in little wagons made of plaited straw, and the liquid gurgled on the rough uneven road in a most tantalizing manner.

"Stand still! Stand still!" was again heard from both parties and they fled to either side. The joyful band was in confusion. The girls gave a piercing shriek and drew back. The servants, however, and the older men sprang forward in order to protect the girls from the unexpected attack. Zagloba sprang forward close to them and, flourishing his sword right under the eyes of the terrified peasants, began to scream:

"Ha! You shrivelled blockheads, you dogs' teeth, you rebels! You want to mutiny! You belong to Krshyvonos you ragamuffins! You are going out as spies! You are sending the soldiers in wrong directions! You are raising your hands against the nobles! I wil show you, you vile souls of dogs, I will have you placed on the block, impaled, oh, you rascals, oh, you heathen, you shall now pay for all your crimes!"

An old, white-headed wedding guest sprang from his horse, approached the nobleman, took hold of his stirrup, bowed low and said in a humble tone:

"Have mercy, illustrious knight, do not destroy us poor people. God is our witness! We are not going to rebel. We have just come from the church, from Hushiatyn, where we have just married our relation Dymitri the blacksmith to Xenia the cooper's daughter. We were just going to the wedding feast with the dancers."

"Those are innocent people, Sir," whispered the sergeant.

"Go away! They are rascals. They have been to a wedding with Krshyvonos," shouted Zagloba.

"May the plague take him!" cried the old man. "We never even saw him. We are poor people. Have mercy on us, illustrious Colonel. Let us go on. We are doing no harm to anyone and we know our duty."

"You will go to Yarmolints in chains."

"Wherever you like, sir! It is yours to command, ours to obey; but grant us one mercy. Command your soldiers not to harm us, and you yourself—pardon us simple people if we entreat you humbly—drink with us to the health of the married couple. Drink, your grace, to the welfare of us, simple people; as God and the Holy Gospel have commanded."

"Do not think that I will overlook anything even if I do drink," said Zagloba sharply.

"No sir," cried the old man joyfully, "we will not think it."

"Hey! Hey! musicians," he cried, "play for the illustrious Pole, or he is kind; and you boys, run and get the mead, sweet mead, for our illustrious gentleman. He will not do the poor people any harm. We thank the gentleman."

The young people set to work to open the barrels and during this time, the drums sounded, the fiddle squeaked, the bagpipers puffed out their cheeks and began to squeeze their bagpipes and the bridemaidens waved the wreaths at the end of their poles. When the soldiers saw this they came closer, twisted their moustaches and looked laughingly across the shoulders of the young men, at the girls. The songs began afresh, fear disappeared and here and there one even heard joyous cries of "Uha! Uha!"

But Zagloba was not perfectly at ease; even when they brought him a quart of mead, he still growled, "Oh you rascals, you ragamuffins!" and, even when his moustache was plunged into the dark surface of the draught, he looked into the goblet gloomily. He raised his head and, blinking his eyes, tasted the mead. As he smacked his lips, astonishment but also anger were visible on his countenance.

"What times are these," he growled, "the mob drink such mead as this! God, thou seest this and dos not strike them with a thunderbolt."

As he said this, he raised the mug and emptied it to the bottom. The wedding guests, having gained confidence, now approached him all together, and prayed him not to harm them but let them continue their journey; and the bride Xenia, rosy and beautiful as the dawn, but trembling and with tears in her eyes, added her voice to the entreaties. She folded her hands and kissing Zagloba's yellow boot, she said:

"Have mercy on us, sir."

The nobleman's heart melted like wax.

Loosening his leather belt, he seemed to be looking for something, and finally brought forth the last golden crown that he prince had given him. Handing this to the girl, he said to her:

"Take this! God bless thee, as he does all innocence!"

His emotion prevented him from continuing, for this slender dark eyed Xenia reminded him of the princess whom Zagloba loved in his own way. "Where might the poor girl be now? Were the Holy Angels watching over her," he thought, and he was so moved that he was just in a mood to embrace them all as brothers.

The wedding guests, however, delighted at his generous treatment, began to shout and sing for joy, to press towards him and to kiss the flaps of his coat. "He is good!" they repeated, "A golden Pole. He gives us red gold, does not harm us, the kind gentleman. May he have glory and fortune!" The fiddler was dancing and playing his fiddle, the bagpiper's eyes seem starting from his head and the drummer's hands fell at his sides. The old cooper, evidently a born coward, who had kept himself in the background now pressed forward with his wife and the blacksmith's old wife, mother of the bridegroom and, amid bowings, begged Zagloba to come to the wedding at the farm with them; as it would be a great honor for them to have such a guest and a happy omen for the young couple; and it would not be right not to come with them. The bridegroom and the black-eyed Xenia were also urgent in their entreaties; for the simple maiden had recognized at once that her people would derive the most benefit. And the bridesmaids said that it was not far to the farm; that the knights would not have to go out of their way; and that the old cooper was rich and could tap even better mead. Zagloba cast his eyes over his soldiers and saw that they were as anxious as hares for a little enjoyment and saw that the prospect of drink and dancing filled them with anticipation and delight. As, however, they did not dare to ask him on their own account, Zagloba took pity on them, and, in a few minutes, the wedding procession and the soldiers marched in the most beautiful harmony towards the farm.

It was, as they said, not very far off; and, as the old cooper was rich, the wedding feast was so abundant that they all got very drunk, and Zagloba became so merry that he took the lead in everything. Remarkable ceremonies were performed. The older women led Xenia into her bedroom and shut themselves in there with her. They remained there some time and when they came out alone and announced that the bride was like a dove, like a lily. Great joy immediately seized all those assembled and loud shouts arose of "To glory! To fortune!" The women clapped their hands and screamed, "What? Did we not say it?" The young men stamped their feet and danced about, singly, holding their drinking-cups in their hand; and, then, going to the door of the bedroom, emptied the cup crying, "To glory!" Zagloba also danced, upholding the dignity of his noble birth by drinking half a gollon of mead instead of a cupful. Then the old cooper and the blacksmith's wife led young Dymitri into the room and as he had no father they begged Zagloba to act in that capacity, to which he agreed at once and went in with them. Now the room became quiet. The only noise that was heard was made by the soldiers who were drinking in the courtyard before the house amid the Tartar cries of "Allah," and the firing of muskets. But the greatest joy broke forth when the parents came back into the room. The old cooper hugged the blacksmith's wife for joy. The young couple put their arms round the feet of the the old cooper's wife and the women congratulated themselves that they had preserved their daughter as the apple of their eye like a little dove and as a lily, upon which Zagloba took her by the hand and led her out on the floor. They tripped about, opposite each other. He clapped his hands, bobbed down, with his knees turned out, then, suddenly bounded into the air, bringing his iron heels to the floor with such a clatter that splinters flew from the planks and great drops of perspiration came out on his forehead. Other couples followed their example and, when there was no room inside, they danced in the courtyard; the girls with the young men and the soldiers. The cooper tapped fresh barrels of mead. Soon, the whole wedding company went out into the court before the house. They lighted bundles of brier and pitch-pine, for it was already late and quite dark. The revelry had become a drinking-bout and the soldiers were firing off their rifles and muskets, as though they were in a battle. Pan Zagloba, his face crimson, soaking with perspiration and staggering, had completely forgotten what was going on. Through the smoke that surrounded him, he saw the faces of the revellers; but, if he had been threatened with a stake, he could not have told who they were. He remembered he was at a wedding,—but whose? "Ha! It was Skshetuski's wedding with the princess." This thought appeared to him the most probable, for he could not get it out of his head; and it filled him with such happiness that he began to shout as if he were possessed: "Long may they live! Gentlemen and brothers! Let us love one another!" and he emptied another half-gallon of mead. "Take your glasses, brothers! To the health of our illustrious prince! May all go well with us. If only this paroxsym might pass by!"

Here, he burst into tears and, as he walked towards the barrel, his gait grew more and more unsteady, especially as there lay on the floor a number of apparently lifeless bodies, as on a field of battle. "Oh God," cried Zagloba, "there are no more brave men in the Commonwealth; but one, Pan Lashch knows how to drink; the other is Zagloba—and the rest, O God! O God!" he turned his eyes sadly towards the sky, and noticed that the heavenly bodies no longer looked like golden buttons in the firmament, but some of them trembled as though they were about to spring from heir places; others described circles, and others seemed to be dancing the "Cossack" opposite one another. Zagloba was more and more astonished and said to himself,

"Am I the only sober person in this world?"

But, presently, the earth seemed to tremble, just as the stars were doing. It turned round in a mad whirl, and Zagloba fell his full length on the ground. He was soon troubled with bad dreams. It seemed to him as if he had a mountain on his chest, which was crushing him to the ground and binding him hand and foot. At the same time, his ears were filled with a noise of what sounded like firearms. A blinding light flashed over his closed eyelids and hurt his eyes dreadfully. He tried to get up to open his eyes, but he could not; he felt that something unusual was happening to him; that his head was falling backward, as if it did not belong to him. Presently, a dreadful fear came upon him. He felt sick, very sick, very heavy. He soon regained his senses; but, strange to say, he was so intensely weak that he could not remember ever having experienced a similar sensation. He tried to move but could not do so. Then he became perfectly wide awake and opened his eyelids. As he did so, his eyes met another pair of eyes, that were fastened on him intently. They were coal-black eyes, and had such an evil expression that Zagloba, now perfectly wide awake, thought at the first moment that his Satanic Majesty was looking at him, and closed his eyes quickly; to open them again, just as quickly. These eyes continued to look at him obstinately—the face seemed familiar. Suddenly, Zagloba trembled, to his very marrow, a cold sweat covered him and all down his back thousands of ants seemed to be crawling.

He had recognized Bohun's face.

CHAPTER VII

Zagloba lay bound, his hands and feet trussed with his own sword, in the very room in which the wedding had taken place; and the terrible Chieftain sat beside him on a stool and looked with evident enjoyment at his prisoner's terror.

"Good evening, sir," he said, when he noticed his victim's eyes were opened.

Zagloba did not answer, but in a moment he was as sober as though no drop of mead ever passed his lips. Only a sensation, as if ants were creeping down to his heels and came back to his head, and the marrow in his bones seemed turning to ice. It is said that a drowning man at the last moment sees clearly his whole past; that he remembers everything, and is conscious of all that is happening to him. This bright vision and memory was Zagloba's experience at this moment; but the only evidence of this clairvoyance was the silent, unspoken cry:

"Now he will flay me!"

And the Chieftain repeated in quiet tones:

"Good evening, sir."

"Ugh!" thought Zagloba, "I wish he would fly into a rage."

"Do you not recognize me, noble sir?"

"I bow, I greet you! How is your health?"

"Not bad. And yours, I myself will take care of."

"I did not ask God for such a physician, and I doubt if I could digest your medicine; but God's will be done."

"Well, you cured me; Now I will repay you. We are old friends. Do you remember how you tied up my head in Rozloga? Eh?"

Bohun's eyes gleamed like two carbuncles and a horrible laugh came from his lips.

"I remember," said Zagloba, "that I could have stabbed you, and I did not do it."

"And I, did I stab you? or do I think of doing it? No, you are my friend, my beloved. I will guard you as the eye."

"I always said that you were a noble knight," said Zagloba,

pretending that he took Bohun's words in earnest; but at the same time the thought came into his mind, "I see that he is preparing something quite special for me. I shall not die any ordinary death."

"You have well said," sneered Bohun, "you are also a noble knight, we have sought and found each other."

"To tell the truth, I did not seek you, but I thank you for your kind words."

"You will thank me more, later, and I will thank you for taking the girl from Rozloga and bringing her to Bar where I found her. And now, I should like to ask you to the wedding; but it is not to-day nor to-morrow. Now it is war and you are an old man; perhaps you will not survive it."

In spite of the terrible position in which he found himself, Zagloba pricked up his ears:

"To the wedding?" he growled.

"And what do you suppose?" said Bohun. "Am I a peasant that I should take possession of her without a priest? Or, perhaps it might occur to me to be married in Kiev. You did not bring her to Bar for a peasant but for an ataman and a hetman. . . ."

"Good," thought Zagloba.

Then, turning his head towards Bohun, "Take those fetters off me," he said.

"Lie still! Lie still! You are going to take a journey and you're old and must rest beforehand."

"Whither are you going to take me?"

"You are my friend; I will take you to my other friend, to Kshyvonos. We will both see that you are well taken care of over there."

"It will be warm," growled the nobleman, and, again the ants began to crawl through his frame. Finally, he said:

"I know that you hate me, but unjustly, unjustly, God knows. We lived together and in Chigrin we drank many a bottle of wine together, for I took a fatherly interest in you on account of your knightly exploits; and you could not have found a better friend in the whole of Ukraina. And now, did I get in your way? If I had not ridden with you to Rozloga, we should be the best friends in the world to-day. And why would I have gone with you if I had not liked you? And if you had not been enraged you would not have killed those unfortunate people and, (God is my witness) I would not have opposed you. What do I care about other people's affairs? I would rather you had the girl than any other but, amid your Tartar wooing, my conscience reproached me for that was a noble house. You yourself would not have acted differently. I could have put you out of the world, to my own advantage—and yet I did not do it because I am a noble-man and was ashamed of such an act. So be ashamed of yourself, for I know that you will avenge yourself on me. The girl is in your hands; what more do you want from me? Did I not guard her, your greatest treasure, as the apple of my eye. That you have not wronged her, is a proof that you also possess knightly honor and conscience. But how can you give her your hand that you have stained with my guilt-less blood; how say to her, 'I have given over to torture that man who led you safely among the Tartars and through the peasant mob. You are yet young and do not know what may happen to you; and, for my death, God will punish you in what is dearest to you."

Bohun sprang from his stool, pale with rage, and, stepping up to Zagloba, said, in a voice choking with fury.

"You unclean boar! I will have straps torn from you, I will roast you on a slow fire, will drive nails in your body, and tear you in shreds."

And in a paroxysm of fury, he seized the knife that hung at his belt, held it convulsively in his grasp for a moment, and it was already flashing before Zagloba's eyes, when the chief-tain grew calm again; put the dagger back in its sheath and cried:

"Cossacks!"

Six Zaporojians sprang into the room.

"Take this carcass, throw it into the pig-sty and guard it as the eye in your head?"

The Cossacks carried Pan Zagloba, two at his head and two at his feet and one by the back hair of his head and carried him out of the room across the yard and threw him upon a dung heap in a pig-sty that stood at a distance. Then they shut the door and the prisoner was left in the midst of total darkness, except for the cracks between the beams and the holes in the thatched roof a feeble light penetrated here and there. Zagloba's eyes soon became accustomed to the twi-light. He looked about him, and noticed that in the pig-sty their were neither pigs nor Cossacks. But he heard distinctly the talking of the latter through all the four walls, evidently the whole building was surrounded closely. In spite of these guards, Zagloba breathed freely.

In the first place, he was alive. When Bohun flourished the knife over him, he was sure that his last hour had come. He had commended his ghost to God, for he was really in the greatest terror.

But Bohun had the intention of reserving him for a death of unheard of barbarity. He did not only wish to avenge himself, but wished to gloat over the tortures of the men who had snatched the beautiful girl from him, who had diminished his renown as a soldier, and had covered him with ridicule by tying him, as if he were a child. A sad outlook was before Zagloba but, for the moment, he was comforted in the thought that he still lived; that he would be led to Kshvonos for examination, so that he would have a few, or perhaps several days, before him; and, meantime he lay lonely here in the pig-sty, and had plenty of time in the stillness of the night to think about devices. That was the one and only redeeming point in the case. But when he thought of the other side, the creeping sensation came over him like a thousand ants creeping over his body.

"Devices . . . . ! If a hog or a sow lay in this pen, it would have better prospects than I have," murmured Pan Zagloba, "for it would not be tied, would not be fastened with its own sword. If Solomon had only been tied like this, he would not have been any wiser than his trousers or stockings. Oh God, Oh God, why dost thou punish me! Of all men in the world, this thief was the sole one I wished most to avoid; and now, it is my fate to run right into his hands. My skin will be combed like Svieboda cloth. If anyone else had caught me, I should declare that I had joined the rebellion, and then run away. Possibly, another might not believe me and, how much less this man? The devil led him here—Oh God! Oh God! I can move neither hand nor foot. O God! God!"

Presently, however, Zagloba reflected that if his hands and feet were free, he might more easily find a way of escape Suppose he should try to free himself. If he only could succeed in getting his sword away from under his knees, he could manage the rest; but how could he draw it out. He turned on one side,—no use. He reflected again.

Then he began to roll about on his back, faster and faster, and, each movement brought him half an inch forward. He became very warm and his brow perspired more than at the dance. Occasionally, he interrupted his labor; because it seemed to him that one of the soldiers was approaching the door; but, on being reassured he began with new zest until he had rolled himself over to the wall.

Now he began to wriggle in a different manner. Not from his head to feet, but from side to side; so that, at each turn, the end of the sword gently struck the wall. It glided each time a little more from beneath his knees and the handle came a little more to one side.

His heart beat like a hammer for he saw that his efforts would be rewarded. He kept on wriggling, endeavoring to strike the wall as gently as possible; and, only when the Cossacks were making such a noise outside that they would not hear him. At length, came the moment when the point of the sword was on a line with one knee and elbow so that he could not push it against the wall any longer.

At the opposite end it extended considerably and this was the heaviest portion taking the handle into consideration.

On the hilt of the sword was a cross as is usual in these weapons and Zagloba counted on this cross.

For the third time he began to squirm but the object of his endeavors, now, was to turn his feet towards the wall. When he had succeeded in doing this, he began to push himself lengthwise. His sword was still between his kneecaps and hands but the hilt at each jerk caught against the uneven ground. The hilt had now stuck fast and Zagloba twisted more violently again, for the last time; and, for a moment, he was unable to move for joy.

He had disengaged the sword completely.

Now the nobleman drew his hands from his knees and although they were still tied together he was able to seize the sword. He held the sheath fast between his feet and drew the sword. It was the work of an instant to cut the thongs that held his feet.

It was difficult to free his hands. He was obliged to put the sword on the dung heap, lying with its edge upturned, and to work away at his bonds until he cut them through.

When he finished that, he was not only unbound but also armed. He took a deep breath and, crossing himself, thanked God.

But, from cutting his fetters to escaping from Bohun's hands, was a long stretch.

"What's to be done next," said Zagloba to himself.

But he found no answer. The pig-sty was surrounded with

Cossacks—there must have been at least a hundred men—and a mouse could not have crept by them unperceived, much less a big man like Zagloba.

"I see that I must take to my heels. My wit is worth as much as shoeblacking, although one can get very good blacking at the market in Hungary. If God does not give me any good ideas, I shall be a roast for the crows; but, if an idea comes to me, I will make a vow to observe chastity, like Pan Longin." The loud conversation of the soldiers interrupted his thoughts. He jumped up and put his ear to a crack between the beams. The dried, pine boards gave back the sound as the sounding board does the tones of a lute. He heard quite clearly.

"And whither are we going from here?" asked a voice.

"I do not now, probably to Kamenets," answered another.

"Bah, the horses cannot do it." They can hardly drag one foot after the other."

"That is why we are waiting here. They can rest till to-morrow."

A pause followed, then the first voice said more quietly.

"And it seems to me, father, that the ataman will go to Yampol from Kamenets."

Zagloba held his breath.

"Silence! if it suits your young head," was the answer.

Another silence followed but, from the opposite wall, came whispering tones.

"They are everywhere; they are watching everywhere," grunted Zagloba.

And he went to the opposite wall. Now, he heard the horses crunching their oats and snorting, as they stood outside the wall. He judged that the soldiers were lying down and conversing, for the second seemed to come from beneath him.

"Hey," said one, "we have ridden here without sleeping, without eating, without giving the horses a rest, and all, only that we may be impaled in Yeremy's camp."

"Is it certain that he is here?"

"The people who fled from Yarmolints saw him just as plainly as I see you. What they relate is dreadful. He is as tall as a fir-tree, has two torches in his head, and his horse is a dragon."

"Oh Lord, have mercy on us!"

"We ought to take this Pole and his soldiers and make our escape."

"How would you fly. The horses are dying already?"

"It looks bad, brother. If I were the ataman I would stick this Pole through the throat and would go, even if it were on foot, to Kamenets."

"We are going to take him with us to Kamenets. The ataman wants to have some fun with him."

"The devil will have some fun with you, first," growled Zagloba.

It is strange! In spite of his great dread of Bohun and, perhaps, for that very reason, he swore that he would not give himself up alive. He was now free from his bonds and, with his sword in his hand, he would defend himself. If they killed him, well, that could not be helped; but, alive, they should never catch him. The snorting and groaning of the horses, who were more than ordinarily exhausted, drowned the rest of the conversation but brought a better idea to Zagloba.

"If I could only get through this wall, and unexpectedly jump on a horses' back," he said. "It is night and, before they knew what had happened, I should be out of sight. It is hard to carry on a pursuit in these hollows and valleys by daylight, how much more in the darkness of night! God help me to do it!"

But the means were not easy. He would be obliged to break through the wall and to do that one would need be a Podbipyenta; or to burrow like a fox, and even then he would be seen and heard; and, before his foot was in the stirrup, he would be caught.

A thousand such thoughts passed through his mind; but, just because there were so many, no single one gave him any clear solution of the difficulty.

"There is nothing for it, but to lose my head," he thought and went to the third wall.

Suddenly, his head struck something hard. He felt it and found it was a ladder. This was not a pig's sty, then, but an ox-stable, and half of it was a space which served to store hay and straw. Without reflecting Zagloba climbed the ladder. Arrived at the top he puffed for breath a while and then slowly drew the ladder up after him.

"Now I am in a fortress!" he grunted. "If they cannot find a second ladder, they will not get up here so easily. If I do not cleave the first head in two that shows itself, I will let myself be made into smoked meat. "Oh, the devil," he said suddenly, "that is a fact, they might not only smoke me but roast me, and melt me into tallow, but let be, let be! If they wish to burn the pig sty—it is well. They will then not be able to catch me alive; and it is all the same, whether the ravens eat me raw or cooked. If I can only escape from the hands of these assassins, the rest does not trouble me, and I hope that something may yet occur."

As we see, Zagloba turned easily from despair to hope. Un-expectedly, he had become filled with as much confidence as though he were already in Prince Yeremy's camp, and yet, his position had changed very slightly. He was sitting in the loft with his sword in his hands, and could in fact defend him-self for a long time; but that was all. From the loft to free-dom, the road was still worse now, for below him the swords and pikes of the Cossacks who were guarding him, awaited him outside.

"How will it end?" mumbled Zagloba and, as he neared the roof, he began to tear away the thatch carefully, in order to open for himself an outlook upon the world.

This was easy for him, as the soldiers, to lighten the tediousness of their watch, were carrying on a lively conver-sation. Besides this, a strong wind had risen and, the noise of the leaves in the neighboring trees drowned the rustle made by the removal of the thatch.

Before long, he had made a hole in the thatch. He stuck his head through and looked round him.

It was near dawn and, in the East, could already be seen the first gleams of morning light. Zagloba saw, by the pale light, that the courtyard before the house was completely filled with horses. Immediately before the house, lay long rows of sleeping Cossacks. Beyond was the crane of the well, and the trough, in which the water gleamed, and close by another row of sleeping men and several soldiers with un-sheathed swords in their hands, keeping guard over them.

"Those are my men whom they have tied," said Zagloba. "Bah," he added, in a moment, "if they only were mine, but they are the prince's. I was a good leader, truly. I led them into the jaws of the dog. If God gives me my freedom, I shall be ashamed to show my eyes. And what was the cause of all this! Love and drink. What did the marriage of that mob matter to me? I had as much business with that wedding as with a dog's wedding. I renounce that traitor, mead, which paralyzes my feet, instead of mounting to my head. All the evil in the world comes from drink; for, if they had attacked us when we were sober, as true as I live, I should have conquered them and shoved Bohun in the pig-sty." Here, Zagloba's eyes fell upon the cabin in which the chieftain was sleeping, and remained fixed on the door.

"Sleep, rascal," he growled, "sleep! May you dream that the devil is flaying you, for you will not escape him in the end. You wanted to make a sieve of my skin, but we will see if I cannot prepare your skin in such a manner that it will not be even good for dog's boots. Only just dare to come up here to me. If I could only get away from here, if I only could! But how?" Indeed, this wish seemed incapable of fulfillment. The whole courtyard was so packed with men and horses that, even if Zagloba had succeeded in getting out of the stables, if he really could have slid down from the roof and sprung on the back of one of the horses that were standing before the stable, he could not, in any case, have forced his way through, to the gate, and how could he get beyond the gate?

And yet it seemed to him as though he already completed half of the task. He was free, armed, and sat in the loft as in a fortress.

"What the devil," he thought, "is getting out of the snare if you are to be hung afterwards."

And again plans began to rush through his head, but they were so many that he was unable to choose one of them.

Meanwhile day was dawning, the surrounding of the cabins stood out from the darkness and the roof seemed to be overlaid with silver. Zagloba could already distinguish the different groups in the yard; could recognize the red color of the uniform of his men, who were lying near the well, and the sheep skins of the Cossack who were lying beside the cabin.

Suddenly a form arose from the ranks of the sleepers and walked slowly across the yard, pausing a moment beside the men and horses and speaking for a while with the Cossacks who were watching the prisoners; then he approached the stable. In the first moment, Zagloba thought it was Bohun; for he had noticed that the sentries had spoken to him as subordinates.

"Ah," he grunted, "if I only had a gun in my hand, I would show you how to cover yourself with your feet."

At this moment, the figure raised its head and the gray light of dawn fell upon its face.

It was not Bohun; it was the sotnik Holody, whom Zagloba recognized at once, for he remembered him very well from that time when he and Bohun were companions in Chigrin.

"Boys," said Holody, "have you not slept yet?"

"No, little father, if we had been sleeping it would be time to change (guards)."

"I will change soon. And the rascal has not escaped?"

"No, little father! Only his soul could have escaped, for he has not budged."

"He's a regular fox. Just see what he is doing, for he is quite equal to sinking through the earth."

"Immediately," answered some of the Cossacks, and approached the door of the stable.

"Throw down some hay from the loft, rub down the horses. We shall set out at sunrise."

"Right, little father."

Pan Zagloba hastily left his position near the hole in the roof, and crept to the entrance to the loft. Presently he heard the grating of the door hinges and the rustling of straw beneath the step of the Cossacks. His heart was beating like with a hammer. His hand grasped more firmly the hilt of his sword, while he renewed his vow in his mind, that he would rather be burned alive with the pigsty or allow himself to be chopped like straw for fodder, than give himself up alive. He expected also, at any moment, that the soldiers would raise a terrible alarm; but he was mistaken. He only heard them running about more quickly in the stable and finally, one said:

"What a devil is there! I cannot feel him. We certainly threw him down here."

"Is he not a magician or what? Strike a light. It is as dark as in the forest."

There was silence for a moment. Vasil was probably looking for flint and tinder. The others began to call him softly.

"Answer, Pan Nobleman."

"Kiss the dog's ear," murmured Zagloba.

Then he heard them strike the flint and a shower of sparks lighted up the dark interior of the stable and the heads of the soldiers that were covered with caps. And, then it became darker than ever.

"He is not here, he is not here," cried several voices.

Then one of them sprang to the door. "Father Holody! Father Holody!"

"What's the matter?" cried the sotnik stepping into the door.

"The Pole has gone."

"How! is he gone?"

"He must have sunk into the ground. He is nowhere to be seen. Oh, God pity on us! We struck fire. He is gone."

"That is impossible! Oh, the ataman will pay you off for that. Has he escaped, or what? Did you go to sleep?"

"No, little father, we did not sleep. He did not come out of the pig-sty on our side."

"Quiet, do not wake the ataman. If he did not get out, he must be somewhere about. Did you look everywhere?"

"Everywhere."

"Also in the loft?"

"How could he get into the hayloft, if he was tied."

"Fool! If he had not untied his fastenings he would be here. Look in the hay loft! Strike fire!"

Once more the sparks flew. The news was quickly spread among all the sentries. They all hastened, with the speed that is usual in sudden emergencies, and went into the stable. Quick steps were heard; hasty questions and still more hasty answers crossed each other like swords in battle.

"To the loft! To the loft!"

"And keep watch outside!"

"Do not wake the ataman or it will be the worse for you!"

"There is no ladder here!"

"Bring another!"

"There is none anywhere."

"Rush into the cabin and see if there is not one there!"

"Oh, the cursed Pole!"

"Climb up on the roof, and come through the roof into the loft."

"We cannot do that, for it is overhanging and has boards nailed across the underside."

"Bring pikes, we will climb up on those. This dog has taken the ladder up with him."

"Bring pikes," commanded Holody.

The Cossacks hurried away for pikes. Others looked up towards the loft. The morning light poured through the open door into the stable and, by its gray gleam, one saw the black square opening that led to the hayloft. From below, cried some voices:

"Come, Pan Nobleman, let the ladder down, and come

down yourself. You will not get away like this, so why do you give people trouble. Come down! Come down!"

There was a silence.

"You are a wise man! If that could help you stay there; but this will not help you, so better come down willingly, good man."

Silence. . . .

"Come down. If not, we will scalp you, and throw you down on the dung heap."

Pan Zagloba remained quiet, deaf to the threats as to the flatteries. He sat in the dark, like a badger in its hole, prepared for the most obstinate resistance. He only grasped his sword more tightly, panted a little and prayed in silence.

Meanwhile, they brought pikes. Three of these were tied together and placed with their points upwards beneath the opening to the loft. Zagloba was thinking whether he could not snatch them away and pull them up, but he reflected that they were too far beneath him, and he might not be able to pull them up entirely. Besides, they would have brought others immediately.

The whole stable was now full of Cossacks. Some lighted pieces of pitch pine; others dragged various poles and racks with them, which of course proved too short, so they tied them together with straps; for it was really very hard to climb up on the pikes, but there were some who wanted to climb.

"I will go," cried several voices.

"Wait for the ladder," said Holody.

"What harm would it do to try climbing the pikes?"

"Vasil can get up. He climbs like a cat."

"Well try it."

Others began to joke.

"Carefully there; he has a sword and will cut off your head. You will see."

"He will seize you by the head and drag you up and then he will finish you as if you were a bear."

Vasil could not be frightened.

"He knows," said he, "that if he were to touch me only with his finger, the ataman would give him to the devil to swallow, and you, too, brothers."

That was meant for a warning for Zagloba, who sat still and did not budge.

But the Cossacks were soon in a good humor, as is the case among soldiers; for the whole proceeding appeared to then as good humor, so they continued joking.

"There will be one fool the less in this white world,' they said. "He will not care if we pay him for your neck. He is a bold fellow."

"Aha! He's a magician. The devil knows what he has changed himself into, the wizard. You, Vasil, you do not know what you may find under the roof."

Vasil, who had just spat on his hands and was about to climb the pikes, suddenly took his hands off them.

"I will look for the Pole," he said, "but not for the devil."

Meanwhile, they had fastened the racks together, and stood them up.

It was difficult, however, to mount them, for they gave where they were tied together, and the thin steps cracked beneath their feet when they attempted to step on them. Holody himself stepped on them and said, as he climbed:

"You see, Pan Nobleman, we are not joking. You have taken it into your head to sit in the loft and you may sit there; but do not defend yourself. We will take you anyway, if the whole stable has to be torn down. Listen to reason."

Presently his head reached the opening and disappeared slowly. Then, one heard a swish and a terrible scream and the Cossack staggered and fell among the crowd, with his head cloven in two.

"Cut! Cut!" screamed the Cossacks.

A frightful confusion ensued. Screams and cries were raised, which were drowned by Zagloba's voice of thunder.

"Ha! You thieves, you cannibles, you vipers! I will kill every last one of you, you mangy rascals. You shall feel a knight's hand. To think of attacking honorable men by night! To fasten a nobleman in a pig's sty—ha, you mob! Come and fight with me, single handed, or two at a time, for all I care! But come on! You will leave your heads behind in the dung heap, for I will cut them off, as sure as I live!"

"Cut! Cut!" screamed a soldier.

"We will burn down the stable."

"I will burn it down myself, you fools. . . . But, with you in it."

"Several go up at once," cried an old Cossack. "Hold the steps. Support them with pikes. Put bundles of straw round your heads, and go ahead. We must have him." As he said this, he mounted the steps and, with him, two companions. The steps began to break; the ladder was more and more

shaky; but more than twenty strong arms grasped them below, and, higher up, they were supported by pikes. Others
poked their pikes through the hole in the loft, in order to
keep off the sword thrusts.

A few minutes later, three fresh heads fell down on the
heads of those standing below. Zagloba excited by his success was bellowing like a buffalo, and such frightful oaths
came from his mouth that the world never heard before; and
they would have terrified the hearts of the Cossacks, if these
had not been filled with wild madness and rage. Several stuck
their pikes at hazard through the opening to the loft; others
forced their way up the steps, although certain death awaited
them. Suddenly, a cry was heard at the door, and Bohun
himself sprang into the stable. He was bareheaded, in his
stockings and shirtsleeves. He held his drawn sword in his
hand, and his eyes darted flames of fire.

"Through the roof, dogs!" he cried. "Tear away the thatch
and take him alive!" When Zagloba saw him, he bellowed:

"You peasant, only come here! I will cut off your nose and
your ears, but not your neck, for that is the hangman's property. What? Are you afraid? Coward! Are you terrified,
you mean servant? Bind this rascal and I will have mercy
on the rest of you. Come here, you gallows bird, come here,
you Jew-pudding. Stick your head through, come, come, I
shall be glad. I will receive you in such a manner that your
father, the devil, and your mother, the wench, will stand before your eyes."

During this time, the beams of the roof were beginning to
crack. The Cossacks were probably above there, and beginning to take off the thatch. Zagloba heard it, but fear no longer robbed him of his strength. He was as if drunk from
fighting and blood.

"I will jump into a corner and end my life there," he
thought.

But at this moment, firing was heard outside, all over the
courtyard and, at the same time, several Cossacks broke into
the stable.

"Little father, little father!" they cried, "come quickly."

Zagloba could not understand at first what had happened
and stood bewildered. He looked down through the opening, but no one was there. The rafters had ceased to creak.

"What does it mean? What has happened?" he cried aloud.
"Ah, I know, they want to set the stable on fire and are firing
their pistols at the thatch."

The noise outside grew louder and was increased by tramping of horses, shouts, firing, mingled with yells and clashing of iron.

"God, that sounds like a fight," thought Zagloba. He ran to his peep-hole in the roof. He looked out—and his legs bent under him for joy.

A fight was raging in the courtyard, and Zagloba could see that Bohun's men had been frightfully routed. Suddenly attacked, and frightened by pistols that had been placed at their heads and breasts, they crowded against the fences, in the cabin and in the sheds, hewn down with swords, crushed and trampled by those who had come swarming in on horseback and had overcome them, almost without resistance. The ranks of soldiers in red uniforms crowded and fired on the fugitives, so that it was impossible for them to form in any order, to draw their swords, or to mount their horses and ride away. Only a few groups defended themselves. Others who tried, amid the noise and confusion, to saddle their horses, were cut down before their feet reached the stirrup. Others, again, threw away their pikes and swords and fled behind the fence; some got caught between the posts; others ran away uttering unearthly cries and howls. The unfortunates believed that Prince Yeremy himself had attacked them, unexpectedly, like an eagle, and was destroying them with his whole army. They had no time to come to their senses or to look round them. The war-cry of the assailants, the swishing of the swords and the reports of the shots drove them along like a wind-storm. The hot breath of the horses fell on their necks. "Men, fly," was heard on all sides. "Fight, kill!" answered the attackers.

And, finally, from his hiding-place, Zagloba saw little Pan Volodiyovski, who was standing near the gate, at the head of several soldiers, giving verbal instructions and with his baton and, occasionally dashing with his bay horse into the crowd. And every time he turned, a man fell, without a sound coming from his lips. Oh, little Pan Volodiyovski was a master of masters and a soldier, blood and bone. He never lost sight of the battle, advised here and there, then turned again and looked round him, then again took part himself; just like a leader of a orchestra who, in the midst of directing, sometimes himself joins in; sometimes stops and listens attentively to see that each one is playing his part.

When Zagloba saw that, he stamped his feet on the floor

of the loft so that clouds of dust arose, and clapped his hands and bellowed:

"Kill the dogs! Strike! Slay! Flay them! Hew them! Slash! Cut! Stab! Thrust!"

He cried thus, running hither and thither, his eyes blood-shot with straining them, so that for a moment he could see nothing. But, when his sight returned, there was a more beautiful spectacle, for behold—surrounded by several dozen of his soldiers, was Bohun, flying without his cap on, just as Zagloba saw him last, in his shirt; and, behind him, at the head of his soldiers, little Pan Volodiyovski.

"Kill!" cried Zagloba. "That is Bohun!"

But his voice did not reach the soldiers. Meanwhile Bohun had crossed the fence with Pan Volodiyovski after him. Some of them remained; the horses of others fell while jumping. Zagloba saw Bohun on the plain as well as Volodiyovski. Presently, they were all running; some to escape, others pursuing; each one after his man. Zagloba held his breath. His eyes almost started from their sockets—for what did he see? Volodiyovski overtakes Bohun; he springs towards him, like a boarhound on the boar. The chieftain turns his head, raises his sword.

"They are fighting!" cries Zagloba.

In another moment, Bohun's horse falls with him and Pan Volodiyovski tramples him down and pursues the others.

But Bohun lives. He rises from the ground and runs over to the rocks that are overgrown with bushes.

"Stop him! Stop him!" cries Zagloba. "That is Bohun!"

Now, a fresh band of Cossacks comes on the scene who had formerly been creeping round the other side of the rocks, but, being discovered, are seeking a new outlet of escape.

In the background, at a distance of a few rods, soldiers are approaching. They overtake Bohun, surround him and lead him away with them. Finally they disappear behind the bend of the narrow path, the other soldiers following them.

In the farmyard all was still and deserted, for Zagloba's soldiers, who had been freed by Volodiyovski, had mounted their horses and joined the other soldiers in pursuit of the enemy.

Zagloba now let down the ladder, climbed down from the loft and said, as he stepped from the sty into the yard:

"I am free."

He looked about him; the farmyard was covered with the

"I WILL KILL EVERY LAST ONE OF YOU."

With Fire and Sword.

dead bodies of the Zaporojians and a few other soldiers. The nobleman walked slowly among them, observed each one carefully and, finally, knelt down beside one of them. Presently he rose again with a tin flask in his hand.

"It is full," he murmured.

And, placing it to his lips, he bent his head back.

"Not bad!"

Again, he looked round him and repeated, but in a much louder voice:

"I am free!"

Then he went into the cabin and, on the threshold, stumbled against the body of the old cooper whom Bohun's men had killed, and disappeared inside. When he came out again, he wore over his dirty coat, that was all covered with manure, Bohun's gorgeous, gold-embroidered girdle, in which was a dagger with a large ruby in its hilt.

"God has rewarded bravery," he murmured, "for the pocket of the belt is full also. Ha! this horrid murderer. I hope he will not escape. But this little pigmy. I will put a bullet in him. He is a spiteful little fellow, just like a wasp. I knew that he was a brave soldier but I did not expect him to ride upon Bohun like a grey mare. It is strange that such a soul and so much couraage should hide in such a litle body. Bohun could easily carry him on a string at his belt, as if he were a little kid. May the bullets strike him or, better still, God give him luck. He certainly could not have known Bohun or else he would have killed him. Ugh! Ugh! how it smells of powder here! It fairly chokes one! Well, I have managed to wriggle out of such dangers as I never before experienced. God be praised! Well, well, but to think they have not killed Bohun! I must look closer at this Volodiyovski, for the devil must be in him."

Thus talking to himslef, Zagloba sat in the threshold of the stable and waited.

Presently, in the distance, appeared the soldiers returning from the pursuit, with Volodiyovski at their head. When he saw Zagloba, he quickened his horse's pace and, dismouning, came to meet him.

"What, I see you still alive!" he asked, from a distance.

"Myself, and no one else," said Zagloba. "God reward you for coming to help me."

"Let us praise God that it happened at the right time," answered the little knight, shaking Zagloba's hand heartily

"But how did you knew of the danger in which I was placed?"

"The peasants from the farm sent me word."

"Oh, and I thought they had betrayed me!"

"What made you think that? They are good people. The boy and his wife hardly escaped with their lives; as for the rest of the wedding-party, I do not know what became of them."

"If they were not traitors they have been killed by the Cossacks. The proprietor of the farm is lying over there beside the cabin. But never mind that, tell me, Pan, is Bohun alive? Did he escape?"

"Was that Bohun?"

"The one without a cap, in his shirt; whom you knocked over, together with his horse."

"I cut his hand through. It is too bad I did not recognize him. But you, but you, Pan Zagloba, what have you done?"

"What have I done," repeated Zagloba, "Come, Pan Michael and see!"

Then Zagloba took Volodiyovski by the hand and led him into the stable.

"Look,' he repeated.

Pan Volodiyovski, at first, saw nothing, for he came from outside into the darkness; but, as his eyes became accustomed to it, he noticed the dead bodies lying on the dung-heap.

"Who killed these men?" he asked in astonishment.

"I," said Zagloba, "you asked what I did, look there."

"Hm," said the young officer, shaking his head. "And how did you do it?"

"Up there," Zagloba said, pointing to the loft, "I defended myself while they attacked me from below and through the roof. I do not know how long it lasted, for in the heat of battle, one does not reckon time. It was Bohun, Bohun with his cruel strength and his picked men. He will remember you, but he will also remember me. Another time, I will tell you how I happened to become a prisoner, all that I suffered, and how I settled Bohun, for I had a war of words with him. To-day, I am so exhausted that I can hardly stand on my feet."

"Well!" repeated Pan Volodiyovski, "I cannot deny that you defended yourself bravely, but one thing I must tell you. That you are better as a fighter than as a leader."

"Pan Michael," said the nobleman, "now is not the time

to argue. Let us, rather, thank God that he has given us both such a great victory, the remembrance of which will long remain in the memory of men."

Voldiyovski continued to observe Zagloba. Until this moment, he had imagined that he had gained the victory that Zagloba now sought to share with him.

But he merely made his own mental comment and, shaking his head, said:

"Well, so let it be."

An hour later, the two friends, at the head of their united divisions were marching to Yarmolints.

Hardly one of Zagloba's soldiers was missing, for they had been sound asleep and offered no resistance; and Bohun, who was commissioned principally to look for people who would give him information, had them all taken prinsoners, instead of killing them.

CHAPTER VIII.

Bohun, although a valiant and careful leader, had no luck with this expedition that he had undertaken against Prince Yeremy's divisions. He was firmly convinced that the prince was marching with his whole army against Kshyvonos, for the prisoners he had taken from Zagloba told him that the prince was following them, and they believed it themselves; so there remained nothing for the unfortunate ataman to do but to retreat as quickly as he could to Kshyvonos and the undertaking was not easy. Scarcely did he succeed in three days in collecting a troop of a little over two hundred men. The rest had either fallen in fight, or remained upon the field of battle, or were wandering among the ravines or in the rushes; not knowing what to do, or whither they should turn their steps. And this troop was not of much use to Bohun for, beaten, terrified, and demoralized, they were ready to fly at the least alarm, and, yet, they were the best picked soldiers; it would be difficult to find better ones in the whole of Sich. But the Cossacks did not know how small the force was which Volodiyovski had against them, or, that thanks to his agility and his surprising them, that he was able to attack and defeat the sleeping and unprepared men. They thought that they were dealing, if not with the prince himself, yet with a strong and considerable division of the army. Bohun was burning like fire; his hand was cut; he had been trampled by his horse, ill and beaten. His accursed enemy had slipped out of his hands; his glory was tarnished. And the very warriors, who on the eve of the defeat, would have blindly followed him not only to the Crimea but even to hell against the very dreaded Yeremy. They had lost faith; they had lost spirit; and were only thinking how they could save their throats and escape total defeat. And, yet Bohun had done all that a leader could do. He had omitted nothing, had stationed sentries around the farmyard, and was only taking a rest because the horse, that had traveled hither from Kamenets, had hardly stopped for breath and were utterably incapable of traveling any farther.

But Volodiyovski, who during his young life, had experience in sorties and hunts upon the Tartars went, like a wolf in the night, on the watch; taken them prisoners before they could scream or even fire; and attacked the rest so quickly that even he, Bohun was obliged to fly, just as he was, in his trousers and his shirt sleeves. As the chieftain thought of these things, a mist came before his eyes, his head grew dizzy and despair gnawed at his heart, and he was enraged like a mad dog. He, who had snatched the Turkish galleys in the Black Sea; he, who had penetrated to Perekop and role across the necks of the Tartars and had held burning torches beneath the eyes of the Khan; he, who had hewn down at the side of the prince a regiment in Vasiloots close to Lubni, had been obliged to fly in his shirt sleeves without his cap or sword—for he had lost the latter in his fight with the little knight. And, when they stopped to feed the horses and no one saw him the chieftain seized his head with both hands and cried: "Where is my Cossack fame? Where my beloved sword?" and, as he thus cried, a wild madness seemed to seize him, and he took to drinking like an inhuman being. He wanted to march against the prince, attack his whole army; die, and perish and be lost forever.

He wished to do this—but the Cossacks did not. "If you should kill us, little father, we would not go," they answered gloomily, to his outbreak of fury—and it was useless, in such outbreaks of fury, to slash them with the sword or blacken their faces with gunpowder from his pistol—they would not go and they did not.

It seemed as if the ground were giving way beneath the feet of the ataman, for his misfortunes were not yet at an end. Fearing that he would be pursued and believing that Kshyvonos had already given up the siege, he did not go immediately towards the south, but turned in the direction of the east and met Longin's division. Watchful as a crane, Longin did not let himself be surprised by stealth, but attacked the ataman first and routed his forces; the more easily, as the soldiers themselves were not anxious to fight, and drove them towards Skshetuski; who defeated them so thoroughly that Bohun, after wandering for some time in the steppes, finally arrived at Kshyvonos camp without glory, without officers or soldiers, without prisoners and with only a few horses.

But the savage Kshyvonos, who was usually so cruel to those under him whom fortune had not favored, was not angry this time. He knew, from his own experience, what it meant to fight with Yeremy's army. He was kind to Bohun, comforted him and calmed him and, when the Cossack leader became a prey to a violent fever, he had him watched, tended, healed and kept as the pupil in his eye.

Meanwhile, the four officers of the prince, after filling the country with terror and horror, returned joyfully to Yarmolints where they remained several days in order to rest the men and horses. After they had taken up their quarters together houses, each of them gave an account of all that had happened to Pan Skshetuski and all that he had endured; and then they took to drinking wine, in order to ease their hearts by cheerful conversation and to satisfy their common curiosity.

But Zagloba would hardly give any of them a chance to speak. He did not wish to listen but expected everyone to listen to him, and it proved that he had the most to relate.

"Gentlemen," he said, "I was taken prisoner, that is true, but the wheel of fortune turned. Bohun has been fighting all his life, and to-day we have conquered him. That is the luck of war. To-day you tan them; to-morrow they tan you. But God punished Bohun for having attacked us when we were sleeping the sleep of the just, and waking us in such a shameless manner. Ha, ha! he thought he would frighten me with his dirty tongue; but I tell you, sirs, as soon as I answered him back, he at once lost courage, became confused, and blabbed out just what he did not intend. I could tell you volumes! If I had not been taken prisoner, Pan Michael and I would not have beaten him. I say, he and I, for on this occasion—I have done most of it. I shall never cease to affirm this till the day of my death. So may God grant me health. Listen further to my story; that if Pan Michael and I had not beaten him, neither Podbiyenta nor Skshetuski would have overtaken him; and if we had not defeated him he would have defeated us—and what would not have happened. Who prevented it?"

"Ah, you're like a little fox," said Longin, "here you wag your tail, there you slip away, and, in every case, you manage to get out of the trap."

"Only a foolish boarhound runs close behind the game, for he catches nothing and does not get even good scent and finally loses the trail altogether. How many men have you lost?"

"About twelve altogether, and a couple wounded. They did not attack us fiercely."

"And you, Pan Michael?"

"About thirty, for I attacked them unexpectedly."

"And you, lieutenant?"

"As many as Pan Longin."

"And I lost two; now tell me who was the best leader? Let's see how matters stand? With what object did we come here? We were sent by the prince in order to collect news about Kshyvonos. Well, I will tell you that I was the first to get news about him, and that from the best source, from Bohun himself. I knew that he is encamped at Kamenets but that he is afraid and will raise the siege. I know that from the people; but I know something else, that will make you all very happy, gentlemen, and I did not mention it, as yet, because I wished to consult you all about it. Besides I did not feel well, because my labors were too much for me and my stomach rebelled at those murderous thongs. I thought my blood would have been poured out.'

"Speak, for God's sake," cried Volodiyovski, "Did you hear anything of our poor girl."

"You have guessed it, may God bless her!" said Zagloba.

Pan Skshetuski stood up, to his full height, but immediately sat down again. There was such a complete silence, that one could hear the humming of the mosquitoes at the little window. Then Zagloba continued:

"She lives, I know it for certain, and is in Bohun's hands. Gentlemen, they are dreadful hands, but God has not allowed any wrong or evil to come near her. Bohun, himself, confessed that to me; that he might deal wrongly with anyone else, but not with her."

"How can that be? How can that be?" asked Skshetuski feverishly.

"If I lie, may I be struck by lightning," answered Zagloba earnestly. "The matter is too sacred with me. Listen to what Bohun told me when he was mocking me, before I roused him fully. 'What did you imagine,' (he said) 'that you were bringing her to Bar for a peasant? Am I a peasant that I should wish to take advantage of her? I would rather take her to Kiev and be married to her in the church and have the people sing songs for us and let three hundred candles be lighted, to me, the ataman and hetman!' He stamped his foot and threatened me with his knife for he thought he would frighten me; but I said to him he could not frighten a dog."

Skshetuski had recovered himself. His monk's face had brightened and fear, hope, joy and uncertainty were once more depicted in his countenance.

"Where is she then? Where?" he asked hastily. "If you found out that, you are a messenger from heaven."

"He did not tell me that, but a wise man needs only a couple of words. Consider, gentleman, that he was insulting me without ceasing until I roused him to a pitch of fury; but he said this: 'First I will lead you to Kshyvonos, and then I would like to invite you to the wedding; but now we have war and so it cannot take place so soon.' Consider that gentlemen, not 'so soon'—so we still have time. Also mark his words, 'I will lead you to Kshyvonos then I would like to invite you to the wedding,' so, in any case, she cannot be with Kshyvonos but in some other place, where the war cannot penetrate."

"You're a man as good as gold," cried Volodiyovski.

"I at first thought," said Zagloba, delighted, "that he had perhaps taken her to Kiev—but, no, for he said that he would take her to Kiev to get married so if he is going to take her there, that proves that she is not yet there. He is too clever to take her there, for if Bogdan Khmyelnitski goes to Cher-Vona Russ, (Red Russia), Kiev would easily fall into the hands of the Lithuanian army."

"That is true; that is true," cried Longin, "that is true, as God lives! Many would like to have your intelligence."

"But I would not like to exchange with theirs, for fear I might get beet soup instead of understanding; which might easily happen to me, among the Lithuanians."

"He is beginning to ridicule me again," said Longin.

"Allow me to finish. Well, she is not with Kshyvonos, not in Kiev; where then can she be?"

"Here is the difficulty!"

"If you can guess, tell me quickly, for I am burning to know," cried Skshetuski.

"Beyond Yampol!" said Zagloba, looking triumphantly round with his sound eye.

"How do you know that?" said Volodiyovski.

"How do I know it? Look here! I was sitting in the pig-

sty, for that rascal had shut me up in the pigsty,—may a hog
eat him, and the Cossacks were conversing all around, outside, so I put my ear close to the wall, and what did I hear?
One said 'the ataman will now ride to Yampol,' the other
answered, 'Keep still, if you value your young head.' I would
wager my neck that she is in Yampol."

"Oh, as true as God is in Heaven," said Volodiyovski.

"He cannot have taken her into the Wild Lands, so he
must have taken and hidden her somewhere between Yampol
and Yahorlik. I was in that region once when the King's
judges met those of the Khan to settle questions, arising from
the seizure of cattle on the frontier. As you gentlemen,
know, it was in Yahorlik that the frequent border questions
about driven-off cattle were settled. There are enough ravines and hiding-places there, all along the Dnieper, and a
number of woods, in which people have farms and live in a
state of lawlessness, dwell in deserted places; and do not even
see any neighbors. He may have hidden her with some of
those wild hermits because, she would be perfectly safe
there."

"Pshaw, but how can one get there, as Kshyvonos has possession of the road," said Longin. "I hear that Yampol is
also a nest of banditti."

"And if I should wage ten heads," said Skshetuski, "I will
save her. I will disguise myself and look for her and God
will help me—I will find her."

"I will go with you Yan," said Volodiyovski.

"And I will go as a beggar with my teorbane. Believe
me, sirs, I have more experience than any of you and as
I am really sick of the teorbane, I will take the bagpipes."

"Then, can I be of any assistance to you, little brother?"
said Longin.

"Certainly!" answered Zagloba, "If it is necessary to cross
the Dnieper, you can carry us over like St. Christopher."

"I thank you with all my heart, gentlemen," said Skshetuski, "and I accept your offer with a joyful heart. There is
nothing like true friends in adversity, and Providence has
not denied me these, as I see. The Great God grant me that
I may be enabled to recompense you with my health and
means."

"We shall all be like one man," cried Zagloba, "God ap-
proves of concord, and you will see that our labor will not
be in vain."

"Well, there's nothing left to me," said Skshetuski, after
a silence, "but to lead the men back to the prince and to
start out with you at once. We will go along the Dniester
until we pass Yampol and get to Yahorlik, and search
everywhere, and, if, as I hope, Khymelnitski is already
beaten, or will be before we reach the prince, we shall not
be delayed by public duty. The regiments will surely go to
the Ukraine, to subdue the rebellion there, but they will get
on without us."

"Wait a minute, gentlemen," said Volodiyovski, "after
Khmyelnitski, Kshyvonos will probably come to the front.
Perhaps we may all march with the cavalry to Yampol."

"No, we must get there first," answered Zagloba, "First
we will take the men back, in order to be unencumbered. I
hope that the prince will be contented with us."

"Especially with you."

"It is so, I shall bring the best news. Believe me, I expect a reward."

"Well, shall we set out?"

"We must wait till to-morrow," said Volodiyovski, "However, Skshetuski must give orders, for he is our leader, but,
if we start to-day, I warn you that my horses may not carry
us."

"I know that it is impracticable," said Skshetuski, "but
I think that, after the horses have been well fed, we can venture it to-morrow."

The following morning, they set out. According to the
prince's orders, they were to return to Zbaraj and there await
further orders. They rode, therefore, by way of Kujmin,
passing to one side of Felshtin to Volochisk where the old
highway led past Khlebanovka to Zbaraj. The journey was
unpleasant, for it was raining; but they travelled without disturbance, and Pan Longin, alone, who had ridden ahead with
a hundred horse, defeated a few bold bands who had collected
in the rear of the army of the commander-in-chief. It was
not till they reached Volochisk that they halted for a night's
rest. But, hardly had they fallen asleep after their long
journey, when the alarm of the watch announced that a division of horse was approaching. Soon after, came the news
that it was Vyershul with his Tartar squadrons, consequently
their own people.

Zagloba, Longin and Little Volodiyovski gathered at once
in Skshetuski's room; and, following immediately behind

them, an officer of the light cavalry dashed into the room like a whirlwind, out of breath and completely covered with mud. When Skshetuski saw him he cried:

"Vyershul!"

"It is I . . . " said the new comer, gasping for breath.

"From the prince?"

"Yes. . . . Oh, give me some air for breath!"

"What kind of news? Is Khmyelnitski defeated already?"

"All. . . over. . . with the Commonwealth!"

"By Christ's wounds, what are you saying there? Defeat?"

"A defeat, disgrace and ignominy! Without a battle. . . a panic! Woe! Woe!"

"I cannot believe my own ears. Speak, speak! By the Living God. . . . and the Commander?"

"They have fled."

"Where is our prince."

"He is retreating . . . without an army . . . I have come from him . . . the command is . . . to go at once to Lemberg . . . they are following us."

"Who? Vyershul, Vyershul! Think what you're saying man, who?"

"Khymelnitski—the Tartars!"

"In the name of the Father, the Son and the Holy Ghost!" cried Zagloba, "The world is out of joint."

But Skshetuski understood what was at stake.

"We will ask questions later,' 'he said, "now let us mount."

"To horse! To horse!"

The hoofs of Vyershul's Tartars horses were heard clattering outside the windows. The inhabitants of the place, awakened by the entrance of the soldiery, came with lanterns and torches out of the houses. The news spread like lightning over the town. Alarm bells were presently sounded The little town only a moment before was so peaceful, was now filled with screams, tramping of horses, cries of command and the wails of the Jews. The inhabitants wanted to leave the town in the company of the soldiery. Wagons were got ready, and children, women, and bedding were placed in them. The burgomaster, at the head of some of the residents, came to entreat Skshetuski not to leave them behind, but to allow them to accompany him, at least as far as Tarnopol. But Skshetuski would not listen to it, as he had direct orders from the prince to hasten to Lemburg.

They set out, therefore, and, not till they started, did

Vyershul, after having recovered himself to some extent, relate to them what had happened.

"No such misfortune," said he, "has ever befallen the Commonwealth since she came into existence; Tsetsara, Zolta Woda, and Korsun are comparatively nothing!"

And Skshetuski, Volodiyovski, and Longin bent towards the horses' necks, now taking hold of their own heads, now lifting up their hands.

"The thing passes human understanding,' 'he said, "where is the prince?"

"Forsaken, intentionally put into the background by all. He has not power, even over his own division."

"Who has the command?"

"No one, and every one. I have served a long time and have already cut my teeth in the war, but such soldiers and such leaders I never saw."

Zagloba, who had no special liking for Vyershul, and did not know him well, shook his head and smacked with his lips.

At last he said:

"My good sir, either you did not see clearly, or perhaps you regard a partial as a total defeat; for what you have told us, entirely passes in imagination."

"I grant it; but I tell you, sir, that I would willingly let my head be chopped off if, by some miraculous chance, I should be shown that I am mistaken."

"Then," continued Zagloba, "how is it that you are the first to come to Volochysk after the defeat? I will not presume that you were the first that took to your heels. Where is the army? Whither is it fleeing? What happened to it? Why, if it ran away, did it not get here before you? I am waiting in vain for an answer!"

Vyershul, at any other time, would not have let these questions pass without remark; but now he could think of nothing but of the calamity. Therefore he only said:

"I came here first, because the others have retreated by way of Ojygovts. And the prince sent me here on purpose, because he judged that you were here, gentlemen, and he wished to warn you about the enemy, that you might not be overtaken; and, secondly, because the five hundred horses that you have are no small comfort at this time, as the other division are almost all killed or separated."

"These are wonderful things," murmured Zagloba.

"It is frightful to think of it, despair seizes one, one's heart

breaks, tears flow," said Volodyovski, wringing his hands; "the
country is lost, death has become inglorious—such splendid
armies scattered . . . . destroyed! It cannot be otherwise
than that the end of the world is here, the last day of judgment approaches."

"Do not interrupt him," said Skshetuski, "let him tell it
all."

Vyershul was silent awhile, as though he would gather
strength. Nothing was to be heard but the splashing of
hoofs in the mud, for it was raining. It was late at night
and very dark as the heaven was covered with thick clouds.
And, in the midst of this darkness, this cloud, Vyershul's
words sounded weird and gruesome, as he continued:

"If I did not hope to fall in battle, I should lose my reason.
You, gentlemen, speak of the day of Judgment and say it will
soon dawn—I believe it is now here. Everything is falling
to the ground; wickedness is getting the upper hand of virtue;
anti-Christ is abroad in the world. You did not see all that
happened, but, if you cannot even stand the description of
it, how shall I describe to you the whole misfortune, the
whole ignominy, which I witnessed with my own eyes! God
gave us a favorable beginning to this war. Our prince, after
he had passed sentence on Lashch at Cholhanski Kamyen,
forgot everything else, and made friends with Prince Dominik. We were all delighted at this reconciliation and God's
blessing seemed to rest upon it. The prince was victorious
at Konstantinov and, even took the town, for the enemy forsook it after the first attack; then we went to Pilavyets,
although the prince was opposed to it. But, on the way, we
became aware of intrigues against him, envy and disaffection
and open agitation. In the councils, his advice was not
listened to; no attention was paid to it; and especial pains was
taken to divide our forces, so that the prince should not have
them all under his control. If he had then opposed them,
he would have received all the blame for the defeat, so he
was silent and patiently endured everything. Thus, the light
cavalry by order of the commander-in-chief with Vurtsel and
his cannon with Captain Makhnitski, remained in Konstantinov. They separated the Lithuanian field-commander Osinski and Korytski's squadron; so that all that remained with the
prince were the Hussars under Zatsvilikhowski, two regiments
of dragoons and a portion of my regiment under my command; in all, there were hardly two thousand men. From

that time, they seemed to despise him. I even heard some of Prince Dominik's favorites say, "If we can gain a victory now, they will not be able to say any longer that it was Vishnyovy-etski's work alone;' and they talked and said that if the prince gained so much glory, his candidate Prince Charles would probably be elected when a king was chosen; and they did not wish him, but Prince Casimir. The whole army was affected by the contagion of their example, and groups of disputants were formed just as if Delegates were sent to the Diet—one thought of everything but the battle; just as if the enemy had already been defeated. If I were to tell you, gentlemen, about the dinners and vivats, and the luxury there, you would hardly believe me. The armies of Pyrrhus, gleaming with gold, jewels, and ostrich plumes, were nothing in comparison with this army. With two hundred thousand followers and a multitude of carriages followed us; the horses swayed beneath the weight of the gold stuffs and silk tents and the carriages beneath the weight of crockery, etc. It would appear that we were setting out to conquer the whole world. The noblemen belonging to the militia cracked their whips day and night. 'How can we keep the peasants in order without drawing our swords,' said they. And we, old soldiers, foresaw evil at the sight of this unparalleled pride. And now began the trouble about Kisyelov. Some maintained that he was a traitor, others that he was an honorable Senator. Heated with drink, men fought with swords. There were no sentries, no one maintained order, no one carried on any supervision; each did as he wished, went where it seemed to him best, stood where it pleased him best. The servants created a disturbance—Oh merciful God, that was a pleasure trip, no military expedition; a carnival upon which the honor of the Commonwealth was danced away, drunk away, ridden away—and, finally, traded away."

"We are yet alive," said Pan Volodiyovski.

"And God is in heaven," added Skshetuski.

Another pause, and then Vyershul continued:

"We are totally ruined, unless God works a miracle; ceases to punish us for our sins and shows us undeserved mercy. There are moments, when, what I have seen, appears incredible to me and I feel as if it was all a nightmare. . . ."

"Go on, sir," said Zagloba, "you came to Pilavyets, and, after that?"

"And stopped there. What the commanders decided

there,—I do not know. At the Day of Judgment, they will give an account of it; for, if they had then attacked Khmyelnitski suddenly, he would have been beaten and completely routed, as true as God is in Heaven; in spite of the disorder, the want of discipline, the tumult and the lack of a leader. The 'blacks' there were already filled with fear; they were consulting how they should deliver up Khmyelnitski and the captains; and he, himself, was thinking of taking to flight. Our prince rode from tent to tent, praying, entreating, threatening, 'Let us make an assault otherwise the Tartars will come, let us attack them'—and he tore his hair—and the other leaders looked at one another, and nothing, nothing! They were drinking and holding a council. There was a rumor that the Tartars were coming; that the Khan was approaching with two hundred thousand horsemen—they continued their council. The prince shut himself up alone in his tent, for they had rebuffed him completely. It was already common talk among the soldiers that the Chancellor had forbidden Prince Dominik to begin a battle—that negotiations were being carried on. The disorder increased—finally the Tartars came, but God was yet with us on the first day. The prince attacked them; Osinski and Pan Lashch held out bravely; obliged the horde to vacate the field; killed a considerable number and then—"

Here Pan Vyersul's voice became inaudible.

"And then?" asked Zagloba.

"Then came a terrible, indescribable night. I remember, that I was keeping watch with my men beside the river, when, suddenly, I heard the thunder of cannon and a screaming in the Cossack camp, as if they were firing a salute. Then I remembered that they had told me yesterday that the whole Tartar force had not arrived, but only Tukhay Bey with a portion of them. I thought, therefore, when I heard them firing salutes, that the Khan must have come himself; until, all at once a tumult arose in our camp. I sprang forward with some of my men. What has happened? They answered 'the commanders have fled!' I hastened to Prince Dominik, he was gone; to the cup-bearer—he was gone; to the crown ensign—he was gone. Jesus of Nazareth! the soldiers were running about on the square; screams, shouts, crying, noise, tumult, the flash of torches in every direction. Where are the commanders? Where are the commanders? Others cried, To horse! To horse! Others, again, save yourself, brothers! Treason! Treason!' Holding their hands in the air with wild looks, their eyes starting out of their heads, crowding each other, trampling, crushing each other, they mounted their horses and hurried off, blindly without their weapons. Others cast away helmets, armor, weapons, tents. Finally, the prince, in his silver armor appeared at the head of his hussars. Six torches were carried beside him. He stood up in his stirrups and cried, 'Gentlemen, I am still here; come to me!' His call remained unanswered; they heard nothing. They crowded upon the hussars, threw them into confusion, trampled men and horses to the ground, and we hardly succeeded in saving the prince. Then, the whole army, plunging over trampled fires in the darkness, like a rushing stream, like a swollen cataract; the whole army fled in wild terror, out of the camp; scattered, disappeared, fled. . There is no longer any army, no leaders, no commonwealth, only ignominy; and the Cossacks' foot is on the neck. . . "

Pan Vyershul groaned and pulled on the reins, for madness and despair had possession of him; and this despair was shared by the rest, who rode through the night and rain like men bereft of reason.

They had ridden for some time, Zagloba interrupted, "Without fighting a battle! Oh ye knaves, oh ye dogs! Do you remember how boastful they were in Zbaraj, how they were going to eat Khmyelnitski, without pepper and salt? Oh you knaves!"

"Why," cried Vyershul, "they fled after the first battle they won against the Tartars and the 'blacks'. After a battle in which even the militia fought like lions."

"This is the finger of God," said Skshetuski, "but there is some mystery here which must be cleared up."

"It is not unusual for soldiers to run away," said Volodiyovski, "but in this case, the leaders were the first to leave the camp; as though they would intentionally make the victory easier for their enemies, and give over their army to slaughter."

"That's just it, that's just it!" said Vyershul, "it is said that it was done on purpose."

"Done on purpose? By God's wounds that cannot be!"

"So it is said, but why? What is behind that? Who can guess?"

"Oh may the earth swallow them up, may their race die out and their memory be covered with everlasting ignominy," said Zagloba.

"Amen," said Skshetuski.

"Amen," said Volodiyovski.

"Amen," said Volodyovski.

"Amen," repeated Pon Longin.

There is only one man who can yet save the country; if they will give him the baton and the remaining powers of the Commonwealth. There is only one, for neither the nobility nor the army will hear of any other."

"The prince!" said Skshetuski.

"It is he."

"We will stand and fall with him—long live Yeremy Vishnyoyetski," cried Zagloba.

"Long may he live," answered about a score of unsteady voices. But the cry died away, for it was no time for cheers when the ground seemed to be opening under their feet, and the heavens seemed threatening to fall down on them. There was no time for shouts and vivats. Meanwhile, day was breaking and, in the distance, the walls of Tarnopol became visible in the dim morning light.

CHAPTER IX.

The first fugitives from Pilavyets reached Lemburg at day-break on the 26th of September, at the moment that the gates of the town were opened. The dreadful news spread with the rapidity of lightning through the whole town, awakening in some, doubt and terror; in others, and these the greater number, the desire for a desperate battle. Skshetuski had arrived with his division two days later, when the town was already full of fugitive soldiery, nobility and armed citizens. They were already thinking of preparing for defence, as the Tartars were expected to arrive at any moment; but they did not yet know who would place himself at their head and what steps would be taken. Consequently, panic and disorder reigned. Many fled from the town to seek safety for their families and their possessions; but the dwellers in the vicinity, on the contrary, sought shelter in the town; the departing and entering crowds blocked the streets and caused tumults for the right of way. Everywhere might be seen carriages, packages, bundles and horses, also soldiers of the most varied uniforms. On all faces might be seen uneasiness and feverish expectation, despair or resignation. At every moment, like a sudden blast of wind, came fresh terror. Loud cries were heard; "they come! they come!" and the crowd rolled forward blindly like a wave, driven by mad fear, until they saw that a new company of fugitives was approaching; and these companies increased in number. But what a sad sight was presented by these soldiers, who, a short time before had marched out from here in gold and plumes; with songs on their lips and pride in their eyes to march against the peasant mob! To-day they came back, tattered, famished, haggard and covered with mud on weary horses, the signs of disgrace in their faces, more like beggars than knights. They might have aroused pity, if there had been time for any such feeling in this town, against whose walls the entire force of the enemy might soon be raging. And each one of these disgraced knights comforted himself with the knowledge that he had so many thousands of companions in shame. All hid themselves in the first hour, in order to recover themselves, to make complaints, to utter curses and threats, to prowl about the streets, to drink in the wineshops and to increase, if possible, the disorder and the panic.

For each one repeated the same thing, "the Tartars are on our heels!" Some said they had seen smoke behind them; others swore by all the saints that they had already been obliged to defend themselves against their pursuers. The crowds who surrounded the soldiers, listened attentively to these tidings. The roofs and church towers were packed with thousands of anxious citizens, the alarm bells were rung; and a crowd of women and children choked the churches, in which, amid the glow of wax candles, gleamed the sacred host.

Skshetuski forced his way gradually with his company from the Halitski gate through crowds of horses, wagons, soldiers, and through groups of citizens who were standing beneath their banners and through the people who looked in astonishment at this squadron which moved in perfect battle order through the town. They began to shout to one another that help was coming and, at once a most baseless joy took possession of the populace, who crowded round Skshetuski in order to seize his stirrup; other soldiers approached with the cry, "Those are Vishnyovyetski's men! Long live Prince Yeremy." Such a crowd collected that the regiment could only move forward a step at a time.

Suddenly a division of dragoons, with an officer at their head came towards them. The soldiers separated the crowd, the officer crying, "Out of the way! Make room!" and striking with the flat of his sword those who did not immediately move out of his way.

Skshetuski recognized Kushel.

The young officer heartily greeted his friend.

"What times! What times!" he said.

"Where is the prince?" asked Skshetuski.

"He would have died of sorrow if you had remained away much longer. He was already very anxious about you and your men. He is now in the Convent of St. Bernard. I am sent out to keep order in the town but Grozvayer has already taken hold of the thing. I will ride with you to the church. They are going to hold a council there."

"In the church?"

"Yes, they want to offer the prince the baton of field-marshal; for the soldiers declare that they will not defend the town under any other leader."

"Let us go, then, I also am in a hurry to see the prince."

The two companies united and rode off together. On the way, Skshetuski enquired about everything that had happened in Lemburg and if they had decided to defend it.

"They are just considering the matter," said Kushel, "The citizens want to defend it. What times these are! The men of lower rank show more heart than the nobles and the soldiers."

"And the Commanders? What has happened to them? Are they in the town, and will they not make difficulties for the prince?"

"If he only does not make any himself! There have been more favorable opportunties of giving him the field-marshal's baton; now it is too late. The commanders dare not let themselves be seen. Prince Dominik rested for a short time in the archbishop's palace and then went on his way. It was well he did so, for you cannot believe how bitter the soldiers are against him. Although he has gone, they still keep crying, 'Give him to us! We will cut him down!' He would not have escaped an attack. The cup-bearer arrived here first, and he actually began to complain of the prince; but now he is quiet, very quiet; for he has been threatened, too. They accuse him to his face, and he only swallows his tears. Everything is dreadful; what these times are! I tell you, I thank God that you were not at Pilavyets; that you did not need to fly, for it is a wonder that all who were there did not go crazy."

"And our division?"

"No longer exists! Hardly one man remains! Vurtsel is lost, Makhnitski and Zatsvilikhovski are also lost. Vurtsel and Makhnitski were not at Pilavyets for they remained in Konstantinov. That Beelzebub, Prince Dominik, left them behind there in order to weaken our prince's power. No one knows if they escaped or were taken by the enemy. Old Zatsvilikhovski has disappeared like a stone in the water. God grant, he may not be killed."

"Are many soldiers gathered here?"

"Enough; but what good does that do? The prince, alone, can restore order, if he takes the command; for they will obey no one else. The prince was terribly anxious about you and the soldiers. Yours is the only entire regiment that is left. We were already mourning for you."

"Anyone who is mourned at this time, may count himself happy."

They rode for a time in silence, looking at the crowd and listening to the noise and the cry, "The Tartars! The Tartars!" They came across the horrible spectacle of a man torn in pieces, whom the crowd suspected of being a spy. The bells rang unceasingly.

"Will the horde be here soon?" asked Zagloba.

"The Devil knows. Perhaps they may be here to-day. This town cannot defend itself long. Khmyelnitski is coming with two hundred thousand Cossacks, beside the Tartars."

"The town is lost," answered the nobleman. "It would have been better for us to have ridden away at breakneck speed. To what end have we won so many victories!"

"Over whom?"

"Over Kshyvonos, Bohun, God knows over whom besides."

"But, . . . " said Kushel, and, turning to Skshetuski, he asked in a low voice: "And you, dear Yan, has not God comforted you? Have you not found what you sought? Have you at least heard any news?"

"Now is no time to think about that," cried Skshetuski. "Of what consequence am I and my affairs, in comparison to what has happened! All is vanity, vanity until at length death comes."

"That is true," said Kushel. "The whole world must be coming to an end very soon."

They had reached St. Bernard's church, which was brightly lighted. An enormous crowd of men stood before the church, but no one could enter, for a cordon of halberdiers defended the entrance and allowed only the more important officers to enter.

Skshetuski formed his men in two ranks. "Let us go in!" said Kushel. "Half the Commonwealth is in the church."

They entered. Kushel had not exaggerated much. All who were prominent in the army and in the town, had assembled to the council. There were in the church, Voyevodas, castellans, colonels, cavalry captains, foreign officers, spiritual dignitaries, a crowd of nobility, a number of officers of lower rank, and some civil officers under Grozvayer, who was in command of the citizens. There were present, also the prince, Cup-Bearer, one of the commanders, the Voyevoda of Kiev, the Starosta of Stobnitski, and Vessel and Artsishevski, and the Lithuanian field marshal Pan Osinski. These sat before the high altar so that the public could see them. They took council in feverish haste, as is usual in such cases. The speakers rose on benches and conjured the chief officers not to give the town into the hands of the enemy without resistance. "And though we should ourselves be destroyed in the attempt, the town will hold out, the Commonwealth will recover! What do we need for defence? The walls are there, the soldiers are there and the determination is there—only the leader is lacking!" And, as this was said, a murmur arose in the crowd, which soon resolved itself into a loud shout. The people were seized with enthusiasm. "We will die, we will willingly die," they cried, "to wipe out the disgrace of Pilavyets; to save the country!" And now was heard a clashing of swords and the bare blades gleamed in the candle light while some called out, "Calm yourselves, let us take council quietly. Shall we defend ourselves, or shall we not?"

"We will defend ourselves! We will defend ourselves!" cried the crowd, so that the walls rang. "We will defend ourselves! Who will lead us, who is our leader? Prince Yeremy —he is our leader, he is a hero! He will defend the town and the Commonwealth will give him the command—long live Yeremy!"

Now, from a thousand throats arose a shout that made the walls tremble and the panes in the church windows rattle.

"Yeremy! Yeremy! Long live the Prince! Long live the Prince! Victory to him!"

A thousand sword-blades glittered; all eyes were turned towards the prince and he rose quietly with a furrowed brow. Instantly there was a deep silence:

"Gentlemen," said the prince in a sonorous voice which, amid the silence, reached every ear, "when the Cimbri and the Teutons attacked the Roman Commonwealth, no one cared to undertake the consulate, until Marius took it. But Marius had the right to seize it, for no leader had been chosen by the Senate. . . . And I would not seek flight amid this danger, but would dedicate my life to my beloved fatherland; but I dare not accept the baton, as, by so doing, I might offend my country, the Senate and the higher authorities. I will not be a self-appointed leader. Among us is the man to whom the Commonwealth would give the baton—that is the Crown Cup-Bearer. . . . "

The prince was forced to stop speaking, for he had no sooner mentioned the name of the Cup-Bearer than a frightful noise and clashing of swords ensued. The crowd became restless, gave vent to their feelings and flamed up like powder to which a spark has been applied. "Away with him! Kill him! Pereat!" echoed through the crowd. "Pereat, pereat!" sounded in louder tones.

The Cup-Bearer sprang from his seat, pale, with large beads of cold perspiration on his forehead. Threatening forms approached nearer the altar, and, already, were heard the ominous words, "Give him to us!"

The prince, who saw what turn things were taking, stood up and stretched forth his right hand.

The crowd stopped short. They thought the prince was going to speak. In a moment all was quiet. But the prince only wished to quiet the storm, to quell the tumult, to allow no shedding of blood in the church; and he sat down again when he saw that the danger was over. Separated from him only by the Voyevoda of Kiev sat the unfortunate Cup-Bearer. His gray head had sunk on his breast, his hands hung listlessly at his side and, from his mouth came these words, broken with sobs:

"Lord! for my sins I am willing to bear my cross."

The old man might have awakened pity in the hardest heart; but the mob is usually unmerciful; and the noise began afresh. Suddenly the Voyevoda of Kiev stood up, and motioned with his hand that he was about to speak. He was a companion in arms of Prince Yeremy, so that the people listened to him willingly.

"He, however, turned to the prince and conjured him in the most touching manner not to refuse the offer of the baton and not to fail to save his country. "When the Commonwealth is in danger, let all private discord cease. She will not be saved by him who has been appointed, but by him who is most competent to save her."

"Take the baton, thou unconquered hero! Take it! Save her! Not the town alone, the whole Commonwealth. In her name, I, the old man, entreat thee; and, with me, all ranks, all men, all women and children entreat thee, save us—save us!"

Something now occurred which moved all hearts. A woman in deep mourning approached the altar and, casting some jewels and gold ornaments at the feet of the prince, she kneeled before him and cried, sobbing loudly, "We bring thee our possessions! We give our lives into thy hands. Save us! Save us!—or we are lost."

At this sight, the Senators, the soldiery, and, with them the whole crowd broke into loud weeping and, with one voice, the cry resounded through the church:

"Save us!"

The prince covered his eyes with his hands and, when he raised his face, his lashes were wet with tears; but still he hesitated. What would be the effect on the Commonwealth if he should accept the dignity of Commander.

Now the Cup-Bearer arose.

"I am old," he said, "unhappy, and bowed with care. I ought to lay down the burden which is beyond my strength. In the sight of the Crucified One, and of the assembled knights, I deliver up my baton—take it!"

And he handed the symbol of his office to Prince Vishnyovyetski. There was a moment of such deep silence that one might have heard the winging of a fly, then Prince Yeremy's voice was heard, saying in solemn tones:

"For my sins—I will accept it."

Now ensued a wild scene in the crowd. They pressed forward, fell at the feet of the prince and cast their treasures and gold before him. The news flew like lightning through the whole town, the soldiers were almost crazy with joy, and cried that they would march against Khmyelnitski, the Tartars and the Sultan. The citizens no longer thought of giving themselves up, but only of defending themselves, to the last drop of blood. The Armenians brought voluntary gifts of money to the town hall some time before there was any talk of an assessment. The Jews, in their synagogues, raised a cry of gratitude. The cannon on the ramparts announced the joyful news; in the streets, muskets, guns and pistols were fired. The cry, "Long live Yeremy!" continued the whole night. Whoever did not understand the situation might have thought that the town was celebrating a great triumph, or was keeping a feast.

And, yet, at any moment, three hundred thousand of the enemy, a larger army than the emperor of Germany, or the French king, could call into the field, and more savage than Tamerlane's forces, might besiege the walls of this town.

CHAPTER X.

A week afterwards, on the morning of the sixth of October, the terrible and unexpected news was spread in Lemburg that Prince Yeremy, taking with him the greater part of the army, had left the town and no one knew whither he had gone.

Groups of people collected before the archbishop's palace; at first they would not believe the news. The soldiers surmised that if the prince had really gone it must have been at the head of a large division of the army to explore the neighborhood. It was said that deserters had spread false reports, for they affirmed that at any moment Khmyelnitski and the Tartars might appear. And since the twenty-sixth day of September, ten days had already passed without any sign of the enemy. The prince wished to convince himself with his own eyes whether there was any danger and would probably return when he had verified the reports. Besides, he had left several regiments, and everything in readiness for defence.

This was what really happened. All kinds of orders were given, posts assigned and the cannon brought on the ramparts. In the evening Captain Tsikhotski arrived with fifty dragoons. They were surrounded at once by an eager crowd, but he would not talk with them, but went straight to General Artsishevski. They both sent for Grozvayer, and after a consultation went to the Town Hall. Tsikhotski there told the terrified audience that the prince had gone, never to return.

At the first moment, all were thunder-struck and bold voices cried, "Traitor!" But Artsishevski at once arose. He was an old man, celebrated as a leader for his great services in the Holland army, and he spoke as follows to the soldiers and the councillors:

"I have heard insulting words that had better never been spoken, for despair could not justify them. The prince has gone away and will never return—that is true; but what right have you to demand that a leader, upon whose shoulders rests the salvation of the whole country, should defend your little town alone; what would happen if the rest of the army of the

Commonwealth were surrounded by the enemy? We have here neither provisions, nor arms, nor food, for such a large army. Moreover, I tell you, and you may believe my words, that the more soldiers you have shut up here, the shorter the time of defence will last, for hunger would besiege us sooner than the enemy. Khmyelnitski cares more for the person of the prince than he does for your town. When he finds out, therefore, that he is no longer here; that he has collected a new army and may come here to garrison it; he will be the more likely to give in to you and listen to negotiations. To-day you grumble, but I tell you that the prince, in leaving this town and threatening Khmyelnitski from outside, is protecting you and your children. Contain yourselves, defend yourselves, keep off the enemy for a time, and you will not only save the town, but render the Commonwealth an ever-lasting service. For the prince can meanwhile gather new forces and garrison other fortresses. The torpid Commonwealth will rouse itself from slumber and hasten to your assistance. He has opened the only way of salvation; for if he had fallen a sacrifice to hunger with his forces, no one would have remained to repulse the enemy; who might then go without resistance to Cracow and Warsaw and swarm over the whole country. Therefore, instead of grumbling, run to the walls to defend yourselves, your children, the town, and the whole Commonwealth."

"To the walls! To the walls!" repeated several bold voices.

Grozvayer, an energetic and courageous man, remarked:

"Your silence, gentlemen, pleases me, and let me tell you that your prince has not gone away without arranging everything for the defence. Everybody knows what to do. What has happened, had to happen. I have charge of the defence and I will protect you till death."

Hope kindled anew in the anxious hearts, and Tsikhotski then took up the word:

"His Excellency sends word that the enemy is at hand. Lieutenant Skshetuski with one of his wings came across a Tartar chambul of two thousand men and defeated them. The prisoners say that an enormous force is following them."

This news made a great impression. There were a few moments of silence and all hearts beat joyfully. "To the ramparts!" said Grozvayer.

"To the ramparts! To the ramparts!" repeated the assembled officers and citizens.

At this moment, a noise was heard outside the windows. Thousands of voices arose from a roaring crowd, that resembled the waves of the sea. Suddenly the door was opened with violence, several citizens dashed through it; and, before the council had time to ask what had happened, a shout arose:

"Flames in the sky! Flames in the sky!"

"And the Word is become flesh!" said Grozvayer. "To the ramparts! ! ! To the ramparts! ! !"

The hall was deserted.

A moment later, the thunder of cannon shook the walls of the town and made the inhabitants tremble, announcing to the suburbs and the outlying villages that the enemy was at hand. The eastern sky was blood red as far as the eye could reach. It looked as though a sea of fire was approaching the town.

*   *   *   *   *   *   *

The prince, meanwhile, had marched to Zamost, and after he had destroyed the little Tartar camp of which Tsikhotski had spoken, he set to work to repair and garrison it, as it was already a natural fortress; and, in a short time, had rendered it impregnable. Skshetuski, with Pan Longin and a portion of the squadron in the citadel, had remained with Pan Veyherz, the Starotsa of Valetsk; the prince proceeded to Warsaw in order to demand from the Diet means to provide a fresh force, and also to take part in the election of the king, which was to be held at that time. Vishnyovyetski's fate and that of the whole Commonwealth hung on this election; for, if Prince Charles were elected, the war party would maintain the upper hand—the prince would receive the chief command over the united armies of the Commonwealth and it would lead up to a decisive battle, for death or life, with Khmyelnitski. Prince Casimir, although well known for his personal courage and for his warlike character, was justly considered a partisan of Chancellor Ossolinski, whose politics tended to negotiations with the Cossacks and the granting to them of great concessions. Both brothers made no end of promises and strove to increase the number of their followers. Consequently, as they each had an equal chance, no one could foresee the result of the election. The chancellor's party feared that Vishnyovyetski, thanks to his ever-increasing fame and the love which the nobility and the knights bore him, would obtain a majority for Prince Charles; and the prince, on account of these apprehensions, desired to support his candidate in person. Therefore he hastened to Warsaw, with the certainty that Zamost was in a condition to stand a long siege against the whole strength of Khmyelnitski and the Crimea. Lemburg might, to all appearances, be regarded as secure; for Khmyelnitski would certainly not waste time in storming this town when he had the far more important Zamost before him; which blocked his way into the heart of the Commonwealth. These thoughts cheered the prince and filled his heart with renewed confidence, which he needed, in his present anxious condition regarding the fate of his country. He hoped surely that, even if Casimir were chosen, he would see that the war had became an unavoidable necessity, and that this terrible rebellion could only be drowned in a sea of blood. He expected also that the Commonwealth would fit out another army; for even negotiations could not be carried on without the assistance of a mighty military force.

Lulled by such thoughts, the prince, under the protection of several regiments, rode alongside Zagloba and Volodiyovski; the former swore by all he held dear that he would bring about the election of Prince Charles, as he knew how to talk to his noble brethren and how to take them. The latter commanded the Prince's escort. In Siennits, not far from Minsk, the Prince was surprised by an agreeable and quite unexpected meeting. He found Princess Grizelda there. She was hastening from Bjesh-Litevsk to Warsaw, so as to be in greater safety, and also with the hope that she might find the prince there. Their meeting was a very happy one and all the more so as it was so unexpected. The princess, although a woman of iron courage, threw herself with sobs and tears into the arms of her husband and could not be quieted for some hours; for how often had she given up all hope of ever seeing him again. And now God had permitted him to return more famous than ever, with more veneration accorded him than any of his race had yet received.

The greatest leader, the one hope of the Commonwealth. The princess, raising her head from his shoulder, looked through her tears at his tanned, emaciated face, at his noble forehead, upon which care and fatigue had traced deep furrows, at his eyes, red and weary from sleepless nights; and her tears flowed afresh and all her ladies of honor wept with her from the depths of their hearts. Gradually she became calmer, and accompanied by the prince went into the spacious house of the provost. And then began questions and inquiries about friends, about courtiers and knights who had been considered as part of their own family, and who were associated in her memory with Lubni. The prince quieted her anxiety about Pan Skshetuski and explained to her that he had only remained in Zamost because, amidst all the sorrow that God had laid on him, he could not endure the noise of the capital, but preferred rough military service, in order to deaden the wounds of his heart. The prince then introduced Pan Zagloba and praised his exploits. "This is an incomparable man," he said, "who not only snatched the young Panna Kurtsevich out of Bohun's hands, but also led her in safety through Khmyelnitski's camp, and through the midst of the Tartars; and also conducted himself in the most praiseworthy manner at Konstantinov." When the princess heard this, she was profuse in her compliments to Pan Zagloba, repeatedly held out her hand for him to kiss and promised him at some future time a better reward. The incomparable man bowed low, maintaining the modesty of a hero; and then he became puffed up and winked over at the court ladies; for, although he was old and did not make any further conquests among the fair sex, he was yet flattered that so many had heard of his bravery and his exploits. But this meeting was not one of unmixed joy; for, apart from the thought of the sad times that oppressed the Commonwealth, the princess was painfully affected when, in answer to her frequent inquiries for this or the other well-known knight, she received the answer, "He is dead, he is dead, he has fallen!" The young ladies were also cast down, for among these names were more than one that they loved.

Thus joy was blended with sadness, and tears with smiles. But the one who grieved the most was Pan Volodiyovski, for in vain he looked round him on all sides and cast his eyes in every direction—Princess Barbara was not to be seen. Indeed, during the fatigues of war, the continual battles, encounters and marches, this cavalier, who was by nature as susceptible in love as he was inconstant, had partially forgotten his fair lady. But now, when he saw the court ladies of the princess and the life in Lubni came vividly to his mind, he thought to himself that, now the hour of rest had arrived, it would be agreeable to sigh and to awaken afresh the flame of his heart. But, as he could not do this and his old inclination, as if out of obstinacy awoke once more, Pan Volodiyov-ski grieved greatly and looked as if drenched by rain. He hung his head, and his slender moustachios, which were usually twisted upwards till the ends almost reached his nostrils like the feelers of a cockchafer, now hung down too. His pug nose seemed to grow longer, his face had lost its ordinary cheerful expression, and he stood still, and did not move, even when the prince in turn praised his courage and his remarkable endowments. What did he care for words of praise if she could not hear them?

Anusia Borzobahata took pity on him, and although they continually had spats she resolved to comfort him. With this intention, after casting a side glance at the princess, she moved gradually nearer to the knight until she was close beside him.

"Good morning, Pan," she said, "we have not seen one another for a long time."

"Alas, Panna Anna," answered Pan Michael, in a melancholy voice, "a flood of water has poured over us since then and we meet in sad times and not all of us."

"It is true, that not all of us are here, for many knights have been killed."

Here Anna sighed and presently continued: "Our number is smaller than it was, for Panna Syenyutovna is married and Princess Barbara remained with the Voyevodovna of Vilna."

"And she will be married, too."

"No, she is not thinking about that yet; but why do you ask, Sir?"

As she said this she dropped her dark little eyes so that only the eyelids were visible and looked askance beneath her lashes at the knight.

"On account of my well wishes for the family," answered Pan Michael.

"That is right, Pan Michael," answered Anusia, "for Princess Barbara is a very good friend of yours. She often asked 'where is my young knight who at the tourney in Lubni has thrown down so many Turkish heads, for which I rewarded him? What is he doing? I wonder if he is alive and still remembers us?'"

Pan Michael raised his eyes gratefully to Anusia and was happy, and then observed that Anna had improved remarkably.

"Did Princess Barbara really say that?" he asked.

"As true as I live and—she remembered how you jumped across the moat for her that time you fell into the water."

"And where is Pani Voyevodovna of Vilnanov?"

"She was with us in Brest Litovski, a week ago she went to Belsk, and from there will go to Warsaw."

Volodiyovski looked at Anusia the second time and could not contain himself any longer.

"And you, Panna Anna," he said, "have grown so beautiful that it fairly blinds one to look at you."

The girl smiled thankfully.

"Pan Michael, you are only saying this to capture me."

"I might have done it once," he said, shrugging his shoulders. "God knows I tried it and could not, and now—I wish Pan Podbipyenta happiness."

"And where is Pan Podbipyenta?" asked Anusia in a low tone, with her eyes cast down.

"In Zamost with Skshetuski. He has been promoted to the lieutenancy and is in active service, but if he had known whom he would see here, as true as God is in heaven, he would have taken leave and ridden here with giant strides. He is a great cavalier who deserves every favor."

"And did he meet with reverses in the war?"

"It seems to me that you don't want to ask that, but whether he has got the three heads that he was determined to cut off."

"I do not believe that he meant that in earnest."

"And yet, you must believe it, Panna; without those heads, he can do nothing. He is seeking every opportunity to find them. At Makhnovka, we even rode into the middle of the battle, in which he was fighting his way in the crowd, in order to look at him. The prince himself was with us, for I must tell you that I have been in many battles, but I never saw such slaughter as I saw there, and I will never forget it. When he fastens your scarf round him, he can fight terribly. He will find his three heads. Do not be anxious."

"May each one find what they seek," said Anusia, sighing.

Volodiyovski also sighed and turned his eyes to the ceiling. He was suddenly surprised at something he saw in one corner of the room.

In this corner an angry, fiery face entirely unknown to him, was staring at him. This face possessed a gigantic nose, and moustaches that looked like wisps and twitched nervously as if in suppressed passion.

Any one might have been frightened for that nose, those eyes and moustaches, but little Pan Volodiyovski was not at all backward, therefore, as said above, he only wondered, and turning to Anusia, asked: "What kind of man is that in the corner who is looking at me as if he would like to swallow me, which moved quickly, like an old Tom cat at prayers?"

"That, said Anna, showing her little white teeth, "that is Pan Kharlamp."

"What kind of a heathen is that?"

"He is no heathen at all, but the Captain in the light horse, of the Voyevoda of Vilna, who is taking us to Warsaw and is to wait there for the Voyevoda. Do not offend him, Pan Michael, for he is a great man-eater."

"I see that, I see that; but if he is a man-eater there are fatter morsels than 1. Wherefore should he sharpen his teeth on me and not on some one else?"

"Because . . " said Anusia, giggling gently.

"Because what?"

"Because he is in love with me and told me himself that he would tear anyone to pieces who came near me and now— believe me—it is only the presence of the prince and princess that prevents him from seeking a quarrel with you immediately."

"Now you have it!" said Pan Volodiyovski, gladly. "Is that so, Panna Anna? Oh, I see now that it was not in vain that we sang, 'Like unto a Tartar horde, hast thou taken captive the heart.' Do you remember, Panna? You cannot move from one place to another without someone falling in love with you?"

"That is my misfortune," said Anna, with her eyes cast down.

"Ah, what a Pharisee you are! What would Pan Longin say?"

"Is it my fault that this Pan Kharlamp follows me? I cannot bear him; I do not want to see him."

"Well, well, see to it, Panna, that he does not shed any blood on your account. You can dress a wound with Podbipyenta, but when it comes to a question of love it is dangerous to trifle with him."

"I wish he would cut off his ears, I would be glad of it."

As she said this, she whirled round like a top and in a moment was on the other side of the room beside Pan Carboni the prince's medical attendant, to whom she whispered much and entered into a lively conversation. The Italian fixed his gaze on the ceiling as if he were in perfect ecstasy.

Meanwhile Zagloba had approached Volodiyovski, and winked at him roguishly with his sound eye.

"Pan Michael," he said, "who is that crested lark?"

"Panna Anna Borzobahata-Krashyenska, the lady-in-waiting to the princess."

"And a fine creature. Eyes like saucers, little mouth like a picture and a neck—ah!"

"Nothing! Nothing!"

"I congratulate you!"

"Give us peace, Sir; that is Pan Longin's fiancee; or as good as his betrothed."

"Pan Longin? But by God's wounds! He has made a vow of chastity, and besides even if there is this understanding between them, he could hide her behind his coat collar; she could perch upon his moustache like a fly—what now?"

"Yes, she will manage him; Hercules was stronger, and yet a woman outwitted him."

"If only she does not play him false, but I, as true as I am Zagloba, will do my best to bring that about."

"There are many others in your position, although she is a good girl and comes from a good family. It is a pity because she is young and pretty."

"You praise her because you are a true cavalier, but she is a great flirt, I am certain of it."

"Beauty attracts people; as, for example, do you see that captain yonder? they say he is dreadfully in love with her."

"Pshaw! And just look at that crow she is talking to now. Who the devil is he?"

"That is the Italian Carboni, the prince's physician."

"Watch, Pan Michael, how his gig lamps sparkle and look as though they were in delirium. Ah, it is bad for Pan Longin. I know something about it, for when I was young I had many experiences. At a suitable time, I will tell you about all that I went through; but, if you care, I will tell you at once."

Zagloba began to whisper into the little knight's ear and to blink more furiously than ever, but just then came the command to proceed on the journey. The prince got into the carriage with the princess in order to converse freely after their long separation. The young court ladies were in the other carriages, the knights mounted their horses and all

34

set out. In the van, were the court suite, the soldiers a little
behind them; for the country was quiet in this region, and
the escort was only for form not for safety. They went
therefore from Siennits to Minsk and from there to Warsaw,
making frequent stops, as was the custom at that time. The
highway was so packed that they advanced very slowly.
Everyone from far and near was hastening to the elections,
from far and near even from far Lithuania. Here and there
whole noblemen's suites met each other, whole trains of gilt
coaches surrounded by Hayduks dressed in Turkish manner,
behind whom came the court companies, Hungarian and
German; now divisions of Janissaries; now Cossacks, and
finally, the important squadrons of the inconquerable Polish
cavalry. Each of the more distinguished Poles endeavored
to appear with as much gorgeousness, display, and number
of followers as possible. Beside the numerous cavalcades of
the magnates, moved the smaller and less important district
and provincial dignitaries. Every now and then, from out
the clouds of dust, appeared a single nobleman's carriage,
and in each carriage sat a nobleman, or a priest with a crucifix or an image of the Holy Virgin on his breast, attached
to a silk ribbon. All were armed with a musket on one side
and a sword on the other, and among the active or retired
officers, lances protruded nearly two yards at the back of the
saddle. Pointers and greyhounds ran in and out among the
carriages, not for hunting, since it was not on a hunting expedition, but for the amusement of their owners. In the rear,
pages led horses with costly saddles that were covered completely so as to protect the costly equipments from dust and
rain. Then came creaking wagons with wheels made of
woven reeds, carrying the tents and provisions for the masters
and servants. When the wind suddenly blew the dust from
the highway, the procession was wrapped in a cloud and
looked like a hundred colored serpent, or a ribbon embroidered in mystical figures in golden silk. Here and there the
joyous strains of Italian bands or of the Janissaries might be
heard, especially in the ranks of the royal and Lithuanian
regular soldiers, of which there were numbers in that throng.
These accompanied the procession as escort of the royal dignitaries. Everywhere were heard cries, noise, shouts, questions and wranglings, because one would not get out of another's way. From time to time soldiers and officers rode
up to the prince's train with the request that they would

make room for one or the other dignitary, or else to inquire who was traveling here, but, as soon as they heard the answer, "The Voyevoda of Russia," they at once announced it to their masters, who then left the road clear, or if they were ahead turned aside to look at the prince's train. The nobles and the soldiers crowded together at the halting places, looking with eager eyes at the greatest warrior of the Commonwealth. There was no lack of cheers, for which the prince gracefully expressed his thanks, partly from his natural kindliness and partly in order to win adherents for Prince Charles, which were often captivated at the mere sight of him. The prince's regiments, those soldiers that were called Rusinow[1] were also regarded with the same curiosity. They were no longer ragged and worn, as after the battle of Konstantinov, for the prince had bought them new uniforms in Zamost. Nevertheless, the crowd gazed at them as though they were monsters from beyond the sea; for the inhabitants of some of the surrounding towns of the capital, thought that they came from the end of the world. They told one another wonderful stories about those mysterious steppes and forests, in which such knights were born; admired their faces that were browned by the wind from the Black Sea; their proud look, and a certain savagery of appearance that distinguished them from their wild neighbors.

But most of the glances, turned, after the prince, on Pan Zagloba; who, as soon as he noticed the surrounding people who were admiring him, looked sturdily and boldly and rolled his eye so frightfully, that the crowd began to whisper to one another, "He must be the most distinguished of all the knights," others said, "This fierce dragon must have driven many souls from their bodies." When such words reached Zagloba's ears, he endeavored to conceal his inward satisfaction by a still more fierce demeanor.

Now he spoke to the crowd; now he ridiculed them, and especially the companies of the Lithuanian horsemen, whose heavy cavalry wore a golden loop across their shoulders, while the light cavalry wore a silver one.

"What is it you have on, Pan Loop," cried Zagloba, at sight of them, and more than one ground their teeth and grasped their swords; but when they remembered that he belonged to a regiment of the Voyevoda of Russia they let it pass, spat on the ground, and avoided any quarrel.

---

[1] Russians.

Near Warsaw, the crowd became so dense that one could hardly advance at all. The election of the king appeared to assemble more people than usual, for the nobility thronged hither from the farthest Russian and Lithaninan regions; not only on account of the election but also to seek safety in Warsaw. And yet the election would not be for several days, as the first assembly of the Diet had hardly begun; but everyone went there one or two months in advance in order to find quarters in the city; to bring themselves to the remembrance of this one or the other one; to look for promotion and invitations to dinner at the different lord's houses; and, in fact, after the harvest to enjoy the luxury of the capital. The prince looked through the windows of his carriage at this crowd of knights, soldiers and nobles; at this wealth; at these gorgeous clothes; and thought how many soldiers he could have armed with that money; what an army he could have sent into the field. How did it happen that a Commonwealth that was so thickly populated and so rich and full of valiant knights should be so powerless that she could not protect herself against a Khmyelnitski and the wild Tartars, why was it? He could not understand. Khmyelnitski's thousands could be answered by more thousands, if this nobility, these soldiers, these riches and abundance, these regiments and squadrons would have served the public interests as readily as they did their own private interests. "There is no more virtue in the Commonwealth," thought the prince, "the great body is beginning to decay, the old valor has become enervated in the delights of comfort. The nobles and the soldiery no longer love the fatigues of war." The prince was partially right, but he considered the situation of the Commonwealth from the standpoint of a warrior and a leader who would willingly have turned every man into a soldier and would have led him against the enemy. Valor was still to be found and came to the front, when a little later, much more serious wars threatened the Commonwealth. She lacked another thing that the martial prince did not foresee at this moment, but that his enemy the Crown Chancellor, who was a more experienced statesman than Prince Yeremy, well understood.

The pointed towers of Warsaw gleamed in the gray distance. The Prince's reflections were interrupted and he gave orders which the officers on duty imparted to Volodiyovski, the leader of the escort. Consequently, Pan Michael left his place at the side of Anusia's carriage, where he had been riding, in order to join his company, which was some way behind and bring them up with the rest. He had not gone many steps when he heard somebody coming up behind him. He looked round—it was Pan Kharlamp, Captain of the Voyevoda of Vilna's light cavalry, Anusia's adorer. Volodiyovski reined in his horse for he understood at once that he would have to meet this man; and Pan Michael loved such things with his whole soul. Pan Kharlamp rode up beside him and, at first, said nothing; but panted and tugged fiercely at his moustache, evidently seeking for words. Finally he said :

"I greet you, Pan Dragoon."

"I greet you, Pan of the Line."

"How dare you call me that?" asked Kharlamp, grinding his teeth, "me, a captain, and a companion in arms, eh?"

Pan Volodiyovski began to throw into the air the little axe, which he had in his hand, his whole attention apparently being only directed to endeavoring to catch it by the handle at every turn, and he answered indifferently:

"Because I do not recognize your rank by your loop.'

"You insult officers with whom you are not equal."

"And why?" innocently asked the rascal Volodiyovski.

"Because you are serving in a foreign regiment."

"Calm yourself," said Pan Michael, "even if I am in the dragoons, I am an officer and not one of the least, but in the highest rank of the Voyevoda's service. You can therefore speak to me as your equal, or as your superior."

Pan Kharlamp began to understand that he was not dealing with a person of no importance, as he imagined; but he continued to grind his teeth, for Volodiyovski's indifference made him still more angry. He said, therefore:

"How did you dare to get in my way?"

"Oh, I see you are anxious for a quarrel."

"Perhaps, and I will tell you one thing," here Pan Kharlamp leaned over to Volodiyovski and said in a low tone:

"I will cut your ears off if you get in my way where Panna Anna is concerned."

Volodiyovski again twirled his little axe, as if his right hand were accustomed to such play, and said mockingly to Pan Kharlamp.

"Oh, gracious sir, permit me to live a little longer—permit me—permit me."

"No, that will not do, you cannot escape me so easily," said Pan Kharlamp seizing the little knight by the arm.

"I will try not to escape you," said Volodiyovski, gently; "but, at present, I am on duty and am hurrying to execute my master's orders. Let go my sleeve, sir, let it go, I beg you; for otherwise there will be nothing left for me to do but to —to cut you over the head with this axe and knock you from your horse."

The voice which had commenced so gently now hissed so dangerously that Pan Kharlamp involuntarily looked at the little knight in astonishment and let go his sleeve.

"Oh, that makes no difference," he said, "you will have to meet me in Warsaw. I will not let you out of my sight."

"I will not hide myself, but how can we settle this affair in Warsaw? Have the goodness to tell me. I a simple soldier have never yet been there, but I have heard of court martials that punishes the unsheathing of a sword in the presence of the king, or his representative with death."

"One can see that you have never been in Warsaw and are a boor, as you fear the court; and do not know that during the interregnum the chapter dispenses justice. And in this case an explanation will be easy, and for the sake of your ears they would not be likely to cut off my head—believe me."

"I thank you for your information and beg for further instructions, for I see you are not a bad instructor and are also a well-informed man. And I, as a man who has only studied the minor sciences and hardly know how to make an adjective agree with a noun, should I venture, which may God forbid, to call you a fool, only wish to know if I should say stultus and not stulta or stultum."

Here Pan Volodiyovski again tossed his axe. Pan Kharlamp became embarrassed, and his face flushed, and drew his sword. At the same moment the little knight raised forth his axe and it gleamed in the air. They looked at one another for a moment like two aurochs, with distended nostrils and eyes flashing fire—but Pan Kharlamp was the first to remember that he would have to answer to the Voyevoda himself if he should attack any officer in his service, so he was the first to sheath his sword:

"Oh, I will find you, you son. . . .. " he said.

"You will find me? You will find me? You beet-broth!" said the little knight.

And they separated. One rode to join his cavalcade, the other to his regiment which had advanced during this time, and clouds of dust filled the air from the hoofs of the approaching horses. Pan Michael did not take long to place his regiment in order and to ride at their head. Presently, Zagloba trotted up to him.

"What did that sea-scarecrow want with you?" he asked Volodiyovski.

"Pan Kharlamp? Oh, nothing, he was only calling me out."

"Now you have it," said Zagloba. "He will bore you through with his nose. Look out, Pan Michael, if you fight with him, that you do not cut off the largest nose in the Commonwealth, for it would require an unusually large grave mound? How happy is the Voyevoda of Wilna! Others are obliged to send out military expeditions against the enemy, but this nobleman of his can scent the enemy from afar. But why does he call you out?"

"Because I rode beside Panna Anna Borzobahata's carriage."

"Pshaw! You should have told him to go to Pan Longin at Zamost. He would have received him with pepper and ginger; this beet-broth swiller's fortune is not so great as his nose."

"I said nothing to him about Pan Podbipyenta;" said Volodiyovski, "for how could I, as long as he left me in peace? Just out of obstinacy, I will make desperate love to Anusia; I shall get some enjoyment out of it and what can we find better to do in Warsaw?"

"We shall find something to do, Pan Michael, do not fear," said Zagloba, winking. In my young days when I was the regiment tribute collector we marched over the whole country; but nowhere did I find such gay life as in Warsaw."

"Do you think it is different from our life beyond the Dnieper?"

"There is no comparison."

"I am quite curious," said Pan Michael, and added, after a pause, "and I will nip this beet-broth swiller's moustache, for he wears it too long."

CHAPTER XI.

Several weeks had passed. Fresh nobles came crowding every day to the election. In the town the population had increased ten-fold; for, beside the crowd of nobles, thousands of merchants and bazaar traders came thither from different parts of the world, from distant Persia to the coasts of England beyond the sea. In the quarter of the town called Woli they had put up a wooden building for the Senate and round about it, might be seen already thousands of tents which completely covered the ground. No one knew as yet which of the two candidates would be elected, the king's son Casimir, the Cardinal, or Charles Ferdinand, the bishop of Plotski.

Both parties exerted themselves to the utmost. Thousands of circulars were distributed, setting forth the virtues and faults of the candidates. Both sides had many and powerful adherents. To Charles's party belonged, as we know, Prince Yeremy; and this was all the more dangerous for the opposite party that it seemed more and more probable that he would carry with him the nobility, who were very devoted to him and on whom everything depended; but Casimir was not lacking in strength. The provincial governors were on his side, and he had the influence of the chancellor. The Primate also seemed to favor him, and behind him stood the greater number of the magnates, each of whom had a considerable following. And, among these magnates was Prince Dominik Zaslovski-Ostrogski, Voyevoda of Sandomier, who, although actually dishonored after the affair of Pilavyets and even threatened with justice, was still the greatest Lord in the Commonwealth; yes, even in the whole of Europe; and had besides unlimited wealth to throw into the balance for his candidate.

Nevertheless, Casimir's adherents had many moments of bitter doubt; for, as we have said, everything finally depended on the nobility, who, from the fourth of October, had begun to pour into Warsaw and were still coming in by thousands from all parts of the Commonwealth; and carried away by

536

the greatness of Vishnyovyetski and the prince's interested generosity, declared one and all for Prince Charles. Charles was able and hospitable and did not fail on this occasion, to give considerable sums towards forming fresh regiments, which were to be placed under Vishnyovyetski's command. Casimir would willingly have followed his example and it was not stinginess, but on the contrary, a too great open-handedness which had caused continual depletion of his treasury that now prevented him from giving. During this time, active consultations were going on between the two parties. Messengers were sent daily between Nyeporenta and Yablonna. Casimir, on account of his seniority and in consideration of brotherly love conjured Prince Charles to withdraw and leave the field clear for him, but the bishop would not listen to this request, and wrote that it was not right to turn away any fortune that might come to him, especially as this fortune was in accordance with the suffrage of the whole Comonwealth which had nominated him for its ruler. And meanwhile the time passed, the six weeks interval was coming to a close and, with it, the terror of the Cossacks; for news had arrived that Khmyelnitski had raised the siege of Lemburg, after storming it several times, and that he was now before Zamost, the last rampart of the Commonwealth, which he was storming day and night.

It was also said that besides the ambassador whom Khmyelnitski had sent with a letter, and an announcement that, as a Polish nobleman, he declared in favor of Prince Casimir, he had sent to Warsaw a whole swarm of disguised Cossack captains who had sneaked into the ranks of the nobility without being recognized. They were dressed like the true nobility, and could not be distinguished from them even in their speech; and were especially like the nobility from the Russian district. Some had gone there, it was said, out of pure curiosity; in order to see the election festivities and to see Warsaw; others had gone to find out what was said about the coming war; how many soldiers the Commonwealth could put in the field and what money she had to spend on it. Much that was told about these guests might be true; for, among the Zaporojian captains there were many noblemen who lived in the Cossack fashion and also understood Latin, which made it all the more difficult to recognize them. In the farther steppes, Latin did not flourish and people even like the princess Kurtsevich did not understand it, as well as Bohun and other atamans.

These and similar umors which had circulated in the town, as well as in the election camp, combined with the news of Khmyelnitski's approach and the expeditions of the Cossacks and Tartars who were advancing to the Vistula, filled men's hearts with fear and unrest, and often gave rise to tumults. It was quite enough among the assembled nobility to suspect anyone of being a Zaporojian in disguise and, in a moment, before he could justify himself, he was cut to pieces by their swords. In this manner, several innocent men came to their death and the dignity and earnestness of the election suffered in consequence; especially as, in those times, drunkenness was not looked upon with much disfavor. The Chapter for the security of the place could not restrain the continual disputes which at the first opportunity turned into a fight. But if earnest men who were filled with love of good and of peace lamented these tumults in the face of the danger which threatened their country, the frivolous, the fighters and the drunkards, the dice throwers and ruffians who were in their element, considered this time as their period of harvest and committed all sorts of misdemeanors with the greatest audacity.

It is not necessary to say that Pan Zagloba was their leader, as one might have supposed from his distinguished position, as well as his insatiable thirst for drink, and his fluent tongue, which was equalled by none, and his absolute self-confidence which nothing could shake. At times he was even attacked by melancholy and then he shut himself up in his room or in the tent, saw no one; and, when he came out, he was in a horrible temper and ready for serious quarrels and fighting. It transpired that, in a similar humor, he had wounded Pan Dunchevski of Ravianina severely; for no other reason than, that in passing by, he had pushed against Zagloba's sword: At such times, he could endure the company of no one but Pan Michael, to whom he then complained that a longing to see Skshetuski and the 'poor girl' was consuming him. "We have forsaken them, Pan Michael," he would say, "like traitors we have given them over into ungodly hands and you cannot excuse yourself with your nemine excepto! What do you suppose is happening to her, Pan Michael?"

It was in vain that Pan Michael told him that if the catastrophe at Pilavyets had not overtaken them they would have sought the "poor girl;" but that now it was impossible,

as the whole might of Khmyelnitski's forces separated her
from them. The nobleman however would not be comforted,
but became more furious; and even swore that the world now
consisted only of feather quilts, childishness and Latinity.

These attacks of sadness, however, only lasted a short time;
and, after they were over, Zagloba drank and caroused more
than ever, as though to make up for lost time. He passed
most of his time in the wine shops, in the company of the
greatest sots or women of the town, and Pan Michael was his
faithful companion.

Pan Michael, an excellent soldier and officer, had not the
slightest degree of that earnestness which misfortune and
sorrow had developed in Skshetuski. He fulfilled his duties
to the Commonwealth, in striking wherever he was told, and
did not bother himself about anything else. He did not understand public affairs. He grieved over a mischance of war,
but it did not occur to him that these tumults and brawls
were just as injurious to the country as a defeat in battle.
In one word, he was a flighty youngster and, having once
been swallowed up in the whirlpool of the capital, was sub-
merged to his ears and hung like a chain round Zagloba who
was his master in deviltry. He rode about, therefore, with
the other nobles, to whom Zagloba told the most incredible
things over the wine, gained adherents for Prince Charles,
drank with Zagloba, screened him in emergencies, and went
everywhere with him, to the electioneering camp and about
the town together like flies in boiling water, there was no
corner they did not penetrate. They were seen in Nyeporenta in Yablonna and at all the dinners and suppers at the
houses of the magnates and in the inns; in fact everywhere,
and they enjoyed everything. Pan Michael's young palm
itched to make itself felt and to prove that the Ukranian
nobles were better than any other; and that the Prince's soldiers are above all others. So they rode off to look for adventure among the Lenchytsans who were the best swords-
men, and especially among the partisans of Prince Dominik
Zaslavski whom they both hated above all. They entered
into disputes only with the most desperate ruffians whose
reputation was well-known and could not be doubted, and
at once began to seek a quarrel.

"You, sir, seek a quarrel," said Pan Michael to Zagloba,
"and then I will take it up." Zagloba who was not to be
beaten in a war of words, and who in single fight with a

brother nobleman was no coward, did not always agree to playing second fiddle, especially in disputes with the Zaslavskis; but, when it was a question of fighting with any Lenchytsans, he halted; and, even if the other man had drawn his sword, Zagloba would say: "My good sir, I should have no conscience if I were to expose you to an inevitable death by fighting with you. Perhaps you had better try with my little son and pupil, but I do not know if you will fare any better with him." After this speech Volodiyovski would come to the front, with his pointed little moustache twirling upwards, his pug nose, and a stupid expression on his face; and, whether his substitution was accepted or not, he would intervene as he really was a master above all masters began at once to fight and usually laid his opponent low, after a few rounds. They both, therefore, sought such entertainment. Their fame continued to increase among the restless spirits of the nobility; especially Zagloba's fame, for they said, "if that is his pupil, what must the master be." But it was a long time before Volodiyovski could find Pan Kharlamp—he even thought that he had been sent back to Lithuania on some business.

Six weeks had elapsed, during which time public affairs had made a great advance. The struggle between the two candidates, and brothers, the exertions of their adherents, the violence and excitement of the partisans, had all pretty nearly passed from remembrance. It was already known to all that Yan Casimir would be elected, for Charles had withdrawn and left the field clear for his brother. It seemed strange that Khmyelnitski's voice should be heard and that it should have any weight.

It was thought that he would bow to the majesty of the king, especially such a king; one who had been chosen according to his wishes. These surmises for the most part were verified by the event. This turn of the wheel of fate was a heavy blow to Vishnyovyetski who, like Cato of olden times, had never ceased to advise the destruction of this Zaporojian Carthage. Now, under these circumstances, the only step to take was that of negotiation. The prince saw, indeed, that these negotiations would result in nothing or, in a short time, would be brought to nothing by the force of circumstances. And he saw nothing but war in the future and was filled with anxiety at the thought of whither this war would lead. After the conclusion of these negotiations, Khmyelnitski would become stronger and the Commonwealth weaker. And who would then venture to lead their forces against such a celebrated leader as Khmyelnitski? Would not new defeats new misfortunes come to pass, which would exhaust their resources to the uttermost? For the prince did not deceive himself. He knew, that he, the most dreaded of Prince Charles' adherents, would not receive the chief command. It was true that Prince Casimir had promised his brother that he would honor his adherents as he did his own, for he had a noble soul. But Casimir sided with the political party of the chancellor, consequently, another would obtain the baton, not he. Woe to the Commonwealth, however, if this one should not be a more experienced leader than Khmyelnitski. A twofold sorrow filled the soul of Prince Yeremy—anxiety about the future of the mother-country and that indescribable feeling that takes possession of a man who sees that his services are not valued; that he does not obtain justice, and that others are allowed to supplant him. Yeremy would not have been a Vishnyovyetski if he had not been haughty. He felt in himself the power to wield the baton and he had deserved it; consequently he suffered a two-fold disappointment.

It was said even among the officers that the prince would not wait for the end of the election, but would leave Warsaw; but that was not true—the prince not only did not leave, but even went to Nyeporents to see Prince Casimir, by whom he was received most graciously; and, after a long audience, returned to the town, because military affairs demanded his presence. It was a question of the transport of provisions to the soldiers, which the prince had earnestly urged; besides this, new regiments, dragoons and infantry, had to be formed at Prince Charles' expense. The first were to be sent at once to Russia, the others were to be trained. For this purpose, Yeremy sent, in all directions, officers who were experienced in the organization of troops, in order to bring those regiments and squadrons into the desired condition. Kushel and Vyershul were also sent out, and, at last, it came to Volodiyovski's turn.

He was summoned one day before the prince who gave him the following orders:

"You are to go to Zaborova by way of Babits and Lipki, where horses intended for the regiment are waiting. Look them over and make your selection and pay Pan Tshakovski, and then bring them home for the soldiers. You can draw the money here in Warsaw on my account from the pay-master."

Volodiyovski lost no time in setting to work, drew the money and, that very day, rode off with Zagloba to Zaborova, accompanied by ten men and a wagon to convey the money. They rode slowly, for the whole region this side of Warsaw was swarming with noblemen, servants, wagons and horses. Every hamlet was so crowded on the road to Babits that every cabin was filled with guests. One might easily meet with an accident among this crowd of men of the most varied dispositions; and the two friends, in spite of their polite be-havior, did not escape some adventure. When they reached Babits they noticed, outside the inn, several noblemen who were just mounting their horses in order to ride away. Both parties were just about to pass each other with a friendly salute when suddenly, one of the riders spied Pan Michael and, without saying a word, sprang towards him on horseback.

"So here you are, little brother," he cried, "you hid your-self, but I have found you. You will not escape me. Hey, gentlemen," to his comrades, "wait a little; I have some-thing to say to this little officer and would like you to hear my words."

Volodiyovski smiled, for he had recognized Kharlamp.

"God is my witness, I did not hide myself," he said, "I was looking for you, myself, to see if you were still cherishing your hatred against me, but we could not find each other."

"Pan Michael," whispered Zagloba, "you are under orders."

"I remember!" growled Volodiyovski.

"Stand forth!" shouted Kharlamp. "Gentlemen, I prom-ised this youth, this beardless boy, that I would cut off his ears, and I will cut them off, as sure as my name is Khar-lamp. Yes, Kharlamp! Be witnesses, gentlemen; and you, youngster, prepare to fight!"

"I must not, as I love God! I must not; allow me a few days time."

"What? Cant! Coward! You are afraid! If you do not stand up on the instant, I will thrash you so that you will call on your grandmother and grandfather. Oh, you gad-fly, you poisonous insect, you can get in a man's road and insult him and sting him with your tongue; but, when it comes to a duel, you are not to be found."

Here Zagloba intervened:

"It seems to me, gentlemen, that you are dodging the question," he said to Kharlamp. "Look out that this gad-fly does not really sting you; for, then, no plaster will help you. Fie! To the Devil! Do you not see that this officer is under orders. Look at this wagon full of gold, which we are taking to the regiment, and understand, that he is guarding a treasure, and that you dare not injure his person, dare not touch him. Whoever cannot understand that, must be a fool and no soldier. We are in the service of the Voyevoda of Russia and we don't fight with such fellows, to-day it cannot be. Delayed does not mean run away."

"That is really the case, if they are travelling with money; they dare not," said one of Kharlamp's companions.

"What do I care for their money?" screamed the furious Kharlamp. "Let him stand forth or I will thrash him."

"I will not fight to-day; but, on the word of a knight," said Pan Michael, "I will meet you in three or four days, wherever you wish, as soon as my duties are at an end. And if you, gentlemen, are not satisfied with this promise, I will give the order to fire on you; for I shall believe that I am not dealing with noblemen—not even with soldiers, but with bandits. Choose, therefore, by all the devils; for I have no time to stand here!"

At Volodiyovski's last words, the escort of dragoons at once aimed their muskets at the assailants; and this movement, together with the decided words of Pan Michael, made an evident impression upon Pan Kharlamp's comrades.

"Give in," they said to him, "you are a soldier yourself and know what duty means, and it is certain that you will get satisfaction; for this is a bold fellow like all the men of the Russian companies. Calm yourself, we beg you."

Pan Kharlamp fumed for a few moments longer and, then, he noticed that he should either make his comrades angry, or force them into an unequal fight with the dragoons, so he turned to Volodiyovski and said:

"Promise me that you will meet me?"

"I will look for you myself, if for no other reason, than because you have twice demanded it. In four days, I shall be ready for you. This is Wednesday—let it be Saturday afternoon at two o'clock. Choose the spot."

"There are too many people in Babits," said Kharlamp. "There might be some unpleasantness. Let us meet here, near Lipki, for it is quieter and nearer for me, for my quarters are in Babits."

"And will you gentlemen appear in full force?" said Zagloba, the careful.

"Oh, that is unnecessary," said Kharlamp, "I will bring my two relations, Pans Syelitski. You, sir, will also appear without your dragoons?"

"It may be the custom with you to ride to a duel with a military escort," said Pan Michael. "With us it is not usual."

"Well, then, in four days, on Saturday in Lipki, near the inn. And now, God be with us!" said Kharlamp.

"God be with us," answered Volodiyovski and Zagloba.

The adversaries parted peacefully. Pan Michael was pleased at the idea of this approaching pastime and promised himself that he would take Kharlamp's moustache, after cutting it off, as a present to Longin. They rode at a fair speed to Zaborona, where they found Prince Casimir, who had come here for the hunting. But Pan Michael only saw his future king at a distance, for he was in a hurry. In two days he had finished his affairs, chosen the horses and, having paid Pan Tshakovski for them, returned to Warsaw and finished his journey by going to Lipki, for the duel, accompanied by Zagloba and Pan Kushel, whom he had invited to be his seconds.

They arrived in good time, a full hour before the event was to come off. When they reached the inn, which was kept by a Jew, they stepped inside to wet their throats with a little mead and converse over the glasses as they drank.

"Scab, is the landlord at home?" asked Zagloba of the innkeeper.

"The master is in the town."

"And are there many noblemen here in Lipki?"

"No, the place is almost empty. I have only one gentleman here. He is sitting in the parlor; a rich man with servants and horses."

"Why did he not go to the castle?"

"Probably he does not know our Lord. Besides, the castle has been closed for a month."

"Perhaps it is Kharlamp," said Zagloba.

"No," said Volodiyovski.

"But, Pan Michael, it seems to me that it is."

"What now?"

"I am going to see who it is. Jew, has the gentleman been here long?"

"He only arrived to-day. He has not been here quite two hours."

"And do you not know where he comes from?"

"I do not know, but it must be from a long distance, for his horses are very tired. The men say from the other side of the Vistula."

"Why did he come to Lipki?"

"Who can tell?"

"I will see about it," repeated Zagloba, "perhaps it is a friend, an acquaintance."

And approaching the closed door of the parlor, he knocked with his fist and asked:

"May I come in, sir?"

"Who is there?" cried a voice from within.

"A friend," said Zagloba, opening the door. "Pardon, sir, perhaps I am disturbing you?" he added, sticking his head into the room.

Suddenly, he drew back, slammed the door as if he seen death. On his face was depicted horror, mingled with utter astonishment and, with his mouth open, he looked in bewilderment at Volodiyovski and Kushel.

"What is the matter?" asked Volodiyovski.

"By Jesus' wounds, keep still!" said Zagloba. "Yonder! . . . Bohun!"

"Who? What happened to you?"

"In there—Bohun!"

Both officers sprang to their feet.

"Have you lost your senses? Think, again, who is it?"

"Bohun! Bohun!"

"It is not possible."

"As true as I live! As true as I stand before you! I swear by God and all the saints!"

"Why are you so frightened," said Volodiyovski. "If he is there, God has given him into our hands. Calm yourself! Are you quite certain it is he?"

"As true as I am speaking. I saw him. He is dressing himself."

"And did he see you?"

"I do not know. I think not."

Volodiyovski's eyes flashed like live coals.

"Jew," he cried softly, waving his hand furiously, "come here. Does a second door lead into that room."

"No, only the one into this room."

"Kushel, go to the window," whispered Pan Michael. "Oh, now he will not escape us again."

35

Kushel without saying a word hurried out of the room.

"Come to your senses," said Volodiyovski. "The sword does not hang over your neck, but over ours. What can he do to you? Nothing!"

"I simply cannot recover from my astonishment," answered Zagloba, and thought to himself, "It is true; why should I fear? Pan Michael is with me, let Bohun be afraid."

And, assuming a fierce look, he grasped the hilt of his sword.

"Pan Michael, he cannot escape us again!"

"I wonder if it is really he. I can hardly believe it. What could he be doing here?"

"Khmyelnitski has sent him out as a spy; that is certain. We will catch him and give him his choice; either he must give up the princess, or we will threaten to hand him over to justice."

"If he would only give up the princess, devil take him!"

"Pshaw! But are there not too few of us. We two, and Kushel, the third. He will defend himself like mad and, especially, as he has some attendants with him."

Kharlamp will come with two men; then we shall be six, more than enough."

At this moment, the door opened and Bohun stepped into the room.

He evidently had not seen Zagloba looking in at the door; for, at sight of him, he started, his face became crimson and his hand flew like lightning to the hilt of his sword;—but it was the work of a moment; the glow faded out of his face and he became paler than usual. Zagloba looked at him and said nothing. The ataman also stood in silence. One could have heard the wings of a fly in the room. And these two men, whose fate was so strangely interwoven, acted at this moment as if they did not know each other.

They stood thus for some moments. To Pan Michael, it seemed an eternity.

"Jew," said Bohun, suddenly, "is it far from here to Zaborova?"

"No, it is not far," answered the Jew. "Is your lordship going to set out at once?"

"I am," said Bohun, putting his foot on the step which separated his room from the inn parlor.

"With your permission," exclaimed Zagloba.

The chieftain stood, as if rooted to the spot; and, turning to Zagloba, fixed his black, dreadful eyes on him:

"What do you wish?" he asked curtly.

"Why, it seems to me that we have met somewhere? Did we not see each other at that wedding at the farm in Russia?"

"We did," said the chieftain proudly, placing his hand again on the hilt of his sword.

"How is your health?" asked Zagloba, "for you rode away so hastily from the house that day that I did not even have time to take leave of you."

"And you were sorry?"

"Certainly, I was sorry. We would have had a little dance. The company had become more numerous." Here, Zagloba pointed to Volodiyovski. "This cavalier had just arrived and wanted to make your acquaintance."

"Enough of this!" cried Pan Michael, suddenly springing forward. "Traitor, I arrest you!"

"And, by what right?" asked the ataman, raising his head proudly.

"Because you are a rebel, an enemy of the Commonwealth, and have come hither as a spy."

"And who the devil are you?"

"Oh, I do not need to introduce myself; but you will not escape me."

"We shall see," said Bohun. "I would not hesitate to tell you who I am, sir, if you were to call me out with swords, like a soldier; but as you threaten me with arrest, so let it be. See here, is a letter that I am bringing from the Hetman of the Zaporojians to Prince Casimir; and, as I did not find him in Nyeporenta, I am travelling to Zaporova to see him. How is that? Will you arrest me now?"

Then Bohun looked proudly and disdainfully at Volodiyovski, and Pan Michael looked as embarrassed as a boarhound whose prey is about to escape. He knew not what to do and turned his questioning glance on Zagloba. For a moment, there was a deep silence.

"Ah!" said Zagloba, "that will not help you. As you are an ambassador we dare not arrest you; but you dare not meet this cavalier with your sword, for you fled before him once and the earth fairly groaned."

Bohun's face became purple, for now he recognized Volodiyovski. Shame and wounded pride overcame the fearless warrior; the remembrance of that fight burned like fire. It was the one indelible stain on his soldier's honor, which he prized more than his life; more than anything else.

And the merciless Zagloba continued in a cold blooded manner.

"Your trousers were flapping, and this cavalier took pity on you and gave you your life. Fie! Pan warrior; you have a woman's face, but also a woman's heart. You were courageous enough in presence of the old princess, and the boy princes, but before a knight you play a different tune. Carrying letters, kidnapping girls, that is your business; but not making war. As true as I love God, with my own eyes, I saw your trousers flapping. Fie! Fie! and, even now, you speak about the sword, when you are carrying a letter. How can one fight with you when you hide yourself behind a letter? Sand in one's eyes, sand in one's eyes! Fie! Sir Cossack. Khmyelnitski is a good soldier, Kshyvonos is good, but there are many cowards among the Cossacks."

Bohun suddenly sprang forward on Zagloba, who sprang just as quickly behind Volodiyovski, so that the two young knights stood face to face.

"I did not flee from you out of fear, but in order to save my soldiers," said Bohun.

"I do not know why you fled, I only know that you did run away," said Pan Michael.

"I am ready to call you out, even this very moment."

"Do you call me out?" Volodiyovski asked, his eyes twinkling.

"You have robbed me of my soldier's honor, you have insulted me, I must have your blood!"

"Good," said Volodiyovski.

"*Volente non fit injuria.*" (If they are willing there is no harm), said Zagloba. "But who will take the letter to the prince?"

"Do not let your head ache on that account; that is my affair."

"Fight away, then, if it cannot be helped," said Zagloba. "If you, Chieftain, have luck with this cavalier, remember, I come in as second. And now, Pan Michael, come into the hall, I have something of importance to say to you."

The two friends went out, calling Kushel from the window of the parlor; and Zagloba said:

"Gentlemen, we are in a bad way; he has really a letter to the prince. If we kill him, it is a criminal offence. Think of it! The Chapter, propter securitatem loci, exercises justice within a circuit of two miles—and this man is as good as

an ambassador. A hard case; we shall be obliged to hide ourselves afterwards or, possibly, the Prince might shelter us;
otherwise it might go hard with us. But, again, if we let him
go free it is still worse. It is our only opportunity to free our
poor girl. God evidently wishes to help her and Skshetuski—
what shall we do? Let us consider, gentlemen."

"You will certainly find a means," said Kushel.

"I have brought it as far as this, that he has called us out,
himself; but we need witnesses, strangers. My idea is, that
we should wait for Kharlamp. I will take it upon myself to
relinquish his right to come first; and, if necessary, to bear
witness that we were challenged and had to defend ourselves.
We must also find out particularly from Bohun where he has
hidden the girl. If he should die, she would be of no use to
him. Perhaps he will tell us, if we conjure him; and, if he
will not tell us, it is better that he should not live. We must
move carefully and with consideration. My head is bursting,
sirs."

"Who will fight with him?" asked Kushel.

"Pan Michael first; then I," said Zagloba.

"And I will be the third."

"That must not be," interrupted Pan Michael. "I, alone,
will fight him. If he cuts me down, that is his luck. Let him
go off safe and sound."

"Oh! I told him I would," said Zagloba. "But if you are
determined, gentlemen, I will give it up."

"Well, that is his own affair; if he wishes to fight you and
no one else. Shall we go to him?"

"Let us go."

They entered the room and found Bohun in the parlor
drinking mead. The chieftain was perfectly calm.

"Listen, sir," said Zagloba, "for we wish to talk to you on
important matters. You called out this cavalier—that is all
right; but you must know that, as you come as an ambassador,
the law protects you, for you are among civilized people, and
not among wild beasts. We cannot challenge you, but we
ask you to acknowledge, before witnesses, that you challenged
us of your own free will. Several noblemen are coming here,
with whom we are to fight. You must explain this all to
them. We, however, will give you our word, as knights, that,
if fortune favors you in your encounter with Volodiyovski,
you may go free and no one will hinder you; unless you wish
to try your luck with me."

"Good," said Bohun, "I will explain it to the gentlemen, and will tell my servants that they shall deliver the letter and tell Khmyelnitski, if I fall, that I, myself, gave the challenge. And, if God gives me luck in recovering my lost honor with this knight, I will then request you to draw your sword." As he said this he looked into Zagloba's eyes, which much embarrassed the nobleman, who coughed and spat on the floor and answered:

"Good, when you have tried your luck with my pupil, you will know what task lies before you. But, that is a secondary matter. There is another, more important point, with regard to which we will appeal to your conscience; for, although you are a Cossack, we wish to treat you as a knight. You have kidnapped princess Helena Kurtsevich, the betrothed of our companion in arms and our friend, and are hiding her away. Now, if we should call you out on that account it would matter not that Khmyelnitski had made you an ambassador; for this is abduction, a capital offence, which would be very soon dealt with. But, as you are going to fight and may probably be killed, consider what would happen to this poor girl, if you should fall. Do you, who love her so much, desire her shame and unhappiness? Must she be deprived of protection, be given over to shame and misfortune? Do you wish, even after your death, to be an executioner?"

Here, Zagloba's voice became unusually serious. Bohun grew pale, and said:

"What do you want me to do?"

"Tell us where she is imprisoned, so that, in case of your death, we may find her and take her back to her betrothed. God will have mercy on your soul if you will do this."

The chieftain buried his face in his hands and became absorbed in thought. The three friends noted carefully each change in that mobile countenance, which had suddenly assumed an expression of such deep sadness that one might have thought that anger, fury, or any other cruel feeling had never been reflected there, but that this man had been created only for love and tenderness. The silence lasted some time, until Zagloba's voice broke it, saying:

"But, if you have already wronged her, may God damn you; and may she, at least, find refuge in a convent." . .

Bohun raised his sad, moist eyes and said:

"If I have wronged her! See here! I do not know how you gentlemen of the nobility, you knights and cavaliers love;

but I am a Cossack. I preserved her from death and shame in Bar, and then took her into the wilds and watched her as the eye of my head. I have not touched a hair of her head, but have fallen at her feet and bowed my forehead to the ground before her, as before an image. She told me to go away—I went, and have not seen her since, for my mother, war, has kept me a prisoner."

"God will reward you for that at the last day," said Zagloba, sighing deeply. "But, is she perfectly safe there, Kshyvonos and the Tartars are there."

"Kshyvonos is encamped near Kamenets and sent me to Khmyelnitski to ask if he should go to Kudak. He has probably gone,—and where she is, there are neither Cossacks, Poles nor Tartars—she is safe there."

"Where is she then?"

"Listen, gentlemen, Poles! Let it be as you say. I will tell you where she is and will allow her to be given up to you; but, in return for this, give me your word as knights that, if God helps me, you will not look for her. Promise me this on your own account, as well as for Skshetuski, and then I will tell you."

The three friends looked at one another.

"We cannot do that," said Zagloba.

"No, by our soul, we cannot," cried Kushel and Volodiyovski.

"Indeed!" said Bohun, knitting his brows and his eyes flashing. "Why can you not do that, gentlemen?"

"Because Skshetuski is not here. Besides, you must know that no one of us will cease to search for her, even though you have buried her beneath the ground."

"This, then, is the kind of way you wish to deal with me: 'Thou, Cossack, give thy soul and we will pay thee for it with the sword!' Oh, you cannot do that! Do you think, perhaps, that my sword is not made of steel, that you can already croak over me like crows over carrion? Must it be I that fall, and not you? You demand my blood, I seek yours; we will see who has the most luck."

"Then, you will not tell us?"

"What should I say more—death and destruction to you all."

"Death and destruction to you yourself! You deserve to be cut to pieces."

"Try it! said the chieftain, suddenly rising to his feet

Kushel and Volodiyovski also sprang to their feet; threatening glances were exchanged; the angry breasts heaved more quickly; and who knows what would have happened, if Zagloba, who was looking out of the window, had not called out:

"Kharlamp is coming, with his seconds."

"In a few moments, the light-cavalry captain, with two companions, Pans Syelitski stepped into the room. After the first greeting, Zagloba took him aside and began to explain the matter to them. And he was so plausible that he persuaded them to wait, especially by assuring them that Pan Volodiyovski requested only a short delay and would be ready as soon as he should have finished with the Cossack. And, then, Pan Zagloba explained the terrible hatred that all the prince's soldiers had long cherished for Bohun, that he was an enemy of the whole Commonwealth, and one of the most dreaded rebels; and last, but not least, that he had stolen the princess, a young lady belonging to a noble house and the betrothed of a nobleman who was a model of knightly virtue.

"And as you, sirs, belong to the nobility and count yourselves among the brotherhood of companions in arms, the insult should be felt by all of us, as any injury to one is felt by the whole brotherhood. Would you suffer it that she should go unavenged?"

Pan Kharlamp demurred at first and said that if this was the case it was fitting that they should fight Bohun on the spot. "And Pan Volodiyovski, as previously arranged, can meet me."

Zagloba had to explain to him why this could not be and that it was not knightly for so many to attack one man. Fortunately the two Pans Syelitski agreed with him, as they were both steady, sensible men; and at length the obstinate Lithuanian let himself be persuaded and agreed to delay.

During this time, Bohun had gone to his men and had returned with Sergeant Elyashenka. He told him that he had challenged two noblemen to a duel, which he repeated aloud in presence of Kharlamp and the two Syelitskis.

"But we wish to say," said Pan Volodiyovski, "that if you are the victor it will depend on yourself whether you fight with Pan Zagloba; on no account shall one of the others challenge you. You shall also not be attacked by this crowd of men, but may go away, whither you will—on our word as knights. And I beg you, gentlemen, who have just arrived, to make the same promise on your part."

"We promise!" said Kharlamp and the two Syelitskis, solemnly.

Bohun now handed Khmyelnitski's letter to the prince to Elyashenka and said:

"Give this writing to the Crown Prince and, if I die, tell him and Khmyelnitski that it was my own fault and that I was not killed by traitors."

Zagloba, who was observing everything, remarked that Elyashenka's earnest face betrayed not the slightest uneasiness—one saw that he had perfect confidence in his ataman's skill.

Meanwhile, Bohun, turning proudly to the noblemen, said:

"Well, who is to die and who is to live? Let us go."

"It is time, it is time," they all said, tucking their coats into their belts, and carrying their swords under their arms.

They went out of the inn and towards the river which flowed between thickets of bramble, wild-roses, flags, and young pine trees.

October had scattered the leaves but the bushes grew so closely that they extended like a gray veil across the desert prairie, far away to the forests. The day was cloudy, but there was that peculiar mixture of sadness and cheerfulness which is seen only in the beauty of an Autumn day. The sun tinged with gold the branches of the trees and lighted up the yellow sand-hills which stretched along the right bank of the stream. The duellers and their seconds went toward these sand-hills.

"We will stop here," said Zagloba.

"Agreed," they all answered.

Zagloba's uneasiness increased and, at last, he approached Volodiyovski and whispered.

"Pan Michael . . . . "

"What is it?"

"For God's sake, Pan Michael, do your best! Skshetuski's fate lies in your hands, the freedom of the princess, your own life and mine; for, may God prevent it, but if you should be unlucky, I know of nothing that will save me from this murderer."

"Why did you call him out then?"

"The word is spoken. . . . I depended upon you Pan Michael; for I am getting old, my breath is short and I am clumsy; and this rascal can bound like a cricket. He is a rascally hound, Pan Michael."

"I will do my best," said the little knight.

"May God be with you! Do not lose your presence of mind!"

"Eh, why should I?"

At this moment, one of the Pan Syelitskis approached.

"Your Cossack is a queer fellow," he whispered, "he acts as if he were our equal or even better than we are. He has a sense of chivalry; his mother must have looked at a nobleman."

"Eh!" said Zagloba, "more probably a nobleman looked at his mother."

"That is what I think," said Volodiyovski.

"Let us take position!" said Bohun suddenly, "stop here!"

"Let us take position! Let us take position!"

They took position; the nobles in a semicircle and Volodiyovski and Bohun opposite one another.

Volodiyovski, with an air of experience in such matters which belied his youth, tried the ground with his foot to see if it was hard enough; then, he looked about him to take in all the inequalities of the ground, and it was evident that he took the matter seriously. He had to settle with a knight, the most celebrated in the Ukraine, in whose honor popular songs were sung, and whose name was known to the extremest limits of Russia, even to the Crimea. Pan Michael, a simple lieutenant of dragoons, counted a great deal on this duel, as he would either meet with a glorious death or an equally glorious victory. He, therefore, omitted nothing that might render him worthy of such an opponent. His face consequently became so earnest that Zagloba, when he noticed it, was fairly frightened.

"He is losing courage," he thought. "It is all up with him, as it is with me!"

Volodiyovski, after investigating the ground thoroughly, unbuttoned his coat.

"It is cool," he said, "but we shall be warm enough soon."

Bohun followed his example. They both took off their coats and stood in their shirt sleeves, with the right sleeve turned back. But how small little Pan Michael looked beside the tall, powerful ataman; one could hardly see him. His seconds looked uneasily at the Cossack's broad chest and powerful muscles which appeared under the turned back sleeve, looking like knotted cords. It was as though a little bantam should undertake to fight with an enormous hawk of the steppes. Bohun's nostrils were distended as if they smelt

IN THE NAME OF GOD, BEGIN!

blood; his face appeared to be drawn up, so that the black locks over his forehead almost reached his eyebrows; his sword twitched in his hand; the fierce eyes seemed to pierce through his opponent; he awaited the signal.

And Volodiyovski held up his bare sword to the light once more, tugged at his yellow mustache and took his position.

"It will be a regular butchery" growled Kharlamp to Syelitski.

Then Zagloba's voice said, rather unsteadily:

"In the name of God, begin!"

CHAPTER XII.

The swords swished through the air and blade clashed blade. They soon changed their ground, for Bohun attacked so furiously that Pan Volodiyovski was obliged to spring back a few steps, and his seconds did the same. Bohun's strokes fell like lightning and the excited beholders could not follow them with their eyes. It seemed to them as though Pan Mishael was completely surrounded and covered with sword thrusts and that God alone could save him from this attack. There was continuous swishing of swords, which fairly disturbed the air as though a wind were blowing in their faces. The fury of the chieftain increased; he was possessed with the madness of battle, and drove Volodiyovski before him like a hurricane. The little knight continued to retreat and to defend himself. His outstretched right arm hardly moved, the wrist alone describing small but rapid semicircles quick as thought, as he warded Bohun's wild strokes. He caught each stroke, parried it, again guarded, and retreated at the same time, fixing his eyes on those of the Cossack, and remaining perfectly calm in the midst of the serpentine-lightning strokes; only on his cheeks were two red spots.

Zagloba shut his eyes and listened to stroke upon stroke, clash upon clash.

"He is still defending himself," he thought.

"He is still defending himself," whispered the two Syelitskis and Kharlamp.

"He is already driven to the bank," added Kushel softly.

Zagloba opened his eyes again and looked up.

Volodiyovski's back was against the bank, but he did not appear to be wounded and his face only grew redder and a few drops of sweat stood out on his forehead.

Zagloba's heart beat with hope.

"Pan Michael is a fighter of fighters," he thought, "and the other man will finally become exhausted."

Bohun's face grew pale, sweat covered his forehead; but his opponent's resistance only increased his rage, his white teeth

556

gleamed beneath his moustache and a growl of anger escaped him.

Volodiyovski never took his eye off him and continued to guard.

Suddenly, feeling the bank beside him, ne pulled himself together; his seconds thought he was about to fall; but he bent forward, crouched, and threw himself like a stone at the breast of the Cossack.

"He is attacking," cried Zagloba.

"He is attacking," repeated the others.

It was really the case. Now, the chieftain retreated and the little knight, who had found out the whole strength of his opponent, pressed on him with so much energy that his seconds gasped for breath. He was evidently becoming excited—the little eyes flashed fire. Again he crouched and again sprang forward, changing his position at every moment, describing circles around the chieftain and forcing him to turn round constantly.

"An adept! an adept!" cried Zagloba.

"You are lost!" said Bohun, suddenly.

"You are lost!" answered Volodiyovski like an echo.

Here the Cossack used a trick, which was only known to the most practised fighters. He suddenly changed his sword from the right to the left hand and made such a powerful stroke that Pan Michael fell to the earth as though struck by lightning.

"Jesus Maria!" cried Zagloba.

But Pan Michael had fallen intentionally, and Bohun's sword cut through the empty air. The little knight at once sprang up like a wild-cat, and slashed with almost the whole length of his sword across the breast of the Cossack.

Bohun tottered, took a step forward, and with an effort gave a last blow, which Pan Volodiyovski parried with ease. Twice, he struck his opponent's bowed head, and the sword dropped from Bohun's powerless hands and the warrior fell on his face in the sand, which presently became a wide pool of blood beneath him.

Elyashenka who had been present at the fight, threw himself upon the body of the ataman.

The seconds were unable to speak a word for some time, and Pan Michael also was silent he leaned both hands on his sword and panted heavily.

Zagloba was the first to break the silence.

"Pan Michael, come to my arms!" he said, in an unsteady voice.

They all surrounded him.

"You are a fighter of the first rank. May the balls strike you!" said Pan Syelitski.

"I see you are a tough knot," said Kharlamp, "I will stand up with you, so that no one may say I was afraid; but if you should punish me like that I should still say, 'I congratulate you, I congratulate you.'"

"Let that go, gentlemen, for, to tell the truth, you really have no good reason to fight," said Zagloba.

"That will not do, for it is a question of my reputation," said the light-cavalryman, "for which I would willingly sacrifice my head."

"I care nothing about your head, but let us give it up," said Volodiyovski, "for I am really not standing in your way as you think; there is another in the case who is more fortunate than I."

"How so?"

"On the word of a knight!"

"Make it up," cried the Syelitskis and Kushel.

"Let it be so!" said Kharlamp, holding out his arms.

Volodiyovski threw himself into the outstretched arms and they kissed one another till the banks re-echoed, and Kharlamp remarked:

"I had no idea that you could give that giant such a beating! And yet he understood how to wield a sword?"

"I never would have believed him to be such a swordsman, where can he have learned it?"

Here the general attention was directed to the prostrate form of the Cossack chieftain. Elyashenka had turned his master over so that his face was upturned; and he looked with tears for any sign of life. Bohun's face was not recognizable for it was covered with blood, which flowed from the wounds in the head and congealed in the cool air; the shirt on his breast was also soaked with blood, but he still gave signs of life. He was evidently in the death convulsion, his feet twitched and his hands were clenched and dug in the sand. Zagloba looked at him and motioned with his hand.

"He has had enough," he said, "he is taking leave of the world."

"Ah!" said one of the Syelitskis, looking at the body, "he is quite dead."

"Bah! he is almost hacked through and through."

"He was not a bad knight," murmured Volodiyovski, shaking his head.

"I have something to say about that," added Zagloba.

During this time Elyashenka was trying to lift the unfortunate ataman, to carry him away; but, as he was no longer young and strong, and Bohun was almost a giant, he was unable to do it. It was some furlongs to the inn and Bohun might expire at any moment. When the sergeant saw this, he turned to the gentlemen.

"Gentlemen!" he cried, folding his hands, "help me, for God and the Holy Virgin's sake; do not let him die here like a dog. An old man like me cannot manage it alone, and there is no one near!"

The gentlemen looked at one another, their hatred for Bohun had vanished from all hearts.

"True; it is not fitting that we should leave him here like a dog," murmured Zagloba, "as we fought a duel with him, we can no longer consider him a peasant, but as a soldier who needs assistance. Who will help me to carry him, gentleemen?"

"I," said Volodiyovski.

"Carry him on my cloak," added Kharlamp.

In a few minutes Bohun was placed on the cloak at either end of which was Zagloba, Volodiyovski, Kishel and Elyaskenka and the procession moved with slow steps towards the inn, accompanied by Kharlamp and the two Syelitskis.

"He has a strong hold on life," said Zagloba, he is still moving. Good God! if anyone had told me that I should be his nurse and carry him as I am doing now, I would have laughed. What a fool I am! I have a very tender heart, I know, but it cannot be helped. I will bind up his wounds once again. I hope that we shall never meet again in this world and I want him to have a pleasant remembrance of me in the other."

"Do you really think, then, that he will not recover?" asked Kharlamp.

"He, recover! I would not give an old rag for his life. It was so ordained and can't be changed. Even if he had escaped from Volodiyovski's hands, he would not have got away from me. But I am glad it happened as it has, for I am already looked upon as a slayer without mercy. What can I do if anyone puts himself in my way? I had to pay Pan

Dunchevski five hundred gold zlatos indemnity, and you all know that the Russian property does not bring in any income at present."

"That is true. They have completely plundered you over there," said Kharlamp.

"Ugh! This Cossack is heavy," said Zagloba. "I am quite out of breath. Plundered! I should say they had plundered. But I hope that the Diet will make some provision for us. If it does not, we shall all starve to death. . . How heavy he is, how heavy! Look, his wounds are beginning to bleed again. Pan Kharlamp run to the inn and tell the Jew to knead up some bread and cobwebs. It is true it will not be of much use to a dead man, but it is our Christian duty to stanch the wounds; he will die more easily. Lively! Pan Kharlamp."

Pan Kharlamp ran ahead, and, as soon as they had finally brought Bohun into the room of the inn, Zagloba set to work to bandage him with great skill and deftness. He stanched the blood, closed the wounds, and then, turning to Elyash-enka, said:

"You, old man, are no longer needed here. Ride speedily to Zaborova and entreat that they will allow you to see the Leader at once. Give him the letter and relate all that you witnessed, just as you saw it. If you lie, I shall find it out, for I am the confidant of the illustrious prince—and I will have your head chopped off. Greet Khmyelnitski from me, for he knows and loves me. We will give the ataman honorable burial; and you, attend to your business. Do not wander out of your way, for someone may kill you before you have time to find out who it is. God be with you, go, go!"

"Permit me, sir, to wait until he is perfectly cold."

"Go, I tell you!" said Zagloba, angrily. "If not, I will have you given up to the peasants in Zaborova and greet Khmyelnitski for me."

Elyashenka bowed low and went out. Zagloba, however, said to Kharlamp and the Syelitskis:

"I sent away the Cossack, he had nothing to do here; and if he should be killed, as may easily happen, they would blame us. The Zaslavskis and the chancellor's mongrels will be the first to cry out that the prince's men, contrary to God's commands, have murdered the whole Cossack embassy. But a clever head is of use in all emergencies. We will not let ourselves be pounded into grits by these fools, these barley-porridge eaters, and you, gentlemen, give your testimony, should it be necessary, and tell how everything happened; and that he, himself, called us out. I must also give orders to the bailiff here to have him buried somewhere. No one here knows who he is, and they will think he is a nobleman and bury him with honors. It is time to set out, Pan Michael, for we must bring word to the Prince Voyevoda.

The death-rattle in Bohun's throat interrupted Zagloba's speech.

"Oh, the soul is seeking its way," said the nobleman. "It is growing dark already, he will find the darkness in the other world. But, as he has not wronged our poor girl, may God grant him everlasting rest, Amen! Let us mount, Pan Michael, I forgive him everything from my whole heart, although, in truth, I got more in his way than he did in mine. But now, this is the end. Farewell, sirs, I am pleased to have met such noble knights. Do not forget to give your testimony should it be necessary."

CHAPTER XIII.

Prince Yeremy received the news of Bohun's death with indifference, especially when he learned that men who did not belong to his regiments were ready to bear witness that Volodiyovski had been challenged. If the affair had not taken place a few days before it was publicly announced that Yan Casimir had been chosen; if the struggle of the two candidates, Yeremy's opponents, with the chancellor and Prince Dominik at their head, had still been going on, they would have made of this circumstance a weapon against him, in spite of all witnesses and all testimony. But, after Charles' withdrawal, men's minds were otherwise engaged, and probably the whole event would be completely forgotten.

Khmyelnitski might possibly make use of it to show that he had again suffered an injustice, but the prince expected rightly that the king's son, in answering the letter, would also point out the manner in which his ambassador had come to his death, and Khmyelnitski would not dare question the royal word.

The prince was particularly anxious that his soldiers should not be brought into any political difficulty. He rejoiced on Skshetuski's account that this had happened, for the recovery of the young Princess Kurtsevich was now much more possible and practicable. She might be found, freed or rescued, and, no matter at what cost, the prince would spare nothing, not even the greatest cost to release the sorrow of his favorite knight, and to give him back his happiness.

Volodiyovski had gone to the prince in fear and trembling, for, though in general he was no coward, he feared the prince's frown as he feared fire. How great then was his astonishment and joy, when, after receiving his message and reflecting for a few moments, the prince drew a costly ring from his finger and said:

"I esteem your self-restraint, gentlemen, for if you had been the first to attack him, great and serious trouble might have resulted in the assembly; and if the princess is found,

Skshetuski will owe you everlasting gratitude. I hear that you, Volodiyovski, cannot keep your sword in its sheath as some cannot restrain their tongue, and you deserve a penalty on that account; but, as you acted in the interests of your friends and maintained the reputation of our regiments in a duel with such a well-known warrior, take this ring in remembrance of the day. I knew that you were a good soldier and swordsman, but I hear that you are a master of masters."

"He!" cried Zagloba, "he would cut off the devil's horns in the third round. If your Highness should ever wish to cut off my head, may I entreat that no other than he should be given the task, for I know my transit to the other world would be rapid. He cut Bohun twice across the breast and then gave him two strokes on the brain-box."

The prince loved knightly deeds and good soldiers so he smiled pleasantly and asked: "Have you ever found anyone who equals you with the sword?"

"Once, Skshetuski wounded me slightly, but I also wounded him; at the time your Highness put us in the tower. Among others, Pan Podbipyenta would be a match for me, for he has superhuman strength,—and even perhaps Kushel, if he had better eyes."

"Do not believe him your Highness," said Zagloba, "no one can withstand him."

"Did Bohun defend himself long?"

"I had hard work with him," said Pan Michael, "he knew how to fight with his left hand."

"Bohun told me himself," interrupted Zagloba, "that he spent whole days practising with the Kurtseviches and I saw him practising with others in Chigrin."

"Do you know what, Pan Volodiyovski," said the prince with pretended earnestness, "supposing you ride to Zamost, call out Khmyelnitski to fight with swords and, with one stroke, deliver the Commonwealth from all its sorrow and misery."

"If your Highness commands, I will go; if Khmyelnitski will only fight with me," answered Volodiyovski.

The prince replied:

"We are joking, while the world is going to ruin. But you really must ride to Zamost gentlemen; I have word from the Cossack camp that as soon as Prince Casimir's election is announced, Khmyelnitski will raise the siege and retreat to Russia. He does this either from real or pretended respect to the king, or because his forces might be easily routed at Zamost. So you must go there and tell Skshetuski what has happened and that he must look for the princess. Tell him that he may take as many men as he needs for his expedition from our regiment under the Starosta of Valet's command; and I will grant him leave and a safe conduct, which you will take to him, for I am deeply interested in his happiness."

"Your Highness is a father to all of us," said Volodiyovski, "and we will serve you faithfully to the end of our days."

"I do not know if my following may not diminish before long," said the prince, "if all my possessions in the Dnieper land are lost—but as long as they last, what is mine is yours."

"Oh," cried Pan Michael, "our poor property will always be your Highness's property."

"And take mine with the rest," said Zagloba.

"I do not need it, as yet," said the prince graciously, "besides, I hope that even if I should lose everything the Commonwealth will take care of my children."

The prince spoke these words in a moment of clairvoyance of what might come to pass. Some ten years later, the Commonwealth gave his only son the best that it had to offer—the crown; but at the present time the prince's gigantic fortune had decreased considerably.

"Well, we got out of it finely," said Zagloba, after he and Volodiyovski had left the prince. "Pan Michael, you are sure of promotion. Let me see the ring! By God! it is worth a hundred zlotas (florins); the stone is very beautiful. Let us ask an Armenian in the bazaar about it to-morrow. One could carouse for its value in eating and drinking and other delights; what do you say, Pan Michael? That is a soldier's maxim, 'Live to-day, perish to-morrow,' and the meaning is that it does not pay to think of to-morrow. Man's life is short, very short, Pan Michael. The most important thing is, however, that from now on the prince has taken you to his heart. He would have given ten times as much to have made Skshetuski a present of Bohun; and you have done it. Believe me, you are on the high road to promotion. Has not the prince given villages in life-tenure to his knights, or even given them out and out? A ring is of no value; he will certainly give you something else, and probably marry you at last to one of his relations."

Pan Michael almost jumped.

"How do you know that. . . "

"That what?"

"I only meant what notion have you got in your head? How could such a thing come to pass?"

"Does not everything come to pass? Are you not a noble, and are not all nobles equal? Have not all the magnates distant cousins among the nobility, and do they not give them in marriage to their favorite attendants? Has not the Suffchynski in Siench a distant relation of the Vishnyovyetski for a wife. They are all brothers Pan Michael, all brothers, even if one serves another, for we all descended from Japhet; and the whole distinction in rank and riches depends on whether you can obtain them or not. It is said that, in other places, there are considerable differences in rank among the nobility; but that is a mangy nobility. I understand differences between dogs, as for instance; setters, greyhounds and bloodhounds, by their voice in hunting; but, consider, Pan Michael, with the nobility it is not so, or we should all be hounds and not nobles, which disgrace to this noble condition our good Lord does not permit."

"You are right, sir," said Volodiyovski, "but the Vishnyovyetski are almost of royal blood."

"And you, Pan Michael, might not you be chosen for king? I should be the first to insist on nominating you; like Pan Zygmunt Skarshevski who swears that he would elect himself if he were not a dicer. Everything with us thank God is by free suffrages; and our poverty, alone, not our birth, stands in our way."

"That's just what it is," sighed Pan Michael.

"What is to be done! They have robbed us completely and we shall be completely ruined, if the Diet does not give us some help; utterly ruined. Is it any wonder that a man who is naturally abstemious should take to drinking under such circumstances. Come Pan Michael, let us drink a glass of beer, perhaps that may comfort us somewhat."

During this conversation, they had reached the old town and stepped into a wine room before which stood several boys holding the furs and cloaks of their masters, who were drinking inside. They sat down at a table, ordered a bottle, and considered what was best to do, now that Bohun was dead.

"If it is true that Khmyelnitski is raising the siege of Zamost and there will be peace, the princess is ours," said Zagloba.

"We must go as soon as possible to Skshetuski. We will not leave him again until we have found the princess."

"We will go together, but now it is impossible to reach Zamost."

"That makes no difference, if God only helps us later."

Zagloba emptied his glass.

"He will help us, He will help us," he said, "listen Pan Michael to what I tell you."

"What is it?"

"Bohun is dead."

Volodiyovski looked up in astonishment.

"Pshaw, who knows that better than I do?"

"You deserve all credit, Pan Michael; you know it and I know it. I watched you fighting, I see you now—and, nevertheless, I have to repeat it to myself, for sometimes it seems as if it were only a dream. What an anxiety is removed, what a knot your sword has cut! May the balls strike you! by God! it is incredible; no, I cannot stand it any longer; let me embrace you once more, little Michael. Believe me, when I first met you, I thought to myself, 'H'm, a little creature'— and see what a fine creature it is that has beaten Bohun. Bohun lives no longer, no, not a trace, no ashes left, killed dead, forever and ever, amen!"

Here, Zagloba put his arms around Volodiyovski and kissed him, and Pan Michael was moved to tears, as though he were mourning Bohun. Finally, he managed to free himself from Zagloba's arms and said:

"We did not see him die and he is a tough fellow—supposing he should get well!"

"For God's sake, what do you mean?" said Zagloba. "I am ready to ride to-morrow to Lipki to order him the most splendid funeral, if he is only dead."

"And what good would that do? You would not kill a wounded man! It is often so with sword wounds; if a man does not give up the ghost at once, he generally creeps out of it somehow. The sword is not like a bullet."

"No, it is impossible, the death-rattle was beginning as we rode away. Oh, no, it is impossible, his breast was cut open like the door of a shed, let him rest, you cut him as if he were a hare. We must go to Skshetuski as soon as possible to help him and comfort him, for he is worrying himself to death."

"Or he has gone into a monastery, as he told me himself."

"No wonder! I should do the same thing in his place. I know no cavalier who is more worthy than he, but none who is more unhappy. Oh, God is proving him severely, very severely."

"Stop there, sir," said Volodiyovski, who was a little drunk, "for I cannot keep from tears."

"And how can I then," answered Zagloba, "such an honorable knight, such a soldier. . . and then the girl! you do not know her; . . . she is a dear little worm."

Here Zagloba began to bellow in a deep bass, for he loved the little princess very dearly, and Pan Michael accompanied him in a somewhat higher key, and they drank wine mixed with tears, and their heads sank on their breasts; they sat for some time in gloomy silence. At length, Zagloba brought his fist down on the table:

"Pan Michael, why do we weep, Bohun is slain."

"Ah, that is true," said Volodiyovski.

"We ought rather to rejoice. What fools we are not to go and look for her at once."

"Let us start at once," said Volodiyovski, standing up.

"Let us drink," said Zagloba, "God grant that we may yet hold her children over the font; and all that because we have killed Bohun."

"It serves him right!" ended Pan Michael, who did not remark that Zagloba was already sharing the fame of Bohun's death.

CHAPTER XIV.

At length the Te Deum Laudamus sounded in the cathedral in Warsaw and "the King was enthroned in his majesty;" the cannon thundered, the bells rang, and confidence was restored to all hearts. Now at last the time of interregum, disputes, and unrest, was over, which had been so terrible for the Commonwealth, especially as it happened at a time of general misery. Those who had trembled at the thought of the approaching dangers, now breathed freely; as the election had passed more quietly than any had dared to hope. Many believed that the unexampled civil war was now over, once for all; and that all that remained for the newly-chosen King was to sentence the guilty ones. Khmyelnitski's attitude also confirmed this hope. The Cossacks who were obstinately besieging the fortress of Zamost declared, as one man, for Yan Casimir. Khmyelnitski sent by provost Hunzel Mokrski letters full of assurances of submission and fealty and by other messengers, humble entreaties for himself and the Zaporojian armed. It was also known that the King in accord with the policy of the chancellor Ossolinski wished to make important concessions to the Cossacks. As before the defeat of Pilavyets the word "war" had been in everyone's mouth, now, everyone spoke of peace. It was expected that after so much misfortune the Commonwealth would breathe freely and that all her wounds would be healed under the new regime.

Finally, Sniarovski went with a letter from the king to Khmyelnitski; and, soon after, the joyful news was spread abroad that the Cossacks had left Zamost and were going to the Ukraine, where they would quietly await the commands of the king, and a commission which should investigate the wrongs of which they complained. It seemed to all as though a seven-hued rainbow, promising peace and quiet, overarched the land after a storm.

Indeed, evil prophecies and forebodings were not wanting; but, in face of the happy reality, no great importance was

568

attached to them. The king travelled to Chenstohovo to thank the heavenly intercessor for his election and to place himself under her further protection, and then he went to Cracow for the coronation. The royal officials followed in his train, and Warsaw was deserted. The refugees from Russia alone remained behind, as they did not dare to return to their ruined property; or, perhaps, had none.

Prince Yeremy, as a senator of the Commonwealth was obliged to go with the king, but Volodiyovski and Zagloba at the head of a dragoon regiment, went by forced marches to Zamost in order to announce to Skshetuski the joyful news of Bohun's death; and then to set out with him to look for the princess.

Zagloba left Warsaw, not without a certain sadness; for he was as happy as a fish in the sea among this enormous crowd of noblemen, amid the noise of the election, and the uninterrupted carousing and quarreling, in company with Volodiyovski. But he was comforted by the thought that he was returning to an active life, to adventures and intrigues, which he was planning; and besides he had his own opinion of the dangers of the capital, which he explained to Volodiyovski in the following manner:

"It is true, Pan Michael, that we have done great things in Warsaw, but God preserve us from remaining there too long. I tell you, we should have become effeminate like those celebrated Carthaginians, who were completely ruined by the enervating life in Capua. And the worst of all are the women, they lead one to destruction; for, mark you, there is nothing more dangerous than a woman. I am already old and yet they try to attract me . . . "

"Eh! never mind that," interrupted Volodiyovski.

"I have often said to myself that it is time to get some sense; but I am so warm-blooded. You have more phlegm, but I am choleric. But that is a secondary matter, we are now going to begin another life. There have been times when I was unhappy without war. Our regiment is in good condition and near Zamost there are enough rioters; we can amuse ourselves with them on the way to the princess. We will then find Skshetuski and that giant, that Lithuanian crane, that hop-pole, Pan Longin, we have not seen him for a long time."

"You long to see him and, yet, when you see him, you do not give him any peace."

"Because when he speaks it is as when your horse moves his tail and he stretches out every word as a shoemaker does a piece of leather. It is all strength with him, not intelligence. When he embraces anyone, he squeezes his ribs through the skin; but, on the other hand there is not a child in the Commonwealth who could not hang him up on a hook. Is it not absurd that a man of such fortune should be so stupid?"

"Is he really so rich?"

"He! When I first met him he had a belt that was so full of money that he could not fasten it, and dragged it about with him like a sausage. You might hit it with a stick and it would not bend. He told me himself how many villages he possessed;[1] but who could remember all their heathenish names! He owns half a district; it is a great family among the soup-swillers, the family of the Podbipyenta."

"Are you not over-coloring it somewhat?"

"I am not; for I am repeating only what he told me himself, and he never told a lie in his life, for anyway he is too stupid to tell a lie."

"Well, then Anusia will be in the fullest sense of the word princess. But, as for his stupidity I do not agree with you at all; he is a reticent man and so sensible that no one can give better council in emergency. He is no rascal; but God has given to very few such a fluent tongue as you have, that cannot be denied. He is a great knight and the noblest of men, the best proof of it is that you yourself love him and like to see him."

"He is a scourge of God," growled Zagloba, "the only reason I want to see him is that I like to roast him about Panna Anna."

"I would not advise you to do that, for it might be dangerous. One can amuse oneself at his expense, but in this case he would lose patience."

"Let him lose it, I will cut off his ears as I did Dunchevski's."

"Let it alone, sir, I would not advise my worst enemy to try it."

"Tut, tut, tut, let me only see him."

Zagloba's wish was fulfilled sooner than he expected. When they reached Konskovoli Volodiyovski determined to

---

[1] Myshykishki, Psikishki, Pigvishki, Syrutisiany, Tsiaputsiany Kaputsiany, or rather Kaputsiana—glova (cabbage-head)—Baltupie.

rest, for the horses were very tired. Who can describe the astonishment of the two friends, when, on entering the dark hall of the inn the first person they met was the nobleman, Pan Podbipyenta.

"How are you, sir, it is a long time since I saw you,' said Zagloba. "So the Cossacks in Zamost did not cut you to pieces."

Podbiyenta embraced one after the other with both arms and kissed them on the cheeks.

"Oh, it is good to see you again," he said joyously.

"Where are you going?" asked Volodiyovski.

To Warsaw, to the prince."

"The prince is not in Warsaw, he has gone to Cracow with the king, to carry the orb before him at the coronation."

"And Pan Veyher has sent me to Warsaw with a letter, and to find out where the prince's regiments are going; for, thank God, they are no longer needed in Zamost."

"You do not need to go there, for we are bringing commands."

Pan Longin was annoyed; he had wished with whole heart to see the prince, the court, and especially a certain little person at this court.

Zagloba winked meaningly at Volodiyovski.

"Well, then, I will go to Cracow," he said, after a short pause, "I received orders to deliver the letter and I will do so."

"Let us go into the room and warm ourselves with some beer," said Zagloba.

"And where are you going?" asked Longin.

"To Zamost, to Skshetuski."

"The lieutenant is not in Zamost."

"Old woman, here's a cake, where is he then?"

"Somewhere near Khorosch. He is scattering groups of peasantry. Khymelnitski retreated, but his officers are burning and plundering on the road. The Starosta of Valets has sent Pan Jacob Rogovski to scatter them."

"And Skshetuski is with him?"

"Yes, but they are going separately; for there are great differences between them, of which I will tell you later."

They had entered the room, Zagloba ordered three pots of beer to be heated, and, approaching the table at which Longin and Volodiyovski were already seated, he said:

"You do not yet know the greatest and most joyful news,

Pan Podbiyenta; the news that we, I and Pan Michael have killed Bohun."

The Lithuanian almost jumped from the bench in his astonishment.

"My own dear brothers, can that be?"

"As true as we are both alive."

"And the two of you killed him?"

"We did."

"That is news indeed! O God, God!" said the Lithuanian clapping his hands, "You say you both killed him, how could you both do it?"

"In this way. I managed by craft, to bring him to such a pass that he challenged us—do you understand? upon which Pan Michael fought him and cut him up like an Easter sucking-pig; he laid him out like a roast capon—do you understand?"

"Then you did not both fight him?"

"Now, look here;" said Zagloba, "you must have been bled and your understanding have become weakened. Do you think I could fight with a dead man, or slay one already down?"

"But you said you both fought him."

Zagloba shrugged his shoulders.

"One must have the divine patience with this man. Pan Michael, did not Bohun call us both out?"

"He did," said Volodiyovski.

"Now, do you understand?"

"Well, let it be," answered Longin. "Skshetuski looked for Bohun near Zamost, but he was not there any longer."

"How do you mean that Skshetuski looked for him?"

"I see that I must tell you everything from the beginning, just as it happened," said Longin. "We remained, as you know, in Zamost and you went to Warsaw. We did not have to wait long for the Cossacks. They came in enormous crowds from Lemburg; one could not see the end of them from the walls. But our prince has provided for Zamost so well that it can hold out for two years. We began to believe that they would not storm the fortress and were very sorry on that account; for we were all looking forward to their defeat. As there were also Tartars among them, I hoped that the merciful God would give me my three heads. . . ."

"Pray for one, and that a good one," answered Zagloba.

"Ah, you are the same as ever, sir; that does not sound

well," said the Lithuanian. "Well, we thought they would
not storm the town, but they were almost mad in their obstinacy of heart, and began to build machines and then to
storm us. It appeared later that Khmyelnitski himself did
not wish that; but Charnota, their field commander, stormed
in upon him and said that he was trying to run away, like
a coward and to make friends with the Poles; and then
Khmyelnitski had nothing for it but to send Charnota forward. What then happened, little brothers, I cannot tell
you. There was nothing to be seen but smoke and fire. At
first they attacked us boldly, filled the trench, and sprang
on the walls. We made it so hot for them, however, that they
fled, not only from the walls, but from their own engines;
then we moved out with four regiments, and pursued them
and slaughtered them like cattle."

Volodiyovski rubbed his hands.

"Ah, I am sorry that I was not at that entertainment," he
cried excitedly.

"I too, might have been of some use there,' said Zagloba
with quiet assurance.

"And those that fought the best there were Skshetuski
and Jacob Rogovski," continued the Lithuanian. "Both
noble knights, but very antagonistic to each other. Rogovski,
particularly, sought a quarrel with Skshetuski and would
have undoubtedly called him out if Pan Veyher had not forbidden the duel under pain of death. We could not understand at first, why Pan Rogovski wanted to fight, until we
discovered that he was a relation of Pan Lashch whom, you
remember, the prince drove out of the camp on Skshetuski's
account. This accounted for Rogovski's anger towards the
prince, and towards all of us; and especially towards the lieutenant. This was the discord between them, between two
men who, during the siege covered themselves with glory;
and who, before that, had wished to kill each other. They
were both first on the walls, first in a sally, until Khymelnitski finally got tired of attacking us and the regular siege
began, not omitting any treachery which might bring about
the fall of the town."

"He trusts in cunning more than anything," said Zagloba.

"A mad and, at the same time, an obscure man," added
Podbipyenta. "He thought that Pan Veyher was a German
—probably he knew nothing of the Voyevoda of Pomerania
of the same name, for he wrote a letter with the intention of

persuading the Starosta to betray the town, as if he were a stranger and a hireling. But Pan Veyher told him in a letter what he thought of him and that he had come with his temptation to the wrong man. In order to make his dignity apparent, the starosta insisted on sending this letter by some person of importance and not by a trumpeter, and, as one was sure to be killed among such wild beasts, none of our men were anxious to go; so I undertook it and now—listen, for the best is to come."

"We are listening attentively," said the two friends.

"Well, I rode there and found the hetman drunk. He received me in a rage, especially when he had read the letter, and threatened me with his baton; and I—humbly commended my soul to God and thought to myself, 'if he touches me I will smash his head with my fist.' What was to be done, little brothers, what could I do?"

"It was noble of you to think that," said Zagloba slyly.

"But his officers sought to calm him and stepped between us," said Longin, "especially a young man, who was so bold as to seize him round the waist and pull him back, saying 'you shall not go, little father, you are drunk.' I looked more closely to see who was protecting me, astonished at his boldness and that he was so familiar with Khmyelnitski and it was—Bohun."

"Bohun" cried Volodiyovski and Zagloba.

"Bohun, himself; I recognized him, for I had seen him in Rozloga—and he recognized me. I heard him say to Khmyelnitski 'That is a good friend of mine' and Khmyelnitski, with a sudden resolve that often comes to a drunkard, said: 'If he is thy friend, little son, give him fifty dollars and I will give him a safe-conduct.' And he gave me the safe-conduct; but, as for the money, I said, so as not to irritate the animal, that he should save it for the Haiduks for it is not the custom among officers to receive tips. They treated me with great respect as I left the tent, but I had hardly got outside when Bohun came up to me, 'We met each other once in Rozloga,' he said. 'Yes, I remember,' I said, 'but at that time I did not expect, little brother, that I should see you again in this camp,' and he answered, 'It is not my own will, but misfortune that has brought me here.' During the conversation I told him also how we had beaten him behind Yarmolints. 'I did not know with whom I was dealing at that time,' he said, 'I was wounded in the hand and had poor soldiers; for they imagined that Prince Yeremy was fighting them.' 'And we did not know who you were,' I said, for if Pan Skshetuski had known it, one of you would not be alive to-day.'"

"You were right, but what did he think of it," asked Volodiyovski.

"He became embarrassed and said no more about it. He then told me that Kshyvonos had sent him with letters to Khymelnitski near Lemburg, that he might recover himself a little; and that Khmyelnitski would not let him return because he needed him as a representative on other missions. Finally, he asked 'Where is Pan Skshetuski?' and when I said, 'In Zamost,' he answered 'then perhaps we may meet' and then we parted."

"I judge that immediately after that Khymelnitski sent him to Warsaw," said Zagloba.

"He did; but wait a minute, sir. I returned to the fortress and reported to Pan Veyher about my mission. It was already late at night. The following day, they stormed us again, more obstinately than at first. I had no opportunity to see Skshetuski for three days, when I told him that I had seen Bohun and spoken to him. There were a number of officers standing near, among them Rogovski. When he heard that, he said mockingly I know that it is a question of a lady. If you are such a knight as people claim, there is Bohun; challenge him to a duel with swords, and be sure that this duellist will not let you off. We shall enjoy a fine spectacle from the walls, they make more fuss about you Vishnyovyetski men here than you deserve.' Skshetuski looked at Pan Rogovski as if he would bite him 'Do you advise me?' he asked, 'that is well, but I do not know if you, who make little of our valor, have the courage to go down among the 'blacks' and deliver my challenge to Bohun.' And Rogovski answered 'I have the courage, but I am neither kith nor kin to you—I will not go.' The others now laughed at Rogovski. 'Oh,' they said, 'now you are getting faint-hearted; but, when it was a question of somebody else's skin, you were very brave.' Rogovski, who is very proud, grew angry, and undertook to do it. The following day he took the challenge, but Bohun was not there. We did not believe his report; but now, after what you have told me, I see that he spoke the truth. Khmyelnitski must have really sent Bohun away and that was when you killed him."

"Yes, that was it," said Volodiyovski.

"But tell us," asked Zagloba, "where shall we now find

Skshetuski, "for, find him we must, in order to go with him at once to look for the girl."

"You can learn more about him on the other side of Zamost for they talk of nothing else. He and Rogovski have completely routed Kalin, a Cossack colonel, by driving him towards one another from opposite directions. After that Skshetuski destroyed, on his own account, two Tartar chambuls, defeated Burlay and fought different mobs."

"Does Khmyelnitski allow that?"

"Khmyelnitski would have nothing to do with them and says they were fighting contrary to his orders; otherwise no one would believe in his fealty and obedience to the king."

"How bad the beer is in this Konskovoli!" remarked Zagloba.

"Behind Lublin you will ride through a devastated land," said the Lithuanian; "for the expeditions went beyond Lublin, and the Tartars drag everybody into slavery and God, alone knows what they have plundered beyond Zamost and Hrubiesh. Skshetuski has already rescued several thousand prisoners and sent them back to the fortress. He is working with all his might, paying no attention to his health."

Here, Longin sighed and hung his head thoughtfully. Presently, he resumed:

"See here, I think that God in His great mercy will surely comfort Skshetuski and give him that alone which will make him happy; for this knight's services are many. In these times of destruction and self-interest, where each one thinks of himself, he forgets his own interests. He could have obtained leave from the prince long ago, in order to seek the princess; but, instead of that, when the terrible blow struck our dear mother country, he never slackened in his duty for a moment and worked unceasingly, though his heart was bleeding."

"He has the soul of a Roman, no one can deny it," said Zagloba.

"He might serve as an example."

"Especially to you, Pan Podbipyenta, for all through the war, instead of thinking of your mother country, you are looking for your three heads."

"God sees my heart," said Longin, raising his eyes to heaven.

"God has already rewarded Skshetuski with Bohun's death," said Zagloba, "and also by allowing the Commonwealth a time of rest. Now the time has come for him to think of looking for his lost happiness."

"Will you gentlemen accompany him?' asked the Lithuanian.

"Will not you?"

"I would do it with my whole heart, but what will become of the letters. I have one from the starosta of Yelets to His Majesty the king, another to the prince, and a third from Skshetuski, also to the prince, with a request for leave."

"We are bringing him his leave."

"Pshaw, but I must deliver the letters."

"You must go to Cracow, there is nothing else to be done. But, I tell you frankly that, in our expedition to look for the princess, I should like to have such fists and such shoulders as yours in our company; but I do not want you on any other account, for there we must simulate. The safest thing would be to put on Cossack dress and pretend we are peasants, but you would attract so much attention by your enormous height that everyone would ask, 'What kind of pole is that? Whence comes such a Cossack'—besides you cannot understand much about their language. No, no, you go to Cracow and we shall have to get along without you."

"I am of your opinion," said Volodiyovski.

"Then we will let it remain so," answered Longin. May God in His mercy bless and guide you. Do you know where she is hidden?"

"Bohun would not tell me, we know only what I heard when Bohun kept me a prisoner in the pig-pen; but that is enough."

"How will you find her?"

"That is my affair," said Zagloba. "I have succeeded in doing more difficult things. The chief thing now is to get to Skshetuski as soon as possible."

"Ask about him in Zamost. Pan Veyher must know where he is; he corresponds with him, and Skshetuski delivers the prisoners up to him. May God bless you!"

"The same to you," said Zagloba, "when you are in Cracow with the Prince, remember us to Pan Kharlamp."

"Who is that?"

"He is a Lithuanian of such great beauty that he has turned the heads of all the Princess's ladies in waiting in the capital."

Pan Longin started.

"Sir, you are joking?"

"Good-bye sir! the beer in Konskovoli is wretched," concluded Zagloba, winking at Volodiyovski.

37

CHAPTER XV.

Pan Longin set out for Cracow with a heart pierced by an arrow, and cruel Zagloba, accompanied by Volodiyovski, went to Zamost, where they did not even stay one day. The commandant Starosta of Velets had told him that it was a long time since he had heard anything of Skshetuski; and he thought that the regiments which Skshetuski commanded had gone to garrison Zbaraj, in order to protect that region from the bands of freebooters. This was all the more probable from the fact that Zbaraj, being the property of the Vishnyovyetski, was especially liable to the attacks of the prince's deadly enemy. A long and weary road lay before Volodiyovski and Zagloba; but, as they were obliged to travel this road in their search for the princess, and it mattered not whether sooner or later, they started without delay, resting no longer than was absolutely necessary, or than was required to rout the wandering bands.

They rode through regions so desolate where sometimes, for days at a time they never saw a human soul. The little towns lay in ashes, the villages were burned down and desolate, their inhabitants killed or taken into slavery. They found nothing on their way but corpses, ruins of houses and churches, smoking remains of villages, and howling dogs upon the ashes. Whoever had survived the Tartar-Cossack invasion, crept away into the depths of the forest and endured cold and hunger, not daring to come out of the forests for fear the danger might not be over yet. Volodiyovski fed his horse on the bark of trees, or cobs of half burned corn, which they picked up amid the ruins of what had been granaries; but they hurried forward seeking their subsistence chiefly in the provisions which they took from the marauding companies. It was already the end of October and in proportion as the former winter, much to the astonishment of all, had passed without snow, frost, or ice, this winter was more severe than usual. The whole course of Nature seemed changed. The earth was frozen hard, snow lay upon the plains; and,

578

along the margin of the rivers, a thin coating of ice could be seen in the mornings. The weather was dry, the pale sunbeams gave a little warmth at midday, but morning and evening a dark red glow was seen in the sky, the sure sign of an early and severe winter.

In addition to war and famine, a third deadly enemy threatened the wretched people—frost; and, yet, everyone looked for it longingly; as it was a far surer impediment to war than any negotiations. Pan Volodiyovski, as a man of experience and one who knew the Ukraine thoroughly, was full of hope that the expedition to find the princess would surely be successful; for the chief hindrance, the war, had been removed for some time.

"I do not believe in Khmyelnitski's sincerity," he said, "or whether he is returning to the Ukraine out of love for the king, or from the cunning of a fox. He knows that the Cossacks are good for nothing if they cannot fight behind earthworks. And in the open field, although they were five times our number, they could not stand against our regiments. They are now going into winter quarters and will drive the herds into the snow. The Tartars also want time to drive their captives home. If the winter is severe, we shall have peace until the grass is green once more."

"Perhaps longer, for they certainly respect the king's authority; but we do not need so much time. God willing, we shall arrange Skshetuski's wedding for Shrovetide."

"If only we do not miss him now, that would be a fresh trouble."

"He has three regiments with him, so it will not be like looking for one grain in a bushel; perhaps we may overtake him before we reach Zbaraj, if he is detained anywhere among the haydamaks."

"We cannot overtake him, but we ought to hear something about him on the road," answered Volodiyovski.

This, however, was not easy, for the peasants had seen regiments passing by, had heard of encounters with the marauders; but no one could tell whose men they were, as they might have been Rogovski's men just as easily as Skshetuski's. The two friends had no certainty in the matter. But they heard definite news of the defeat of the Cossacks by the Lithuanian soldiers. The rumor was already taking shape on the eve of Volodiyovski's journey from Warsaw, but it was doubted at first. Now the news with all details was circulated through the whole country as an absolute certainty. The Lithuanian victory made up for the defeat of the royal forces by Khmyelnitski. Polksienjyts and savage Nebaba had lost their heads, and the still more redoubtable Kshechovski who, instead of a Starostship and a Voyevodaship and other honors, had earned impalement among the ranks of the rebels. It seemed as though a strange Nemesis had avenged the German blood which he had shed in killing colonels Flick and Werner in the reeds of the Dnieper, for he fell into the hands of the German regiment Radzivil. Although sorely wounded, he was dragged away to the stake, upon which the unfortunate man lingered in agony the whole day long before he finally gave up his black soul. This was the end of one who, through his courage and warlike genius might have become a second Stefan Khmyelnitski; but whose insatiable desire for wealth and position led him into treachery and perjury and in the end sent him to the most frightful of deaths, a death fit for Kshyvonos himself.

Polksienjyts and Nebaba who were with him, had lost almost twenty thousand Cossacks on the field of battle, all who had not perished in the swamps of the Prypets. Fear spread like a storm-wind across the thriving Ukraine, for all believed that after the great triumphs at the Zolta Woda, Korsun and Pilavyets, a time of defeat had arrived, similar to those which the rebels had experienced at Solonits and Kumeyka. Khmyelnitski himself, although at the height of his fame and more powerful than ever, vacillated when he heard of the death of his friend Kshechovski and began anew to seek for knowledge of the future among the fortune-tellers. They prophesied various things, among others, that a new war would take place; they spoke of conquests and defeats—but could not tell the hetman what would happen to him personally.

Through Kshechovski's death and on account of the winter, the truce was of longer duration; the country began to settle down; the devastated villages were once more inhabited and confidence returned to all the despairing and troubled hearts.

With the aid of this confidence, after a long and difficult journey, our two friends arrived happily in Zbaraj, where, after announcing themselves at the castle, they at once went to the commandant, in whom, to their great astonishment, they recognized Vyershul.

"And where is Skshetuski?" Zagloba asked, after the first greetings were over.

"He is not here," answered Vyershul.

"Have you the command of the garrison?"

"Yes. Skshetuski was in command, but he went away and left me as commandant until his return."

"And when did he promise to return?"

"He did not say; indeed he did not know himself, but he said when he left, 'if any one should come for me, tell them to wait for me here.'"

Zagloba and Volodiyovski looked at one another.

"How long has he been gone?" asked Pan Michael.

"Ten days."

"Pan Volodiyovski," said Zagloba, "let Pan Vyershul give us some supper, for we cannot take council on hungry stomachs; we will continue our conversation at the supper table."

"I am only too delighted to wait on you, gentlemen, for I am just going to sit down to table myself. Besides, Pan Volodiyovski, as my superior officer, will now take the command, so I am his guest and not he mine."

"Keep the command, Pan Kryshtof,' said Volodiyovski, "for you are older than I am and, besides, I must leave again soon."

It was not long before supper was ready. They sat down and ate and drank with enjoyment; and, after Zagloba had somewhat satisfied his hunger, with two plates of soup he said to Vyershul:

"You have no idea, Sir, where Pan Skshetuski is gone?"

Vyershul ordered the servants to leave the room and, after a moment's reflection, he said:

"I have an idea, but Skshetuski is very anxious to keep the matter a secret, and that is why I would not speak before the servants. He took advantage of a favorable opportunity—for we shall probably remain here quietly until the spring—and in my opinion has gone to look for the princess, who is in Bohun's hands."

"Bohun is no longer alive," said Zagloba.

"How is that?"

Zagloba now related for the third or fourth time all that had happened; for he always enjoyed telling it.

Vyershul, like Longin, could not sufficiently express his astonishment, and finally said:

"Well, then, it will be easier for Pan Skshetuski."

"It just depends on whether he finds her. Did he take any men with him?"

"No one, he rode alone, with one little Russian boy and three horses."

"Then he set to work prudently, for one can do nothing there except with cunning. One might get as far as Kamenets with a regiment, but in Ushyts and Mohilov there are nothing but Cossacks. There are good winter-quarters there. There is a nest of them in Yampol, and one must go there either with a whole division or quite alone."

"But how do you know that he has gone into that region?" asked Vyershul.

"Because she is hidden somewhere behind Yampol and he knew that; but there are so many glens, hollows, and bush that it would be hard enough to find her if one knew the exact spot; and how much harder when one does not know. I rode to Yahorlik with horses, and also to a council, that is how I know. If I were with him, it might be more easy; but as he is alone, I doubt very much if he finds her, unless some accident should show him the way, for he would not dare to ask any one."

"Then, you, gentlemen, wished to accompany him?"

"Yes. But what shall we do now, Pan Michael, shall we follow him or not?"

"I leave that to your good judgment."

"H'm! ten days have passed since he left—we cannot overtake him, and besides, he said we were to wait for him. God knows what way he may have taken; he may have followed the old highway, that leads through Ploskir and Bar, or he may have gone by way of Kamenets Podolski. It is hard to decide."

"Remember, also, gentlemen, that there are only surmises and we have no certainty that he has gone to look for the princess."

"That's just it, that's just it," said Zagloba. "He may have only gone to get information, and then return to Zbaraj, for he knew that we would go with him and he may be expecting us just at this time. It is a difficult matter."

"I would advise you to wait ten days," said Vyershul.

"Ten days is nothing. Shall we wait or not?"

"I think perhaps we had better not wait, for what should we lose by setting out to-morrow? If Skshetuski does not find the princess, perhaps God will give us better luck."

"See here, Pan Michael, we cannot undertake this thing without due consideration. You are young and anxious for

adventure," said Zagloba, "but there is a danger; for if he is
looking for her alone, and we are also looking for her, it might
easily arouse suspicion among the people in that neighborhood. The Cossack people are sly and fear that any one may
discover their plans. They may be arranging with the Pasha,
whose territory borders on Khotsim, or with the Tartars beyond the Dnieper for a war—who can tell? In that case they
will keep a watchful eye on strangers and, especially, on any
who may be asking their way. I know them; we might easily
betray ourselves, and what then?"

"Well, it would be all the more easy for Skshetuski to fall
into some trap, and we ought to hasten to his assistance."

"That is very true."

Zagloba sank into deep thought, so that his temples
twitched. Presently he roused himself and said:

"Taking everything into consideration, I think we ought
to set out."

Volodiyovski breathed freely.

"And when?"

"After we have rested here about three days, so that we
may be fresh in body and soul."

The following day, the two friends began their preparations for the journey, but, suddenly and quite unexpectedly,
the evening before they were to start, Skshetuski's boy, the
young Cossack Cyga arrived with news and letters for Vyershul. When Zagloba and Volodiyovski heard of it they went
at once to the commandant's quarters and read what follows:

"I am in Kamenets whence the road through Satanov is
safe. I am going to Yahorlik with Armenian merchants to
whom Pan Bukovski directed me. They have Tartar and
Cossack safe-conducts which will insure them a safe journey
as far as Akerman. We are going to Ushyts, Mohilov, and
Yampol, with silks, stopping in every place where there is the
slightest trace of life. Perhaps God will help us to find what
we seek. Tell my comrades, Volodiyovski and Pan Zagloba,
to wait for me in Zbaraj if they have nothing else to do; for
the road I have left behind me cannot be travelled by large
numbers on account of the great mistrust of the Cossacks,
who are wintering in Yampol and along the Dniester to Ya-
gorlik, and have turned their horses out in the snow. What
I cannot do by myself, three of us could not do, and I can
easily get through as as an Armenian. I thank you, Pan
Kryshtof, from my whole soul for your decision, which I shall

never forget as long as I live. But I could not wait for her any longer, for I passed every day in torture. I could not tell whether they would come, and this was just the time to set out, when all the merchants are setting out to buy candied fruits and silk stuffs. I am sending back my faithful boy. Take him under your protection; I have no need of him and I am afraid that as he is so young he may chatter about our affairs. Pan Bukovski vouches for those merchants that they are honest, and I believe it. In the belief that everything rests in the hands of the Almighty, who, if He will, may show us His mercy and shorten our tortures, Amen."

Pan Zagloba, after reading the letter through, looked at his companions, who were silent. At last, Vyershul said:

"I suspected that he had gone there."

"And what remains for us to do?" asked Volodiyovski.

"Well, what?" said Zagloba, shrugging his shoulders. "There is nothing for us to do there. I am glad that he is travelling with the merchants, for he can spy round everywhere without any one being suspicious. They will buy something in every cabin and every country-house, for half the Commonwealth has been plundered. It would be difficult for us, Pan Michael, to get beyond Yampol. Skshetuski is as dark as a Wallach, and could easily pass for an Armenian; you would easily be recognized by your flaxen moustache. Even a peasant's disguise would not be of much use. . . God bless him! We are of no use there, I must confess, although I am sorry to think that we cannot lift a hand to rescue that poor child. However, we have done Skshetuski a great service in killing Bohun; for, if he were alive, I would not answer for Yan's life."

Volodiyovski was much disappointed, he had looked forward to a journey full of adventure, and, now, he had the prospect of a tedious sojourn in Zbaraj.

"Perhaps we can ride to Kamenets," he said.

"And what would we do there, what should we live on?" answered Zagloba. It does not make any difference within what walls we vegetate, we must wait in any case! for such a journey will take Skshetuski a long time. A man remains young as long as he is occupied"—(here Zagloba let his head droop in a melancholy manner)—"and he grows old in inaction, but what is to be done? . . . Let him go without us To-morrow we will have a solemn mass said that God may give him good luck. We have killed Bohun—that is the principal thing. Let the horses be unsaddled, Pan Michael—we must wait."

The following morning, long, monotonous days of expectation began for the two friends; and neither drinking mead nor throwing dice was able to enliven them; they stretched out endlessly. The severe winter made itself felt; snow, two feet deep, covered everything like a shroud, the roofs of Zbaraj as well as the whole earth. Wild animals and flocks of birds approached human habitations. All day long was heard the croaking of innumerable flocks of crows and ravens. December passed, January, February—and still no news of Skshetuski. Zagloba became melancholy and declared he was growing old.

CHAPTER XVI.

The commissioners who had been sent by the Commonwealth to carry on negotiations with Khmyelnitski, finally made their way to Novosiolek amid the greatest difficulties; and remained there waiting for an answer from the victorious hetman, who during this time remained in Chigrin. They waited sadly and anxiously for, during their whole journey, they had been exposed to death; and their difficulties increased at every step. They were continually surrounded, by night as by day, by swarms of "blacks," who had become perfectly savage from war and slaughter, and howled for the death of the commissioners. From time to time they came upon bands without a leader, consisting of murderous and savage herders, who had not the slightest conception of the law of the land and thirsted for blood and booty. The commissioners had indeed an escort of a hundred horse, commanded by Pan Bryshovski and, besides that, Khmyelnitski, foreseeing what might occur to them, had sent Colonel Donyets to protect them with four hundred Cossacks. But the escort might at any time prove insufficient, for the crowd of "blacks" increased every hour and assumed an ever more threatening attitude; and whoever wandered for a moment from the train, or from his regiment, disappeared forever. They were like a handful of travellers surrounded by a herd of hungry wolves. Thus, whole days and weeks passed until one night in camp at Novosiolek they all believed that their last hour had come. The company of dragoons and the escort under Donyets had been carrying on a regular battle to protect the lives of the commissioners, who were already saying their prayers and commending their souls to God. The Carmelite Lentovski gave them absolution, one after another, while, from outside, each gust of air brought frightful cries, firing, hellish laughter, the clash of scythes, and cries of death and destruction, as well as demands for the head of the Voyevoda Kisiel, who was an especial object of their hatred.

It was a long, dreadful, winter night. The Voyevoda Kisiel

sat motionless for several hours, his head buried in his hands.
He did not fear death, for since the time he left Hushch he
was so exhausted, so weary and sleepless, that he would have
gladly stretched out his arms to death—but his soul was filled
with boundless despair. Was it not he who as a Russian in
blood and bone had first undertaken the role of a peacemaker
in this unexampled war; was it not he who, everywhere, in
the Senate and at the councils, had stepped forward as the
most zealous advocate of negotiations; he, who had supported
the policy of the chancellor and the Primate; he, who had
condemned most fiercely Prince Yeremy; who had worked
in good faith for the welfare of the Cossack people and of the
Commonwealth, and had believed, with the whole might of
his earnest soul, that negotiations and concessions would settle everything, soothe and heal the bleeding wounds. And
now, at the very moment that he was taking the baton and
the concessions for the Cossacks to Khmyelnitski, he despaired of everything—for he saw with his own eyes the
futility of his exertions, and beheld before him emptiness
and an abyss.

Did they then demand nothing but blood, desire no other
freedom than the freedom to rob and burn, thought the Voyevoda, suppressing the groan that sought to escape from his
noble heart.

"The head of Kisiel! the head of Kisiel! and destruction
to him," was the answer to his thoughts from the mob.

And the Voyevoda would willingly have sacrificed his white,
careworn head, if one last spark of belief had not restrained
him. The belief that something else was needed for their
salvation and that of all the Cossacks, as well as for the welfare of the Commonwealth. Let the future teach them how
to demand that.

And as he thought of this, a ray of hope and a certain
amount of confidence lightened for a moment the darkness
with which despair had clouded his soul, and the unhappy old
man persuaded himself that these "blacks" did not represent
the whole Cossack people, not even Khmyelnitski and his
colonels, and that negotiations must be entered into with
him.

But would they be lasting so long as half a million of
rabble were under arms; would they not be disregarded at the
first breath of spring and vanish like the snow which now lay
on the steppes? . . . . Here he thought of the words of

Prince Yeremy: "One can show mercy only to the conquered," and again his thoughts became gloomy and again the abyss opened at his feet.

It was past midnight; the noise and the confusion had lessened, but the storm outside was raging more fiercely, and the snow was forming drifts. The weary rabble scattered in the various houses, and hope returned to the commissioners' breasts. Voytsiekh Miashovski, the under-Chamberlain of Lemburg, rose from the bench on which he was sitting, listened at the window which was covered with snow and said:

"It seems to me that we shall, with God's help, survive until the morning."

"Perhaps Khmyelnitski may send us a larger escort, for we cannot get to him with this one," said Sniarovski.

Zielanski, the Cup-Bearer of Bratslav, laughed bitterly.

"Who would take us for peace commissioners?"

"I was sent repeatedly as an envoy to the Tartars," said the standard bearer of Novogorod, "but in all my life I never made such a mission as this. In our person, the Commonwealth is suffering more humiliation than she underwent at Korsun and Pilavyets. I tell you, gentlemen, we ought to turn back, for there can be no question of negotiations."

"Let us turn back," repeated Bjozovski, the Castellan of Kiev. "As we cannot have peace, let us have war!"

Kisiel raised his brows and fixed his glassy eyes on the Castellan.

"The Zolta Woda, Korsun, and Pilavyets," he said gloomily.

And they were all silent until Kulchinski, the Treasurer of Kiev, began to tell his beads aloud, and the Master-of-the-Hounds Kshetovski put his hands to his head and repeated:

"What dreadful times! what dreadful times! God have mercy on us!" . . . .

The door was here opened and Bryshovski the dragoon captain of the Bishop of Posen, who was looking for shelter, stepped into the room.

"Illustrious Voyevoda," he said, "a Cossack desires an audience."

"That is well," answered Kisiel, "have the 'blacks' already scattered?"

"They have gone, but to-morow they will come again."

"Did they attack you badly?"

"Frightfully, but Donyets's Cossacks killed several of them. To-morrow they are going to burn us out."

"Well, let the Cossack come in."

Presently the door was opened and a tall, black-bearded form stood on the threshold.

"Who art thou?" asked Kisiel.

"Yan Skshetuski, lieutenant of the Hussars of the Prince Voyevoda of Russia."

The Castellan Bjorzovski, Kulchinski, and the Master-of-the-Hounds Kshetovski sprang from their seats. They had all served the year before under the prince, and had been at Makhnovka and Konstantinov and knew Pan Yan well, and Kshetovski was even related to him.

"Can it be! Is it true! then you are Pan Skshetuski?"

"What are you doing here, how did you get here?" asked Kshetovski, putting his arms around him.

"In the disguise of a peasant as you see," said Skshetuski.

"Illustrious Voyevoda," cried the Castellan Bjozovski, "this is the bravest knight of the regiments of the Voyevoda of Russia, celebrated in the whole army."

"I greet him with a joyful heart," said Kisiel, "he must be a very determined knight to have managed to get as far as this." Then, turning to Skshetuski:

"What is your request from us?"

"That you will permit me to travel with you, gentlemen."

"You are putting yourself into the jaws of the dragon, but if you wish it we have no objection."

Skshetuski bowed in silence.

Kisiel looked at him in astonishment. He was struck by the earnestness and sorrow in the stern face of the young knight.

"Tell me, Sir," he asked, "what motive drives you into that hell which no one visits voluntarily?"

"Unhappiness, illustrious Voyevoda."

"That was a useless question," said Kisiel. "You have lost someone you love and wish to seek them there?"

"That is it."

"Is it long since?"

"Since last spring."

"What! and you have only now started out to find them? It is almost a year! What have you been doing all this time?"

"I have been fighting under the Voyevoda of Russia."

"Would not that magnanimous master grant you leave?"

"I would not take it."

Kisiel looked once more at the young knight and there was a silence, which was interrupted by the castellan of Kiev.

"All of us who have served under the prince know of this young cavalier's misfortune; we have all shed tears over him, and we often regretted that he preferred to serve his country as long as the war lasted, instead of thinking of his own happiness. But it was only the more praiseworthy; he has set a rare example in these degenerate times."

"If it prove that my word has any weight with Khmyelnitski, believe me, sir, I will bespeak his kindness in your undertaking," said Kisiel.

Skshetuski bowed again.

"Go and rest now," said the Voyevoda, graciously, "you must be very tired, as we all are, for we have not had a moment's rest."

"I will take him to my room, he is a relative," said the Master of the Hounds Kshetovski.

"Let us go and take some rest also," said Bjozovski, "as we do not know if we shall get any sleep to-morrow night."

"Perhaps an everlasting sleep," answered the Voyevoda.

Then he retired to his room, at the door of which his boy was awaiting him, and the others also retired. Kshetovski took Skshetuski into his quarters, which were only a few doors away; the boy lighted them with a lantern.

"How dark the night is, the snow is is falling harder than ever," said the Master of the Hounds. "Ah, Pan Yan, what hours we have passed through to-day! I thought that our last hour had come. The 'blacks' had almost placed their knives at our throats. Bryshovski had lost courage and we were beginning to take leave of each other."

"I was among them," answered Skshetuski. "To-morrow evening, they expect a new band of murderers whom they have informed of your presence here. To-morrow, we must set out, no matter what happens. You are going to Kiev, are you not?"

"That depends on Khmyelnitski's answer which Prince Chetvertynski has gone to obtain. This is my room, step in, Pan Yan. I ordered some wine to be heated and we will fortify ourselves before going to sleep."

They stepped into the room, where a mighty fire burned in the chimney; the steaming wine was standing on the table. Skshetuski eagerly reached for a glass.

"I have touched nothing since yesterday," he said.

"You look wretched, it is easy to see that you are wasted by sorrow and fatigue. But tell me about yourself, for I know

your affairs. You intend, then, to seek the princess among
those people?"

"To seek her, or death," answered the knight.

"You will sooner find your death. How do you know that
the princess is there at all?" asked the Master of the Hounds.

"Because I have already looked for her elsewhere."

"Where?"

"Along the Dniester, as far as Yahorlik. I travelled with
some Armenian merchants, for I had proofs that she was hidden there. I have been everywhere, and now I am going to
Kiev because Bohun is said to have taken her there."

Skshetuski had scarcely mentioned Bohun's name, when
the Master of the Hounds raised both hands and clasped his
head.

"By God!" he cried. "I have not told you the most important thing. I heard that Bohun was killed."

Skshetuski turned pale.

"What?" he said. "Who said so?"

"That nobleman who had already rescued the princess and
who fought so bravely at Konstantinov. I met him as he was
riding to Zamost; we passed each other on the road. Almost
before I had asked him what news he had, he answered that
Bohun was dead. 'Who killed him?' I asked. He answered,
'I did'—and we separated."

The color which had mounted into Skshetuski's face suddenly paled.

"That nobleman," he said, "is always joking. One cannot
believe him; no, no, he cannot possibly have killed Bohun."

"And did you not see him, Pan Yan? For I remember that
he said he was going to Zamost to see you."

"I did not expect him in Zamost, he must now be in Zbaraj.
But I was in a hurry to overtake the commissioners, so I did
not come from Kamenets by way of Zbaraj and have not seen
him at all. God only knows if all that he told me about her
that time was true. He pretends that while Bohun had him
prisoner he overheard that he had hidden her behind Yampol, and was then going to take her to Kiev for the marriage
ceremony. Perhops there is no more truth in that than in
anything else that Zagloba says."

"Why do you want to go to Kiev?"

Skshetuski did not reply and, for a time, no sound but the
howling of the wind was to be heard.

"For," said the Master of the Hounds, putting his finger on

his forehead, "if Bohun is not dead you would fall into his hands."

"I am going there to find him," answered Skshetuski gloomily.

"Why?"

"God shall decide between us."

"But he will not fight with you, but will put you in chains at once and kill you or sell you to the Tartars."

"I shall go with the commissioners, under their protection."

"God grant that we may manage to keep our own heads out of the noose, and how can we talk of the protection we grant!"

"If it is hard to live, it will be easy to die."

"Have mercy on yourself, Yan; for in this case it is not a question of death only, for no one can escape that, but they may sell you to the Turkish galleys."

"Do you think so, Pan Kshetovski? Do you think that it will be worse for me than it is now?"

"I see you are in despair, you have no confidence in God's mercy."

"You are mistaken, sir. I say that it fares badly with me on earth, but, by God's help, I have been reconciled long ago. I desire nothing, do not complain, do not curse, do not run my head against a wall; I only try to fulfill what seems to be my duty, as long as life and strength hold out."

"But sorrow is wasting you like a poison."

"God gave the sorrow that it might waste me and will send a remedy when he sees fit."

"That is an unanswerable argument," said the Master of the Hounds. "God alone can help you; our hope for ourselves and for the Commonwealth rests in Him. The King has gone to Chenstohovo. Perhaps he will entreat the most Holy Virgin for us; otherwise we are lost."

A silence ensued, broken only by the challenge of the dragoons outside, "Wer da!"

"Yes, yes," said the Master of the Hounds after some time, "we all belong more to the dead than to the living, the people of this Commonwealth have forgotten how to laugh, they only sigh, like the wind in the chimney; but I believed that better times would come, before I set out to come here with the others. I see now that my hope was unfounded; ruins, war, hunger, and death—nothing else, nothing else."

Skshetuski was silent, the flames which darted from the hearth up the chimney lighted up his stern emaciated face. Presently he raised his head and said earnestly:

"All is transitory; all passes, vanishes, and nothing remains."

"You speak like a monk," said the Master of the Hounds.

Skshetuski did not answer. The wind moaned ever more sadly in the chimney.

CHAPTER XVII.

The following morning the commissioners, accompanied by Skshetuski, left Novosiolek. It was a melancholy journey, for, at every halting place, in every little town, they were threatened with death, and everywhere met with insults that were worse than death; more particularly as the commissioners in their person and office, represented the majesty of the Commonwealth. Pan Kisiel became ill and they had to carry him in his sleigh into all the inns where they stopped for the night and into the houses and bakeries. The Under-Chamberlain of Lemburg shed tears at the insults to himself and to the fatherland; Captain Bryshovski also fell ill from annoyance at the abuse they received and from their fatigues; so Skshetuski took his place and led the unfortunate cavalcade farther into the crowds of rebels; amid insults, threats, rough treatment, and fighting.

In Byalogrod it seemed as though the last hour had come for the commissioners. The mob beat Bryshovski, who was sick, killed Pan Jniazdovski and, nothing but the arrival of the metropolitan, to hold an interview with the Voyevoda, prevented the intended slaughter. In Kiev, they would not allow the commissioners to enter the town. On the eleventh of February, Prince Chetvertynski returned without an answer from Khmyelnitski. The commissioners did not know what to do or in what direction to turn. If they returned, they would leave behind them the enormous bands of peasantry who were waiting only for the breaking off of negotiations to murder the embassy. The mob became bolder; they seized the bridles of the dragoons' horses, blocked their way, threw stones, pieces of ice, and frozen snow-balls into the Voyevoda's sleigh. In Gvozdova, Skshetuski and Donyets were obliged to fight a bloody battle, in which they routed several hundred of the "blacks." The soldiers of Novogorod and Sniarovski rode again to Khmyelnitski, to represent to him that he should come to Kiev for further negotiations. But the Voyevoda had little hope that they would reach him alive. In Khvastova, the commissioners were obliged to remain inactive and look on, while the people killed prisoners of both sexes. They drowned them in holes in the ice, poured water over them in the icy air, thrust them with hay-forks, and flayed them alive with their knives. Eighteen such days had passed, before an answer finally came from Khmyelnitski, saying that he would not go to Kiev, but would wait in Pereyaslav for the Voyevoda and the commissioners. The unfortunate envoys breathed freely once more, in the hope that their tortures were now at an end; and, after they had crossed the Dnieper at Tripol, they went for the night to Voronkov, which was only six miles from Pereyaslav. Khmyelnitski came half a mile on the road to meet them, apparently out of respect for the royal embassy. How he had changed from the time when he had exalted himself in order to avenge the supposed insult—"quantum mutatus ab illo!" as the Voyevoda of Kisiel justly wrote.

He came with a number of horses, with officers, sergeants and military music, with the bunchuk and red uniform as though he were a ruling prince. The commissioners' suite at once stopped; but Khmyelnitski sprang forward to the foremost sleigh in which sat the Voyevoda, looked for a time into his reverend countenance, raised his fur cap slightly, and said:

"I greet you, Pan Commissioners, and you, Voyevoda. You should have undertaken to negotiate with me earlier, when I was less important and did not know my own strength; but, as the king sends you to me, I will receive you joyfully into my country."

"We greet you, hetman," answered Kisiel. "His Majesty, the King, sends us to inform you of his forgiveness, and to grant you the justice you seek."

"For the forgiveness, I thank him, and the justice I have already obtained myself, by holding this"—here he tapped his sword, "at your necks, and I will continue to procure it, if you do not give me satisfaction."

"You do not receive us very graciously, Hetman of the Zaporojians, as ambassadors of the King."

"I will not negotiate with the snow on the ground; but at a more convenient time," answered Khmyelnitski, roughly. "Let me get into your sleigh, Kisiel, and then I will do you the honor of driving with you."

As he said this, he dismounted and approached the sleigh.

Kisiel, however, moved over to the right side, leaving the left free for Khmyelnitski.

When he saw this he frowned and said:

"Let me sit at the right side."

"I am a senator of the Commonwealth."

"What do I care for that. Pan Pototski is the first senator and Crown hetman, and I hold him a prisoner and will let him go when I see fit; perhaps to-morrow, with some others, to be impaled.

Kisiel's pale cheeks flushed.

"I represent the king in my person."

Khmyelnitski's face lowered, but he restrained himself and sat down at the left of Kisiel, murmuring:

"He may be king in Warsaw, but I am king in Russia. I have not yet humbled you enough, I see."

Kisiel did not reply, but raised his eyes to heaven. He had a foretaste of what awaited him, and he thought rightly that if the way to Khmyelnitski was a Golgotha, a sojourn with him was martyrdom itself.

The horses hastened to the town, twenty shots were fired from the cannon and all the bells rang. Khmyelnitski, as though he wanted to prevent the commissioners from considering the salute as an exceptional honor granted to him, said to the Voyevoda:

"I have received not only you, but other ambassadors sent to me, in the same manner."

And Khmyelnitski spoke the truth. Ambassadors had been sent to him as though he were a reigning prince. On his return from Zamost, while he was yet impressed by the election and by the defeats he had suffered from the Lithuanian army, the hetman did not possess half his present pride, but since Kiev had received him with torches and flags; since the academy had greeted him in the following words: *"Tanquam Moisem, servatorem, salvatorem, liberatorem populi de servitute lechica et bono omine Bogdan*—by the Grace of God!" and, when they finally called him *"Illustrissimus Princeps"* "there was aroused the beast in him, according to the word of one of his contemporaries. He actually felt his own power on a firm footing, which he had hitherto lacked.

The embassy was a tacit recognition, not only of his power but also of his sovereignty. The faithful friendship of the Tartars, which he had bought by an abundance of booty and many unfortunate prisoners; which this leader of the people had allowed them to pick from among the people, was an assurance of assistance against every enemy. Consequently, Khmyelnitski, who at Zamost had bowed to the royal majesty and to the will of the monarch, was now blinded with pride; and, convinced of his own strength, of the disorder in the Commonwealth and of the inefficiency of her leaders, was now ready to lift his hand even against the king. His ambitious soul was already dreaming, not of the independence of the Cossacks, not of the restoration of the former privileges of the Zaporojians, not of justice for himself; but of a sovereign state, in which he would wear the prince's cap and bear the sceptre.

And he felt himself master in the Ukraine. Zaporoj stood by him, for, under no commander had it been so swamped with blood and booty. The naturally savage people thronged to him, for while the Mazovians and the Vielkopolska bore without murmuring that burden of authority and oppression which all over Europe rests on "Ham's descendants," the Ukraine peasant breathed in with the air of the steppes such an intense, passionate love of freedom as could flourish nowhere else but in the wide steppes. How could he follow his master's plow, when his glance was bounded by God's, and not by man's, desert; when, from beyond the rapids, Sich called to him, "leave your masters, come to freedom;" when the cruel Tartar had taught him to fight, and his eyes had become accustomed to the smoke of the cannon and to slaughter, and his hands to handling firearms? Why not rather raid with Khmyelnitski and snap his fingers at his masters, than bend his proud back before a sub-governor.

And another reason why the people flocked to Khmyelnitski was, that whoever did not do so was made prisoner. In Stambul, they gave ten cartridges for one slave and three slaves for one bow seasoned in the fire, so plentiful were they. The rabble had no choice, a curious song descended from the memory of those times and was long sung by subsequent generations around their fires, a curious song about that leader who was called the Moses of the Zaporojians.

"Oh, that the first, best bullet might not miss this Khmel!"

The towns, the villages and the hamlets disappeared; the land was changed into a desert and a ruin—a wound which centuries could not heal. But that leader and hetman did not or would not see it—for he never looked behind him. He grew more important and fertilized the land with blood, and fire, and destroyed his own people, his own country, in his frightful selfishness. And, even now, he was conducting the commissioners to Pereyaslav amid the thunder of salutes and the ringing of bells; as if he were a sovereign lord, a hospodar and a prince.

The commissioners moved forward into the lion's den with bowed heads as the last spark of hope was extinguished in their hearts.

Skshetuski, who was riding behind the second sleigh, looked eagerly at the faces of the officers who had come with Khmyelnitski, to see if Bohun was among them. After his fruitless search along the Dniester, as far as beyond Yahorlik, he had come to one decision, as his last and only hope of solving the difficulty. He determined to seek Bohun and challenge him to a duel, for life or death. The unhappy knight knew indeed, that, in this game of chance, Bohun might take him without any fight, or give him over to the Tartars. But he thought better of him than that; he knew his bravery, his rashness, and was almost sure that, without any hesitation, Bohun would decide on an honorable duel for the sake of the princess. He, therefore, arranged his plans in the midst of his sorrow, and decided to bind Bohun by an oath, in case he should fall, to give Helena her liberty. Skshetuski did not think of himself, and, on the consideration that Bohun might say "If I die, she is neither for you nor for me," he was ready to agree to that and to swear to it, if he could only get her out of his hands. She could seek refuge in a cloister for the remainder of her life. He hoped to find peace in the war, and, if he should not fall, he would become a monk as soon as peace was declared; as all suffering souls did in those days. Pan Skshetuski saw his way plainly and clearly, and, as the idea of a duel with Bohun had been suggested to him in Zamost and, as his search among the ravines of the Dniester had been unavailing, this seemed to be the only resource left him; for this purpose he had hastened without resting from the Dniester till he reached the commissioners, hoping that he would inevitably find Bohun among Khmyelnitski's attendants, or in Kiev. He hoped it all the more earnestly as, according to what Zagloba had said in Yarmolints, the Cossack was going to Kiev to his wedding, with three hundred candles.

Skshetuski now sought him in vain among the colonels, but

in return he found many acquaintances, whom he had known in former times of peace; such as Dziadzial, whom he had often seen in Chigrin; Yashevski, who had come as an envoy from Sich to the Prince; and Yarosha, a former officer of the prince Naokolo Paltsa, and Hrusha, and many others. He determined to ask them.

"We are old acquaintances," he said, approaching Yashevski.

"I knew you in Lubni, you are Prince Yeremy's favorite," answered the officer, "we drank and caroused together in Lubni! And what is your prince doing?"

"He is well."

"He will not feel quite so well in the spring; he and Khmyelnitski have not met yet. But they will meet and then one of them will have to die."

"As God ordains."

"Come! God is gracious to our little father Khmyelnitski, your prince will never return across the Dnieper to his Tartar coast. Khmyelnitski has many warriors, and whom has the prince? He is a true soldier. Are you not serving any longer under his banner?"

"I am travelling with the commissioners."

"Well, I am glad to have met an old acquaintance."

"If you are glad, you can do me a service; and I will ever be grateful to you."

"What kind of service?"

"Tell me where Bohun is, the famous ataman, formerly of the Pereyaslav battalion, who must be in high standing among you to-day."

"Silence," answered Yashevski threateningly, "it is fortunate for you that we are old acquaintances and that we have drunk together, otherwise I would have laid you out in the snow with this club."

"Skshetuski looked at him in astonishment, but, as he had a good deal of self-restraint, he simply closed his hand on his club.

"Are you mad?"

"I am not mad, and I do not wish to threaten you; but Khmyelnitski has given orders once for all, that if any of you, or even the commissioners, should ask any questions, we were to kill you on the spot. If I do not do it, some one else will, so I warn you out of kindness."

"But I am asking as a private matter."

"Well that makes no difference, Khmyelnitski gave the order to his colonels and told them to repeat it to the rest, 'should anyone ask you for a bundle of wood for the stove, or for potash, kill him dead.' Tell that to your people."

"I thank you for the advice," said Skshetuski.

"I warned you; but any other Pole I would have killed."

A pause followed. The cavalcade had arrived at the gate of the town. Along both sides of the road and in the streets were swarms of "blacks" and of armed Cossacks, who, out of respect for Khymelnitski, did not curse or throw snow, but looked gloomily at the commissioners, clenched their fists, and grasped the hilts of their swords.

Skshetuski formed his dragoons into a square, raised his head and rode quietly and proudly through the wide street, paying not the slightest attention to the threatening glances of the crowd. In silence, however, he thought how much presence of mind, sang froid, and Christian patience would be required to do what he had undertaken; so as not to fall a victim, at the first step, in this sea of hatred.

CHAPTER XVIII.

On the following day, the commissioners held long consultations as to whether they should at once present Khmyelnitski with the king's gifts, or whether they should wait until he had become more humble and showed some regret. It was decided to endeavor to win him over by kindness and the king's favor, by handing him the gifts at once. It was announced that the presentation would take place and the ceremony was appointed for the following day.

From early morning, bells rang and shots were fired. Khmyelnitski waited outside his residence, in the midst of his colonels and all the officials, and an immense crowd of Cossacks and "blacks." He wanted to show the whole nation what honor the king was bestowing upon him. He sat therefore in the midst of his regiments, with the bunchuk on an elevation, clad in a white cloak lined with sable, and, beside him, the envoys from neighboring countries. With his hands placed on his sides, standing on a velvet cushion with gold fringe he awaited the commissioners. There came from the "blacks" at every moment, a murmur of joy and gratification at sight of the leader, in whom, prizing power as they did above everything else, they saw the embodiment of this power. He was just such a figure as the popular fancy pictured, this unconquered hero, the victor of the hetmans, of the nobility and especially of the Poles, who, before his time, had enjoyed the fame of being invincible. Khmyelnitski had grown somewhat older during this war, but he still held himself erect, his giant shoulders still betrayed the old ability to overthrow kingdoms or erect new ones. His strong face bore the impress of an unyielding will, and uncurbed pride, and the consciousness of security gained by victories; but it was red from excessive drinking; anger and fear were slumbering in the furrows of his face; it was easy to guess that if they should be aroused, the people would give way beneath their terrible power, as a forest before a storm; his eyes, whose lids were inflamed, were already flashing with impatience, that the commissioners had not come earlier with their gifts. The frost froze his breath which looked like two clouds of steam, coming from his nostrils, like the two columns of smoke that come from Lucifer's nostrils, and in this mist that came from his lungs, he looked proud and gloomy in his festal array, with the envoys at his side; in the midst of his colonels, with a sea of "blacks" around him.

Presently, the commissioners drove up; before them came the drummers, beating their drums, and behind them the trumpeters with their trumpets to their mouths, and their their cheeks blown out giving forth a melancholy, long-drawn-out sound, as though it were the funeral of the glory and dignity of the Commonwealth. Behind the band the Master of the Hounds Kshetovski, bore upon a cushion of velvet the baton; Kulchynski, the treasurer of Kiev bearing a red flag with the eagle and the inscription on it, came next; then came Kisiel, walking alone, tall and thin, his white beard flowing down to his waist; with suffering depicted on his aristocratic face, and his soul filled with boundless despair. O few steps behind the voyevoda came the rest of the commissioners and the procession closed with the dragoons of Bryshovski under Skshetuski.

Kiesiel walked slowly, for this moment showed him plainly that, beneath the tattered veil of negotiations; beneath the appearance of welcoming the king's favor and his pardon; something else, the humiliating truth peeped out, and even a blind man could see it; and even deaf ears could hear it; because it cried aloud to all. "Thou, Kisiel, dost not go now as a bearer of favors; but thou goest on foot in order to beg for favor. in return for the baton and the standard, to this leader of peasants, in the name of the whole Commonwealth· thou, her Senator and voyevoda. . . " The soul of the lord of Brusilov was crushed, he felt as powerless as a worm, as lowly as dust and, in his ears, counded the words of Yeremy: "It is better not to live than to be the slave of peasants and heathen." What was he, Kisiel, in comparison with this Prince of Lubni, who had opposed this rebellion with a frowning brow, amid the sulphurous fumes of war; wrapped in the smoke of gunpowder like Jupiter? What was he? Under the burden of these thoughts, the heart of the Voyevoda was broken; smiles forsook his face forever; joy had fled from his heart; he felt only that he would a hundred times rather die than take one more step forward on this road. But he went on, nevertheless; for his whole past life, all his efforts and endeavors; and the whole, pitiless logic of his earlier attempt at negotiations drove him forward.

Khmyelniski awaited him with his hands placed on his side, with pouting lips and frowning brow.

The train advanced and Kisiel stepped forward until he reached the elevation; the trumpeters ceased their music; the drums stopped beating—a deep silence fell on the crowd, only the frosty air moved the flag that Pan Kulchynsi carried.

Suddenly the stillness was broken by a voice, curt but commanding, in which was expressed the unspeakable might of despair, which takes no count of anything or anybody.

"Dragoons, to the rear, follow me!"

It was Skshetuski's voice.

All heads turned in that direction, even Khmyelnitski raised himself in his chair to see what was happening. The commissioners paled. Skshetuski was standing in his stirrups, erect, pale, with flashing eyes, his unsheathed sword in his hand, and, partly turned towards the dragoons, he repeated, in thundering tones, the command, "follow me!"

Through the silence was heard the clatter of the horses' hoofs on the frosty streets; the practised dragoons faced about on the instant; the lieutenant placed himself at their head, gave a signal with his sword and the whole procession returned slowly towards the dwelling of the commissioners.

Astonishment and bewilderment were depicted on all faces, not excepting Khymelnitski's for, in Skshetuski's voice, there was something unusual, but no one knew exactly whether this sudden return of the escort did not belong to the ceremonies of the day. Kisiel alone, understood it all. He understood that the negotiations as well as the lives of the commissioners and their escort hung at this moment on a hair. But, before Khmyelnitski had time to recover himself, he mounted on the elevation and began his speech. He began with the assurance of royal clemency for Khmyelnitski and for all the Zaporojians, but his speech was presently interrupted by another incident, which had one advantage, that it completely turned all attention from what had previously occurred. Dziedzial, an old colonel, who stood beside Khmyelnitski, threatend the voyevoda with his staff and cried angrily:

"What are you saying there, Kisiel? The king? What king?—but you, kinglets, princes and nobles, have roused much trouble and you, Kisiel, bone of our bone, hast deserted us and stand by the Poles. We have had enough of thy speech, for we can obtain with the sword all that we need."

The Voyevoda looked into Khmyelnitski's eyes with a grieved expression.

Do you keep your colonels under such discipline, hetman."

"Silence, Dziedzial," cried the hetman.

"Silence, silence! He got drunk this morning," repeated the other colonels, "take yourself off or we will take you by the neck."

Dziedzial wished to make his voice heard still further, but he was literally taken by the collar and removed from the circle.

The Voyevoda spoke on in well arranged and well chosen words. He set before him the great testimonials he would receive, and that they would be the tokens of the justification of a dignity, which he had hitherto usurped by his own might. The king might have punished him; but he forgave him, as Khmyelnitski had shown himself obedient at Zamost, and as his late acts had not occurred during the rule of the present king. It would, therefore, be advisable that Khmyelnitski, after committing so many crimes, should show himself grateful for such mercy and distinction; should stop the shedding of blood, restore peace among the peasantry and begin negotiations with the commissioners.

Khmyelnitski received in silence the baton and the flag, which he at once ordered to be unfurled above his head. At this sight, the "blacks" broke out into a howl of joy, that for a time drowned every other sound. A certain satisfaction beamed upon the face of the hetman who said, after a pause:

"I thank His Majesty, the King, most humbly for the great favor that he has shown me through you, as also for the symbol of authority over the army, and for his pardon of my late transgressions. I always said that the king was on my side and against you, false knights and princes; the best proof of it is that he has expressed his satisfaction that I cut your throats. And I will continue to cut, if you do not obey me and the king in everything."

Khmyelnitski had spoken the last words in a loud voice, frowning and scolding as though his anger were rising; the commissioners were astonished at this unexpected ending to his answer. Kisiel, however, said:

"The king commands you, hetman, to cease the bloodshed and to commence negotiations with us."

"I do not shed blood, the Lithuanian army does that; for I have received news that Radzivill has destroyed my possessions of Mozyr and Turov. If this is confirmed, 1 have enough distinguished prisoners from among you whose throats I will order to be cut at once. I shall not hurry about the negotiations, it would be difficult to conclude negotiations now, as the army is separated; I have only a handful of colonels with me, the rest are in winter-quarters; I can do nothing without them. Besides, why should we stand here talking in the cold? What you were commissioned to give me, you have given me; and all see that I am now hetman appointed by the king. And now come and take some dinner and gorzalka with me, for I am hungry."

Saying this, Khmyelnitski strode towards his residence, followed by the commissioners and colonels. In the large, middle room, stood a table, which bent beneath the weight of plundered silver ware, among which the Palatine Kisiel might have found some that had been robbed from him the previous summer in Hushch.

On the table stood mounds of pork, beef, Tartar pilav and the whole room smelt of millet vodka, which stood in silver flagons. Khmyelnitski sat down and placed the Voyevoda of Kiev at his right, and the Castellan Bjozovski at his left, and, putting his hand on the flagon of gorzalka, said:

"They say in Warsaw that I drink Polish blood; but I prefer gorzalka and leave the other to the dogs."

The colonels broke into a loud laugh.

This was the insult that the Hetman aimed at the commissioners before the meal, who gulped it in silence, in order, as the sub-treasurer of Lemberg wrote, "not to irritate the beast."

Heavy perspiration stood on Kisiel's pale forehead.

The entertainment began.

The officers took up great pieces of meat from the plates in their hands. Khmyelnitski himself waited on Kisiel and Bjozovski: The dinner began in silence, for everyone was satisfying his hunger. The silence was only broken by the crunching of bones between the teeth of the feasters or by the sound of gulping drink. From time to time, one or the other would venture a word, which remained unnoticed, until at length, Khmyelnitski, who had partially satisfied his hunger and tossed down several goblets of millet gorzalka, turned suddenly to the Voyevoda, and said:

"Who commands your escort?"

Kisiel became uneasy.

Skshetuski, a noble knight," he said.

"I know him," said Bogdan, "and why would he not stay when you handed me the presents?"

"Because he was only sent with us as a protection and not to assist us, and he had his orders."

"And who gave him the orders?"

"I," answered the Voyevoda, "because I thought it was not fitting that the dragoons should be at our elbow when I was handing you over the presents."

"But I think it was something else, for I know that this soldier is stiff-necked."

Yashevski here interrupted the conversation.

"We do not fear the dragoons in the least," he said. "They had some mighty Poles among them at one time, but at Pilavyets we learned that they are no longer the same Poles who formerly beat the Turks, the Tartars, and the Germans . . ."

"No longer the Zamoyskis, the Zolkievskis, the Khodkieviches, the Khmyeletskis, and the Konyetspolkis," interrupted Khmyelnitski, "but Tkhorzovski and Zayontskovski,[1] men, children clothed in iron armor. They nearly died of fright when they caught sight of us, although, on that Wednesday, we had only three thousand Tartars there . . ."

The commissioners were silent, but their meat and drink became even more bitter to them.

"I beg you most humbly to eat and drink," said Khmyelnitski, "for, if you do not, I shall believe that our simple Cossack fare is not agreeable to your noble palates.'

"If your throats are too narrow, we can cut them," cried Dziedzial.

The colonels, who were already quite drunk, laughed loudly once more; but Khymelnitski looked at them threateningly and they were silent.

Kisiel who had been ill for several days, was as white as a sheet.

Bjozovski's face was so red that it looked as though the

---

[1] Tkhorzovski and Zayontskovski are fictitious names; the former means "coward" and the latter "hare," intended as a direct insult to the Polish Commissioners.

blood would start through the skin; he could not contain himself any longer, and shouted:

"Have we come here to dinner or to listen to insults?"

Khmyelnitski answered:

"You came here to enter into negotiations and, in the meanwhile, the Lithuanian army is burning and slaughtering. They have destroyed Mozyr and Turov I hear; and, if it is true, I will have the heads chopped off four hundred prisoners, before your eyes."

Bjozovski, who was foaming with rage a minute before, now controlled himself. It was, indeed, as Khmyelnitski said. The life of the prisoners depended on the hetman's mood, a wink of his eye. One must bear all and endeavor to soothe his anger, and to bring him back to a "milder and healthier mood of mind."

With this intention, the naturally timid and gentle Carmelite Lentovski began in a soft voice:

"The good God grant that the news from Lithuania about Mozyr and Turov may not be confirmed."

But, hardly had he spoken, when Fedor Vyeshnyak a Cherkass colonel, leaned over and swung his staff in order to strike the Carmelite on the neck. Fortunately, he did not reach him, for four other diners were sitting between them, so he cried out:

"Silence, priest, it is none of your business to show us our faults, come outside and I will teach you to honor the Zaporojian officers."

The rest endeavored to quiet him, and, as they could not succeed, they threw him out of the room.

"When do you wish to open the negotiations, Hetman?" asked Kisiel, with the intention of giving a different direction to the conversation.

Unfortunately, Khmyelnitski was no longer sober, and he returned a quick and decisive answer.

"To-morrow we will take counsel and pass sentence. I am drunk now; why do you bother me now about the commission, instead of letting me eat and drink in peace. I am tired of all that, we must now have war" (bringing his closed fist down on the table so that the glasses and plates rattled.) "In the next four weeks I will sweep out everyone, from the lowest to the highest. I will trample on you all and finally sell you to the Turkish Sultan. The king will be king to exterminate the nobles, dukes, princes; if it is a prince he cuts his throat, if it is a Cossack, he does the same. You threatened me with the Swedes, but, even they, will not compel me. Tukhay Bey, my brother, my heart, the only falcon in the world, is near me and ready to do all that I wish."

Here, Khmyelnitski, with the peculiarity of drunkenness, suddenly changed from anger to the deepest emotion, his voice trembled with suppressed tears at the remembrance of Tukhay Bey.

"You wish me to draw my sword against the Turks and the Tartars, but nothing will come of it. I will march against you with my good friends. I have already sent out regiments to command that the soldiers shall feed their horses and hold themselves in readiness to march, without wagons, without cannon; for I can find all that among the Poles. Whoever takes a wagon from a Cossack shall have his throat cut. I am not taking any myself, or, at most, only saddles and provision sacks. Thus, I will go to the Vistula and shout: 'Sit still and keep silence, Poles!' and if you shout from behind the Vistula I will find you there. I have had enough of your nobles, your dragoons, you cursed insects, who live only on lies."

He sprang to his feet, kicked away the stool on which he was sitting, tore his hair, stamped on the floor and shouted:

"We must have war, for I have received the absolution and the blessing for it! What do I care for commissioners and commissions; I do not want a truce."

Presently, he became aware of the terror of the commissioners. It suddenly occurred to him that, if they should at once go away, the war would have to begin in winter; therefore, at a time when the Cossacks could not throw up earthworks, and would not be able to offer resistance to the enemy on the open field. So he quieted himself somewhat, and sat down again on the stool. His head sank on his breast, he placed both hands on his knees and breathed heavily. Then, he once more seized the goblet of gorzalka, "Here's to the health of His Majesty the King," he shouted.

"To his health and glory," repeated the colonels.

"Come, Kisiel, do not worry," said the hetman, "and do not take what I said to heart, I am drunk. The fortune tellers told me that we must have war, but I will wait until the new grass grows; and then I will enter into negotiations; and then I will set the prisoners free. They tell me you are ill, we will drink to your health."

"I thank you, Hetman of the Zaporojians," said Kisiel.

"You are my guest, I do not forget that."

As he said this, Khmyelnitski was again overcome by his emotions and, placing his arm around the Voyevoda's neck, he laid his great red face beside the other's pale, emaciated cheeks.

The other officers followed his lead and, approaching the commissioners, shook their hands warmly, clapped them on the shoulders and repeated after the hetman: "When the new grass grows." The commissioners suffered tortures. The peasants' breath, reeking of brandy, covered the faces of these highborn noblemen, who endured the handshakes of their perspiring hands with as much aversion as they did the insults. There was, however, no lack of threats, in between these expressions of good will. Some called out to the Voyevoda: "We will enjoy cutting down the Poles, but you are our man!" Others said, "And what do you think, gentlemen; formerly you beat us, now you beg us for mercy! Death and destruction to the white handed gentlemen!" The ataman Yovk, a former miller from Nestevar cried: "I have cut up my master Prince Chetvertynski." "Give us Yeremy," cried Yashevski staggering, "and we will give you your health."

It had become unbearably warm and close in the room. The table covered with the remains of the meat and bread, and soaking with vodka and mead was a disgu ting sight. Presently, some fortune tellers came into the room, with whom Khmyelnitski generaly sat and drank until midnight, while listening to their foretelling. They were strange figures, old and bent, yellow with age, or still young; and read the future in wax, grains of wheat, fire, the foam of water, the bottom of bottles, or in human fat. Jokes and laughter were heard among the younger of these and the colonels. Kisiel was ready to faint.

"We thank you for your dinner, Hetman," he said in a weak voice.

"I will come to you to dinner to-morow, Kisiel," answered Khmyelnitski, "and now go. Donyets will conduct you with his soldiers into your house, that the 'blacks' may not do you any harm."

The commissioners bowed and went out. Donyets was awaiting them on the outside with his soldiers.

"O God! God! God!" whispered Kisiel to himself, cover-

ing his face with his hands. They proceeded slowly to the
commissioners' houses. It turned out, however, that these
were no longer beside each other. Khmyelnitski had intentionally placed each one in a different quarter of the town
that they might not meet and consult so easily. The Voyevoda Kisiel, weary, exhausted, hardly able to stand on his
feet, at once retired and would see no one until the next day;
only towards evening, he sent for Skshetuski.

"What have you done?" he said to him, "what have you
done, sir? Your life and ours are at stake."

"Illustrious Voyevoda, mea culpa!" answered the knight.
"But I was beside myself and I would rather have died a
hundred times than have witnessed such things."

"Khmyelnitski guessed your motive and I had difficulty in
quieting the animal in him and accounting for your act. But
he will come to see me to-day and will certainly ask for you,
so tell him that I had commanded you to lead the soldiers
away."

"From to-day Bryshovski will take the command again, he
feels better."

"So much the better, you have too proud a neck for the
present times. We have no fault to find with your behavior,
except that you are not cautious enough; but we know that
you are young and have a sorrow that you can hardly bear."

"I am accustomed to sorrow, illustrious Voyevoda, but I
cannot endure disgrace."

Kisiel shuddered slightly, as though someone had touched
an open wound; then he smiled, sadly and resignedly, and
said:

"Such words have become my daily bread. At first, when
I heard them I wept bitter tears; but now I can no longer
weep."

Skshetuski's heart was filled with pity at the sight of this
venerable man, with the face of a martyr, who was passing
his latter days in a double pain, that of the body as well as
the soul.

"Illustrious Voyevoda," he said, "God is my witness that I
was thinking only of the present dreadful days; when the
crown officials and senators must bend their heads before
these vagabonds, for whom the stake should be the only reward."

"God bless you, for you are young, upright, and I know had
no evil intention; but what you are saying is what the prince

says and what the army, the nobles, the Diet, and half the Commonwealth says—and the whole burden of contempt and hatred falls upon me."

"Each serves his country as he thinks best; may God judge the good intention. But, as regards Prince Yeremy, he serves his country with his life and his property."

"And he is covered with fame and suns himself in it," replied the Voyevoda. "But what has happened to me? Oh, you said rightly, may God judge a good intention, and grant rest, in the grave at least, to those who suffer so unspeakably in this life."

Skshetuski was silent, and Kisiel turned his eyes to heaven in silent prayer and in a few moments spoke again:

"I am a thorough Russian, bone and blood. The remains of the Princess Viatoldych rest in this land, therefore I love her, and the favored people who have been nourished at her breast. I saw the injustice on both sides; saw the wild lawlessness of the Zaporojians, but also the unbearable pride of those who sought to crush this wild, warlike people and enslave them. What remained for me to do, for me, a Russian, and at the same time a faithful son and senator of the Commonwealth, I united with those who said "Pax Vobiscum," as both my nature and my heart bade me; for among these was the blessed king, our father, the chancellor, the primate, and many others; and I saw that civil war was destruction for both parties. I desired to devote my whole life, till my latest breath, to securing peace; and, even after some blood had been shed, I thought, I will be an angel of union; and I went thither and worked, and still work although in pain, amid tortures, disgrace and desperation, which are more dreadful than anything else. And now, by the love of God, I do not know if your prince took up his sword too soon, or if I came too late with the olive branch; but one thing I know, that my work is in vain, that my strength is leaving me, that I have too late run my grey head against a wall; that I am going to the grave, seeing before me only darkness and destruction. Great God!—general destruction."

"God will send help."

"Oh, that He might send me a ray of hope before my death, that I may not die with despair in my heart, I would thank Him for all my sorrows, for the cross that I have borne my life long, for the fact that the mob desired my life, that I was called a traitor at the Diet, for my lost fortune, for the disgrace in which I am living, for all the bitter reward that I received from both parties."

As he said this, the Voyevoda raised his emaciated arms to heaven and two big tears, possibly the last in life, flowed down his cheeks.

Skshetuski could stand it no longer, he sank on his knees before the Voyevoda, seized his hand and said, in a voice trembling with emotion:

"I am a soldier, and am going a different road from you, but I honor your service and your sorrow."

With these words, this nobleman and knight of Vishnyovyetski's army, pressed to his lips the hand of this Russian, whom a few months before, he had called a traitor as did others. And Kisiel laid both hands on his head, and said, gently:

"My son, may God comfort thee, guide and bless thee, as I bless thee."

The complicated business of the negotiations began this very day. Khmyelnitski came very late and in a very bad humor to dine with the Voyevoda. He announced at once, that all that he had said yesterday about a commission at Whitsuntide and about the setting free of the prisoners, at the time of the negotiations, had been said while he was drunk, and that he saw now that people must have been trying to make a fool of him. Kisiel again humored and quieted him, allowing him to be in the right; but, according to the words of the Chamberlain of Lemburg, "surd tyranno fabula dicta." Khmyelnitski treated the commissioners so rudely that they preferred even the Khmyelnitski of the day before. He struck Pan Pozovski with his baton, simply because he had not introduced himself to him soon enough, although Pozovski was dangerously ill and then almost dying.

Neither kindness nor the persuasions of the Voyevoda were of any use, and it was not until he had drunk some gorzalka and some excellent Hushch mead, that his humor improved. But now, he would on no account permit any allusion to the matter in hand, only saying, "Let us drink—drink—the day after to-morrow we will attend to business. If you do not agree to that I will go." At three o'clock in the morning he insisted on going into the Voyevoda's sleeping room. The latter opposed this, under all sorts of pretexts; as he had shut Pan Skshetuski in there, for fear that, if this unyielding soldier should meet Khmyelnitski, something might happen that would be ruinous to the officer. Khmyelnitski, however, insisted, and went into the room, Kisiel following. How great, then, was the astonishment of the Voyevoda, when the hetman, spying the knight, nodded to him and cried:

"Skshetuski, why don't you drink with us?"

He stretched his hands invitingly towards him.

"Because I am ill," answered the lieutenant bowing.

"Why did you ride away yesterday? That spoiled my whole enjoyment."

"He had orders to do it," said Kisiel.

"Do not say a word, Voyevoda; I know him, and know that he did not wish to look on when you were honoring me. Oh, he is a case! But what would not go unpunished in another, I will forgive him, for I love him; he is my dear friend."

Kisiel's eyes opened wide in astonishment, but the hetman turned again to Skshetuski.

"And do you know why I love you?"

Skshetuski shook his head.

"You think it was because you rescued me from the noose that time at Omelnik, when I was only a poor fellow and was being hunted like a wild animal; but it is not for that reason. I then gave you a ring, containing some dust from the grave of Christ; but, you, horned soul, did not show me the ring when you fell into my hands—well, I let you go, we were quits. But that is not why I love you; you have done me another service which has made you my warm friend, and for which I am indebted to you."

Skshetuski looked up in astonishment at Khmyelnitski

"See, how astonished they look," said the hetman, as if he were talking to a third person. "I will tell you what I heard in Chigrin, when I came there from Bazavluk with Tukhay Bey. I enquired everywhere for my enemy Chaplinski whom I could not find; but they told me what you did to him after our first meeting; that you had taken him by the neck and the seat of his trousers and had banged him up against the door and had thrashed him like a dog until he bled. Ha!"

"That is true, I did so," said Skshetuski.

"Oh that was good, that was good, you did well; but I will find him yet. What are the negotiations and commissions for, otherwise. I will find him and will settle with him in my own way. But you gave him pepper."

Then he turned to Kisiel and told the story again.

"He took him by the coat collar and by the seat of his

trousers, and lifted him up as if he were a little fox; pushed the door open with him, and threw him into the street."

Here Khmyelnitski began to laugh, so that the echo resounded in the parlor and was heard in the dining-room.

"Sir voyevoda, send for some mead, I must drink to the health of this knight, my friend."

Kisiel opened the door and called to a servant, who immediately brought three goblets filled with Hushch mead.

Khmyelnitski clinked glasses with the Voyevoda and with Skshetuski and drank until his head steamed and his face brightened with a smile. He became very jovial and, turning to the lieutenant, said:

"Demand what you will?"

Skshetuski's pale face flushed a bright red, but no one spoke.

"Fear nothing," said Khmyelnitski, "my words are not smoke; demand what you will, not about anything about Kisiel's business."

Although he was drunk, Khmyelnitski always knew what he was doing.

"If I may be allowed to benefit by the interest which you, hetman, have taken in me, I demand justice from you. One of your colonels has done me a wrong . . . "

"I will cut his throat!" interrupted Khmyelnitski, angrily.

"I do not care for that; let him only fight a duel with me."

"I will cut his throat," repeated the hetman, "who is he?"

"Bohun!"

Khmyelnitski's eyes flashed, and he struck his hand to his forehead.

"Bohun?" said he, "Bohun is dead, the king wrote me that he fell in a duel."

Skshetuski was astonished. Zagloba then had spoken the truth.

"And what has he done to you?" asked Khmyelnitski

Skshetuski's face flushed a deeper red. He dreaded to mention the princess before this half drunken hetman, lest he should hear some unpardonable insult.

Kisiel helped him out.

"It is a serious matter, about which the castellan Bjozovski told me. Bohun has stolen this knight's betrothed, hetman, and has hidden her no one knows where."

"Are you looking for her?" asked Khmyelnitski.

"I looked for her along the Dniester, because he has hidden

her there; but I could not find her. I heard, however, that he was going to take her to Kiev for the wedding. Give me the commission, hetman, to go to Kiev and look for her there. I ask nothing further."

"You are my friend, you have beaten Chaplinski, I give you not only the right to go and seek her there, wherever it pleases you; but I command that whosoever is detaining her shall deliver her into your hands, and I will give you a safe conduct and a letter to the Metropolitan, that he may search for her in the nunneries. My word is not smoke," and, he opened the door and called Vyhovski to come and write the order and the letter. Charnota, although it was four o'clock in the morning was obliged to go and fetch the seal. Dziedzial brought the safe conduct and Donyets, received orders to accompany Skshetuski to Kiev, with two hundred horsemen; and as far as the first Polish settlement.

The following day Skshetuski left Pereyaslav.

CHAPTER XIX.

If Zagloba found time hang heavy on his hands in Zbaraj, it was still more tedious for Volodiyovski, who longed for war and adventure. It happened, indeed, that, from time to time, certain regiments left Zbaraj to drive away the swarms of freebooters who were setting fire along the banks of the Zbruch. But this was not regular war, only little expeditions which the cold weather and the severe winter made difficult and which caused great labor but brought in little honor. Consequently Pan Michael daily urged Zagloba to hasten to the assistance of Skshetuski of whom they had heard nothing for some time.

"He has certainly been exposed to dangers yonder and has perhaps already lost his life," said Volodiyovski. "We must set out at once, even though we should lose our lives with him."

Zagloba resisted no longer, for he felt as though he should die of ennui in Zbaraj, and was astonished that mushrooms had not already began to sprout all over him. But he delayed the journey in the hope that at any moment they might receive news of Skshetuski.

"He is brave, but very cautious," he replied to Volodiyovski's entreaties, "let us wait a couple of days longer; perhaps a letter may come and prove that our expedition is quite unnecessary."

Volodiyovski recognized the justice of this argument and tried to possess his soul in patience, but the time seemed to creep along. Towards the end of December, the cold prevented even skirmishes, and the neighborhood became peaceful. The only interest they had was the news which penetrated the gray walls of Zbaraj from the outside.

They discussed the coronation, and the Diet, and whether Prince Yeremy would be made commander-in-chief, as he certainly deserved to be, in preference to any other warrior. Many were annoyed with those who maintained that the present direction of things in favor of negotiations with

Khmelnitski, Kisiel alone could be promoted. Volodiyovski had to fight several duels on this account; Zagloba, to undertake several drinking-bouts; and there was even danger of his becoming a confirmed drunkard, as, not satisfied with drinking among the officers and noblemen, he was not ashamed to drink even in the citizen's drinking-shops; and to go to baptisms and weddings in their houses, where the mead, for which Zbaraj was noted, pleased him exceedingly well.

Volodiyovski took him to task and did it was particularly unbecoming for a nobleman to put himself on a familiar footing with persons in such low position, and that the whole nobility suffered through his want of self-respect. Zagloba answered that the laws were at fault in allowing the lower classes to thive and to attain to comfort that were properly fit only for the nobility. He prophesied that no good could come of such prerogatives. But he continued to act as heretofore and, really, one could hardly blame him, in those dreary winter days; full of expectation, uncertainty, and ennui.

The regiments of the prince came gradually in greater numbers to Zbaraj, which led people to expect war in the spring. Meanwhile, everyone's courage seemed to rise. Among others, Pan Longin arrived with Skshetuski's hussar regiment. He brought word that the prince had fallen into disfavor at court, and also told that Pan Yanush Tyshkievich, the Voyevoda of Kiev were dead, the man who, according to general opinion, was to be Kisiel's successor in office. And, last of all, he told of the severe illness which had overtaken Pan Lashch the field commander in Cracow. As for the war Pan Podbipyenta had heard from the prince, himself, that it could only be continued through the force of inevitable necessity; as the commissioners, provided with instructions to make all possible concessions to the Cossacks, had already set out to see Khmyelnitski.

Podbipyenta's report was received with regular fury by Vishnyoveyetski's officers, and Zagloba proposed that they should enter a protest at court and should form a confederation; for, as he said, he did not wish to see his services at Konstantinov made of no account.

Amid these stories and uncertainty, the whole of February passed and almost the half of March; and yet, no news came of Skshetuski.

Volodiyovski insisted more and more that they should set out.

"We are bound to seek not only the princess, but also Skshetuski," said he.

And yet Zagloba was right in deferring their journey from day to day, for, towards the end of March, the Cossack Zakhar arrived and brought a letter from Kiev, addressed to Pan Volodiyovski. Pan Michael at once called Zagloba and, after they had shut themselves up with the messenger in a room apart, he broke the seal and read as follows:

"All along the Dniester, as far as Yahorlik, I found no trace. Thinking that she must be hidden in Kiev, I joined the commissioners and went with them to Pereyaslav. Having, quite unexpectedly, received a safe-conduct from Khmyelnitski, I went to Kiev and looked everywhere, assisted by the metropolitan himself. There are a number of our men here, among the residents and hidden in the cloisters; but, for fear of the 'blacks', they do not let themselves be seen, and consequently it makes it more difficult to look for anyone. God has not only guided and protected me, but he has given me favor in Khmyelnitski's eyes; and, therefore, I trust that He will continue to help me and have mercy on me. I have requested Father Mukhovietski to perform a solemn votive mass, at which I hope you will pray for my success."

Skshetuski."

"Praised be God Everlasting," cried Volodiyovski.

"There is a postscript," said Zagloba, who was looking over the knight's shoulder.

"So there is," said Pan Michael, continuing to read:

"The bearer of this letter, the sergeant of the Mirgorod camp, served me faithfully when I was imprisoned in Sich, and has helped me also in Kiev; and he undertakes to deliver this letter to you at the peril of his life. Take him under your protection, Pan Michael, and see that he wants for nothing."

"Come, that is a brave Cossack, perhaps the only one," said Zagloba, reaching his hand out to Zakhar.

The old man shook it without servility.

"You can count surely upon a reward," said the little knight.

"He is a falcon!" answered the Cossack, "how I love him! I did not do this for money."

"Many a nobleman would be proud of your sense of chivalry," said Zagloba. "So you are not all beasts over there, not all of you; but, never mind that. So Pan Skshetuski is in Kiev?"

"Yes, Sir."

"And in safety? for I hear the "blacks" are carousing there."

"He is staying with Donyets the colonel. Nothing can harm him, for Khmyelnitski, our little father, has commanded Donyets to watch over him at peril of his life as the eye in his head."

"Wonders will never cease! How did Khymelnitski develop this affection for Skshetuski?' '

"He has loved him for a long time."

"And did Skshetuski tell you what he was looking for in Kiev?"

"Why should he not tell me when he knew that I was his friend. I helped him to search, or I searched alone—and of course he had to tell me what I was to look for."

"And have you found no trace yet?"

"None! the Poles that are concealed there know nothing of each other, so it is not easy to find her. You heard that the 'blacks' were committing murder, but I saw it for myself. They murder, not only Poles, but those who conceal the Poles; even monks and nuns. In the convent of Saint Nicholas there were twelve Polish women among the nuns; they smoked them out, together with the nuns, and, when the poor things ran into the street, they hunted them and threw them into the Dnieper. Ah, how many of them have been drowned there!"

"Then perhaps she is dead."

"Perhaps.'

"But no," interrupted Volodiyovski, "if Bohun took her there, he certainly put her somewhere in safety."

"Where would she be safer than in a convent? That is the only place where one would be sure of finding her."

"Ugh!" said Zagloba. "Do you believe Zakhar, that she is dead?"

"I do not know."

"It is evident that Skshetuski is in good spirits," said Zagloba, "God proved him, but he has also comforted him. And you, Zakhar, is it long since you left Kiev?"

"Some time ago, sir, I left Kiev at the time that the commissioners passed through there on their homeward journey. A crowd of Poles wanted to escape with them, and fled across the snow-fields, the steppes, and through the forests to Byalogrod; but the Cossacks followed them and slew them. Some were left behind, some were killed, and many were ransomed by Pan Kisiel, as long as he had a coin left."

"Oh, the dog-souls! So you travelled with the commissioners?"

"I travelled with them as far as Hushch and from there to Ostrog and then I came on alone."

"You are an old acquaintance of Skshetuski's?"

"I made his acquaintance in Sich and took care of him when he was wounded; and there I learned to love him as though he were my own child. I am old and have no one to love."

Zagloba called a boy and ordered some mead and meat to be brought and they sat down to supper. Zakhar eat with enjoyment as he was tired and hungry, and he eagerly dipped his grey moustache into the dark liquid, he tasted it, smacked his lips, and said:

"Excellent mead!"

"It is better than the blood that you drink," said Zagloba, "but I think that as you are a good fellow and love Pan Skshetuski you will not return to join the insurrection, but will remain with us. You will not suffer."

Zakhar raised his head.

"I have brought the letter, I shall return; I am a Cossack, I will remain with the Cossacks, not fraternize with the Poles."

"And will you fight against us?"

"That will I, I am a Cossack of Sich. We have chosen Khmyelnitski, our little father, as hetman; and now the king has sent him the baton and the standard."

"There you have it, Pan Michael!" said Zagloba, "did I not tell you that we must protest?"

"From what camp are you?"

"From the Mirgorod camp, but it is not in existence any longer."

"What happened to it?"

"Pan Charnyetski's hussars destroyed it at the Zolta Woda; and I, and all who survived, are now with Donyets. Pan Charnyetski is a brave soldier; he is our prisoner; the commissioners asked for him."

"And we have also prisoners belonging to you!"

"So it is. In Kiev, they say that our best warrior is in captivity with the Poles; although others say that he is dead."

"Who was it?"

"Oh, the celebrated ataman Bohun."

"Bohun received his death-wound in a duel."

"And who fought him?"

"This knight, here," Zagloba answered, pointing to Volodiyovski.

Zakhar's eyes almost started out of his head, and his face became crimson. He was about to put the second quart of mead to his mouth, but it spluttered through his nose as he broke into a loud laugh.

"This knight kill Bohun?" he asked choking with laughter.

"What, the devil!" cried Volodiyovski frowning, "this messenger takes too much upon himself."

"Do not be angry; Pan Michael," interrupted Zagloba, "he is a good man, it is evident. He does not know how to flatter—but then he is a Cossack. And, on the other hand, it does you all the more honor, that, in spite of your small stature, you have already carried off so many victories. You have a puny body, but a mighty soul. Do you know that I, myself, looked at you after the duel, although I had seen you fight with my own eyes; for it seemed impossible that such a little fellow. . . . "

"Enough of that," growled Volodiyovski.

"I am not your father; you need not bear me any malice. But I tell you one thing, that I wish I had such a son; and, if you wish it, I will adopt you; will leave you my whole fortune; for it is no disgrace to have a great soul in a little body. The Prince himself is not much taller than you, yet Alexander of Macedon is not worthy to be his squire."

"But what makes me angry is that one can see no results in Skshetuski's letter," said Volodiyovski, already pacified, "thank God that he did not lose his own life on the banks of the Dniester. But, up to this, he has not yet found the princess; and who can vouch that he will find her?"

"That is true, but, as God, through our hands, has freed him from Bohun and has led him safely through so many dangers and accidents; has filled Khmyelnitski's stony heart with an extraordinary love for him; it cannot be that he should be finally consumed by torture and sorrow. If you do not see the hand of Providence in all this, Pan Michael, your intelligence is blunter than your sword; but it is a fact that a man cannot possess all the virtues at the same time.' '

"I see only one thing," said Volodiyovski, tugging at his

moustache, "that there is nothing for us to do over there, and that we must continue to remain here until we are completely dried up."

"I shall dry up sooner than you, for I am older than you, and it is well known that a turnip shrinks and bacon becomes rusty from old age. Let us thank God that all our cares seem to be coming to a happy termination. I have worried not a little about the princess, more than you, at any rate, and not less than Skshetuski; for she is my little daughter, and I could not love my own child as well as I do her. They even say that we are as alike as two goblets, but I love her, in any case; and you would not see me as happy or peaceful as I am, if I were not confident that her misery will shortly come to an end. To-morrow, I will begin to compose an epithalamium, for I write beautiful poetry, and have only lately slighted Apollo for Mars."

"What have we to do with Mars?" answered Volodiyovski. "May the devil take the traitor Kisiel, with all the commissioners and their negotiations. There will be peace in the spring as sure as two and two are four. Pan Podbipyenta, who has spoken to the prince, says the same thing."

"Pan Longin understands as much about public affairs as a goat does about pepper. He dangled at the court after that crested lark, more than he did anything else, and stood sentry over her like a setter before a covey of partridges. God grant that someone else may snatch her away from him—but that is of no consequence. I do not deny that Kisiel is a traitor, the whole Commonwealth knows that well enough, but as regards the negotiations, I think that old witch prophesies equivocally."

Here Zagloba turned to the Cossack.

"And what do your people say, Zakhar? Is it war or peace?"

"There will be peace until the new grass grows; and in spring it will be death and destruction—either to us or the Poles."

"Be comforted, Pan Michael, I heard that the blacks were arming everywhere."

"That will be such a war as has never yet been seen," said Zakhar. "They say, with us, that the Turkish Sultan is coming; and the Khan with all his hordes; and that our friend Tukhay Bey is near the border and has never been home."

"Take comfort, Pan Michael,' 'repeated Zagloba, "there is a prophesy of a new king, whose whole reign will be filled with bloodshed. So it is probable that it will be a long time before we can sheathe our swords. We shall be worn out from constant war, as a broom is by constant sweeping; but that is the lot of a soldier. When we begin to fight again, keep near me, Pan Michael, and you will see glorious deeds and learn how we fought in former, better times. My God! people are no longer what they used to be; you, yourself, are not, Pan Michael, although you are a fierce soldier, and killed Bohun."

"You are right, sir," said Zakhar, "there are no such men as there used to be."

And he looked at Volodiyovski searchingly and shook his head.

"But that this knight should have killed Bohun—no, no, I cannot believe it."

CHAPTER XX.

Old Zakhar returned to Kiev after resting a few days and, during this time, news was received that the commissioners had returned home without any great hope of peace; indeed, they almost despaired of it. They had only succeeded in arranging a truce to last till the Russian Whitsuntide; and then a new commission would undertake to conclude negotiations, with the whole army at their back. Khmyelnitski's conditions and demands were so mountain-like that no one believed that the Commonwealth would accept them; consequently, both sides made preparations for arming themselves completely.

Khmyelnitski sent one envoy after another to the Khan, requesting him to come to him with all his forces; he sent also to Stambul, where Pan Byechinski had been staying for some time, as an envoy from the king. In the Commonwealth, a call for a general arming was expected at any moment. News was received of the appointment of new leaders; Ostorog, Lantskorontski and Firley and of the absolute retirement of Prince Yeremy Vishnyovyetski from all military affairs. He could henceforth only protect the mother country with the assistance of his own troops. Not the Prince's soldiers alone, not only the nobility of Russia, but even the supporters of the former Commanders were indignant at this selection and slight; for they decided, justly, that, if Vishnyovyetski's sacrifice had received recognition, as long as there was a hope of negotiating; his retirement, in the event of war, would have been an unpardonable mistake, as he, alone, was competent to measure his strength with Khmyelnitski and to conquer this celebrated rebel leader. Finally, the prince himself came to Zbaraj in order to collect as many troops as possible and to stand prepared for war. A truce had been concluded; but appeared futile from moment to moment. Khymelnitski, indeed, beheaded several officers here and there, when, in spite of the truce, they attacked castles and troops; but he was powerless against the countless crowds of wandering "blacks" and marauders who, either knew nothing of the truce, or did not wish to know, or were perhaps ignorant of the very meaning of the word. These flocked unceasingly into the territory that was protected by the truce and thus set at naught all Khmyelnitski's promises. On the other hand, private regiments and border soldiery; in pursuit of the robbers, frequently crossed the Prypets and Horyn into Kiev territory; or, in their zeal, hunted them into the interior of the province of Bratslav, and there, while resisting Cossack attacks, fought regular battles, which were carried on frequently with great energy and loss of life. Consequently, incessant disputes arose between the Poles and Cossacks on account of breach of faith, which no one, in fact, had the power to prevent. The truce existed therefore only in so far as Khmyelnitski, himself, on one side, and the king and the hetmans on the other did not take the field. But war had actually begun before the authorities had engaged, and the first warm beams of the spring sun lighted up, as formerly, burning villages, towns, and castles; and shone on slaughter and human misery.

Whole bands of rebels came from Bar, Khmyelnik and Makhnovka burning, plundering, and killing, close under the walls of Zbaraj. These were cut down by Yeremy's officers by his orders, though he, himself, tok no part in the petty battles; but was ready to move with his whole force into the field, as soon as the hetman should do so. He therefore sent out companies with orders to avenge blood with blood, and robbery and murder with the stake. Among others, Longin started out and fought at Charny Ostrov; but he was only a knight terrible in battle; with the prisoners he was so gentle that they did not send him out any more. Volodiyovski, especially, distinguished himself in these expeditions as a fighter, and perhaps had his equal only in Vyershul. No one understood how to surprise the enemy with such lightning speed, no one could creep up so unperceived behind them and scatter them to the four winds in a total rout, make prisoners, kill or hang them up; in short, he struck terror all around and won the favor of the prince. From the end of March to the middle of April, Volodiyovski destroyed seven bands of freebooters, each of which was three times as powerful as his own force. He never ceased fighting and became more greedy for war, as though the sight of bloodshed gave him new energy.

40

The little knight, or rather the little devil, never ceased urging Zagloba to accompany him on these expeditions, for he enjoyed his society above all things, but the more sedate nobleman withstood all his inducements, and excused his inaction in the following manner:

"I have too big a belly for these shocks and violent exertions, Pan Michael; and, besides, one man cannot do everything. To hew my way with the hussars among the close ranks of the enemy in the broad daylight, to destroy camps, to conquer flags—that is in my line, that is what God created and fitted me for; but nightly hunts among the bushes for ragamuffins, I leave to you; for you are as slippery as an eel and can get through anywhere. I am a knight of the old days and would rather tear my prey, like the lion, than to look for it behind the bushes like a pointer. And, besides, I have to go to sleep immediately after supper, that is my time to retire."

Pan Volodiyovski rode off alone and conquered alone until one day after setting out towards the end of April he returned about the middle of May, sad and troubled, as though he had suffered a defeat and lost his men. So it appeared to all, but this was a mistaken surmise. On the contrary, Volodiyovski had penetrated, during this long and difficult expedition, as far as Holovni, beyond Ostrog and had found there not an ordinary band of "blacks" but several hundred Zaporojians, about half of whom he cut down and took the others prisoners. Consequently, this deep sadness which covered his naturally joyous face like a cloud, was the more remarkable. Many wished to know the cause of it at once, but Volodiyovski said not a word, but went, the instant he dismounted, to a long interview with the Prince, accompanied by two unknown knights; and, after that, betook himself to Zagloba with the utmost haste, although several inquisitive friends tried to hold him back by the sleeve.

Zagloba looked with a certain astonishment at the two gigantic men whom he had never seen before; the gold stripe on whose shoulders showed that they belonged to the Lithuanian army.

Voldiyovski said, however, "Fasten the door, sir, and let no one in, for we have weighty matters to talk over."

Zagloba gave his servant the order, then looked uneasily at the new arrivals; judging from their manner that they had nothing good to tell.

"These," said Volodiyovski, pointing to the youths, "are the princes Bulyhov-Kurtsevich, Yur and Andrey."

"Helena's cousins," cried Zagloba. The princes bowed, and answered at the same moment,

"The cousins of the deceased Helena."

Zagloba's red face turned as pale as the sky; he threw up his hands as though a bullet had struck him and, with gasping breath and glaring eyes—said, or rather, moaned:

"What do you say!"

"We have news that the princess was killed in the Convent of St. Nicholas," said Volodiyovski sadly.

"The 'blacks' smoked out twelve young ladies and several nuns in one cell, and our cousin was among these," added Yur.

Zagloba answered nothing this time; but his face, just now so pale, became so flushed that his friends feared a stroke of apoplexy. Then his eyelids gradually drooped, and he covered his eyes with both hands; while from his lips came a groan once more.

"Oh! what a world! what a world!" Then he was silent.

And the princes and Volodiyovski began to mourn.

"We have gathered relations and friends together to rescue thee, sweetest maid," said the little knight, over and over again, amid his sighs; "but we came too late with our assistance. Our good intentions, our courage, our sword are in vain, for thou dwellest now in another, better world than this; in the train of the Queen of Heaven."

"Sister!" cried the gigantic Yur whose sorrow seized him afresh, "forgive us our fault and we will, for every drop of thy blood, shed a pail of the enemy's blood."

"And may God help us?" added Andrey.

Both men raised their arms to heaven. Zagloba rose from the stool on which he was sitting, went out a few steps towards the bed, staggered as though he were drunk and fell on his knees before the crucifix.

Presently the castle bells chimed midday. They sounded as mournful as though they were tolling for a funeral.

"She is no more," said Volodiyovski again. "The angels have taken her to Heaven and left us only sighs and tears."

Zagloba's stout body was shaken with sobs while the others kept on mourning. The bells continued ringing. After a while, Zagloba became calmer and they thought he had even fallen asleep on his knees. But it was not very long before he raised himself from the ground and sat on the edge of his bed. He was like another man, with his bloodshot eyes and sunken head. His underlip hung down on his chin and on his pallid face was an expression of bewilderment and decrepitude unusual to him; so that it really appeared as though the jovial, lively, and effervescing Zagloba had died, and left in his place an old man, bowed with age and weakness.

Presently Pan Longin stepped into the room in spite of the protests of the servant who was watching the door, and the moans and the sorrow began afresh. The Lithuanian recollected Rozloga and his first meeting with the princess, her sweetness, her youth and beauty. But, presently, it occurred to him that there was some one who was far more unhappy than any of them; and that was her betrothed, Pan Skshetuski—and he began at once to ask the little knight about him.

"Skshetuski remained with Prince Koretski in Korets whither he came from Kiev and he is lying ill and unconscious," said Volodiyovski.

"And must we not go to him?" asked the Lithuanian.

"We should do no good there," answered Volodiyovski. "The prince's physician promises that he will get well; and Pan Sukhodolski, one of Prince Dominik's officers, and a great friend of Skshetuski's is there, and also our old Zatsvilikhovski; and they are both nursing him. He lacks nothing and it is all the better for him that he is delirious."

"Oh, almighty God," said the Lithuanian. "Did you see Pan Skshetuski with your own eyes."

"I saw him; but if they had not told me who it was, I should not have recognized him. Pain and sickness have so changed him."

"And did he recognize you?"

"Yes, indeed, he recognized me, although he said nothing; but he smiled and nodded his head. And it made me so sad that I could not stay any longer. Prince Koretski is coming here with his regiment to Zbaraj, and Zatsvilikhovski is coming with him and Pan Sukhodolski swears that he will also go with them, even though he should receive contrary orders from Prince Dominik. They want to bring Skshetuski here also if he can survive the journey."

"And whence did you get the news of the princess' death?" asked Pan Longin. "Have these knights brought it perhaps?" he added pointing to the princes.

"No, these knights learned it accidentally in Korets whither they had gone from Vilna with messages from the voyevoda; and now they have come here with me because they have letters from the voyevoda to our prince. War is certain. The commission of inquiry will have no results."

"We knew that also; but tell me, sir, who told you about the death of the princess?"

"Zatsvilikhovski told me and he heard it from Skshetuski. Khmyelnitski had given Skshetuski permission to search for her in Kiev, with the assistance of the Metropolitan. They sought her chiefly in the nunneries, for all of our people who remained in Kiev concealed themselves there. They thought, also, that Bohun had placed the princess in a convent. They searched and searched, and were quite cheerful although they knew that the 'blacks' had burned out twelve young girls in the convent of the good St. Nicholas. The Metropolitan, himself, was confident that no one would dare touch Bohun's beloved, until events proved otherwise."

"Then she was in the convent of the good St. Nicholas?"

"Yes. Skshetuski found in one convent Panna Yoakhima Yerlicha concealed and, as he asked everyone about the princess, he also asked her. She told him that all the maidens had been carried away by the Cossacks and twelve only had remained in the convent of St. Nicholas, which was afterwards burned. Princess Kurtsevich must have been among these. Skshetuski did not believe her at first, as she was a refugee and was half crazy from terror. So he went once more into the convent of the good Nicholas to seek her. Unfortunately, the nuns, three of whom had been suffocated, did not know her name; but, when they heard the description of Skshetuski's princess, they said that such a one had been there. Skshetuski at once left Kiev and fell ill."

"I am astonished that he is still alive."

"He certainly would have died, had it not been for that old Cossack who took care of him during his imprisonment in Sich and who brought us the letter from him, and on his return again helped him to search. This man had him taken to Korets and delivered him to Pan Zatsvilikhovski."

"May God preserve him, for he will never be comforted," said Longin.

Volodiyovski was silent and no one uttered a word. The princes sat with their elbows on the table with frowning foreheads, and perfectly motionless. Longin raised his eyes heavenward. Zagloba fixed his glassy eye upon the opposite wall, as though he were sunk in deep thought.

"Wake up, sir," said Volodiyovski, presently, shaking him by the shoulder, "What are you thinking of? You cannot think up anything more and all your inventions lead to nothing."

"I know that," answered Zagloba in a broken voice. "I am only thinking that I am old and no longer of any use in this world."

CHAPTER XXI.

"Only think, sir," said Volodiyovski to Longin, a few days later, "that this man changed so in one hour that he seemed to be twenty years older. He was so joyous, so chatty, and full of life, that Ulysses himself could hardly compare with him. To-day, he hardly opens his mouth, but broods all day long; complaining about his age and talking as if he were in a dream. I knew that he loved her, but I did not dream that he was so fond of her."

"It is not to be wondered at," answered the Lithuanian, heaving a sigh. "He loves her all the more because he rescued her from Bohun's hands, and experienced so many dangers and adventures during his flight with her. Therefore, so long as there was hope, he kept up and exerted his ingenuity to save her. Now that there is actually nothing more for him to do in this world, he feels lonely. His heart has no object to which it can cling."

"I have already tried to get him to drink with me, in the hope that drink might restore his former vigor—but that is no good. He drinks, indeed, but does not think as he did formerly; never tells of his deeds, but becomes maudlin; his head sinks on his breast and he falls asleep. I do not know if Pan Skshetuski is any more desperate than he is."

"It is an unutterable pity, for he was a great knight. Let us go to him, Pan Michael. He liked to tease me and was always gnawing at me. Perhaps it will please him to do so now. My God! What may happen to a man! What a jolly fellow he was."

"Let us go," said Volodiyovski. "It is indeed pretty late, but at the worst it is only evening with him. He cannot sleep at night, as he sleeps all day."

As they conversed thus, they went to Zagloba's quarters, where they saw him sitting at the open window with his head leaning on his hand. It was late. Everything was still in the castle. The sentries alone called to one another in drawling tones and in the bushes which separated the castle from the town, the nightingales filling the night with melody singing, sighing and trilling, in such quick succession that it was almost like a spring shower. Through the open window, the warm breath of May entered the room and the bright mooonlight shone on Zagloba's troubled face and bowed head.

"Good evening, sir," said the two knights.

"Good evening," answered Zagloba.

"What are you thinking of here at the window, instead of going to sleep?" asked Volodiyovski.

Zagloba sighed.

"I am not sleepy," he said slowly. "It is just a year since I fled from Bohun with her to the Kahamlik and these same little birds were trilling then just as they are now; and where is she now?"

"God has ordained it so," said Volodiyovski.

"Only tears and sorrow, Pan Michael, there is no longer any consolation for me."

They were silent. Only the song of the nightingales which filled the beautiful night came ever more clearly through the open window.

"Oh God, God!" sighed Zagloba. "Just as it was at Kahamlik."

Pan Longin shook a tear off his fair moustache, and the little knight said, after a pause:

"Eh! Do you know what, sir? Leave sorrow to its sorrow. Drink with us a cup of mead, for there is nothing better as a remedy for care. We will think of better times over our glasses."

"Let us drink," said Zagloba resignedly.

Volodiyovski ordered the servant to bring a candle and a flask of mead and, as he knew that the sight of the latter was enough to enliven Zagloba, he asked:

"Then it is a year now since you fled with the poor little one from Bohun in Rozloga?"

"It was in May, in May," answered Zagloba. "We passed through Kahamlik to fly to Zolotonosha. Oh! how sad life is!"

"And she was disguised?"

"As a Cossack. I had to cut off the poor girl's hair with my sword to complete the disguise. I know the very spot where I hid her tresses under a tree along with my sword."

"She was a sweet lady," said Longin sighing.

"I tell you that I loved her from the first day as though I had brought her up. And she only folded her little hands and thanked me for rescuing and protecting her. I wish they had cut me to pieces, rather than that I had lived to see this day. I wish I were dead!"

Again there was a silence. The three knights drank their mead mingled with tears, and then Zagloba continued:

"I thought to pass a peaceful old age near her and now . . . ."

He let his hands fall helplessly.

"Where is there comfort but in the grave?"

But, before Zagloba had finished the last words, they heard a noise in the hall. Some one was trying to get in and the servant held him back. A loud argument arose and it seemed to Volodiyovski as though he recognized a well-known voice, and he called to the servant not to deny entrance. The door was opened and, in the doorway appeared the puffy-cheeked red face of Jendzian, who let his eyes wander over those present, bowed himself and said:

"Praised be Jesus Christ!"

"For ever and ever," answered Volodiyovski. "You are Jendzian?"

"That is my name," said the boy, "and I fall at your feet, sir. Where is my master?"

"Your master is lying very ill in Korets."

"Oh, for God's sake, what are you saying, gracious sir! And is he very sick? May God preserve him!"

"He was very sick, but now he is better. The doctor says he will get well."

"For I have come with news to my master about the young lady."

The little knight shook his head sadly.

"You hurried here for nothing, for Skshetuski knows about her death already; and we have been shedding burning tears on her account."

Jendzian's eyes nearly started from his head.

"Help! Help! What do I hear? The young lady is dead?"

"She did not die, but was murdered in Kiev."

"In what Kiev? What are you saying, good sir?"

"In what Kiev? As if you did not know Kiev!"

"In God's name, gracious sir, you are joking! What should she be doing in Kiev, when she was in the ravine near the Valadynka not far from Rashkov. The witch had orders not to let her move one step from the ravine, until Bohun's return. As true as God lives! This is enough to drive one crazy."

"What kind of witch?" What are you talking about?"

"Well, Horpyna. I know the virago."

Zagloba suddenly sprang to his feet, and beat the air frantically with his hands; like one who is trying to save himself from drowning.

"By the Living God, be silent!' 'he said to Volodiyovski. "By God's wounds, let me question him!"

Those present were frightened, for Zagloba was deathly pale. His forehead was covered with sweat. He jumped over the bench towards Jendzian; and, seizing the boy by the shoulders, asked in a hoarse voice.

"Who told you that she . . . was concealed near Rashkov?"

"None other than Bohun."

"Boy, are you crazy!" bellowed Zagloba, shaking him like a pear-tree. "What Bohun?"

"For God's sake, why are you shaking me so, gracious sir," cried Jendzian, "let me alone, let me collect myself; otherwise you will turn my head. What Bohun! Does the gracious Pan not know him then?"

"Speak, or I will stab you!" cried Zagloba again. "Where did you see Bohun?"

"In Vlodava. What do you gentlemen want of me," cried the terrified boy. "Am I then a murderer? . . . "

Zagloba was almost beside himself. He gasped for breath and sank panting on the bench. Pan Michael ran to his assistance.

"When did you see Bohun?" he asked the boy.

"Three weeks ago."

"Then he is alive?"

"Why should he not be alive? He told me himself how the gracious Pan had wounded him, but he managed to get over it. . . "

"And he told you the young lady was near Rashkov?"

"Who else would have told me?"

"Listen, Jendzian. It is a question here of the life of your master and of the young lady. Did Bohun tell you himself, that she was not in Kiev?"

"No, gracious sir. How could she be in Kiev, when he

had concealed her near Rashkov, and forbidden Horpyna, on pain of death, to let her escape; and given me his ring and a safe-conduct, that I might ride to where she is; for his wounds had opened afresh and he is obliged to lie still, for I know not how long."

Jendzian's further speech was interrupted by Zagloba, who sprang up again; and, seizing with both hands the few remaining hairs on his head, began to scream like a madman.

"My little daughter is alive! By God's wounds, she lives! It was not she who was killed in Kiev; she lives, she lives, my beloved!"

And the old man, stamped his feet, laughed, sobbed and, finally, seized Jendzian's head and pressed it to his breast and kissed him so hard, that the boy almost lost his head.

"Let me be, good sir . . . I am almost choked. Of course she lives. If God is willing, we can go together to fetch her. Please sir, oh, that hurts good sir!"

"Let him go, sir, let him explain; we cannot understand everything," said Volodiyovski.

"Speak, speak!" cried Zagloba.

"Tell us all, from the beginning, little brother," said Longin, on whose moustache was a heavy dew.

"Allow me, sirs, to get my breath first and to shut the window, for those nightingales are singing so in the bushes that one cannot understand a single word."

"Mead!" cried Volodiyovski to the servant.

Jendzian, with the deliberation peculiar to himself, shut the window; then, turning to those present, he said: "Will the gentlemen allow me to sit down, for I am tired?"

"Sit down!" said Volodiyovski, pouring him out a glass of mead from the bottle which the servant had just brought in. "Drink with us, for you have deserved it for your news; but tell us quickly."

"This is good mead," said the boy, holding the glass to the light.

"May you be cut to pieces! Will you talk!" scolded Zagloba.

"Ah, the gracious Pan gets angry so quickly. I will talk if the gentlemen desire it, for my business is to obey; that is why I serve. But I see, already, that I must begin from the beginning and tell everything exactly."

"Begin at the beginning!"

"You remember, gentlemen, that when the news came of

the taking of Bar, we thought it was all up with the young lady. At that time, I returned to Jendziani, to my parents and to my grandfather, who is already—let's see—ninety, no ninety-one years old."

"Nine hundred so far as I am concerned," grumbled Zagloba.

"God grant that he may live as long as possible! I thank the kind gentleman for his good word," answered Jendzian. "Well, I went home to take my parents what I had, by God's help, collected among the banditti—for the gentlemen must know that the Cossacks had kept me in Chigrin the year before, for they took me for one of themselves; and I nursed the wounded Bohun while there and became very confidential with him. And from those robbers I got some silver and a few jewels."

"We know, we know," said Volodiyovski.

"Well, I came to my parents, who were very glad to see me, and could not believe their eyes when I shewed them all I had collected. I had to swear to my grandfather that I had gained it all honestly. At first they were particularly delighted; for, the gentlemen must know, they have a law-suit with the Yavorski on account of a pear-tree, half of whose branches stretch over on the Yavorski land and half on ours. So, when the Yavorski shake the tree our pears also fall off and some fall on the boundary-line. They say that those on the boundary-line belong to them, and we . . . ."

"Do not make me angry, fellow!" said Zagloba. "And talk of nothing but what concerns this affair."

"First, with your permission, good sir, I am no fellow; but a nobleman with a coat-of-arms, although I am poor; to which Pan Volodiyovski and Pan Longin, as friends of Pan Skshetuski, can testify. And, secondly, the lawsuit has been going on for fifty years. . . ."

Zagloba closed his teeth tightly and undertook not to speak another word.

"Well, my little fish," said Longin sweetly, "but you must tell us about Bohun, not about pears."

"About Bohun?" said Jendzian. "Well, then, about Bohun. Well—Bohun thinks, sir, that he has no more faithful friend and servant than myself, although he almost cut me through the body in Chigrin. But I really watched and nursed him after the princes Kurtsevich had wounded him so badly. I lied to him then, and said that I was sick of serving noblemen and would rather be with the Cossacks, because there was more to be gained with them; and he believed me. Why should he not believe me when I cured him? He grew very fond of me and to tell the truth he rewarded me generously; but, without knowing, of course, that I had made a vow to avenge myself for the insult I had received in Chigrin. The only reason I did not kill him for that was, that it did not seem fitting for a nobleman to stab a sick enemy in his bed as though he were a pig."

"Well, well," said Volodiyovski, "we know all about that. But how did you come across him this time?"

"Well, see here, sir, it was like this. When we had put the thumb screws on the Yavorski (they would have to go beg, there was no help for it) I thought to myself, 'well, now, it is time for me to look for Bohun and settle with him for what he did to me.' I told my parents my secret and also my grandfather, who, with his sense of chivalry, said to me, 'If you have sworn to do it, you must go, or you would be a fool.' I set out, therefore, for I also thought that if I found Bohun I might perhaps hear something about the young lady, whether she was alive; and I also thought that if I were to shoot him dead and bring my master the news, I should not go unrewarded."

"Certainly not, and we will reward you also," said Volodiyovski.

"And from me, little brother, you will get a horse and bridle," added Longin.

"I thank you, humbly, gracious sirs,' said the delighted boy. "It is true that one generally gives a reward in return for good news, and I never drink up what is given me. . . ."

"The devil!" grunted Zagloba.

"Well, then, you rode away from home . . . " added Volodiyovski.

"Well, I rode away from home," continued Jendzian, "and I thought to myself, 'whither now? why not to Zbaraj, for Bohun is not far from there and I could find out about my master?' So I rode, good sir; I rode past Byala and Vlodava. When I reached Vlodava, the horses were rather tired and I stopped to feed them. It was fair time there, and all the inns were full of noblemen. I went to the citizens' houses, they were also full of noblemen. Then a Jew told me I could have had a room with him, but a wounded nobleman had just taken it. 'That's just the thing' I said, for I understand bandaging, and your barber-surgeon is probably so busy during fair time that he has not time to turn round. The Jew told me that the nobleman attended to himself and would not allow anyone into his room; but he went to ask him. The fellow inside must have been feeling pretty sick, for he let me enter. I stepped into the room and, who should I see there, lying in bed, but—Bohun! I crossed myself, in the name of the Father, and the Son, and the Holy Ghost; I was so dreadfully frightened. And he recognized me at once, and was perfectly delighted to see me (for he thought I was his friend) and said 'God has sent thee to me; now I shall not die.' And I said, 'what brought you here, gracious sir?' But he put his finger on his lips and it was not till later that he told me of his adventure; how Khmyelnitski had sent him to His Majesty the King in Zamost, and how Lieutenant Volodiyovski had done for him in Lipki."

"Did he think of me with affection?" asked the little knight.

"I must say, gracious sir, that he spoke very kindly, 'I thought,' said he, 'that he was scrapings, a mongrel; but he is a fighter of the first class, and almost cut me in two,' but he speaks worse than ever of Pan Zagloba. He grinds his teeth with rage to think that Pan Zagloba dragged him into that fight."

"The hangman take him! I am not afraid of him now," said Zagloba.

"We soon got back to our old confidential footing," continued Jendzian, "or even more confidential. He told me everything; how near he had come to dying; how they had taken him for a nobleman and, consequently, had taken him in at the country house at Lipki, and that he had given his name as Pan Hulevich from Podolia, how they had cured him and had treated him with the greatest kindness, and that he had made a vow of gratitude to them till his dying day."

"And what was he doing in Vlodava?"

"He was on his way to Volhynia but in Parcelva his wounds opened again, for his carriage had overturned. He had to remain behind, therefore; although he was very much afraid to do so, as he might be discovered and killed. He told me this himself. 'I was sent out with letters,' he said 'but now I have no credentials, only the safe-conduct; and if they should discover who I am, not only the nobles would hack me to pieces, but that charming colonel would have me strung up without asking permission.' I remember that when he said that to me I answered 'I am glad to know that any arbitrary colonel may string one up' and he asked 'Why is that?' I said, 'So·that I may be careful and not tell anything I know—and I am telling you this for yourself, sir.' Then, he began to thank me and to assure me of his gratitude and also that he would not fail to reward me. 'I have no money just now' he said 'but whatever jewels I have shall be yours; and, later on, I will shower you with gold, but do me one favor.' "

"Ah, now we are getting to the princess," said Volodiyovski.

"You are right, sir. I must tell everything in order. When he told me then that he no money, I lost all compassion for him and thought to myself, 'wait awhile, I will serve you!' And he said 'I am sick, I have no strength to travel, and a long and dangerous road is ahead of me. If could only get to Volhynia—and that is not far, I should be with my own people. But, yonder, along the Dniester, I cannot travel; for I am not strong enough. And, besides, one has to go through the enemy's country, castles and troops—you go in my place.' I asked him, 'And whither?' He answered 'To the vicinity of Rashkov, for she is hidden there with Donyet's sister, Horpyna, the witch.' I said, 'the princess?' 'Yes,' he answered, 'she is concealed so that no human eye can discover her; but she fares well and sleeps on gold brocade, like the Princess Vishnyovyetski.' "

"Speak faster, for God's sake!" cried Zagloba.

"What is sudden is of the Devil," answered Jendzian. "Well, when I heard that, gracious sirs, I rejoiced greatly, but I did not show it and said, 'And is she really ther ' It must be a long time since you took here there.' He began to assure me that Horpyna was his faithful wench, and would keep her there, if necessary, ten years until he should return; and that the princess was truly there, as true as that God is in heaven, and that neither Poles, nor Tartars, nor Cossacks could come near her and that Horpyna would obey his commands."

As Jendzian was telling this, Pan Zagloba shook as with a chill, the little knight nodded his head in satisfaction, and Podbipyenta looked up to heaven.

"It is quite certain that she is there," continued the boy,

"and the best proof of it is that he sent me to her. But I restrained myself at first, that he might notice nothing, and said: 'But why should I go there?' He answered, 'Because I cannot go. If,' he said, 'I escape with my life from Vlodava and reach Volhynia I will have myself carried to Kiev, for our Cossacks are all over that country. And you,' he said, 'ride and command Horpyna to drive the princess thither and place her in the convent of the Holy Virgin.'"

"What then she did not go to the convent of Saint Nicholas?" broke in Zagloba. "I said at once that Yerlicha was crazy or was telling a lie."

"To the convent of the Holy Virgin," repeated Jendzian. " 'I will give you this ring,' he said, 'and a safe-conduct and the knife—and Horpyna will know what that means, for we arranged it. And another proof that you are sent me by God,' he said, 'is that she knows you and knows that you are my best friend. Go at once to her; and do not fear the Cossacks; but beware of the Tartars. Wherever you hear of any, avoid them, for they do not respect the safe-conduct. In a certain spot in the ravine, there is money buried, ducats; take it with you in any case. On the way you can say it is Bohun's wife—and you will want for nothing. Besides,' he said, 'the witch will know what to do as soon as you come from me; for whom can I send, unhappy man that I am, whom can I trust in a strange land, among enemies?' . . Well, sirs, he begged me, amidst a torrent of tears, and, finally, I allowed the beast to make me swear that I would go. I swore, right enough, but added, in my mind, with my lord!' He was quite happy, then, and gave me the safe-conduct, the ring, and the knife and all the jewels he had with him. I took them, for I thought they would be safer with me than with a marauder. At parting, he told me which ravine it was near the Valadynka, how I must ride, and in what direction I must turn; all so exactly that I could have found my way there blindfolded. And the gentlemen will see that I am speaking the truth if they, as I think, will set out at once."

"Directly, to-morrow!" said Volodiyovski.

"What, to-morrow! To-day, by daybreak, the horses will be saddled."

Joy took possession of all hearts and was expressed in words of gratitude to heaven, in joyful rubbing of hands, and in ever fresh questionings of Jendzian; to which Jendzian answered with his accustomed self-possession.

"May the balls strike you!" cried Zagloba. "What a servant Skshetuski has in you!"

"How so?" asked Jendzian.

"He will cover you with gold."

"I think that I have deserved something, although I served my master faithfully without any reward."

"And what did you do with Bohun?" asked Volodiyovski.

"That was just what bothered me, gracious sirs, that he was ill again and I could not stab him; for my master would have scolded me. That is fate, what could I do? See here, when he had already told me everything that I was to say and had given me what he had to give, I reflected, 'Why,' said I to myself, 'should such a knave, who has kept the princess prisoner and who cut me down in Chigrin, be permitted to go free in the world. The hangman take him! It would be better if he were not in the world.' And then I thought that he might get well and ride after me with the Cossacks. But I set out, without reflecting any longer, to find Colonel Rogovski, who is stationed with the regiment in Vlodava and informed him that this man was Bohun, the worst rebel of all. By this time they must have hanged him."

As he said this, Jendzian laughed foolishly and looked round him as though he expected the others to follow his example; but was much astonished at receiving no response.

Not for some minutes did Zagloba growl: "That is of no consequence." Volodiyovski, however, sat quite still, and Longin clacked his tongue, shook his head and said finally:

"That was not a nice thing to do, little brother, as one says, not nice."

"How so, gracious sir?" asked Jendzian in astonishment. "Would it have been better for me to stab him?"

"That would not have been nice either, not at all; but I do not know if it is not better to be a murderer than a Judas."

"What are you saying, sir? Did Judas betray a rebel? This man is the worst enemy of the king and of the whole Commonwealth."

"That may be, but all the same, it was not nice. And what was the name of that colonel, speak."

"Rogovski, they said his first name was Jacob."

"It is the same," murmured the Lithuanian, Pan Lashch's relative, Skshetuski's enemy."

But no one heard this remark, for Zagloba began to speak.

"Gentlemen," he said, "this matter will bear no delay.

God, through this boy, has ordained and arranged everything, so that we may seek the princess now, under better conditions than ever, God be praised! To-morrow we must set out. The prince, indeed, is not here, but we will undertake the journey without leave; for we have no time to waste. Pan Volodiyovski will go, and Jendzian and I will accompany him; and you, Pan Podbipyenta had better stay here, for your size and your simplicity might betray us."

"No, brother, I will go too," said the Lithuanian.

"For the sake of her safety, you must remain here. Whoever has once seen you never forgets you during his lifetime. We have a safe-conduct, it is true; but, even with the safe-conduct they would not trust you. You killed Pulyan before the eyes of the whole rebel mob, and if such a bean-pole should appear among them, they would recognize it again. It must not be, you cannot go with us, you will not find your three heads there, and your own head is of not much use. It were better to remain here than to imperil the undertaking."

"I am sorry," said the Lithuanian.

"Sorry, or not sorry, you must remain here. If we ever go birdsnesting, we will take you with us; but not now."

"That does not sound nice."

"Give me your snout, for my heart is very joyful; but remain here. Only one thing more, sirs, a matter of the greatest importance; keep the secret, that it may not reach the soldiers and, through them, the people; say not a word to anyone"

"Bah! And the prince?"

"The prince is not here."

"And Pan Skshetuski, if he returns?"

"Not a word to him above all; he would immediately follow us. He will have plenty of time for happiness, and God preserve him from a fresh disappointment; he would lose his reason. On your word of honor, gentlemen, not a syllable about this matter."

"On the word of a knight," said Podbiyenta.

"On our word! on our word!"

"And, now, let us thank God!"

Zagloba first knelt down, the others followed his example, and they prayed long and earnestly.

CHAPTER XXII.

The prince had, several days before this, actually ridden to Zamost to enlist new regiments. He was not expected to return just yet, so Volodıyovski, Zagloba, and Jendzıan set out in absolute silence, not betraying their secret to anyone. And of all those that remained ın Zbaraj, Longin was the only one who knew ıt. But in accordance wıth his knightly word, he was silent as though bewitched.

Vyershul and the other officers who knew of the death of the princess, did not suspect that the journey of Zagloba and the little knight had anything to do with.the betrothed of the unfortunate Skshetuski; but believed that the two friends were riding to visit him himself, especially as Jendzian was with them and they all knew that he was Skshetuski's servant.

The friends went directly to Khlebanovka, to make their preparations there for theır journey.

The first thing Zagloba did was to buy, with money that he had borrowed from Longin, five strong Podolian horses, fit to stand long journeys; such as were used by the Polish cavalry and the Cossack captains. Such a horse could chase a Tartar pony the whole day long, and was even more swift than the Turkish horses; and was to be preferred to them on account of hıs greater endurance in changes of weather, cold nights and rain. So Zagloba bought five such steeds and, besides, he bought for himself, his companions, and also for the princess, costly Cossack garments. Jendzian busied himself with the horses' harness; and, as soon as everything was thought of and in readiness, they set out on their way, commending their undertaking to God and Saint Nicholas, the patron of virgins.

Disguised as they were, they might easily have been taken for Cossack atamans, and it often occurred that they were stopped by soldiers from the Polish quarters, and by the Polish watches, until they got some distance beyond Kamenets. But Zagloba soon set himself right with these. For some time, they rode through a safe country, which was occupied by the regiments of Lantskorontski, who kept drawing nearer to Bar in order to keep his eye on the Cossack companies who were collecting there. It was already generally known that no negotiations would take place, and war hung over the land; although the principal powers had not yet made a move. The truce of Pereyaslav would not come to an end at Whitsuntide; the skirmishes between the companies of scouts had never ceased, and became daily more serious. Each side was only waiting for the battle-cry. Meanwhile, spring was advancing in the steppes; the trampled and downtrodden earth was once more covered with the carpet of grass and blossoms, which had grown up from the bodies of the fallen knights. The larks soared in the air above the battlefields. Flocks of birds mounted, screaming, into the clouds. The frozen waters once more gathered and formed a gleaming scaly coat of mail beneath the warm breath of the wind, and, in the evening, frogs splashed in the water and carried on their joyful dialogues until late at night.

It seemed as though Nature, herself, desired to heal the wounds; to still the sorrows; and to conceal with flowers the grave-mounds of the war. Light shone in heaven and on the earth. The whole steppes, fresh, joyous, and full of life, gleamed like a glorious picture, and shimmered in all colors of the rainbow, like a gold brocade, or like a wide Polish girdle, upon which all the colors have been embroidered in harmonious relation to each other. The steppes were joyous with the song of birds; and a wide wave of warm air streamed across them, drying the moist places and browning the faces of men.

At such a time, every heart is full of joy, and a boundless sense of confidence fills all breasts. It was thus with our knights, who looked into the future with happy confidence. Volodiyovski sang incessantly. Zagloba stretched himself out on his horse and offered his back with full enjoyment to the warm rays of the sun; and, when he was thoroughly warmed through, he said to the little knight:

"I feel so well; for to tell the truth, next to mead and Hungarian wine, there is nothing better for old joints, than the sun."

"It is good for everything," answered Volodiyovski, "for even the animals love to warm themselves in the sun."

"It is fortunate that we are travelling just at this time to the princess," continued Zagloba, "it would have been hard to travel with her in winter, in the frost."

"If we only once get her into our hands, I am a rogue if she ever escapes me again."

"I must tell you, Pan Michael," said Zagloba, "that I fear only one thing; and, that is, that if the war should break out, the Tartars would flood the country and attack us. But I do not fear the Cossacks. We shall not need to explain ourselves to the Cossacks; for you have noticed have you not, that they take us for leaders. The Zaporojians honor the safe-conduct, and Bohun's name is our protection."

"I know the Tartars, for, among the gentlemen in Lubni, our life passed in incessant skirmishes with them. Vyershul and I never had any rest on account of them," said Pan Michael.

"I know them too," said Zagloba. "I have told you, before now, that I passed many years among them, and might have attained rank and dignity in their midst; but, as I did not wish to become a heathen, I had to throw over everything, for they were about to make me die the death of a martyr, because I tried to convert their oldest priest to the only saving faith."

"You told us once, sir, that you were in Galatz."

"That is a matter by itself, and also that I was in the Crimea. But, if you think that the world ends with Galatz, you do not know where pepper grows. There are more sons of Beliel than Christians in that country."

Jendzian here joined in the conversation.

"It is not only from the Tartars that we must apprehend danger," he said, "I have not yet told the gentlemen what Bohun told me that the glen was guarded by frightful monsters. The giantess herself, who guards the princess, is a witch, in compact with the devil; and who can tell if she may not have received warning of our approach. I have a bullet, it is true, which I cast above some consecrated bread, which will break everything that strikes it; but she has, besides, whole regiments of ghosts and vampires guarding the entrance. The gentlemen must vouch with their lives that no evil shall happen to me, for otherwise I should lose my reward."

"You great dunce," said Zagloba; "as if we had nothing to do but to think of your life. The devil will not wring your neck; but, if he should do so, it would not matter, for you would have deserved it by your avarice. I am too old a sparrow to be caught with chaff. And, mark this, if Horpyna is a witch, I am a still more mighty wizard; for I learned the black art in Persia. She serves the devils, but the devils serve me. I can plough with them as with oxen if I wish it, but I have my soul's salvation to think of."

"That is right, gracious sir; but, for this once, make use of your power, for it is always better to be on the safe side."

"And I," said Volodiyovski, "have more confidence in our good cause and in God's protection. May the devils watch over Bohun and Horpyna; but with us are the Heavenly Hosts, whom the mightiest powers of Hell cannot resist. For this occasion, I will sacrifice seven candles of white wax to the Holy Archangel Michael."

"I will add one more," said Jendzian, "so that Pan Zagloba may not frighten me with perdition."

"I will be the first to send you to Hell," answered the nobleman, "if it should prove that you do not know the exact spot."

"How should I not know it? As soon as we get to the Valadynka, I can find the glen with my eyes blindfolded. We must ride along the bank towards the Dniester and the glen is to our right, we shall recognize it because the entrance is blocked by a rock. At first sight, it appears as though one could not enter; but there is a cleft in the rock, through which two horses can ride abreast. If we once get there, no one can escape us, for it is the only exit from the glen; and all around are such high walls of rock than even a bird can scarcely fly over them. The witch kills people who try to enter the glen without permission. There are many skeletons there; but Bohun told me not to mind that, but to keep on riding and calling Bohun! Bohun! . . . Then, only, will she receive us as friends. Besides Horpyna, there is Cheremis who is a good archer. We must kill them both."

"I agree with you as to Cheremis but the woman—we will bind her."

"If the gracious gentlemen could only do it! She is so strong that she tears a coat of armor as if it were a shirt and crushes a horseshoe in her hand. Podbipyenta is the only one who might conquer her, but not we. Let be, sir, I have a charmed bullet for her—may it bring the last hour to this devil woman; otherwise she might follow us like a she-wolf and howl till all the Cossacks awoke; and then we should not only be unable to save the young lady, but also our own heads."

Amid such conversations and counsels, the journey passed. They hurried forward through towns, settlements, farms, and grave-mounds. Their way led past Yarmolints towards Bar where they first turned off in the direction of Yampol and towards the Dniester. They came through the region where Volodiyovski had once wounded Bohun and delivered Pan Zagloba from his hands; they found the very same farmhouse and remained there over night. Sometimes, they had to take up their quarters for the night in the open air on the steppes; and then Zagloba would vary the monotony and the silence by relating his former adventures, some that he had really experienced and others that had no existence. But the conversation turned chiefly on the princess, her imprisonment with the witch and the rescue that was awaiting her.

When they had finally left behind them the territory that was under the care of Lantskoronski's soldiers, they came into the territory of the Cossacks, in which not a single Pole was left alive. Those who had not fled, had been destroyed with fire and sword. May had come to an end and it was now the warm month of June; but they had hardly travelled a third of their journey for the road was long and full of difficulties. Fortunately, they anticipated no danger from the Cossacks; they had no difficulty with the wandering bands who took them for Zaporojian chiefs; nevertheless, they were asked who they were from time to time, and then Zagloba, if the interrogator were a Nijov would show Bohun's safe-conduct. But if he were an ordinary "black," he did not dismount, but kicked him in the chest with his foot so that he fell on the ground. The others who saw this, at once gave them a free passage; for they believed that they were not only friends, but persons of high position, since they beat them. "Perhaps it is Kshyvonos Burlay or even Khmyelnitski, the little father himself," they would say.

The only thing that annoyed Zagloba was the fact of Bohun's fame; for the incessant questions about him were very tiresome and also delayed them, as they were usually detained some time while answering them. Would the questions never cease? 'Did he live? was he well?' For the news of his death had reached Yahorlik and beyond the rapids.

And when the travellers answered that he was well and in freedom and that they were his messengers, they were kissed and entertained hospitably. All hearts and, even all purses, were opened to them; which Skshetuski's cunning servant did not fail to turn to his own advantage.

In Yampol, Burlay received them. He had come here with his Nij soldiers and the "blacks" to wait for the Budziak Tartars. He was an old and famous commander, who had instructed Bohun, years before in military matters; had accompanied him in his expeditions to the Black Sea, and, together with him, set fire to Sinope. He, therefore, loved him like a son and received his messengers without the slightest mistrust, especially as he had seen Jendzian with him the previous year; and, when he learned that Bohun was alive and was going to Volhynia, he gave the messengers a feast to show his joy, and got quite drunk. Zagloba feared that Jendzian, who was also slightly drunk, might let out their secret; but the foxy young rascal knew enough to tell the truth only when it was advisable, without endangering their expedition; and thus he gained their full confidence. The two knights were amused at this wonderful conversation of Jendzian's; especially as during the whole time, their names were continually repeated by him, with a most obstinate rashness.

"We heard," said Burlay, "that Bohun was wounded in a duel; do you know who fought him?"

"Volodiyovski, an officer of Prince Yeremy's," answered Jendzian quietly.

"Oh, if he could only fall into my hands, I would pay him out or our falcon; I would flay him!"

Volodiyovski twitched his yellow moustache and looked at Burlay, as a hound looks at the wolf at whose throat he dare not spring.

Jendzian continued, "That is just why I am telling you his name, colonel."

"The devil will enjoy getting hold of that boy," thought Zagloba.

"But," contiued Jendzian, "he is not so much to blame; for Bohun challenged him, himself, without knowing with whom he had to deal. There was another nobleman there, Bohun's greatest enemy; who hand once already rescued the princess from his hands."

"And who was that?"

"An old sot, who attached himself to our ataman in Chigrin and pretended friendship for him."

"He will be hanged!" cried Burlay.

"May I be called a fool, if I do not cut off that fellow's ear," murmured Zagloba.

"They wounded him so," continued Jendzian, "that, had it been anyone else, the crows would long since have pecked at him. But our ataman has a soul of steel; he will get well, although he could hardly drag himself to Vlodava and would have been at his wits' end if we had not arrived. We took him to Volhynia where our men have the upper hand and he sent us alone to the lady."

"Those black-eyed wenches are his destruction," cried Burlay. "I told him that long ago. Would it not have been better to have taken the girl in the Cossack fashion, and then have tied a stone round her neck and thrown her into the water, as we did at the Black Sea?"

Volodiyovski could hardly contain himself, so indignant was he at the insult to the fair sex. Zagloba, however, laughed and said:

"Yes, indeed it would have been better."

"But you are good friends of his," said Burlay. "You did not forsake him in his need. And you, young fellow," turning to Jendzian, "you are the best of all; for I saw you in Chigrin, when you were nursing and watching our falcon. Well, I am your friend also. What do you wish, soldiers or horses? I will give them to you so that no accident may happen to you on your homeward journey."

"We have no need of Cossacks, Colonel," said Zagloba, "for we are riding as friends in a friendly land; and may God preserve us from any accident. We can get along better alone than with a great number, but we should like some swift horses."

"I will give you some that cannot be overtaken by any of the Khan's Arab steeds."

Jendzian once more seized the favorable opportunity.

"The ataman gave us very little money as he had not much himself; and, after we leave Bratslav, oats are worth a dollar a peck."

"Come with me to my room," said Burlay.

Jendzian did not need a second invitation and disappeared with the old colonel, behind the door. When he again made his appearance, his chubby face beamed with delight and his gray coat was considerably puffed out around the waist.

"Now God be with you on your journey," said the old colonel; "and, when you have got the girl, come and see me again, for I want to see Bohun's little bird."

"We cannot do that, Colonel," answered the boy, boldly, "for this little Polish lady is very timid and actually tried to kill herself once with a knife. We fear that some harm may happen to her. Let the ataman do as he pleases with her."

"He will, he will; she will not be afraid of him. She is a white-handed Pole! And the Cossack stinks in her nostrils!" growled Burlay. "Go, and God be with you; you have not much farther to travel."

It was not far from Yampol to Valadynka but the road was difficult, or, rather, there was no road. The land stretched away endlessly before our riders, without any path; for in those days this region was yet a wilderness, only built up and settled in places. Therefore, on leaving Yampol, they turned westward, moving away from the Dniester in order to follow the river Valadynka in its course to Rashkov; for only in this way could they find the glen. Morning was breaking in the east, for Burlay's supper had lasted till quite late in the night; and Zagloba calculated that they could not reach the glen before sunset. But that suited him, as, after freeing Helena, he wished to have the night before him. Meanwhile, the friends conversed as they rode, and rejoiced that fortune had favored them so far; and Pan Zagloba, remembering the supper with Burlay, said:

"Just see how these Cossacks who belong to the brotherhood stand up for each other in all dangers! I am not speaking of the rabble, whom the Cossacks despise; and who, if the devil help them to get the upper hand, will make far worse masters; but of the brotherhood itself. One stands up for another, they are ready to go through fire for one another, and do not act as the nobles do."

"Eh, what? gracious sir," answered Jendzian. "I was among them for some time, and saw how they devoured each other like wolves; and if it were not for Khmyelnitski, who keeps them in check, partly by his strong will and partly by concesssions, they would have utterly eaten up one another. But this Burlay is a great warrior among them and Khmyelniski, himself, honors him highly."

"And you, evidently, seem to be in great favor with him,

as he allows you to plunder him. Ah, Jendzian, Jendzian, you will come to a bad end."

"What is written cannot be avoided, gracious sir. Is it not a praiseworthy act and agreeable to God to lead your enemy into a trap?"

"I am not blaming you for that, but for your avarice, this passion of the peasantry, which is quite unworthy of a nobleman, and on account of which you wil be condemned."

"I do not grudge a candle to the Church if I succeed in earning something, that the Lord God may make use of me and may continue to bless me. And that I support my parents, is surely no sin."

"What a rogue on four feet it is!" cried Zagloba, turning to Volodiyovski. "I thought that all cunning would go to the grave with me; but I see that he is a still greater rascal. Through his craftiness, we shall free the princess from Bohun's imprisonment, with Bohun's own permission and with Burlay's horses. Did you ever hear anything like it? And I wouldn't give three mites for him."

Jendzian smiled contentedly and answered:

"Are we any the worse off, gracious sir."

"I like you; and, if you were not so avaricious, I should like to take you into my service. But, as you hoodwinked Burlay, I will even forgive you for calling me a sot."

"I did not call you so, gracious sir, it was Bohun."

"God has punished him for it," answered Zagloba.

Thus chatting, they passed the morning; but when the sun had reached the meridian, they became serious, for in a few hours they would see Valadynka. After a long journey, they were near their goal, and an uneasiness natural on such occasions stole into their hearts. Was Helena yet alive? And, if she were alive, would they find her in the ravine? Horpyna might have taken her away, or, at the last moment, have hidden her in some unknown cleft in the rocks, or have killed her. The impediments were not all overcome, the dangers not all conquered. They had indeed credentials by which Horpyna was to recognize them as Bohun's emissaries; but how would it be if she had been warned by devils or ghosts. Jendzian was the most apprehensive of this and even Pan Zagloba feared it; and, although he was so confident in his own knowledge of the black art, he could not think about it without uneasiness. If this were the case, they would find the ravine empty; or, perhaps even worse, they might find the Cossacks from Rashkov in ambush. Their hearts beat louder and when after several hours ride, from a rising ground at the border of the ravine they saw in the distance a gleam of water like a silver ribbon, Jendzian's chubby face grew somewhat pale.

"That is Valadynka," he said, in a hushed voice.

"Already!" asked Zagloba, in an equally muffled voice, "how near it is . . ."

"May God protect us!" answered Jendzian. "My gracious sir, begin your incantations at once, for I am dreadfully frightened."

"Incantations are foolishness! We will bless the river and the cells that will be of better help."

Volodiyovski was the least disturbed, but he was silent. He only looked carefully at his pistols, loaded them with fresh powder, and saw that his sword could be unsheathed without difficulty.

"I have a consecrated bullet here, in this pistol," said Jendzian. "In the name of the Father, and of the Son, and of the Holy Ghost! Forward! Forward!"

Before long, they found themselves on the bank of the little river, and turned thir horses' heads in the direction of its course. Volodiyovski stopped a moment, and said:

"Let Jendzian take the safe conduct; for the witch knows him, and he can talk to her first, so that she will not be afraid when she sees us and go and hide herself with the princess in some cleft in the rocks."

"I will not go first, no matter what you say, gentlemen," said Jendzian.

"Well, then, ride in the rear, you blockhead."

Then, Volodiyovski rode forward, followed by Zagloba; Jendzian, with the extra horses, bringing up the rear, and looking anxiously about him on all sides. The horses' hoofs clattered on the stones; the stillness of a desert reigned in this place, which was only broken by the chirping of crickets and grasshoppers who were hidden in the rocks, for the day was warm although the sun was already long past the meridian. The horsemen had finally reached a round elevation, which looked like a knight's shield turned over, upon which broken rocks, weather beaten by the sun and air, were scattered like ruins of houses and church towers. It looked as though it was the ruins of a nobleman's castle or a town that had been but yesterday destroyed by the enemy.

Jendzian looked at it and rode up to Zagloba.

"That is the boundary line," said he. "I recognize it by what Bohun told me of it. No one who crosses this at night survives to tell the tale."

"If one cannot pass it by, perhaps one can pass across it," answered Zagloba. "Bah! this is a strange, accursed land; but at least we are on the right road."

"It is not much farther," said Jendzian.

"God be praised," answered Zagloba, and his thoughts turned to the princess.

His courage revived wonderfully at the sight of the wild banks of the Valadynka, of this desert and its silence. It seemed incredible that the princess should be so near; she, for whom he had undertaken so many adventures and passed through so many dangers; she, whom he so loved that, when the news of her death came to him, he no longer knew how he should live out the rest of his days. But on the other hand one becomes habituated even to misfortune. Zagloba had so long been filled with the conviction that she had been stolen and was far away in Bohun's power, that now he hardly dared to say: 'Behold, now sadness and searching have come to an end, the time of peace and happiness is here.' But, other questions forced themselves upon him. What would she say when she saw him? For this rescue from such a long and wearisome imprisonment would surprise her, like a flash of lightning . . . . "God's ways are wonderful," thought Zagloba; "He understands how to direct everything so that virtue shall conquer and injustice shall be put to shame. It was God who first sent Jendzian into Bohun's hands and then made him his friend. It was God who directed that the cruel mother, war, should call the wild ataman from this desert where, like a wolf, he had carried his prey. God, who later gave him into Volodiyovski's hands and led Jendzian to him once more. And so He has so directed everything that now, when Helena is perhaps giving up her last ray of hope and no longer expects assistance, at this very time rescue is at hand.

"Thy tears will cease to flow, my little daughter," thought Zagloba, "and soon thou wilt be overcome with joy. And oh, how thankful she will be, how she will fold her little hands and be thankful!"

Here, Zagloba saw the girl in his mind's eye; and he was filled with emotion and became buried in thought about what was to happen in the next hour.

Jendzian pulled his sleeve from behind.

"Gracious sir!"

"What is the matter?" asked Zagloba, annoyed that the thread of his thoughts had been broken.

"Did you not see, sir?"

"What? Was it only a wolf! Kiss him on the nose."

At this moment Volodiyovski reined in his horse.

"Have we not missed the road?" he asked. "It ought to be here."

"No," answered Jendzian, "we will ride as Bohun said. "I wish to God it were all over."

"If we are on the right road, it will soon be over."

"I want to ask the gentlemen to look at Cheremis, when they are talking to the witch. He must be a hideous creature. But he can shoot splendidly."

" Do not be afraid—go forward!"

They had not ridden many paces when the horses began to snort and to lay back their ears. Jendzian grew as cold as a lizard, for he expected at every moment to hear the howling of a vampire from the clefts in the rocks, or to see some fearful form start up before him; but it turned out presently that the horses were only snorting because they had passed close by the place where the wolf stood, who had frightened the boy a few moments before. The air was perfectly still, not even the crickets chirped, and the sun had almost set. Jendzian crossed himself and became calm.

Suddenly Volodiyovski pulled in his horse.

"I see the glen. Its entrance is hidden by a rock and there is a breach in the rock.'

"In the name of the Father, the Son, and the Holy Ghost! There it is," whispered Jendzian.

"Follow me!" cried Pan Michael, turning his horse.

Before long, they stood at the breach in the rock and rode through it, as into a stone vault. A deep glen lay open before them, the sides of which were thickly overgrown, and spread out in the distance into a wide semicircular level surrounded by gigantic walls of rock.

Jendzian began to cry at the top of his voice.

"Bo—hun! Bo—hun! come here, witch, come, Bo—hun! Bo—hun!"

They stopped their horses and waited in silence. Presently the boy called again:

"Bo—hun! Bo—hun! . . . "

The barking of dogs was heard in the distance.

"Bo—hun! Bo—hun!"

On the left of the glen on which the red beams of the setting sun were falling there was a rustling in the thick bushes of wild plum and hawthorn; and, following upon it, appeared at the extreme summit of the precipice, a human form, which bending over, with her hand screening her eyes, was looking attentively at the new arrivals.

"That is Horpyna," said Jendzian; and, placing his hand to his mouth, he cried again "Bo—hun! Bo—hun!"

Horpyna began to descend, bending her body backwards to preserve her equilibrium. She came down rapidly and, behind her, came plunging a little undersized man with a long Turkish gun in his hand. The bushes cracked under the heavy feet of the witch, the stones rolled clattering to the bottom of the glen, and, in the red evening sunlight, with her body bent backwards, she looked like a gigantic, unearthly being.

"Who are you?" she said, in a loud voice, when she reached the bottom.

"How are you, lass?" said Jendzian, who, at the sight of beings who were not ghosts, had regained his self-possession.

"You are one of Bohun's servants, I recognize you, you little fellow. And those over there, who are they?"

"Bohun's friends."

"A pretty witch!" murmured Pan Michael to himself.

"And why have you come here?"

"Here are the safe-conduct, the knife, and the ring. Do you know what that signifies?"

The giantess took the tokens in her hand and looked at them closely; then she said:

"They are the same! you want the princess?"

"We do; is she well?"

"She is well. Why did not Bohun come himself?"

"Bohun is wounded."

"Wounded? I saw it in the mill."

"If you saw it, why do you ask? You lie, girl!" said Jendzian, with confidence.

The witch laughed and showed her white wolf's teeth; and, clenching her fist, she gave Jendzian a dig in the ribs.

"You little fellow, you."

"Be off with you."

"Will you not kiss me? And when do you want to take the princess?"

"Immediately. But we must rest the horses."

"Well, take her, I will go with you."

"And why do you want to go?"

"My brother is destined to die; he is going to be impaled by the Poles; I will go with you."

Jendzian bent over in his saddle, as though he would converse more privately with the giantess, while his hand, unobserved sought the butt of his pistol.

"Cheremis! Cheremis!" he said, in order to direct the attention of his companions to the dwarf.

"Why do you call him, his tongue has been cut out."

"I am not calling him, I am only astonished at his beauty. You would not leave him; he is your husband."

"He is my dog."

"There are only two of you in the glen?"

"Only two—and the princess."

"That is well, you will not go with us."

"But I will go, I say."

"And I say you will stay here."

In the boy's tone, there was something so peculiar that the giantess became uneasy and turned round; she had become mistrustful.

"What do you want?" she said.

"That is what I want," answered Jendzian, firing his pistol at her breast, and she was so close that the smoke enveloped them both in a moment. Horpyna stepped back with outstretched arms, her eyes started from their sockets, an unearthly cry escaped from her throat, she staggered and fell backwards her whole length on the ground. At the same moment, Zagloba gave Cheremis a blow with his sword; so that the skull cracked under the blade. The monstrous dwarf uttered not a sound, but rolled himself together like a worm, twitching, and opening and shutting his hands alternately, like the claws of a dying lynx.

Zagloba wiped his reeking sword with the sleeve of his coat. Jendzian sprang from his horse, seized a huge stone and threw it upon Horpyna's broad chest and then began to look for something in his breast pocket.

The gigantic form of the witch was still striking the earth with its feet, her face twitched convulsively, the white teeth were covered with a bloody foam, and, from her throat, came a muffled gurgle. Meanwhile, the boy pulled out a piece of consecrated chalk and with it traced the sign of the cross on the stone and said:

"Now, she will never get up again."

Then he sprang into the saddle.

"Forward!" commanded Volodiyovski. They flew along the brook like a whirlwind, and came to a halt in the middle of the glen. They passed several scattered oaks and presently there appeared before their eyes a cabin and a tall mill, whose dripping wheel glistened like a red star in the rays of the sun. Two huge black dogs were fastened by ropes outside the cabin. They tried to spring at the newcomers, and tugged at their opes with howls of rage. Volodiyovski was ahead and arrived first. He sprang to the ground and, stepping to the door of the house, opened it, and entered the hall, his sword clattering at his side.

At the right of the hall, could be seen an open door leading into a large room with a fireplace in the middle, filled with chips of wood, and smoking fiercely. The door at the left was closed "She must be in there," thought Pan Michael, springing to open it.

He shook the door, opened it, was about to dash into the room, but remained on the threshold as if petrified.

At the farther end of the room, with her hand upon the head of her couch, stood Helena Kurtsevich, pale, with her hair falling over her shoulders; her terrified eyes, turned towards Volodiyovski, seemed to ask: "Who art thou, what dost thou want here?" for she had never seen the little knight.

He, however, stood in bewilderment at the sight of such beauty, and of this room, furnished with velvet and gold brocade. Presently, he recovered himself and spoke hastily:

"Fear nothing, princess, we are friends of Skshetuski."

The princess sank upon her knees.

"Save me," she cried, clasping her hands. But at that moment Zagloba plunged into the room, red, trembling, and panting.

"It is we," he cried, "we, and we are bringing assistance!"

When the princess heard these words and saw that well-known face she bent like a cut-off flower, her hands fell and her lids closed over her eyes. She had fainted.

BOOK IV

CHAPTER I.

The horses had hardly been allowed to rest, but still they flew onward with such speed, that when the moon had risen over the steppes, the party had reached the vicinity of Studenka on the other side of the Valadynka. At the head rode Pan Volodiyovski, looking carefully about him in all directions, behind was Zagloba beside Helena and at the end of the train Jendzian, leading the horses of burden, and two reserve horses which he had not forgotten to take from the stable of Horpyna. Zagloba did not give his tongue a minute's rest, he had indeed many things to tell the princess, who, having been secluded in the wild ravine, knew nothing of what was going on in the world. He told her how a friend had searched for her from the beginning, how Skshetuski had gone to Pereyaslav in order to look for Bohun, not knowing of his defeat, and how finally Jendzian succeeded in worming the secret of her hiding-place from the ataman, and had brought the same to Zbaraj.

"Merciful God!" said Helena turning her beautiful pale face towards the moon, "so Pan Skshetuski has followed my traces beyond the Dnieper!"

"As far as Pereyaslav, I repeat. And surely he would have come hither with us had we had time to send word to him; but we wanted to hurry to your aid without delay. He knows nothing of your rescue yet, and prays daily for your safety—but he needs no pity. Let him suffer a while longer inasmuch as such reward awaits him."

"And I thought I was forgotten by all and prayed to God to let me die."

"We had not only not forgotten you, but were all the time planning how we might rescue you and come to your aid. It was only natural that Skshetuski and myself should have given serious attention to the matter, but this knight too, who rides before us, with an equal self-sacrifice, spared neither care nor trouble nor toil."

"May God reward him for it."

"Both of you evidently possess something that attracts men to you; but to Volodiyovski, you are really indebted, for, as I have said, we together cut up Bohun like a pike."

"Pan Skshetuski in Rozloga spoke about Pan Volodiyovski as his best friend, he said . . . "

"And he was right. There abides a great soul in that little body. Just at present, he is somewhat shy, for your beauty has evidently dazzled him. But when he gets over it, he will come to himself. We together did great work at the election of the king."

"So there is already a new King?"

"So you have not even heard of this, poor soul, in that cursed desert?" Why John Casimir was elected last Fall and has been reigning now for eight months. A great war has broken out with the rebels, and God help us! for Prince Yeremy was forced to resign, and in his stead others were chosen, who were fitted better for feasts than for war."

"And will Pan Skshetuski also go to this war?"

"He is a good soldier, and I doubt if even you can keep him back from it. We are alike in this respect. As soon as we smell powder, no power on earth can hold us back. Oh, last year we made ourselves felt by that mob. The whole night would not suffice for me to tell you all that happened. Of course, we shall go to the war, but the main thing is that we have found you, poor child, without whom life for us was a burden."

The princess turned her sweet face to Pan Zagloba.

"I do not know why you love me so much, sir, but you cannot love me more than I love you."

Zagloba sighed deeply with content.

"Do you really love me so much?"

"As I live, I do."

"God reward you, for this will lighten the burden of my old age. It is an every-day matter for me to attract the attention of women. This was the case during the election in Warsaw. Volodiyovski is a witness. But what care I any longer for the love of women, despite the warmth of my heart—I will content myself with fatherly feelings alone."

Silence followed, then the horses snorted one after another, which was a good omen.

"Good luck! Good luck!" exclaimed the horsemen.

The night was clear. The moon ascended higher and higher in the sky richly set with stars, which grew smaller and paler. The tired horses slackened up and the riders themselves began to grow weary. Volodiyovski was the first to rein in his horse.

"It's about time to rest," said he, "it will soon be dawn."

"Yes, it is time," repeated Zagloba. "I am so tired that I see two heads on my horse."

But before they lay down to sleep, Jendzian prepared supper; he made a fire, and taking off the saddle-bags from a horse, he got out the supplies which he had purchased in Yampol, near Burlay. There was corn bread, cold meat, delicacies and Wallachian wine. At the sight of the two leather bottles, which were filled with beverage and gave out a splashing and pleasant sound, Zagloba forgot all about sleep, and the others also fell to and ate with a good will. There was plenty for all, and when they were satisfied, Zagloba wiped his mouth with his coat-sleeve, and said:

"Till life ends, I shall never cease to repeat, God's ways are marvellous. See, my dear lady, you are free and we are sitting here joyfully under God's sky, drinking Burlay's wine. I will not deny that Hungarian wine would be better, for this smells of leather, but on the journey it is good enough."

"I cannot get over wondering at one thing," said Helena, "and that is that Horpyna gave me up so easily to you."

Zagloba looked at Volodiyovski and at Jendzian and winked at them.

"She consented because she had to. Anyway, why should we conceal it, for it is no shame that we killed her, together with Cheremis."

"What?" asked the princess frightened.

"Did you hear the shot?"

"I heard it; but I thought Cheremis was shooting."

"It was not Cheremis, but this youth here, who shot the witch through and through? The devil is in him, that is sure; but he could not do otherwise, for whether on account of a whim, or whether she divined something, the witch wished to ride with us in any event. We could not allow this, for she would have soon noticed that we were not riding to Kiev. So he shot her then, and I made way with Cheremis. He was indeed an Afican monster, and I do not think that God will count it against me. Even in hell he must arouse general disgust. Shortly before our departure from the retreat, I rode ahead and drew the bodies somewhat aside, so that the sight of the corpses might not frighten you, or that you might not think it an evil omen."

Then the princess said:—

"In these terrible times, I have seen too many persons who were near to me slain, to become frightened at the sight of corpses, still, I should have preferred if no blood had been shed, lest God might punish us."

"Nor was it a chivalrous act," curtly remarked Volodiyovski. "I would not soil my hands with it."

"What's the use of thinking over the matter now," said Jendzian. "It couldn't be otherwise. Had we killed a good man, I would not have a word to say, but to kill enemies of God is allowable. Had I not seen myself that the witch was in a league with devils! I do not regret that matter at all."

"And what does Pan Jendzian regret?" asked the princess.

"That there is money hidden in the ground of which Bohun told me. But because the gentlemen compelled us to hurry, I had no time to dig it up, although I knew the spot by the mill accurately. It also broke my heart that we had to leave behind us so many precious things in the place where your Ladyship dwelt."

"Behold the kind of a servant you are getting," said Zagloba to the princess, "with the exception of his master, he would tear the skin from anyone, from the devil himself, to make a collar of it."

"If it please God, Jendzian will have no reason to complain of my ungratefulness," answered Helena.

"I thank your Grace, very humbly," said the lad, kissing her hand.

Meanwhile Volodiyovski sat silent, drinking wine from the leathern bottle, with his brow contracted in a frown, until his unusual silence drew Zagloba's attention to him.

"And Pan Michael," said he, "hardly utters a word," and turning to the princess, he added:

"Did I not tell you that your beauty had paralyzed his tongue and his intellect."

"You had better get some sleep before daybreak," replied the knight, much confused, and twisting his little moustache to a point.

But the old nobleman was right; the extraordinary beauty of the princess had stunned and entranced the little knight. He looked at her again and again, and asked himself, "Is it possible that such a being live upon this earth?" Doubtless he had seen many beauties in his life, the Pannas Anna and Barbara Zbaraska were beautiful, Anna Borzobahata's beauty

defied all description. Panna Zukovna to whom Pan Rostvorovski was paying attention, was charming also, and Panna
Viershulova Skoropadzka and Panna Bohovitynyanka, but
none of them could compare with this beautiful wild-flower
of the steppes. In the presence of the others, Pan Volodiyovski was always lively and talkative; but now when he
glanced at those sweet half-veiled, velvet eyes, the silky
lashes of which drooped on her rosy cheeks; when he beheld
her luxuriant hair that spread like a hyacinth over her arms
and shoulders, her slender figure, her beautifully-rounded
bosom, which lightly rose and sank, as she breathed; exhaling
warm love, and when he looked on her lily and rose white complexion and the roses on her cheeks, and on her red lips, then
Pan Volodiyovski completely lost his speech, and worst of all,
he appeared to himself so clumsy, stupid and diminutive as to
appear ridiculous. She is a princess, and I am but a school
boy, thought he with bitterness, and he longed for an adventure, possibly with a giant, who might emerge from the
darkness; then poor Pan Michael would show that he was
not as small as he appeared. He was also put out because
Zagloba, evidently delighted that his fair daughter was the
object of so much attention, gave vent to many knowing
winks and nods, and joked him not a little.

Meanwhile she sat before the fire. The white moon and
the red flames cast their light upon her. She sat still and
quiet, looking more and more beautiful.

"Admit, Pan Michael," said Zagloba, the next morning
when they were alone for a moment, "that there is not
such another girl throughout the entire Commonwealth. If
you can show me such another, you can call me a fool, and
demented besides."

"I don't deny it," said the little knight. "She stands
alone, and I have never seen her like before. Even those
marble statues of the goddesses in the palace of Panna Kaz-
anovski, which, though cut from marble, seem to be alive,
cannot compare with her. I am not surprised that the
bravest men risked their lives on her account, for she is
worth it."

"What! As God is my judge," said Zagloba, "one does not
know whether she is more beautiful in the morning or in the
evening, for she seems ever as fresh as a rose. I told you
that I once was also wonderfully handsome, but even in
those days, I should have been obliged to bow to her although
many say that she resembles me as one goblet does another."

"Oh, go to the devil!" exclaimed the little knight.

"Do not treat me with such scorn, Pan Michael, for you frown like Mars already. You gaze at her like a goat at a cabbage, and pucker your brow; one would swear that desires torment you, but the sausage is not for the dog."

"Fie," exclaimed Volodiyovski, "as an old man are you not ashamed to talk such nonsense?"

"Why do you look so downcast?"

"Because you believe that all danger is behind us, that we are in safety and that evil has flown like a bird in the air. But we must consider how we can avoid the one and overcome the other. The way that lies before us is full of danger, God knows what is awaiting us, for the region into which we go is surely now in flames."

"When I abducted her from Bohun in Rozloga, it was worse, because pursuit was behind us and revolution before us; nevertheless, we traversed the entire Ukraine crossing an ocean of flames to Bar. What is the use of the heads upon our shoulders. If it comes to the worst, we are not far from Kamenets."

"Yes, but the Turks and Tartars are not far from there either."

"What are you telling me?"

"I only speak the truth, and that is worth while thinking about. It would be better to skirt around Kamenets and go directly to Bar for the Cossacks respect a safe-conduct and we could easily get through the 'blacks,' but should a single Tartar get sight of us we are lost. I know their tricks by a long experience, and understand how to steal around a Tartar camp like a wolf or a bird, but should we chance upon one now without warning, I should be at loss what to do."

"Well, then let us go to Bar or around it, and may a pest destroy the Lipkovs and Cheremis of Kamenets. You evidently do not know that Jendzian received a safe-conduct from Burlay? We can roam about among the Cossacks singing. We have left the worst desert behind us, we are coming now into an inhabited land. We must take care that we always stop at some farm before nightfall, for this will be safer and more comfortable for the lady. It seems to me Pan Michael, that you look at things too darkly. By Jove, it were a strange thing if three fellows like ourselves, without flattering myself or you, could not take care of ourselves in the steppes. We shall combine our wits with your sabre, and

'Haida! onward! We can do nothing better. Jendzian has his safe-conduct from Burlay, that's the main thing, for Burlay rules the whole of Podolia, and once we have Bar behind us, we shall find Lantskorontski's troops. Haida! Come on Pan Michael, let us lose no time."

They hurried onward towards the northwest as fast as the horses could go. On the heights of Mohilov, they reached inhabited land, so that it was no longer difficult for them to find a farm or village where they could spend the night, but with the dawn they were always on their horses, and on the way. Fortunately the summer was dry, the days were warm, and the nights dewy, and in the morning the steppes glistened like silver frost. The winds had dried the ponds; the rivers were shallow, and could be forded without difficulty. After they had gone for some distance along the Lozova, they stopped for a more protracted rest in Sharagrod where a division of Burlay's Cossack's was encamped. Here they met delegates of Burlay, and among them Captain Setnik Kuna, whom they had seen in Yampol at the feast given by Burlay. The Captain Setnik was somewhat surprised that they did not pass through Bratslav, Raygrod, Skvira to Kiev, but no suspicion entered his mind, especially as Zagloba explained to him that they had not taken that course through fear of the Tartars, having heard that the latter were marching up from the Dnieper. Kuna told them in reply that Burlay had sent him to the regiment to announce the campaign, and that he, himself, with all the Yampol and Budziak-Tartars would come to Sharagrod and push on from there.

Special messengers had come to Burlay from Khmyelnitski with the news that war was declared, and with orders to lead all the squadrons to Volhynia. Burlay, himself, had intended long ago to go to Bar, and only waited for the Tartars to join him, for at Bar things were going badly for the rebels.

Pan Lantskoronski had defeated a considerable body then, and had captured the city and occupied the castle. Several thousand Cossacks had fallen, and these the old Burlay wished to revenge, or at least to retake the castle. Kuna said, however, that the latest orders from Khymelnitski to proceed onward to Volhynia had prevented this action, and that Bar would not be besieged, unless the Tartars insisted upon it at all hazards.

"Now, Pan Michael," said Zagloba, the next day, "Bar lies before us, and I could for the second time find the princess a safe retreat there, but the deuce take that place. I trust neither Bar nor any other fortress since the rebels have more cannon than the army of the Crown. What disturbs me is, that a storm is threatening all about us."

"It is not only threatening, but it is breaking right at our heels in the shape of the Tartars; if they should over-take us, they would not be a little surprised, that instead of going to Kiev, we should be going in an opposite direction."

"And Burlay would be ready to show us another way. May the devil show him first the way which leads directly to hell. Let us make a contract. I will engage to get through these rascals, but when we come among the Tartars, there, you must use your wits."

"It is a simple matter to deal with this mob, as they take us for their own." answered Volodiyovski, "but as regards the Tartars, my advice is to flee from them as fast as possible, so that we may escape their toils. Our horses are good, but wherever an opportunity offers, we must buy new ones on the way in order to have a fresh relay."

"Pan Longin's purse will probably pay our way, but should it not, Jendzian must lend us Burlay's, and now onward!"

And they rushed onward still faster until the foam covered the flanks of the horses and fell like snow on the green steppe. They passed through Derla and Lodava. Volodi-yovski bought fresh horses in Bark. But the old ones were not left behind; for those that Burlay had presented to them were thoroughbreds, and therefore they kept them as re-serves. Shorter and shorter became their pauses for rest, and fewer their stops in sheltered places. They all enjoyed fine health, and although Helena was fatigued by the journey, still she gained strength day by day. In the ravine she had led a secluded life, and had rarely left her gilded cage for fear of meeting the shameless Horpyna, and being compelled to listen to her talk. Now the fresh air of the steppe re-stored her health, her cheeks became rosy, the sun tanned her face, and her eyes gained fresh fire. Often when the winds curled her hair on her forehead, one might have taken her for a gypsy; or a wonderful witch, or have thought that a gypsy queen was prancing across the wide steppe, with flowers pringing up before her, and an escort of knights behind.

Pan Volodiyovski gradually became accustomed to her wonderful beauty, the journey had brought them closer to each other, and he became himself again. He regained his former gayety and spirits, and his speech, and as he rode by her side, he told her many things about Lubni, and especially about his friendship with Skshetuski, for he noticed that she liked to listen to talk about him.

Sometimes he teased her, saying:

"I am Bohun's friend, and I'll take you to him, Princess."

Then she would clasp her hands as if in great fear, and beseech him with soft words.

"Do not do so, dear knight, rather kill me on the spot."

"That I would not do! I cannot do that!" answered the little knight sternly.

"Kill me," repeated the princess, closing her eyes, and extending her neck.

Then a strange flush overcame the knight, he felt as if ants were crawling all over him. "This girl mounts to one's head like wine," he said to himself, "but I shall not get intoxicated, for the wine belongs to another;" and Pan Michael shook himself and galloped away, and when he had plunged into the tall grass of the steppe, like a sea-mew into water, the ants departed; and he turned all his attention to the way they were gaing, looking carefully to see that they were on the right track, and that no danger was threatening them from any quarter. He stood up in his stirrups, and his little moustache rose above the waving grass as he looked all around listening and sniffing like a Tartar, when hunting in the Wild Lands.

Pan Zagloba was also in the best of spirits.

"Our flght is easier now,' said he, "than formerly on the Kahamlik, where we had to run along on foot, panting like dogs, with the tongue hanging out. My tongue was so dry that I could saw wood with it, and now thank God, we can rest at night, and also have something to lubricate our throat with from time to time."

"Do you remember, Sir, how you bore me in your arms across the water?" asked Helena.

"If it please God, you will also see the day when you will carry something in your arms—Skshetuski will see to that."

"Ho, ho!" laughed Jendzian.

"Say no more I pray you," whispered the princess, blushing and with downcast eyes.

Thus they diverted themselves on the steppe as well as they could to pass the time. Finally beyond Bark, and Yoltushka, they entered a region which showed the devastation of war. Until recntly bands of rebels, had camped there, and there Lantskoronski had defeated them, and left everything in ruins behind him, for he had retired only a few days previously to Zbaraj. Our party learned also from the villagers that Khmyelnitski together with the Khan and his entire forces had moved against the Poles, or rather against the commanders, whose troops had mutinied, and who refused to serve except under Vishnyovyetski. Besides there was a general feeling that if Khmyelnitski and Yeremy should meet, either the Poles or the Cossacks would be wiped out. Meanwhile, the whole country rose up in arms, and every one seized their weapons and marched off to the north to join Khmyelnitski. From the low lands of the Dniester, and from Nij, Burlay was advancing with all his forces, and drawing to himself regiments from their winter-quarters and garrisons from the towns, for the order to mobilize had gone forth everywhere. So they marched in divisions of hundreds and squadrons and regiments and following them streamed the disorderly "blacks" armed with flails, pitch-forks, knives and spears. Horse-herders and cattle-drivers threw away their scythes, farmers deserted their lands, bee-keepers their bees, the wild fishermen their banks on the Dniester, and the hunters their forests. Hamlets, villages and towns were deserted. In three provinces there remained only the old women and children, for the maidens had marched out with the men against the poles. At the same time from the east, like a threatening storm came the forces of the Khmyelnitski, who with powerful hand destroyed places and castles on his way, killing all whom former contests had spared. When the party had left Bar with all its sad memories for the princess behind them, they took the old highway that led through Latichov and Ploskirov to Tarnopol, and onwards to Lemberg. Here they often encountered big trains of wagons, divisions of infantry, and of Cossack cavalry, bands of peasants and enormous herds of oxen, which stirred up great clouds of dust as they were driven along to make provision for the Cossack and Tartar soldiery. Now, their journey became dangerous, for they were continually questioned as to who they were, whence they came, and whither they were going. To the Cossack regiments Zagloba showed his safe-conduct from Burlay, and said:

"We are messengers from Burdaj and we are taking the maid to Bohun."

At the sight of the safe-conduct of the dreaded colonel the swarm of Cossacks which surrounded them would fall back, for they thought that if Bohun was alive, he must be already near the main army about Zbaraj, or Konstantinov. But the party had still more trouble with the "blacks" and wild bands of drunken and ignorant herdsmen who had no idea of the meaning of the safe-conduct, issued by the colonel. Had it not been for Helena, Zagloba, Volodiyovski and Jendzian, would have been taken by these half savage tribes for their own kind, as sometimes actually happened, but Helena attracted the attention of all on account of her sex and her beauty, and therefore, there arose dangers, which they could only avoid by taking the greatest precaution.

Sometimes Zagloba showed the safe-conduct; sometimes Volodiyovski showed his teeth, and many a corpse they left behind them? At times they were saved from disaster only by the great speed of Burlay's racers, and the journey which at the outset had begun so favorably, became more difficult day by day. Helena, who though brave by nature, felt the strain of sleepless nights and of continuous alarm, now began to fail in health. She looked like a captive who is dragged unwillingly into the camps of the enemy. Zagloba continually formed new plans which Volodiyovski carried out, and both of them consoled the princess as well as they could.

"We must leave the swarms of ants behind which now confront us and reach Zbaraj," said the little knight. "Here, Khmyelnitski, with the Tartars floods the whole region about."

They had learned on the way that the commanders had assembled at Zbaraj and intended to hold the town. They had gathered there expecting that Prince Yeremy would join them with his division, as a considerable portion of his forces were quartered in Zbaraj. Now our party drew near to Ploskirov. The swarms on the high roads began to grow thinner, for but ten miles away the country was occupied by the royal forces. The Cossack bands did not dare to advance further. They preferred to wait at a safe distance, for the arrival of Burlay on one side, and of Khmyelnitski from the other.

"But ten more miles, but ten more miles!" repeated Zagloba rubbing his hands. "If we can only reach the first squadrons, we surely will get safely to Zbaraj."

Pan Volodiyovski, however, decided to provide new horses

at Ploskirov, for those they had purchased in Bark, were no longer any good, and those which Burlay had given them, had to be spared for a dark hour. This precaution was necessary, for rumors were afloat that Khymelnitski was already near Konstantinov and that the Khan was approaching with all his hordes from Pilavyets.

"It is best for us to remain with the princess here outside the town, and not to show ourselves," said the little knight to Zagloba when they had arrived at a small deserted cottage about two furlongs from the town.

"But you go to the villagers and see if they have any horses for sale or exchange. It is evening already, but we must remain in the saddle all night."

"I'll be back soon," said Zagloba.

He rode onward to the town. Volodiyovski then ordered Jendzian to loosen the saddle-girths so as to give the horses a chance to rest. He then led the princess into the house, and bade here to refresh herself with wine and sleep.

"I would like to have those ten miles behind us by daybreak," he said to her, "then we can all rest."

No sooner had he brought the wine and some provisions, than the sound of horses' hoofs was heard at the door. The little knight looked out the window.

"Zagloba is back already," said he, "he surely has found no horses."

At that moment the door opened, and Zagloba appeared pale, blue, perspiring and breathless.

"Mount your horses," he cried.

Pan Michael was too experienced a soldier to lose time in asking questions. He did not even take time to snatch up the wine-bag, this, however, Zagloba grasped, but immediately led the princess into the yard and helped her into her saddle, and casting a glance at the saddle-girths to see if they were tight, he cried:

"Mount your horses!"

There was a sound of clattering hoofs, and horsemen and horses vanished in the darkness like a dream cavalcade. They galloped for a long time without resting. But not till about a mile separated them from Ploskirov, and the darkness had grown so dense that the pursuit was impossible, did Volodiyovski approach Zagloba and ask:

"What was it?"

"Wait, Pan Michael, wait. I am dreadfully out of breath. My legs were nearly paralyzed. Ugh!"

"But what was it?"

"The devil himself, I tell you, the devil himself, or a dragon on which a second head grows, as soon as the first one is chopped off."

"Speak plainly, I beg of you?"

"I saw Bohun in the market-place."

"Are you delirious?"

"I saw him in the market-place as true as I live, and five or six people with him. I did not count them. I could hardly stand on my feet—they held torch-lights for him—methinks an evil spirit is working against us; I have lost all faith in the success of our enterprise. Is that devil immortal, or what? . . . don't speak to Helena about it, for God's sake."·

"You killed him, Jendzian gave him up? No! And still he lives, is free, and crosses our path again. Ugh! Oh God! God! I tell you, Pan Michael, that I would rather see a ghost in a churchyard than him. What in the devil kind of a fortune have I to always be the first one to see him everywhere. To the dogs with such luck! Are there no other people in the world? Could he not appear to others? No, always me, and only me."

"And did he see you?"

"If he had seen me, you Pan Michael would have never seen me again. That was the only thing wanting."

"It would be well to know," said Volodiyovski, "if he is in pursuit of us, or if he is going to Valadynka, to Horpyna with the intention of catching us on the way."

"It seems to me, that he is going to Valadynka."

"That is probably the case. Then we shall ride in one direction, he in another, and if now one or two miles were between us, there will be five in an hour from now. Before he learns about us on the road and turns back, we shall be not only in Zbaraj but in Jolkov."

"Do you think so, Pan Michael? Thank God. You relieve my mind greatly, but tell me how is it possible that he has regained his freedom since Jendzian gave him up to the commander in Vlodava."

"He simply escaped."

"Oh, the Commander deserves to have his head chopped off. Jendzian, hey! Jendzian!"

"What do you want?" said the lad reining in his horse.

"To whom did you give Bohun up?"

43

"To Pan Rogovski."

"And who is this Pan Rogovski?"

"A fine gentleman; a lieutenant of the cuirassiers of His Majesty, the King."

"You go to ——" said Volodiyovski, snapping his fingers. "Now I can explain matters. Don't you remember what Longin told us about the enmity between Skshetuski and Rogovski? He is a relative of Pan Lashch, and hates Skshetuski on his account."

"I see, I see!" cried Zagloba. "He liberated Bohun out of spite, but this is a criminal offence, whose penalty is the gallows. I shall be the first to report it."

"If God should let me meet him once we shall hardly need to go before a tribunal."

Jendzian did not understand what the trouble was, for after answering Zagloba's question, he rode forward again beside the princess. They had now slackened their pace, the moon had risen, the fog which since the evening had enveloped the earth now lifted, and the night became clear. Volodiyovski became engrossed in thought. Zagloba was still thinking over his terrible experience. Finally, he said:

"How would Bohun have repaid Jendzian, if he had fallen into his hands?"

"Tell him the news. Let him have a taste of the fright. Meantime, I will ride on with the princess," answered the little knight.

"All right, here! Jendzian."

"What's the matter?" asked the lad, checking the horse again.

Zagloba remained silent for a while, until Volodiyovski and the princess had gotten enough ahead not to overhear it. Then he said:

"Do you know what happened?"

"I don't know."

"Pan Rogovski set Bohun free. I saw him in Ploskirov."

"What, in Ploskirov, just now?" asked Jendzian.

"In Ploskirov, just now! Why don't you fall out of your saddle?"

The moonlight illumined the lad's chubby face, but Zagloba could discover upon it no trace of fright, but he saw with astonishment that it had the same expression of almost brutal rage which he had already noticed when Jendzian killed Horpyna.

"Don't you fear Bohun then?" queried the old noble.

"My Lord," answered the lad, "if Rogovski has set him free, I must try to revenge myself once more the insult and ignominy he heaped upon me. I shall not spare him, for I have sworn vengeance upon him, and were we not escorting the princess now, I would instantly follow his tracks that I might redeem my oath. I intend to keep it."

"Well," thought Zagloba, "I am glad that I have done no injury to this lad."

Then he put spurs to his horse, and came up with the princess and Volodiyovski.

After riding for about an hour they crossed the Medvedovka and entered a forest, which from the river bank stretched along their path like two dark walls.

"I know this region well," said Zagloba. "We shall soon be through this wood. Beyond it is open land for a quarter of a mile, crossed by the highway to Charny-Ostrov, then there are thicker forests extending to Matchyna. May it please God that we find Polish troops already in Matchyna."

"It is high time for our deliverance," murmured Volodiyovski.

Again they rode along in silence for a time, on the brightly-illumined highway.

"Two wolves have just run across our path," said Helena, suddenly.

"I saw them," answered Volodiyovski, "and there is the third one."

Indeed, a gray shadow crept across the way, about a hundred paces before their horses.

"There is a fourth," cried the princess.

"No, that is a deer. Look, lady, two—three."

"What the devil!" cried Zagloba. "The wolves are being chased by deer. The world is topsy-turvy."

"Let us ride faster," said Volodiyovski, his voice trembling from anxiety, "Jendzian, come here, and ride ahead with the princess."

They flew along; but as they rode Zagloba bent over towards Volodiyovski, and asked:

"Pan Michael, what is the trouble?"

"Bad!" answered the little knight. "You observe that the beasts have been disturbed from their sleep in their lairs, and are running about in the night."

"And what does that mean?"

"That means that they are being frightened."

"By whom?"

"By soldiers, either Cossacks or Tartars, who are approaching us from the right."

"But perhaps these are our own troops?"

"That cannot be, for the animals are fleeing from the east, from Pilavyets, and it is certain that the Tartars are approaching in a numerous body."

"Let us fly, Michael, for God's sake."

"There is nothing else to do. If it were not for the princess, we could ride up close to their chambuls, and drag some of them out, but with her, the matter would be too difficult, should they spy us."

"Merciful God, Pan Michael, shall we take to the woods behind the wolves, or what?"

"That cannot be, for though we should escape the enemy at the present moment, they would flood the regions before us, and how then could we evade them?"

"Thunder and lightning strike them. This alone was wanting. But Pan Michael, are you not mistaken, do not wolves follow troops, rather than flee before them?"

"Those in the rear of the troops follow them, and gather from afar, but those which are before them, flee. Look, there to your right among the trees. There gleams a fire."

"Jesus of Nazareth, King of the Jews!"

"Keep quiet! Is the forest much longer?"

"We shall soon come to its end."

"And then do we get into open country?"

"Yes! oh Jesus!"

"Keep quiet. Is there another forest beyond?"

"As far as Matchyna."

"Good. If only they do not overtake us in the open field! If we will reach yonder forest, then we shall be at home. Let us keep together now."

"Luckily the princes and Jendzian were mounted on Burlay's horses."

They spurred their horses in order to join their friends who were ahead.

"What kind of a fire is that I see at the right?" asked the princess.

"There's no use in concealment," answered the little knight, "they may be the Tartars."

"Jesus Maria!"

"Do not worry my lady, I'll wager my head that we escape them; and in Matchyna are our troops."

"For Heaven's sake! let us make haste," exclaimed Jendzian.

They rode on in silence, flying along like spectres. The forest grew lighter, and they were beginning to get to its end; the fire-light also grew dimmer. Suddenly Helena addressed the little knight.

"Sir," said she, "promise me that you wil not let me fall into their hands alive."

"That will not happen as long as I live," answered Volodiyovski.

Hardly had they emerged from the forest,and entered the open country, or rather the steppe, which extended for about a quarter of a mile, when they beheld beyond another line of forest. The clearing, open in all directions, gleamed in the silvery beams of the moon, as bright almost as the daylight.

"This is the worst part of our way," whispered Volodiyovski to Zagloba, "for if they be in Charny-Ostrov, they must cross here between the woods."

Zagloba did not reply; he only spurred his horse.

They had gotten over half of the clearing, and they were drawing nearer and nearer to the forest before them, and its outlines showed up distinctly, when suddenly the little knight pointed towards the east.

"Look!" said he to Zagloba, "do you see?"

"I see bushes and thickets in the distance."

"But those bushes are moving."

"On, on, they can't fail to see us."

The wind whistled by the ears of the riders, the protecting forest came nearer and nearer. All of a sudden there came a sound like the roaring of ocean waves from the approaching mass on their right, and at the next moment, one mighty shout filled the air.

"They see us," roared Zagloba. "The dogs; the rascals; the devils; the wolves; the ruffians!"

The forest was so near that the fleeing ones already felt its cool raw air blowing upon their faces.

But the cloud of Tartars also grew more distinct and visible, and the dark body shot out long arms like the feelers of a gigantic monster, approaching with inconceivable speed. Volodiyovski's trained ear could already clearly distinguish their cries:

"Allah! Allah!"

"My horse has stumbled," shouted Zagloba.

"That does not matter," replied Volodiyovski.

But like lightning the question flashed through his brain: "What would happen if the horses gave out, or if one of them broke down?"

They were, no doubt splendid Tartar steeds of iron endurance, but they had already made the journey from Ploskirov without rest after the first mad rush from the town to the forest. They might indeed, mount the reserve horses, but these were worn out also.

"What is to be done now?" thought Volodiyovski, and his heart beat in alarm, perhaps, for the first time in his life, not for himself, but for Helena, whom during this long journey he had learned to love as his own sister. Too well he knew that when once the Tartars began to pursue they would not soon relinquish the chase."

"If they overtake us, they shall not take her," said the knight to himself, grinding his teeth.

"My horse has stumbled," cried Zagloba for the second time."

"That does not matter!" repeated Volodiyovski.

Now they sped into the forest. Darkness enveloped them, but several Tartars were not more than a few hundred feet behind them.

The little knight already had made up his mind how to act.

"Jendzian," cried he, "turn with the lady into the nearest pathway."

"All right, sir," answered the lad.

Then the little knight addressesd Zagloba: "Have your pistols ready in your hand." At the same time he grasped the bridle of Zagloba's horse to check its speed.

"What are you doing?" cried the nobleman.

"Nothing, check your horse!"

The distance between them and Jendzian, who flew along with Helena, grew greater and greater. At length the fleeing pair reached a spot where the highway abruptly turned towards Zbaraj and straight ahead the narrow path trailed through the forest, the entrance to which was almost hidden by branches. This Jendzian entered and shortly disappeared with Helena in the thicket and the drakness. Meanwhile Volodiyovski had stopped his horse and that of Zagloba.

"In the name of God what are you doing?" said the noble.

"We must delay the pursuit. There is no other way of rescuing the princess."

"We are lost."

"Let us be lost! Stop here, right by the side of the road. . . . Here, here."

Both tried to hide themselves in the dark shadows of the trees. The mighty tramping of the Tartar horses approached, and rumbled along like a wild tempest, causing the whole forest to resound.

"It has come," said Zagloba. He lifted the wine skin to his lips and drank and drank. Then he shook himself. "In the name of the Father, Son and Holy Ghost!" cried he, "I am ready to die."

"Wait, wait," exclaimed Volodiyovski, "three of them are riding in advance; there's just what I desired."

On the clear road there appeared three horsemen, who evidently had the best steeds, so-called wolf-hunters of the Ukraine, their name implying power to overtake the speediest wolf. A few hundred steps behind them were some others, and still farther behind was a dense mass of the horde.

When the first three had come close to the ambush, two shots rang out, and then Volodiyovski sprang like a panther into the middle of the road, and in a second, ere Zagloba had time to think, or had time to exactly appreciate what had happened, the third Tartar fell as if struck by lightning.

"Mount!" shouted the little knight.

Zagloba did not wait for further instructions. They fled along the highway like two wolves chased by a pack of bloodthirsty hounds. Meantime, the Tartars in the rear reached their dead comrades, and when they saw that the hunted wolves could inflict deadly wounds, they paused for a while to wait for their other comrades.

"See!" said Volodiyovski, "I knew that we could retard them."

But though the fleeing ones had gained an advantage of a few hundred steps, the pursuit was not interrupted for long, but the Tartars now rode in larger companies, and no small detachment now pushed forward as before.

The horses of the fleeing ones, however, became exhausted by the long ride, and their speed slackened. Zagloba's horse in particular, as it bore considerable burden, stumbled repeatedly; the few remaining hairs on the old man's head stood up like bristles at the thought that he might fall.

"Michael, dearest Michael, do not desert me!" he cried in despair.

"Don't worry about that," replied the little knight.

"This horse, may the wolves—" he did not finish the sentence, an arrow swished by his ear followed by more, whistling and humming about like bees and gadflies. One arrow sped so close to Zagloba's ear, that its haft almost touched him.

Volodiyovski turned and again fired two shots at his pursuers.

Zagloba's horse now stumbled so badly, that its nostrils almost touched the ground.

"By the living God! my horse is breaking down," cried Zagloba in a heart-breaking voice.

"Get off the saddle and into the woods," ordered Volodiyovski.

Then he reined in his horse and springing off disappeared with Zagloba into the darkness.

But this manoeuvre did not escape the eyes of the Tartars. Several of them sprang from their horses, and continued the pursuit.

The branches tore the cap off Zagloba's head, slapped him in the face, and caught his coat, but the noble kept bravely on, and ran as if he were but thirty years old. At times he fell, but he rose again, and ran on still faster panting and puffing like a bellows. Finally he fell into a hole and felt that he could not get out of it, for his strength had deserted him entirely.

"Where are you?" whispered Volodiyovski.

"Here in a hole, all is over with me. Save me, Michael!"

But Pan Michael jumped immediately into the hole and closed Zagloba's mouth with his hand.

"Keep still, perhaps, they won't notice us; at any rate, we will defend ourselves."

Meanwhile, the Tartars came up. Some indeed passed the hole, thinking that the runaways were ahead; others advanced slowly, looking about them carefully in all directions.

The knights held their breath.

"Let one fall in here," thought Zagloba in desperation, "I'll fix him."

Now sparks flew all about, the Tartars began to strike fire. In the light their wild faces could be seen, with protruding cheek-bones and thick lips; how they blew at the flickering wood! For some time they kept going about in a circle, but

THE PERIL OF ZAGLOBA AND PAN MICHAL.

a few steps away from the hole. They approached like ill-omened phantoms of the forest, and came nearer every moment.

A moment later a great uproar arose from the highway and penetrated the silent depths of the forest.

The Tartars ceased striking fire, and stood dumbfounded. Volodiyovski's hand convulsively grasped Zagloba's arm.

The noise grew louder, and suddenly red lights flashed up, and following them, the sound of volleys, the sound of muskets; then another and another mingled with shouts of "Alllah, Allah!" Then was heard the clash of sabres, the neighing of horses, the trampling of hoofs and tumultuous uproar. A battle was taking place on the highway.

"Ours, ours!" shouted Volodiyovski.

"Kill, slay, cut, slaughter!" roared Zagloba.

The next moment several dozen Tartars rushed past the hole in wild confusion in the direction of their comrades.

Volodiyovski could not restrain himself any longer; he followed close upon their heels into the thicket amid the darkness.

Zagloba remained at the bottom of the pit. After a time he attempted to crawl out, but he could not; every bone in his body was aching, he could hardly stand on his feet.

"Wait you rascals," said he, looking about him. "You have run away, but it's a pity one of you didn't stay here. I sigh for company and wouldn't I show him where pepper grows. Oh Pagans, I will slaughter you like cattle! My God, the noise is growing louder! I would that Prince Yeremy himself were there, he would make it hot for you. You shout, 'Allah, Allah!' soon the wolves will yelp 'Allah!' over your carrion; but think of it, Michael has left me here alone. Well, it is no wonder, for he is young and fiery. After this expedition, I will follow him to hell, for he is not a friend that leaves one in distress, he is a wasp. In one moment he stung three of them. If I only had the wine-skin here; but the Devil has surely taken it. The horses must have trampled over it. The insects are biting me in this cursed hole. But what was that?"

The shouting and the sound of muskets now sounded in the direction of the open field and of the first forest.

"Ah!" said Zagloba, "they are at their heels already. Oh, dog-brothers you did not hold your ground. Thanks be to God, most High!"

The shouts grew still fainter.

"They ride valiantly," murmured the nobleman, "but I see that I am doomed to stay in this hole, perhaps, to become the prey of wolves. First Bohun, then the Tartars, and at last the wolves. May God given Bohun to the stake; and madness to the wolves; it was the Tartars who ran, our men will not spare them. Michael! Michael!" But only silence answered to Zagloba's shouts; the forest murmured, and afar off, the noises grew fainter and fainter.

"If matters remain like this, I shall have to sleep here. The devil take it! Hello! Michael!"

But Zagloba's patience had to stand a longer test, for it was dawn when the galloping of the horses was heard again on the road and light broke in the forest.

"Pan Michael, here I am!" called out the nobleman.

"Creep out of there."

"How can I?"

Pan Michael stood at the edge of the hole with a torch in his hand. He stretched out his other hand to Zagloba, and said:

"Well, the Tartars are gone. We drove them beyond the forest.'

"And who was with you?"

"Kushel and Rotzvorovski with two thousand horse. My dragoons were also with them."

"And were there many Tartars?"

"Well, a couple of thousand."

"God be praised! Give me a drink, for I am faint."

Two hours later Zagloba sat in a comfortable saddle among Volodiyovski's dragoons. He had had his fill of food and drink. Beside him rode the little knight, who said:

"Don't worry; for even if we do not reach Zabaraj in company with the princess, it is better anyway, than if she had fallen into the hands of the pagans."

"But, perhaps, Jendzian will convey her to Zbaraj?" asked Zagloba.

"He will not do that. The highways will be occupied. For the chambuls which we have repulsed, wil return soon to follow in our footsteps. Moreover, Burlay may arrive at any moment at Zbaraj, before Jendzian could get there. On the other side Khmyelnitski and the Khan are marching from Konstantinov."

"Oh, my God! then the princess will fall into a net."

"It is Jendzian's lookout to get through between Zbaraj and Konstantinov in time, and here Khmyelnitsi's squadrons and the hordes of the Khan surround them. I believe that he appreciates this fact."

"God grant it."

"The boy is as cunning as a fox. You are a shrewd fellow, I admit; but he is still more crafty. We worried our heads over plans of how to save the girl, but at the end we were helpless. He made everything all right again. He will crawl out of this difficulty like a snake, for his own life is at stake. Trust in God, who has protected her so many times; and remember that in Zbaraj you bade me have confidence when Zakhar came there."

These words somewhat consoled Zagloba, but he became lost in thought.

"Pan Michael," said he, after a time, "have you asked Kushel where Skshetuski is?"

"He is in Zbaraj, and thank God, he is well. He came with Zatsvilikhovski, from Prince Koretski."

"But what shall we tell him?"

"That is a knotty point?"

"He still believes, does he not, that the girl was murdered in Kiev?"

"That's so."

"And have you told Kushel, or any one else whence we came?"

"Not as yet, for I thought it best to talk matters over first."

"It would be better to keep the whole matter a secret," said Zagloba, "for should the girl (God forbid) fall again into the hands of the Cossacks or Tartars, this would be new sorrow for Skshetuski, just as if someone should tear open his recently-healed wounds."

"I will stake my head that Jendzian will get her through all right."

"I would stake my own too, but misfortune stalks abroad like a pestilence. Let us drop the subject, and leave everything to the will of God."

"So be it. But will Podbipyenta keep the secret from Skshetuski?"

"You do not know him, he pledged his word of honor, which is sacred to this strange Lithuanian."

Kushel now joined them, and they rode on together in the early morning discussing public affairs, the arrival of the commanders at Zbaraj in consequence of Prince Yeremy's commands, the expected arrival of the prince himself, and the terrible battle which could not be avoided with the whole force of Khmyelnitski.

CHAPTER II.

At Zbaraj, Volodiyovski and Zagloba found all the royal forces gathered, and awaiting the enemy. Here were the Cup-bearer who had come from Konstantinov and Lantskoronski the Castellan of Kamenets who first warred at Bar, and the third commander, Pan Firley of Dombrovitsa the Castellan of Belsk, Andrey Sierakovski the secretary of the crown and Pan Konyetspolski the standard bearer, and Pan Pshiyemski the general of the artillery, who was especially experienced in the capture of towns and their defence. And with them ten thousand troops besides the forces of Prince Yeremy who had been previously stationed at Zbaraj.

Pshiyemski pitched his camp on the southern slope of the town and fortress behind the two lakes and the Gnierna rivulet, formed a powerful camp which he fortified according to the foreign fashion so that it could only be taken from the front as it was protected on the rear and sides by the lakes, the stream and the castle. In this camp the commanders purposed to resist Khmyelnitski and to hold him in check until the king should arrive with the rest of his forces and the general levy of the entire nobility. But could this plan be carried out against the might of Khmyelnitski? Many doubted that this could be done, and gave good reasons for their doubts, one of them being the disorder in the camp itself. First of all, discord was brewing in secret among the leaders. The Commanders had come to Zbaraj unwillingly, they yielded to the will of Prince Yeremy. They had wished at first to defend Konstantinov, but when news was spread that Prince Yeremy promised to take part in the struggle only on condition that Zbaraj should be selected for the place of defence, the soldiers declared to the royal commanders that they wished to go to Zbaraj, and would fight nowhere else. Neither persuasions nor the authority of the commanders were of any avail, and the commanders soon discovered that should they resist longer, the army, from the hussar regiments down to the last soldiers from the foreign

684

contingent would leave and go over to Vishnyovyetski's standard. This was but another deplorable example of the lack of discipline so frequent in those days, caused by the incompetence of the leaders, the discord among them, and the fear of Khmyelnitski's strength, and the unheard-of defeats, especially that of Pilavyets.

Consequently, the commanders were obliged to go to Zbaraj, where in spite of the royal appointments, the supreme command passed into the hands of Vishnyovyetski; for the army would obey only him, fight and ıe under him alone. But this real leader had not yet come to Zbaraj and therefore the restlessness of the troops increased, discipline was lax, and their hearts grew faint. For it was already known that Khmyelnitski and the Khan were approaching with an army the like of which had not been seen since the days of Tamerlane. Fresh rumors spread through the camp like ill-omened birds, new and more alarming rumors came ever and anon which weakened the courage of the soldiers. It was feared that a panic like the one at Pilavyets might suddenly occur and scatter this handful of troops that barred Khmyelnitski's way to the heart of the Commonwealth. The leaders themselves lost their heads. Their contradictory orders were not carried out, and if at all, unwillingly. Yeremy alone could rescue the camp, the army and the country.

As soon as Zagloba and Volodiyovski arrived with the troops of Kushel they mingled at once in the vortex of military life. No sooner did they reach the square than they were surrounded by officers of different regiments who eagerly inquired after news. At the sight of the captive Tartars new hope arose in the hearts of the curious. "They have stampeded the Tartars, they have taken Tartar prisoners; God has granted a victory," cried some. "The Tartrs are here and Burlay with them," cried others. "To arms, men! To the ramparts!" The report spread through the camp, and Kushel's victory was magnified as it went from mouth to mouth; a rapidly increasing crown gathered about the prisoners. "Kill them," they cried, "what shall we do with them?" Questions fell like snowflakes, but Kushel would not answer and went to the quarters of the Castellan of Belsk to report. Volodiyovski and Zagloba were greeted by acquaintances in the Russian squadron, but they got away as soon as they could, for they wished to see Skshetuski.

They found him in the castle, together with the old Zats-vilikhovski, two monks of St. Bernard that belonged there, and Pan Longin. Skshetuski grew somewhat pale when he saw them. He closed his eyes, for their sight brought him too many sad recollections to bear without pain. But he greeted them calmly, even joyfully, asked them where they had been and was content with any answer they gave, for believing the princess to be dead, he wished for nothing, hoped for nothing, and had not the slightest idea that the long absence of his friends had any bearing upon the princess. Nor did they make any mention of the purpose of their expedition, although Longin gazed at one then at the other, with a questioning look, sighing and twisting about in his place, hunting for even a shadow of hope in their faces. But both were taken up by Skshetuski, whom Pan Michael embraced again and again, for his heart melted at the sight of that faithful friend who had suffered so much and lost so much that life was scarce worth the living.

"You see," said he to Skshetuski, "we shall have all our old comrades with us again and you shall be happy with us. We are on the eve of a war the like of which we have not seen before and which fills the heart of every soldier with delight. If God restores to you your health, you will often find yourself at the head of the hussars."

"God has already restored me my health," replied Skshetuski, "and I wish nothing for myself except to serve as long as service is necessary."

Skshetuski was indeed really well, for his youth and vigorous constitution had overcome his illness. Grief had torn his soul but could not destroy his body. He had merely grown thin and yellow so that his forehead, his cheeks and his nose looked as if moulded of church wax; his former austere look had settled more deeply on his face which had an expression of rigid calmness such as is seen on the face of a corpse. There were now silver threads woven in his dark beard; but in other respects he did not differ from other men, except that contrary to the custom of a soldier he avoided tumults, crowds and drinking bouts, preferring to associate with monks, listening with attention to their discourses about convent life, and the hereafter. But in regard to the war, he performed his duties conscientiously and interested himself equally with the others in regard to the expected siege.

Soon indeed the conversation turned to this subject. for

no one in the camp, in the castle, and in the town, thought of anything else. Then old Zatsvilikhovski enquired about the Tartars and about Burlay whom he had known for a long time.

"He is a great warrior," said he, "and it is to be regretted that he now rebels against his own country with the others. We served together at Khotsim, he was then but a youth but already he gave promise of becoming a remarkable man."

"Why, he comes from the Dnieper regions and leads the Trans-Dnieper men," said Skshetuski, "how is it then, father, that he marches up now from the south from Kamenets?"

"Probably," said Zatsvilikhovski. "Khmyelnitski purposely sent him there to spend the winter, when Tukhay Bey remained on the Dnieper and the Murza greatly hates Burlay from former days. No one has made it so hot for the Tartars as Burlay."

"And now he becomes their messmate?"

"So it is," said Zatsvilikhovski, "such are the times! But Khmyelnitski will take care that they do not eat each other up."

"And when do you expect Khmyelnitski to be here, father?" asked Volodiyovski.

"Any day, who can tell. The commanders ought to send out one scouting party after another, but they don't do it. I had a hard time to get them to send Kushel southward, and Piglovski to Cholhanski Kamyen. I wanted to go myself, but there is council after council here. . . . They should send out some squadrons with the crown secretary. They should make haste lest it be too late. God send us the prince, or disgrace will befall us like that of Pilavyets."

"I saw the soldiers when we rode through the square," said Zagloba, "and it appeared to me that there are more fools among them than good men, they are only fit for shopkeepers and not to be our messmates, who love glory, and value it more than life."

"What are you talking about?" said the old man sharply. "I don't wish to insinuate anything against your bravery, though I have my own opinion about that, but the soldiers here are the flower of the chivalry of the Commonwealth. They need only a head, a leader. Kamyenyetski is a good cavalry officer but no leader; Pan Firley is old, and as to the Cup-bearer, well—he with Prince Dominik made a reputation at Pilavyets. No wonder that no one will obey them.

A soldier sheds his blood readily, if he is sure that it is necessary, but he will not sacrifice himself needlesssly. But now instead of preparing for the siege they are quarreling about the positions they should hold."

"Is there a sufficiency of provisions?" asked Zagloba with alarm.

"Not as much as are needed; but we are worse off in regard to fodder. Should the siege last over a month we shall have only shavings and stones for the animals."

"There is still time enough to make provision," said Volodiyovsky.

"Then go and tell them that. God send our prince, I repeat."

"You are not the only one, who longs for him," interrupted Longin.

"I know it," answered the old man. "Look out upon the square. All who are upon the ramparts are eagerly looking towards old Zbaraj; others mount the towers, and if anyone cries out jokingly 'He comes' everyone goes mad from joy. The thirsty deer pants not more eagerly for the water than we for him. Would that he could get here before Khmyelnitski for I fear that impediments are in his way."

"We pray for his safe arrival all day long," said one of the monks of St. Bernard.

The prayers and wishes of all the knights were soon to be fulfilled, though the following day brought still greater anxiety and was fraught with evil omens. It was Thursday, July 8th, when a frightful storm burst upon the town and over the newly-built ramparts. Rain poured down in torrents. Part of the earthworks was washed away. The Gniezna and both lakes overflowed. In the evening lightning struck a section of infantry under Pan Firley the Castellan of Belsk, killed several men and tore the flag to shreds. This was looked upon as an evil omen—a visible sign of God's wrath, especially as Pan Firley was a Calvinist. Zagloba proposed that a deputation be sent to him with a request that he become converted, for God's blessing could not abide with an army whose leader was living in errors obnoxious to heaven. Many shared this opinion; and it was only the respect due to the Castellan and his dignity that prevented the sending of the deputation. The general discouragement increased. The storm raged without interruption. The ramparts, though strengthened with stones and palisades, became so soft that the cannon began to sink. They were obliged to put boards under the cannons, mortars, and even under the eight-pounders. In the deep trenches the water rose to the height of a man. Night brought no abatement. The tempest drove before it from the east gigantic mountains of clouds that amidst dreadful thunderings in the sky poured their entire store of rain, lightning and thunder upon Zbaraj. Only the baggage attendants remained in the tents, the soldiers, the commanders, with the exception of the commander of Kamenets, sought shelter in the town. Had Khmyelnitski arrived with the tempest he could have taken the camp without resistance.

Next morning the storm had somewhat abated, though it was still raining off and on. Not before five o'clock did the wind dissipate the clouds. The blue sky then showed itself against the camp, and in the direction of old Zbaraj a rainbow of brilliant seven hues appeared, the mighty arch of which extended with one arm beyond old Zbaraj, while with the other it seemed to drink up the moisture of the Black Forest; it gleamed and played against the background of the scudding clouds.

Hope rose in all hearts. The knights returned to camp and mounted the slippery ramparts in order to enjoy the sight of the rainbow. They began at once to converse in lively fashion and to conjecture what this favorable sign might mean, when Volodiyovski, who with others stood close to the trench, shielded his lynx eyes with his hand and cried out:

"Soldiers are approaching from under the rainbow! soldiers!"

A commotion arose as if a whirlwind had stirred the mass of people and shouts arose. The words "soldiers are coming" flew like arrows from one end of the ramparts to the other. The soldiers began to push and crowd and to gather into groups. Then the noise ceased and it became still; all hands shaded their eyes, all eyes gazed into the distance, and all with bated breath and beating hearts continued to look outward.

And then from beneath the seven-colored arch something emerged and became more and more distinct, rising out of the distance and coming nearer and nearer and growing more and more clearly visible, until at last flags and lances and bunchuks appeared, and then a forest of lances; their eyes did not deceive them, these were soldiers.

44

Then a mighty shout burst simultaneously from the throats of all, a shout of triumphant joy.

"Yeremy! Yeremy! Yeremy!"

Frenzy seized even the oldest soldiers. Some hurled themselves from the ramparts, waded through the trench, and ran afoot across the flooded plain towards the approaching regiments, others rushed to their horses, others laughed, others wept, extending their hands towards heaven and crying out: "He is coming, our father! our saviour! our leader!" One might have thought that the siege was over, that Khmyelnitski was vanquished and the victory won. The squadrons of the prince had drawn so near that the ensign could be distinguished. As usual the regiments of the light cavalry of the Prince's Tartars, Semenovs and the Wallachians advanced in front, behind them could be seen the foreign infantry under Makhnitski—then Vurtsel's cannons, with the dragoons and the heavy hussars. The sun's rays flashed upon their armor and upon the points of the up-raised lances. An unusual splendor shone upon the advancing army like the halo of victory.

Skshetuski, who with Longin, stood upon the ramparts, recognized from afar his own squadron which he had left behind him in Zamost, and a faint flush suffused his yellowish cheeks. He drew deep breaths as if freeing himself from some great burden and his eyes brightened. Before him were days of superhuman labors, heroic battles, the best means of healing the wounds of his heart and of banishing painful recollections, forcing them deeper and deeper into the secret innermost depths of his soul.

Nearer and nearer came the squadrons, and now scarcely a thousand steps separated them from the camp.

The chiefs came running, in order to witness the arrival of the prince; the three commanders also, and with them Pshhiyemski the crown secretary, the Standard bearer of the crown, the chief of Krasnostavsk, Pan Korf and all other officers, Polish as well as foreign. All shared the general joy, especially Pan Lantskoronski, who was a soldier, a greater knight than a commander, but who loved the glory of war. He pointed with his baton in the direction whence Prince Yeremy came, and in a voice loud enough to be heard by all, he cried:

"Behold, there comes our greatest leader and I am the first to surrender my command and authority into his hands."

Now the regiments of the prince entered the camp. They numbered altogether three thousand men, but they bore in their hearts the courage of a hundred thousand. They were indeed the victors of Pohrebyshch Niemyerow, Makhnovka, and Konstantinov. Acquaintances and friends greeted each other. At the end, the Vurtsel artillery toiled in wearily, dragging after them four cannon, two eight-pounders and six captured grape-shot guns. Altogether, twelve guns. The prince, who had personally supervised the departure of his troops from old Zbaraj, arrived in the evening after sunset. Everybody ran to receive him; the soldiers bearing pine sticks, lamps and torches and chips of combustible wood surrounded the prince's horse and barred his passage. They seized the bridle of his horse so as to have a longer look at him, they kissed his garments, and almost lifted him on their shoulders. The enthusiasm rose to such a stage that not only the native soldiery but also the foreign contingent declared that they would serve him without pay for three months. The throng about the prince so increased that he could not advance a step; but sat upon his white palfrey surrounded by the soldiers like a shepherd among his flock. There was no end to the shouts and hurrahs. The evening was clear and still. Myriads of stars twinkled in the dark sky; ere long good omens appeared. Just as Pan Lantskorovski with his field marshal's baton in his hand approached the prince in order to hand it over to him, a star fell from the vault of the sky and leaving after it a stream of light like a comet, disappeared in the direction of Konstantinov, from whence Khmyelnitski was known to be advancing.

"That was Khmyelnitski's star," cried the soldiers.

"A miracle! A miracle! A visible sign! Long live Yeremy the victor," exclaimed a thousand voices; and the commander of Konstantinov approached and made a sign with his hand to indicate that he wished to speak. Silence fell and he said:

"The King gave me this baton, but I surrender it into your more deserving hands, O victor! and wish to be the first to submit myself to your orders."

"And we also," exclaimed the two other commanders.

Three batons were extended towards the prince, but he drew back his hand and said:

"It was not I who gave you your rank, and therefore I cannot take it from you."

"Together with the three, let there be a fourth," said Firley.

"Long live Vishnyovyetski! long live the commanders!" exclaimed all the nobles, "we will live and die together."

At this moment the prince's horse raised its head, shook its reddish mane, and neighed mightily, while all the horses in the camp answered in unison.

This also was taken as an omen of victory, the eyes of the soldiers flashed fire, the thirst for battle filled their hearts, and a tremor of enthusiasm ran through their bodies. The chiefs shared the general enthusiasm. The Cup-Bearer wept and prayed, the Castellan of Kamenets and the Starosta of Krasnostavsk were the first to clatter their sabres, exciting the soldiers, who, rushing upon the ramparts, stretched their hands out in the darkness towards the direction from whence they expected the enemy, and cried aloud:

"Come on, you dog-brothers, we are ready for you."

That night no one slept in the camp; and until the dawn broke the shouts lasted and the pine torches burned.

In the morning the crown secretary Sierakovski returned from a scouting expedition to Cholhanski Kamyen and reported that the enemy were about five miles from the camp. The expedition had given battle to an outnumbering horde and the two Mankovski, Oleksich and several other trusty soldiers had fallen. Prisoners that had been taken affirmed that behind the horde, Khmyelnitski and the Khan with all their forces were approaching. The day passed in waiting and preparations for defence. The prince having assumed command immediately put the army in order, indicating where each section should take its position and directing how each should defend itself and give succor to the others. A cheerful spirit displayed itself in the camp; discipline was established, and in place of the former confusion, conflict of authority, and uncertainty, good order and accuracy prevailed. In the forenoon all took up their positions. The sentries thrown forward reported from time to time what was going on in the vicinity. Servants sent out to the neighboring villages brought back as much of provisions and provender as they could lay their hands upon. The soldiers upon the ramparts chattered cheerfully and sang, and passed the night in sleeping about the camp-fires, their swords in their hands, ready for the fray at any moment that the fortress might be stormed.

At dawn indeed something black emerged from the direction of Vishnyovtsa. The bells in the town sounded an alarm, and in the camp the plaintive notes of the trumpets put the soldiers on the alert. The infantry regiments drew up on the ramparts, in the openings the cavalry stood ready to attack at the first signal, and along the entire line of the intrenchment little clouds of smoke arose from the fuses.

At this moment the prince appeared upon his white charger. He wore silver armour but no helmet. His eyes shone with gladness and no shadow of concern clouded his countenance.

"We have guests, gentlemen, we have guests," he repeated, riding along the ramparts.

Silence reigned; nothing was heard but the flutter of banners playing in the breeze. The enemy approached nearer and could now be plainly seen.

It was but the first wave that dashed up now, not Khmyelnitsky and the Khan, but a reconnaissance of thirty thousand picked Tartars, armed with bows, muskets, and sabres. Having taken captive fifteen hundred men that had been sent out for provisions, they advanced in dense columns from Vishnyovtsa, and stretching out in a long semicircle they went around from the opposite side towards old Zbaraj.

The prince perceiving that this was but the vanguard of the approaching army ordered the cavalry to advance from the entrenchments. Words of command were heard, the regiments advanced and poured out from behind the ramparts like bees from a hive. The plain was filled with men and horses. From afar the captains with batons in their hands could be seen riding around in squadrons placing them in line of battle. The horses snorted and occasionally their neighs sounded through the lines. Then from out the mass emerged two divisions of Tartars and Semenovs of the prince and went forward in an easy trot. Their bows shook on their backs,, their caps gleamed—they rode in silence, at their head the fair-haired Vyershul, whose horse reared like mad, throwing its forehoofs in the air as if it wished to toss aside its bit and throw itself into the tumult.

There was not a cloud in the blue sky, the day was clear and serene, the advancing host could be discerned as on the palm of the hand.

At this moment there appeared from the direction of old Zbaraj a small wagon-train belonging to the prince, which had not entered with the army and now hurried on as fast as possible lest the horde should capture it. Indeed it did not escape their vigilance; and soon the long half-moon pushed forward to suround it. Shouts of "Allah!" came to the ears of the infantry on the ramparts. Vyershul's squadrons flew like a whirlwind to the rescue.

But the half-moon reached the train first and surrounded it in a moment like a black ribbon. Simultaneously some thousands of the horde with unearthly howls turned towards Vyershul to surround him also. But here Vyershul's experience and the skill of his soldiers came into play. When he saw that the horde was surrounding him he divided his forces into three parts and galloped to the sides, then he divided them into four parts and then into two; so that each time the enemy had to swing round having no opponent to face. The enemy's wings were thus broken. At the fourth turning they met breast to breast. Vyershul at once attacked the weakest part with his whole strength broke through the line at the first crash and got in the rear of the enemy. Then careless of pursuit he swept towards the wagon-train. Old veterans, who from the ramparts had watched this manoeuvre stuck their arms akimbo and shouted and exclaimed:

"May the balls strike them! only the Prince's captains can lead in this way."

Then in the form of a sharp wedge Vyershul flew towards the wagon-train and struck the ring encircling it as an arrow pierces the body of a man, and immediately penetrated to the centre. Now instead of two combats one raged alone, but all the fiercer. It was a wonderful sight. The wagon-train in the centre of the plain like a moving fortress puffed out clouds of smoke and spat forth fire. Encircling it a black swarm like a mighty whirlwind, horses rushing about without riders; within a wild uproar and the rattling of muskets. In one place some were crowding upon each other, in another they kept unbroken order. As a wild boar that is surrounded tears with his white tusks the bloodthirsty pack of hounds, so that wagon-train defended itself against the Tartars, hoping that other and stronger aid than Viyershul's might come.

Indeed it was not long before the red dragoons of Kushel and Volodiyovski swept along the plain, looking like red flowers driven along by the breeze. They reached the crowd of Tartars and rushing into it as if into a black forest, were soon lost to sight; but the terrible uproar grew louder. The soldiers wondered that the Prince did not send at once a sufficient force to the rescue; but he delayed purposely in order to show the soldiers the kind of warriors that he had brought with him, and so to increase their courage and prepare them for greater dangers.

The firing from the wagon-train grew fainter, there was evidently no time to load, or the musket barrels had grown too hot. But the shouts of the Tartars grew louder. Then the prince gave a signal and immediately three squadrons of hussars, his own under Skshetuski, one under the Starosta of Krasnostavsk, and a royal squadron under Piglovski shot out of the camp into the battle-field. They charged from the rear, broke through the ring of Tartars like an axe, dispersed them over the plain, chased them towards the woods and drove them a quarter of a mile from the camp. The little wagon-train entered the entrenchments in safety amid the shouts of triumph and thunders of cannon.

The Tartars however knowing that Khmyelnitski and the Khan were close behind, remained in the neighborhood and soon appeared again. With shouts of "Allah!" they circled around the camp, occupying the highways and surrounding the villages, from which black columns of smoke soon arose. Quite a number of horsemen came up close to the entrenchments; these were at once attacked by the soldiers of the prince, especially by detachments of Tartar, Wallachian and dragoon regiments.

Viyershul was unable to take part in these sallies. He had received six wounds on his head while defending the wagon-train and lay in his tent as if dead. Volodiyovski, however, who was as red as a lobster from bloodstains, and could scarce appease his thirst for combat, was everywhere to the front. The skirmishes lasted until evening, the infantry and the knights of reserved squadrons watched the fighting from the ramparts as if looking upon a play. Many prisoners were made and when Pan Michael had made an end of one he turned again and his red uniform was seen flying all over the field. Skshetuski from afar pointed him out to Pan Lantskoronski as a curiosity, for whenever he met a Tartar, the man fell as if struck by lightning. Zagloba, though he could not be heard by Pan Michael, kept shouting out encouraging words from the ramparts. From time to time he addressed the soldiers around him, saying:

"Look, gentlemen, that is the way I taught him to use his sabre. Good! keep on! with God's aid he will soon equal me."

The sun had set meantime, and the soldiers began to retire from the field, on which there remained only dead men and horses. In the town the bells rang the Angelus.

Night came on gradually but it did not grow dark, for all about was the glow of fires. Many villages were in flames, Zaloshtsits, Barzynts, Lublanki, Striyooka, Kretovits, Zariedzie, Vakhlovka, and the entire vicinity as far as the eye could see was ablaze. The clouds of smoke appeared red in the night, the stars shone out from a red background. Great flocks of birds frightened out of the woods and from the thickets and ponds, circled in the reddened air like flying flames. The cattle in their enclosures, frightened at the unusual sight, were bellowing pitifully.

"It is impossible that the vanguard alone has caused such a conflagration," said the veterans to one another in the entrenchments, "without doubt Khmyelnitski with the Cossacks and the entire horde is close at hand."

These were not mere surmises for Pan Sierakovski on the day previous had brought news that the Hetman of the Zaporojians together with the Khan were closely following their vanguard, thus they were expected with certainty. All the soldiers were upon the ramparts, the people were upon the roofs and towers. All were greatly excited. Women wept in the churches and raised imploring hands to the most Holy Sacrament. The fearful suspense bore most heavily upon all, in the camp, in the castle, and the town.

But it did not last long, the night had not passed when the first ranks of the Cossacks and Tartars appeared on the horizon. They were followed by more, by tens, by hundreds and thousands, until it seemed as if all the trees of the forests and groves had cut loose from their roots and were marching towards Zbaraj. In vain did the eye seek an end to those lines. As far as the eye could see there appeared a swarm of men and horses the end of which appeared to be lost in the smoke and flame afar off. Like clouds or like locusts they moved on, covering the entire region with a dreadful moving mass. Before them came the threatening murmurs of human voices like the sough of the wind among the tops of hoary pines in the forest. About a quarter of a mile from the camp they halted and spread themselves about and lit their night-fires.

"You see the fires!" whispered the soldiers, "they spread farther than a horse can go in one breathing."

"Jesus Maria!" said Zagloba to Skshetuski. "I have within me the courage of a lion and feel no fear, but I wish that before to-morrow a flaming thunderbolt might wipe them from the earth. By the love of God, there are too many of them. There will not be a greater throng in the valley of Jehosaphat. And tell me, what do the thieves want? Would it not be better if these thieves remained at home and worked quietly on the land. How can we help it if God has made us nobles and them peasants, with the duty of obedience imposed upon them. Puh! I get furious when I think about it. I am a mild sort of a man and could be applied to wounds, but let them not rouse my wrath! They have been allowed too much liberty, too much bread, therefore they have multiplied like mice in a barn and now wish to fight with the cats. But just wait! wait! here's a cat called Prince Yeremy, and another whose name is Zagloba. What do you think? Will such men stop to negotiate? If the peasants were submissive then their lives might be spared, might they not? One thing worries me all the time and that is if there be a sufficient stock of provisions in the camp. To the devil with it! just look, gentlemen, there behind the conflagration new fires arising, and further away still more fires, may the black plague destroy such a gathering."

"Why talk about negotiations," answered Skshetuski, "when they believe they have everything in their own hands and that they can wipe us out to-morrow."

"But they can't do it, can they?" asked Zagloba.

"That rests with God, but at any rate since the prince is here it will not be easy for them."

"You console me indeed. What do I care if it be easy for them or not; the thing that concerns me is whether they can succeed at all."

"It is no slight consolation for a soldier to feel that he is not laying down his life for nothing."

"To be sure! to be sure! . . . But lightning strike it all! and your consolation with it."

At this moment Longin and Volodiyovski approached.

"The Cossacks and the hordes altogether are said to number half a million," said the Lithuanian.

"May your tongue be cut out!" said Zagloba, "you bring cheerful news."

"It will be easier to repulse them in assault than to attack them in the open field," answered Longin mildly.

"Now that the prince and Khmyelnitski have at last met," said Pan Michael, "there will be no talk about negotiations. Either the governor or the monk. To-morrow will be judgment day," he added rubbing his hands.

The little knight was right, in that war the two fiercest lions had not yet met face to face. The one had conquered the hetmans and the commanders; the other had defeated the mighty Cossack atamans. Each had always been victorious, each was the terror of his enemies; but this encounter was to decide whose scale was to rise or fall. Vishnyovyetski beheld from the ramparts the countless myriads of Tartars and Cossacks and in vain strained his eyes to get them all in view. Khmyelnitski from the field beheld the castle and the camp and thought to himself:

"Over there is my most terrible enemy. If I crush him, who then will stand in my way?"

It was evident that the struggle between these two men would rage long and stubbornly, but the ultimate result could not be doubtful. The Prince at Lubni and Vishnyovtsa stood at the head of fifteen thousand men, the camp-servants included; while behind the peasant chieftain stood all the forces from the sea of Azov and the Don to the mouth of the Danube. Then also with him was the Khan leading the hordes of the Crimea, of Byalogrod, Nohaysh, and of the Dobrudja; the tribes living along the banks of the Dnieper and Dniester, the Nijovs, and a countless "blacks" from the steppes, woods, ravines, towns, villages, hamlets, and farms, and all who had formerly served under the crown; all these were with Khmyelnitski. Besides these, Circasssians, Wallachian, Karalash, Silistrian, and Rumelian Turks, and bands of Servians and Bulgarians joined him. It seemed as if a new migration of nations were taking place, that the nations had abandoned their homes in the freezing steppes and were going westward to conquer new lands and to found a new empire.

This was the proportional strength of the contending forces . . . a handful against hundreds of thousands, an island against the sea. It was no wonder therefore, that many a heart beat with alarm; that not only this town, not only this corner of the country, but the whole Commonwealth looked upon this lonely entrenchment circled by a deluge of wild warriors as the tomb of noble knights and of their great leader.

Khmyelnitski also regarded it in the same light, for hardly had the fires been kindled in his camp when there appeared before the entrenchments a Cossack envoy waving a white flag, blowing upon his trumpet and crying out not to shoot at him.

The sentinuels admitted him at once.

"I come from the hetman to Prince Yeremy," he said to them.

The prince had not yet dismounted, and was on the walls, his face bright as heaven. The fires were reflected in his eyes and made a rosy halo about his delicate white face. When the Cossack stood before the prince he lost his power of speech, his legs trembled, and ants seemed to be crawling over his body although he was an experienced soldier and had come as an envoy.

"Who are you?" asked the prince in a quiet tone.

"I am Captain Sokol. . . . sent by the hetman."

"And what is your message?"

The captain bowed his head several times as low as the stirrups of the prince.

"Pardon me, Prince, I repeat what I was commanded to say; I am innocent."

"Speak boldly."

"The hetman commanded me to announce to you that he came as a guest to Zbaraj and intends to visit you at the castle to-morrow."

"Tell him that not to-morrow, but to-day, I give a feast in the castle," answered the prince.

Indeed an hour later the cannons thundered forth salutes, shouts of joy were heard, and the windows of the palace were illumined by thousands of gleaming lights.

When the Khan heard the vivats and the sound of the kettledrums and trumpets, he stepped out in front of his tent in company with his brother Nur-ed-Din, the sultana Galga, Tukhay Bey, and many murzas, and sent for Khmyelnitski.

The hetman, though somewhat intoxicated, appeared at once, and bowing and placing his fingers on his forehead, on his chin, and on his breast, he awaited thepleasure of the Khan.

For a long time the Khan gazed at the brightly-illumined

palace shining in the distance and nodded his head, then he ran his fingers through his thin beard falling in two locks over his fur shuba and pointing to the shining windows, asked:

"Hetman of the Zaporojians, what is going on there?"

"Mighty Tsar," answered Khmyelnitski, "Prince Yeremy is giving a feast."

The Khan was astonished.

"He is feasting?"

"It is a funeral feast," answered Khmyelnitski, "for to-morrow they will all be dead."

Meanwhile fresh salvos arose from the castle and the sounds of trumpets and confused shouts shouts reached the Khan's ears.

"La Allah ila Allah," murmured the Khan, "this Giaour has a lion heart."

After a short silence he added:

"I would rather be with him than with you."

Khmyelnitski trembled. He had paid dearly already for the indispensable friendship of the Tartars, but he was not sure of his terrible ally. The slightest whim of the Khan would turn the horde against the Cossacks and irretrievably ruin them. Khmyelnitski knew that the Khan was only lending his aid for the sake of booty, gifts, and captives, and that he regarded himself as a legitimate monarch, he blushed inwardly that he was supporting an uprising against a king, and that he was an accomplice of a Khmyelnitski against such a Vishnyovyetski.

The Cossack commander often filled himself with drink not only from force of habit but from despair. . . .

"Great monarch," he cried, "Yeremy is our enemy. He has driven the Tartars from the Trans-Dieper, he has hung murzas like wolves upon the trees in order to spread terror, he intended to ravage the Crimea with fire and sword."

"And you? have you committed no depredations in the ulusas?" asked the Khan.

"I am your slave."

Tukhay Bey's blue lips began to tremble and his eyes flashed. He had a deadly enemy among the Cossacks, who once upon a time had destroyed and beaten down a whole chambul and he himself had almost perished. The name of that man forced itself with the power of hateful recollections to the lips of the murza; he could not restrain himself and hissed out "Burlay! Burlay!"

"Tukhay Bey," said Khmyelnitski, "you and Burlay at the exalted and wise command of the Khan poured water on your blades last year."

A new salvo from the castle interrupted their discourse.

The Khan extended his hand and described a circle, enclosing in it Zbaraj, the castle, and the entrenchments. "Will all that be mine to-morrow?" asked he addressing Khmyelnitski.

"To-morrow, they must all die," answered Khmyelnitski, his eyes glued upon the castle.

Then he bowed again, and touched with his hand his brow and chin and breast, considering the interview closed.

The Khan wrapped himself in his fur, for the July night was quite cool and turning towards the tent said:

"It is late . . . "

All nodded, while the Khan deep in thought went slowly to his tent murmuring in a low voice "La Allah ila Allah."

Khmyelnitski proceeded towards his own tent muttering to himself on the way: "The castle, the town, the booty, and the captives I leave to you; but Yeremy belongs to me, even should I have to pay for him with my neck."

Gradually the fires began to die down. Gradually the dull murmur of hundreds of thousands of voices died away; here and there might be heard the sound of pipes, or the shouting of the Tartar herdsmen as they drove horses to pasture during the night; after a while however these sounds became still, and sleep reigned over the countless legions of Cossacks and Tartars.

Only in the castle was there a sound of revelry, as if a wedding were being celebrated there. In the camp it was generally expected that the storm would break on the morrow. Indeed, a throng of Cossacks, Tartars, and other wild warriors advanced from Khmyelnitski at an early hour towards the entrenchments like dark clouds enveloping the summit of a mountain. The soldiers who on the preceding day had been unable to count the camp-fires were now astonished at the sight of this sea of heads. This was not yet an attack, but an examination of the field, the ramparts, the trenches and the entire Polish encampment. And as a swelling wave of the ocean driven by the wind from afar approaches the shore, surges, foams with rage, strikes with a roar and then recedes into the distance, so they made an attack, here and there, receding and advancing again as if wishing to test the enemy's power of resistance and to convince themselves that the mere sight of their numbers would crush the spirit of the enemy before they destroyed its body.

They opened fire also and the balls fell thickly about the camp, which quickly responded with lively volleys. Now there appeared upon the ramparts a procession bearing the most Holy Sacrament in order to encourage the soldiers. The priest Mukhovietski bore the golden Pix, raising it with both hands before his face and sometimes high aloft. He walked beneath an embroidered canopy, his face bore the marks of asceticism, his eyes were closed, and upon his head he wore a hood. Beside him walked two priests who supported him under the elbows—Yaskolski the chaplain of the hussars, formerly a famous soldier and well-versed in the art of war, the other Jabkovski was also an ex-soldier, a gigantic monk of St. Bernard and second in strength throughout the whole camp only to Longin. The poles of the canopy was carried by four noblemen, one of whom was Zagloba, and they were preceeded by little girls with sweet faces who scattered flowers. The procession marched over the entire length of the ramparts and after it marched the officers of the army. The soldiers, when they beheld the shining pix, the calm faces of the priests and the girls dressed in their white garments, felt their hearts swell and became filled with enthusiasm. The wind scattered the powerful odor of burning myrrh in the censers, and the heads of all were bowed in humility. Mukhovietski raised the pix aloft from time to time and elevating his eyes towards heaven intoned the hymn beginning "Before such a great Sacrament."

The powerful voices of Yaskolski and Jabkovski continued "We fall on our faces!" and soon the entire army swelled the chant "Let the old law give way to the new." The deep bass of the cannon accompanied the hymn and at times hissing cannon-balls flew over the canopy or fell within the ramparts, frightening Zagloba, who squeezed himself close to the canopy-post. Especially did fear overcome him when the procession halted for prayer. At such times the whizzing of the cannon-balls could be distinctly heard flying overhead like great birds in a flock. Zagloba grew more red in the face, and chaplain Yaskolski looking aside over the field murmured to himself "they are only fit to tend chickens and should not meddle with cannon." Indeed the Cossacks had very poor gunners and he as an old soldier could not calmly bear the sight of this poor markmanship and waste of powder. Again the procession moved on until it arrived at the other end of the ramparts where there was no great pressure from the enemy. After the Cossacks and Tartars had attempted again and again to strike terror and panic among the besieged, they finally withdrew to their own positions and remained there. Meantime the procession had strengthened the hearts of the besieged.

It was evident that Khmyelnitski was awaiting the arrival of his wagon-train. He seemed to be so sure of capturing the fort at the first assault that he scarcely had any trenches made for the cannon and raised no other earthworks to defend himself from the besieged. The wagon-train arrived on the following day and arranged themselves in several tens of rows of wagons stretching from Vernyakov to Denbina a distance of about one mile. With it also arrived reinforcements, first of which were the splendid Zaporojian infantry, who could almost be compared to the Turkish janissaries, and who were far better adapted to make an assault than the Tartars or the rest of the "blacks" about Zbaraj.

Tuesday, July 13th, was passed in feverish preparations on both sides. There was no doubt that the assault had been ordered, for trumpets and kettledrums sounded the alarm from early morning among the Cossacks, while in the Tartars' camp the great sacred drum, called the Balt, rolled like thunder. Evening fell clear and calm; but from the lakes and the Gniezna light fogs arose—at length the first star twinkled in the sky.

At once sixty Cossack cannons belched forth smoke and flame with a simultaneous roar. Countless legions rushed with frightful yells towards the walls—the assault had begun.

To the soldiers standing on the ramparts, the earth appeared to tremble beneath their feet. The oldest veterans could recall no such scene.

"Jesus Maria! what is that!" asked Zagloba standing beside Skshetuski in a breach between the ramparts giving orders to his hussars, "these are not men that are coming against us."

"You know that they are not men; the enemy are driving oxen ahead so that we may waste our powder first upon them."

The old nobleman grew red as a beet, his eyes started from their sockets, and one word forced its way through his lips which expressed his feelings at the moment "scoundrels."

The oxen, urged on with clubs and burning brands by the wild herdsmen, became mad through fear. They rushed forward with a terrible bellowing, now crowding each other, now hurrying on, now scattering and turning backward; urged by shouts and scourged with raw hides they surged up to the ramparts. Now Vurtsel made his cannons speak, smoke filled the air, the sky became red as scarlet, the frightened beasts scattered as if dispersed by lightning, half of them falling to the ground while the enemy marched over their bodies.

Captives driven by spears and firebrands ran ahead with sand bags with which to fill the trenches. These were peasants from the neighborhood of Zbaraj who had not had time to flee into the town before the enemy arrived, among them were men both old and young, and also women. They ran along weeping, shrieking, and their hands outstretched towards heaven, praying for mercy. That wailing made the hair stand on end but compassion was dead at that moment; from the rear the spears of the Cossacks threatened them, in front Vurtsel's cannon-balls crushed them, grape-shot tore them to pieces and made long furrows amid the rows of these wretched ones; they ran ahead wading in blood, stumbling, rising again, and rushing onward, with a vast pack of Cossacks, Turks, and Tartars close upon their heels.

The fosse was soon filled with corpses, blood and sandbags, soon it was even with the ground and the enemy rushed over with shouts and yells.

One regiment pushed on after the other; by the light of the cannon flashes the officers could be seen driving with their batons fresh masses against the ramparts. The picked troops assaulted the quarters and soldiers of Prince Yeremy, for Khmyelnitski knew well that there would be the greatest resistance. First the soldiers from Sich, behind them the terrible Pereyaslav legions under Loboda, besides these Vorochenko led a regiment of Circassians, Kuak led the Karovovsk regiment, Nechay the Bratlav, Stepka, the Uman, Mrozoyetski the Korsun; there were also the Kalnik and the powerful division of Byalotserkiev, fifteen thousand men, and with them Khmyelnitski looking as red as Satan amid the fires, his breast open and exposed to the shots of the enemy, with the eye of an eagle and the face of a lion, amid all the chaos, smoke, confusion of battle, and flames, planning everything, ordering everything.

Behind the Cossacks came the wild Don Cossacks then the Circassians armed with knives; near by Tukhay Bey led picked troops of Nogais, after them came the Subagazi Byalogrod Tartars, followed by Kurdluk swarthy Astrakhans armed with gigantic bows, and arrows. They followed one another so closely that the hot breath of those behind were felt by those in front of them.

Who can tell or describe how many fell ere they reached the trench filled with the bodies of captives. But they reached it, crossed it, and began to climb the ramparts. It seemed as if this night, bright with stars, was the night of Judgment. Cannon balls which flew over the heads of the nearer, ploughed into the farther ranks. Bombs, with hellish hissing noises, described fiery arcs in the darkness, making the darkest of night as light as day. The German and Polish infantry with the dismounted dragoons of the prince at their side poured fire and lead upon the faces and breasts of the Cossacks.

The front ranks desired to retreat, but pushed from behind, they could not. Thus they fell on the spot. Blood spouted beneath the feet of those that advanced. The ramparts grew slippery; feet, hands, and breasts slid from them. The men clambering up, slid off, climbed up again to be enveloped in clouds of smoke, blackened with soot, stabbed, beaten, but disregarding death and wounds. Here and there hand to hand combats took place. Men could be seen as though possessed and maddened with rage grinding their teeth and with faces covered with blood.   .   . The survivors fought over the quivering bodies of the dead and dying. Commands could no longer be heard, they were drowned in the terrible general uproar that merged all sounds, the thunder of guns, the groans of the wounded and the hissing of the grenades.

The terrible struggle wherein no quarter was given lasted for hours. About the rampart another was formed by corpses, which hindered the assailants. The Sich Cossacks were almost butchered to a man, the Pereyaslav regiment lay in rows about the rampart. The Karkovsk, Bratslav and Uman divisions were decimated—still others pressed forward, pushed from behind by the guard of the hetman, the Rumelian Turks and Tartars of Urumbey. Now confusion rose amid the ranks of the assailants, for the Polish infantry, the Germans, and the dragoons did not yield a step. Panting,

45

covered with blood, streaming with sweat, half mad with
the smell of blood, they flung themselves one after another
upon the enemy like raging wolves upon a flock of sheep.
At this moment Khmyelnitski pressed forward with the
remnants of the first divisions and with his fresh forces of
Byalotserkiev; Tartars, Turks, and Circassians. The cannons ceased thundering, bombs whizzed no more, hand weapons alone made themselves heard along the western rampart. Shouting commenced anew. At last even the firing
of muskets ceased. Darkness enveloped the combatants. No
eye could see what was taking place but something was
rolling along in the darkness like a gigantic body quivering
in convulsions, it was impossible to tell from the cries which
arose whether they were cries of triumph or despair. At
times even these ceased and then nothing could be heard
save one immense and horrible groan from all sides as if
it issued from beneath the earth and from its surface into
the air higher and higher as if the souls of the fallen were
flying aloft and groaning over the battle-field.

But these were but occasional pauses, after which the uproar and howls grew louder and the unearthly noise of combat became fiercer and more terrible.

Again was heard the crackle of muskets, for Major
Makhnitski with the rest of the infantry came up to the aid
of the exhausted regiments. In the rear ranks of the enemy
the trumpets sounded a retreat.

There was a pause in the combat, the Cossacks retreated
about a furlong from the ramparts and placed themselves
under the protection of their cannon; but within half an hour
Khmyelnitski drove them for the third time to the assault.

Now Prince Yeremy appeared on the ramparts. It was
easy to recognize him, for the pennon and bunchuk, insignia
of the hetman's rank, waved above his head, while before
and behind him were borne flaring torches, making a blood
red glare. Soon the enemy's cannon were belching at him,
but the artillery-men aimed badly and the balls flew high
above him, beyond the Gniezna, while he stood calmly and
surveyed the approaching masses.

The Cossacks slackened their pace as if dazzled by the sight
of him. A murmur like the quick whisper of the breeze
swept through their ranks.

"Yeremy! Yeremy!"

On the rampart in the glare of the blood-red torches the

prince appeared to them like a fabulous giant in folk lore.

A tremor ran through their weary limbs and their hands made the sign of the cross.

But Yeremy stood still. He waved his golden baton and at once a swarm of death-dealing bombs hurtled through the air and fell into the enemy's ranks. Like a wounded dragon the dense mass writhed and a cry of terror was heard from one end of the line to the other.

"Forward! Forward!" shouted the Cossack colonels.

The dark mass rushed at full speed towards the ramparts beneath which was shelter from the bombs. But they had not made half the distance when the prince, who was clearly visible, turned towards the west and again waved his baton.

At the signal the cavalry moved forward from beside the pond, out of the gap between it and the rampart, and immediately poured out on the plain. By the light of the bombs could be recognized the great banners of Skshetuski's and Zatsvilikhovski's hussars, the dragoons of Kushel and Volodiyovski and the Tartars of the prince under Rostvorovski. They were followed by fresh regiments of Semenovs and Wallachians under Bychov. Not only Khmyelnitski, but even the last camp-follower of the Cossacks, recognized in a flash that the audacious prince was going to hurl his entire cavalry upon the enemy's flank.

At once trumpets in the lines of the assailants sounded a retreat. "Front face to the cavalry! front face to the cavalry!" voices of command exclaimed in alarm. Simultaneously Khmyelnitski endeavored to change his front and to place cavalry against cavalry. But it was too late. Ere he was able to form his cavalry the squadrons of the prince came rushing as if on wings shouting their battle cry "Strike! Kill!" Banners rustled, plumes waved, and iron weapons clashed. The hussars with their lances hurled themselves upon the wall of the enemy like a hurricane and bore everything before them. No human power, no command, no leader, could hold the infantry against which the first attack was directed. Wild panic seized the picked guard of the hetman. The soldiers of Byalotserkiev threw away their muskets, spears, swords, daggers, and scythes, and shielding their heads with their hands, they rushed in blind terror and roaring like beasts against the Tartars in the rear. The Tartars however received them with a rain of bullets and arrows, so they threw themselves upon the flank and ran along the wagon-train under the constant fire of the infantry and the cannons of Vurtsel, leaving behind them such a great crowd of corpses that they lay one on top of the other.

Now the wild Tukhay Bey together with Subagazi and Urum Murzas pressed like mad upon the advancing hussars. He did not hope to break their power but simply wished to delay them in order to win time for the Silistrian and Rumelian Janissaries to form into squares and to protect the Byalot-serkiev men from the first panic. As if he were a common Tartar and not a chief he rushed at the enemy in the van of his troops and fought desperately, exposing himself to dangers with the rest. The curved swords of the Nogais clashed upon armor and breast plates, and the howl of the warriors drowned all other sounds. But they could not hold their ground. Forced from their position by the terrible attacks of the iron horsemen against whom they were unaccustomed to stand with open front, they were driven back towards the Janissaries, thrown from their saddles, hacked with long sabres, pierced through, beaten and crushed like poisonous reptiles, they still defended themselves with such furious valor that they did actually check the onset of the hussars. Tukhay Bey raged like a destroying flame and the Nogais kept close at his side, like wolves following a she-wolf.

Still they had to give way, leaving more and more corpses behind them. When thundering cries of "Allah!" announced that the Janissaries had formed, Skshetuski threw himself upon the raging Tukhay Bey and struck him upon the head with his sword. But whether the knight had not yet regained his strength after his illness, or whether the helmet of Damascus steel withstood the blow, the blade bent on Tukhay Bey's head and was shattered to fragments.

Tukhay Bey closed his eyes and fell into the arms of his Nogais who escaped with their chief amid the general uproar like clouds scudding before wind. The entire cavalry of the prince was now fronting the Rumelian and Silistrian janissaries and the Mohammedan Serbians who together with the janissaries had formed an immense square and were slowly retreating towards the wagon-train with their front to the enemy, bristling with muskets, spears, javelins, battle-axes, and swords.

The squadrons of heavy dragoon and the Semenovs of the prince rushed like a whirlwind upon the square; at their head, with great noise and rattle of sabres rode Skshetuski's hussars. He himself rushed on in the van and beside him rode Longin upon his Livonian mare, his terrible broadsword "Cowl-trencher" held aloft.

A red band of flame flew from one end of the quadrangle to the other, bullets whistled about the ears of the riders, here and there a man groaned or a horse fell, but still they chased ahead. Now they neared the enemy and the Janissaries can distinctly hear the snorting and blown breath of the horses. The square is formed more closely and a wall of spears is inclined against the onrushing horses. As many points as there were in that cloud, so many knights were threatened.

Just then a gigantic hussar rushes with tremendous speed upon the wall of the square; for a moment the forefeet of the frantic horse rise in the air, then steed and rider fall upon the crowded mass, overturning men, splintering spears, and spreading destruction.

As an eagle swoops upon a flock of white partridges which crowd together in terror and become easy prey, and are torn to pieces with beak and talon, so Pan Longin Podbipyenta swooped upon the enemy and raged with his "Cowl-trencher." A cloudburst could not create greater havoc in a young and dense forest than did he among the throng of Janissaries. He was terrible. His form assumed superhuman proportions; his horse seemed to transform itself into a dragon snorting flame from its nostrils. Kisler-Bak, a gigantic aga, threw himself upon him, but fell cut in two. In vain did the strongest men attempt to check him with their spears, they fell as if struck by lightning. He trampled upon them, forced himself into the densest throng, and whenever he wielded his mighty sword it seemed as if corn were falling beneath the scythe. The crowd thinned out about him; one could hear yells, groans, the thunder of blows, the crash of steel upon the helmets and the snorting of the hellish mare.

"A Div! A Div!"[1] shouted terrified voices.

At this moment the iron mass of hussars with Skshetuski at its head rushed through the breach made by the Lithuanian knight, the walls of the square burst like those of a falling house; the throngs of Janissaries took to flight in every direction.

It was just in the nick of time, for the Nogais under Su-

---

[1] Devil.

bagazi were now returning to the battle like bloodthirsty wolves, and on the other side Khmyelnitski had rallied the Byalotserkiev men and was hurrying to the aid of the janissaries; but now there was general confusion. Cossacks, Tartars, Mussulmen, Janissaries, without offering the slightest resistance, fled in wild terror towards the wagon-train. The cavalry pursued them, hewing down everything in the way. Those who had not fallen in the first assault perished now. The pursuit was so hot that the squadrons rushed ahead of the rear ranks of the fugitives and their hands grew weary from cutting and slashing. The flying men threw away their weapons, flags, caps, and even their coats. The white caps of the janissaries covered the field like snowflakes. The entire picked force of Khmyelnitski's infantry, the cavalry and artillery, as well as the Tartar and Turkish auxiliary forces formed one disorderly mass, senseless, wild, and blind with fright. Entire companies fled before single officers. The hussars having scattered the infantry and cavalry, had done their work; now the dragoons and light squadrons rushed in, and Volodiyovski and Kushel did incredible mischief. The battle field became a great sea of blood which splashed like water beneath the hoofs of the horses and besprinkled the armor and faces of the knights.

The fleeing crowds only drew breath when they reached the centre of the wagon-train and the trumpets of the prince's cavalry sounded a retreat.

The knights returned singing and shouting in triumph, and counting on their way with bloody swords the corpses of the enemy. But who could estimate at a glance the extent of the defeat? Who could count all that had perished when in the trench alone the bodies were heaped up to the height of a man? The soldiers were almost overcome by the smell of blood and sweat. Fortunately quite a strong breeze blew from the lakes and carried the odors to the enemy's tents.

Thus ended the first encounter between the terrible Yeremy and Khmyelnitski.

But the end of the storm was not yet, for while Vishnyovyetski repulsed the attacks directed against the right wing of the camp, Burlay had almost made himself master of the entrenchments. He had surorunded the town and castle with his warriors from the region beyond the Dnieper and had pushed on to the eastern lake and fiercely attacked Firley's quarters. The Hungarian infantry division stationed

there were unable to withstand the attack, for the entrenchments at the pond were not yet finished; the first company
fled from the banner and was soon followed by the entire
regiment. Burlay rode at full speed to the centre, followed
by his men like an irresistible torrent. The shouts of victory were heard at the opposite end of the camp. The Cossacks who pursued the fleeing Hungarians, crushed a small
division of cavalry, took several cannon, and had almost
reached the quarters of the Castellan of Belsk when Pshiyenski at the head of several German companies rushed to
the rescue. Striking down the flag-bearer with a single
thrust he seized the flag and threw himself with it upon the
enemy. The Germans closed with the Cossacks and a terrible
hand-to-hand combat ensued, in which on one side fought
with fury the crushing numbers of Burlay's forces and on
the other the courage of the old lions of the Thirty Years
War. In vain did Burlay like a wounded boar charge into
the densest ranks of the combatants. Neither the scorn of
death nor the fierceness with which the Cossacks fought,
could check the Germans, who pressed upon the Zaporojians
with such force that they swept them from their places,
scattered them, and after a half-hour's struggle, drove them
beyond the entrenchments.

Pshiyemski, covered with blood, planted the flag upon the
half-finished rampart.

Burlay was now placed in a terrible position. He was
forced to retreat by the same road on which he had come;
and since Prince Yeremy had already crushed those who
had attacked the right wing, he could now with great ease
cut off the retreat of Burlay's division. And though Myro-
zovitski at the head of the Korsun Cossack cavalry came to
his aid, at the same moment Konyetspolski's hussars supported by those of Skshetuski, returning from the attack
upon the Janissaries, fell upon Burlay who had been retreating in order.

One shock scattered Burlay's forces in all directions, and a
terrible slaughter ensued. Cut off from retreat to the wagon-
train, death alone remained for the Cossacks. Some without
asking for quarter, defended thmselves singly or in small
groups with the fury of despair. Others in vain stretched
imploring hands towards the cavalry that was thundering
like a tempest over the field. Then began pursuit and a
search for enemies who had hidden themselves in holes or

in uneven places in the ground. In order to light the battle-field, burning barrels of tar were rolled down from the en-trenchments, resembling blazing meteors with fiery tails, as they fell. By their red light the remainder of the Trans-Dnieper horde were destroyed. Subagazi who had on that day performed marvels of valor, flew to the aid, but the valiant Marek Sobieski, the chief of Krasnostavsk, stopped him as a lion stops a wild buffalo. Burlay saw now that all was lost. But he loved his Cossack honor more than life and did not attempt to escape. Others fled in the darkness, hid in clefts, crept away between the feet of horses; he alone still sought the enemy. He struck down Pan Dombka, Pan Rusietski and the young hero Pan Aksak, who had won un-dying fame at Konstantinov. Then his sword cleft Pan Savitski and struck down two winged hussars together; finally, like a flame of fire, he rushed towards a huge noble-man whom he had noticed rushing over the battle-field bel-lowing like a bull.

Zagloba, for it was he, bellowed still louder from terror and spurred his horse to flight. His few remaining locks stood up like oaks with fright, but he did not lose his presence of mind; on the contrary he was meditating stratagems which flashed like lightning through his mind. He spurred onwards towards a dense throng of horsemen and cried out "Gentle-men, whoever believes in God!"   . . .   Then he spurred like a tempest towards the thick mass of cavalry. But Bur-lay rushed at him from one side to head him off. Zagloba closed his eyes and said to himself: "I shall perish now, I and my fleas." He heard the snorting of the horse behind him, saw that no one was coming to his help, that escape was impossible, and that no hand but his own could save him from Burlay.

In this moment of agony his terror suddenly turned into rage, he bellowed more fearfully than a wild aurochs, and wheeling his horse he turned against his pursuer.

"I am Zagloba!" he cried, flourishing his sword in the air.

Just then a fresh lot of tar-barrels were rolled from the ramparts. In the bright gleam Burlay gazed upon Zagloba and was astounded. Not at hearing his name, however, for that he had never heard before, but that he recognized him as the man whom he had entertained in Yampol as Bohun's friend.

But that unfortunate start of surprise was the ruin of the

brave chief of the Zaporojians, for ere he could collect himself, Zagloba landed such a blow upon his temple that he fell lifeless to the earth.

This happened in view of the entire army. Shouts of joy from the hussars were answered by shouts of terror from the Cossacks, who when they beheld the death of this old lion of the Black Sea, completely lost spirit and attempted no further resistance. Those whom Subagazi could not rescue perished to the last man, for no prisoners were taken on that terrible night. Subagazi fled towards the wagon-train pursued by the Starosta of Krasnostavsk and the light cavalry. The attack all along the line of entrenchments was repulsed. No opposition was met on the way and only about the wagon-train did the pursuing cavalry find work to do.

Shouts of triumph and joy resounded over the entire camp of the besieged, and mighty cries filled the air and ascended towards heaven. The blood-spattered, perspiring, dusty, powder-blackened soldiers stood leaning upon their weapons, their faces were lowering, their brows still frowning, their eyes still flashing, panting, but ready to fight again if necessary. Slowly the cavalry also returned from its bloody harvest at the train. Then the prince himself appeared upon the battle-field and with him the commanders, the royal standard bearer Marek, Sobieski and Pshiyemski. The brilliant procession moved slowly along the trenches.

"Long live Yeremy!" cried the army, "long live our father!"

The prince bowed with uncovered head and waved his field-marshal's baton on every side.

"I thank you, gentlemen, I thank you!" he exclaimed in his clear, bell-like voice.

Then he turned to Pan Pshiyemski:

"This trench is too big," said he.

Pshiyemski nodded his head in sign of affirmation.

Thus the victorious leaders rode along the entire line from the eastern to the western lake, inspecting the battle-field and the damages done to the ramparts by the enemy.

Behind the prince's retinue enthusiastic soldiers bore Zagloba on their shoulders to the camp as the hero of the day.

Twenty strong arms lifted the portly figure of the warrior on high; while he, greatly excited, red, perspiring and waving his arms lest he should lose his balance, cried out with all his force:

"Ha! I peppered him, purposely I feigned flight to draw

him on. This dog-brother will bark at us no more. Gentlemen, I had to give an example to the younger men.   . . .
For God's sake be careful or you will let me fall, hold me
tight, do you hear?   . . .   believe me, I had my hands full
with him. All sorts of rascals fought with noblemen to-day,
but they got their deserts.   . . .   Be careful! let me down!
The Devil!   . . .   "

"Long life to him! long life to him!" shouted the nobles.

"Take him to the prince," cried others.

"Long life to him! Long life to him!"

Meantime the Zaporojian hetman rushed into his camp
roaring like a wounded beast, tore his coat from his breast
and tore his own face. The chiefs who had escaped from
the battle surrounded him in gloomy silence, and spoke no
word of consolation. He was almost bereft of his senses; he
foamed at the mouth and tore his hair with both hands.

"Where are my regiments, my warriors?" he repeated in
a hoarse voice. "What will the Khan say, what will Tukhay
Bey? Give me up to Yeremy, let him impale me on the
stake."

The chiefs maintained silence.

"Why did the soothsayers predict victory?" roared the
hetman, "off with their heads. Why did they say that I should
take Yeremy captive?"

Heretofore when the roaring of this lion had terrorized the
entire camp, the captains had preserved a respectful silence;
but now that he was defeated, trampled upon, and forsaken
by fortune, his plight made the officers insolent.

"You can never conquer Yeremy," muttered Stepka.

"You are the cause of your own ruin and of ours," added
Mrozovitski.

The hetman rushed at him like a tiger.

"And who was the conqueror at Zolta Woda, who at Kor-
sum, and at Pilavyets?"

"You," answered Voronchenko harshly, "but Vishnyovyetski was not there."

Khmyelnitski began to tear his hair.

"I promised the Khan that he should sleep in the castle
to-night," howled he, in despair.

Then Kulak spoke: "What you have promised the Khan
concerns your own head. Keep it. Beware lest you lose it.
. . . But do not drive us again to the assault; do not destroy soldiers of God. Put up ramparts against the Poles,
trenches before the cannon, or woe unto you."

"Woe unto you!" repeated gloomy voices.

"Woe unto you," answered Khmyelnitski.

Thus they murmured and rumbled like thunder clouds. At length Khmyelnitski staggered and fell upon a divan covered with sheepskins in a corner of the tent. The captains surrounded him with gloomy brows and in deep silence. At length the hetman called out hoarsely: "Gorzalka!"

"You shall not drink," shouted Vyhovski, "the Khan will send for you."

The Khan was about a mile distant from the battle-field and knew nothing of what had transpired. The night was still and warm, and he sat by his tent among the agas and servants eating dates from a silver dish, and awaiting news. At times he gazed up at the starlit sky, and murmured "Mohammed Rassul Allah!" (Mohammed the messenger of God.)

At this moment Subagazi came riding up at full speed on a foaming horse, breathless and covered with blood; leaping from his saddle, he hurried up to the Khan and bowed low.

"Speak," said the Khan with a mouthful of dates.

The words burned like flames in the mouth of Subagazi but he dared not speak without first repeating the customary titles. He began therefore, making constant obeisances, to speak in the following manner:

"Almighty Khan of all the hordes, Grandson of Mohammed, Absolute Sovereign, All-wise Monarch, Fortunate Lord, Lord of the tree that gives shade from sunrise to sunset, Lord of the blooming tree . . . "

The Khan waved his hand to check the flow of words. He noticed that there was blood on the face of Subagazi and that pain and despair were in his eyes. He spat the half-chewed dates into his hand and gave them to one of his mullahs, who accepted them as a mark of extraordinary honor, and began to eat them. Then the Khan said:

"Speak quickly Subagazi has the camp of the infidels been taken?"

"God has not granted it."

"The Poles?"

"Are victors."

"Khmyelnitski?"

"Defeated."

"And Tukhay Bey?"

"Wounded."

"There is but one God," said the Khan, "how many true believers have gone to Paradise?"

Subagazi raised his eyes and pointed with his blood-stained hand to the sky. "As many as there are lights on Allah's Heaven," he answered solemnly.

The Khan's fat face grew purple, he almost burst with rage.

"Where is that dog," said he, "who promised me that I should sleep to-night in the castle? Where is that venomous serpent whom God will crush beneath my feet? Let him come here and give an account of the splendid promises he made."

Several murzas at once departed to find Khmyelnitski. By degrees the Khan grew calmer and finally he said:

"There is but one God."

Then he turned to Subagazi.

."Subagazi," said he, "there is blood upon your face."

"It is the blood of unbelievers," replied the warrior.

"Tell how you have shed it, rejoice our ears by telling of the bravery of the faithful."

Then Subagazi began to describe the battle in detail, praising especially the bravery of Tukhay Bey, of Galgi and Nured-Din. Nor did he fail to mention Khmyelnitski likewise, praising him as he did the others, and ascribing the disaster only to the will of God and to the fury of the infidels. One circumstance in the narrative impressed itself upon the Khan, and that was that at the beginning of the battle no shots were fired upon the Tartars, and that the Prince's cavalry had only charged upon them when the Tartars stood directly in their way.

"Allah! they did not want to fight with me," said the Khan, "but now it is too late. . . . "

And this indeed was the case. Prince Yeremy at the beginning of the battle had forbidden his soldiers to fire upon the Tartars, in order to instill in them that negotiations were going on with the Khan and that his hordes were standing beside the rebels only for the sake of appearances. Later, circumstances had forced an encounter with the Tartars.

The Khan nodded his head and deliberated within himself whether it would not be better to turn his arms against Khmyelnitski, but suddenly the hetman stood before him.

Khmyelnitski was now calm, and approached the Khan with head held high and a bold look. Craft and daring were expressed in his face.

"Approach, you traitor!" said the Khan.

"The hetman of the Cossacks approaches you, and no traitor, but your faithful ally to whom you pledged your aid under any circumstances," said Khmyelnitski.

"Go, pass the night in the castle, drag the Poles from the trenches by their hair as you promised."

"Great Khan of all the hordes," answered Khmyelnitski, in a solemn voice, "you are mighty, and except the Sultan, the mightiest on earth; you are wise and powerful, but can you shoot an arrow up to the stars, or fathom the depth of the sea?"

The Khan gazed at him in astonishment.

"You cannot," continued Khmyelnitski in a voice growing in volume, "and so I could not fathom the unfathomable pride and daring of Yeremy. How could I divine that your mere name would not terrify him into subjection, that the sight of you would not humble him to submissiveness, and that he would dare to raise his insolent hand against you, and to shed the blood of your warriors, and to insult you, mighty monarch, as well as the least of your murzas? Had I ventured to harbor such a thought I should have dishonored you whom I love and reverence."

"Allah!" said the Khan, more and more astonished.

"But this much I wish to tell you," continued Khmyelnitski, with increasing assurance in voice and manner, "you are great and mighty, from the east to the west nations and monarchs do homage to you and call you 'the Lion,' Yeremy alone does not bow his head to the dust before your beard. If you therefore do not destroy him, if you do not bend his neck and ride on his back, where is your glory and your honor? Men will say that a simply Polish prince has dishonored the Tsar of the Crimea and has escaped punishment —and that he is greater and mightier than you."

A profound silence followed; the chiefs and agas looked upon the face of the Khan as upon the sun and held their breath, the latter had his eyes closed and was lost in thought.

Khmyelnitski leaned upon his baton and waited confidently.

"You have said it," exclaimed the Khan at last. "I will humble Yeremy and will ride on his back so that no one from the east to the west can say that an infidel dog has disgraced me."

"God is great!" came as one voice from the murzas.

Khmyelnitski's eyes shone with joy. With one stroke he had warded off the destruction hanging over his head, and from a dobtful ally he had formed one who could be implicitly trusted. In case of emergency the lion knew how to transform itself into a serpent.

Both camps until late at night were active as a swarm of bees, while on the battle-field the torn and mangled warriors slept the sleep that knows no waking. The moon rose and started on her course over the immense graveyard, and was reflected in the pools of congealed blood, revealing at every moment new heaps of slain, looked into their open, glassy eyes, lighted their bluish faces, the fragments of shattered weapons, and the corpses of horses—her rays grew fainter as if paling at the sight. Here and there ominous groups appeared upon the field, these were servants and camp-followers who had come to rob the slain, as jackals steal after lions. . . . Superstitious fear drove them finally from the field. A dread mystery hung about that field strewn with corpses, about the silence and stillness of those motionless figures not long before human beings, and in the still peacefullness with which the dead Poles, Turks, Tartars, and Cossacks lay side by side. At times the wind rustled in the bushes that grew in spots over the field and it seemed to the sentinels as if this rustle was caused by the souls of the fallen which were circling above their corpses. It was even rumored that when the clock struck the midnight hour from Zbaraj, on a sudden over the whole field there were sounds as if great flocks of birds were rising in the air. Wailing voices, deep sighs, and hollow groans were also heard, making the hair stand up on the head. Those who were yet to perish in this struggle and whose ears were more sensitive to supernatural voices, distinctly heard the heavenward-rising souls of the Poles making supplications "Before Thine eyes, O Lord! we lay down our sins," while the souls of the Cossacks groaned "Christ, Christ, be merciful." For those that had fallen in this fratricidal war could not hasten at once to the eternal life. It was their fate to remain in the outer darkness and to hover in the wind over this vale of tears, to weep and lament by night until they should obtain of God forgiveness for their guilt and obtain at last peace and pardon for their sins at the feet of Christ.

But in those days men hardened their hearts and no Angel of Peace flew over the battle-field.

CHAPTER III.

On the following morning ere the sun had flashed its golden rays over the sky, new entrenchments surrounded the Polish camp. The former had covered too much space; it was difficult to defend them and to render mutual assistance. The prince and Pan Pshiyemski had decided therefore to enclose the troops within narrower entrenchments. All night long they had worked steadily, the hussars as well as the other divisions; it was not until three o'clock in the morning that sleep closed the eyes of the tired knights, and all except the sentries slept; for the enemy also was working all through the night and attempted to make no assault after yesterday's defeat. It was not expected that an attack would be made upon this day.

Skshetuski, Pan Longin and Zagloba sat in their tent drinking beer in small mugs thickened with crumbs of cheese, and diverted themselves in talking over the battle with that satisfaction with which every soldier talks over a recent victory.

"I am in the habit of going to sleep at milking-time in the evening and of rising when they are milking in the morning, the way the ancients did," said Zagloba, "but in war time that would not do; sleep when you have a chance and rise when you are awakened. It angers me to think that we are being disturbed on account of such a mob of rascals, but it can't be helped, in such times as these. Anyhow we paid them out yesterday, if we give them a couple more such receptions they will take care not to wake us."

"Do you know how many of our men have fallen?" asked Longin.

"O, not many, and, as is always the case, more fall of the assailants than of the besieged. You don't understand such matters as well as I do, because you have not been in so many wars. But we old veterans don't have to count the dead, we can estimate by watching the course of the battle."

"I shall attempt to learn all this from you gentlemen," said Longin mildly.

"Certainly you can if you have sufficient wit, but I doubt this fact."

"Oh, let him alone," interrupted Skshetuski. "Longin has seen war before, and God grant that our best knights perform such deeds as his of yesterday."

"I did as well as I could," said the Lithuanian, "but not as much as I wanted to."

"You did pretty well," said Zagloba, assuming a patronizing air, "and that others surpassed you (here he twisted his moustaches) is not your fault."

The Lithuanian listened with downcast eyes and sighed, thinking of his ancestor Stoveyko and the three heads.

At that moment the curtain of the tent was raised and Pan Michael entered as lively and cheerful as a goldfinch on a bright morning.

"Well, we are all here," exclaimed Zagloba, "let him have some beer."

The little knight grasped the hands of his three comrades, and said: "You should see how many balls are lying about in the square; it surpasses imagination, you can't step without stumbling."

"I have seen them too," said Zagloba, "for after rising I took a short stroll about the camp. All the hens of the entire district of Lemberg could not lay so many eggs in two years. Ah! if they were only eggs. wouldn't we have a high time eating omelets. You must know, gentlemen, that I would not exchange omelets for the greatest delicacy. I have a soldier's disposition, so have you. I enjoy something good, but there must be plenty of it; for this reason I am more valiant in battle than the lazy youths of to-day who cannot retain a mouthful in their stomachs."

"Well, you showed us yesterday, with Burlay, what you are capable of," said the little knight. "To cut Burlay down in the way you did it, ho, ho; I did not expect it of you. Why, he was one of the bravest and most famous knights throughout the Ukraine and Turkey.'

"What! Ha!" said Zagloba proudly, "that was not my first deed nor my greatest, Pan Michael. I see we are all searching in a bushel of poppy-seed, but four of us have found each other at the bottom. Such another four you could not find in the whole Commonwealth. By God! with you gentlemen, and our prince at the head, we could make our way on foot to Stambul. Now let me tell you: Pan Skshetuski killed Burdabut, and yesterday Tukhay Bey."

"Tukhay Bey is not dead," interrupted Skshetuski, "I felt how the blade rebounded, then at once we were separated."

"All the same," said Zagloba, "don't interrupt me, Pan Yan. Pan Michael cut down Bohun at Warsaw, as we have said."

"Better not mention that," said the Lithuanian.

"What is said is said," replied Zagloba, "though I should prefer myself to forget it. But let me proceed. Well, Pan Podbipyenta from Myshykishki did up Pulyan, and I, Burlay. I cannot conceal from you, gentlemen, however, that I would give all those fellows for one Burlay, and that I had the greatest work in settling him. That man was a devil, not a Cossack. If I had legitimate sons I would leave them an illustrious name. I would like to know what his Majesty the King and the Diet will say, and how they will reward us, who live more on sulphur and brimstone than on anything else."

"There was a hero who was greater than any of us," said Pan Longin, "but his name nobody knows or remembers."

"I should like to know who he may be,' said Zagloba, offended, "he must have lived in ancient times."

"No, not in ancient times," said the Lithuanian, "it was that little brother who at Tshetstyana upset King Gustavus Adolphus and his horse and captured him."

"I heard that this was at Putsek," interrupted Pan Michael.

"The king, however, tore himself away and fled," said Skshetuski.

"So it was. I can tell you something about it,' said Zagloba, blinking his eye, "for I was then serving under the noble Konyetspolski, father of the royal standard bearer, I know something about it. Modesty prevents me from making known the name of the hero, therefore nobody knows it. Believe me, Gustavus Adolphus was a great warrior, as great as Konyetspolski, but my encounter with Burlay was a much more difficult task, let me tell you."

"Then as I understand it, it was you who overthrew Gustavus Adolphus," said Volodiyovski.

"Why, have I boasted about it, Pan Michael? Let it remain forgotten. To-day I can boast of a deed which will long be remembered. This beer rumbles terribly in the stomach, and the more cheese there is in it the more it rumbles; for my part I prefer wine, though I thank God for

46

what we have. It may be that we shall lack even this. The priest Jabkovski tells me that provisions are scarce, and that worries him a good deal for he has a stomach as big as a barn. He is a huge Bernardine; I have become very fond of him; the blood of a soldier rather than a priest flows in his veins. The man whom he strikes in the snout must order his coffin at once."

"I have not told you, gentlemen, yet," remarked the little knight, "how well chaplain Yaskolski behaved last night. He posted himself in the corner of the tower on the right side of the castle and watched the fight. You must know that he is an excellent shot. He remarked to Jabkovski: 'I won't shoot at the Cossacks, for they at any rate are Christians, although they displease God; but Tartars,' said he, 'I abhor.' Then he began to shoot, and I understand that he knocked over a score and a half of them during the battle."

"I would that all the clergy were like him," sighed Zagloba, "but our Mukhovietski merely folds his hands and weeps that so much Christian blood is being shed."

"Never mind," said Skshetuski, earnestly, "Mukhovietski is a holy friar; and the best proof of this is, that although he is younger than the two others, they nevertheless humble themselves before him."

"Not only do I not deny his holiness," said Zagloba, "I even believe that he could convert the Khan himself. Oh! gentlemen, his Majesty the Khan must be in such a rage that the lice upon him are turning summersaults from fright. If he goes to negotiations, I shall also go with the commissioners. We are old friends; once upon a time he used to be very fond of me. Maybe he still remembers me."

"No doubt that Yanitski will be selected to conduct the negotiations, because he speaks the Tartar language as well as the Polish," said Skshetuski.

"And so do I. The murzas and myself know each other as white-streaked horses. When I was in the Crimea they wanted to give their daughters to me in order to have a beautiful progeny, and as I was young and had made no vow of chastity, like his grace, Pan Podbipyenta of Myshykishki I had some rousing times."

"That is offensive to the ear," said Longin bashfully.

"And you always repeat the same thing like a starling, it is apparent that the Beet-soup-eaters are not conversant with human speech."

The conversation was interrupted by a murmur of voices outside the tent. The knights went out to see what was the matter. A number of soldiers stood on the entrenchments looking at the region about, which had materially changed during the night and was still changing. The Cossacks indeed had not been idle since the last assault. They had made breastworks and placed cannon behind them, longer and more far reaching than any to be found in the Polish camp, and had begun to throw up winding and crosswise entrenchments and approaches. From a distance these heaps of earth looked like thousands of gigantic molehills, the entire slope of the plain was covered with them, the freshly turned up earth showed everywhere in dark spots amid the green of the grass, and everywhere men were toiling at the earthworks. On the front ramparts glittered the red caps of the Cossacks.

The prince, accompanied by the Starosta of Krasnostavsk and Pan Pshiyemski stood upon the intrenchments. A little lower down the Castellan of Belsk surveyed through a field-glass the Cossack works, and said to the royal cup-bearer:

"The enemy is beginning a regular siege, I see that we shall have to abandon the defense within the intrenchments and take refuge in the castle."

Prince Yeremy overheard these words and bending towards the castellan said: "God forbid! for we should be going voluntarily into a trap. Here we must live or die."

"That's my opinion too, even though I should have to kill a Burlay every day," interposed Zagloba, "I protest in the name of the entire army against the opinion of the Castellan of Belsk."

"This is not your business," said the prince.

"Keep quiet," whispered Volodiyovski, pulling the nobleman's coat sleeve.

"We will dig them out of their hiding-places like moles," said Zagloba, "and I beg your Highness to let me take the first sally; they know me now well enough, but they shall know more."

"A sally," said the prince, contracting his forehead, "better wait . . . until the nights are dark." . . .

Then turning to the Starosta of Krasnostavsk, to Pan Pshiyenski, and the commanders, he said:

"I request you, gentlemen, to come to a conference." And descending from the ramparts he was followed by all the superior officers.

"For Heaven's sake! what are you doing?" said Volodiyovski to Zagloba. "What do you mean? Don't you know
that it is against military discipline to interrupt the conversation of your superior officers? The prince is a mild man,
but in war time he will stand no joking."

"That is nothing, Pan Michael," said Zagloba, "the old Pan
Konyetspolski was as fierce as a lion, yet he highly valued
my advice, and may the wolves eat me if it was not just for
that reason that he twice defeated Gustavus Adolphus. I
know how to talk with these gentlemen, didn't you notice how
the prince gave way when I advised a sally? If God grants us
a victory, who will get the credit then—what—you?"

At that moment Zatsvilikhovski approached.

"Look!" said he, "they are rooting, rooting, like swine,"
pointing to the field.

"I would they were swine," answered Zagloba, "we would
have cheap sausages then. But their carcasses are not fit even
for dogs. In Pan Firley's quarters the soldiers have had to
dig a well, you can't see any water in the eastern pond now
on account of the numbers of bodies. At about dawn the
gall-bladders of the curs burst and they rose to the surface.
We shall not be able to eat fish any more on Friday, because
they have fed upon flesh."

"True," said Zatsvilikhovski, "but I have never seen so
many corpses except perhaps at Khotsim, when the janissaries stormed our camp."

"You will see more of them yet, I tell you."

"I think that they will begin to attack us this evening, or
before the evening."

"But I say that they will let us alone until to-morrow."

Zagloba had scarcely finished when white smoke puffed up
from the enemy's earthworks, and balls began to fly over the
intrenchments.

"There you are!" exclaimed Zatsvilikhovski.

"Bah! they know nothing of the art of war," said Zagloba.

Old Zatsvilikhovski was right. Khmyelnitski had begun a
regular siege; he had closed all ways and exits, removed the
pasture, had thrown up entrenchments and approaches, had
dug winding ditches about the camp, but he did not neglect
to make assaults, he annoyed and frightened them. He had
decided to give the besieged no rest, to tire them out, and to
harass them until the weapons should drop from their weary
hands. Therefore in the evening he again attacked Vish-

nyovyetski's quarters, but with no better result than on the previous day, especially as his soldiers did not display the same zeal. On the following day the firing did not stop for a moment. The winding ditches were so near to the camp that musketry-fire reached the ramparts; the earthworks smoked like miniature volcanoes from morning till night. It was not a general battle but an incessant bombardment. The besieged made occasional sorties, when swords, flails, lances and scythes met in the conflict, but whenever some of the Cossacks were swept away, others immediately took their places. The besieged soldiers had no rest all day long, and when the wished-for sunset came, a general assault was begun, a sally was out of the question.

On the night of July 16th, two brave colonels, Hladk and Nebada, attacked the prince's quarters and were terribly defeated. Three thousand of the most active Cossacks were left upon the field, the rest, pursued by the Starosta of Krasnostavsk, fled to their wagon-train, throwing away their arms and powder-horns. The same ill fate befell Fedeorenko, who, under cover of a dense fog, in the early morning, almost succeeded in capturing the town. Pan Korf, at the head of the Germans, repulsed him, and the Chief of Krasnostavsk and the standard bearer of Konyetspolski almost annihilated the attacking party as they fled.

But this was nothing in comparison to the frightful assault which, on July 19th, was made upon the intrenchments. The night previous the Cossacks had heaped up high embankments right opposite the quarters of Vishnyovyetski and from these heavy cannons belched out an incessant fire. At the close of day, when the first stars were twinkling in the sky, thousands upon thousands pushed forward to the assault. A number of awful-looking machines, resembling towers, appeared in the distance and slowly approached the ramparts. At the sides of these were things that looked like outstretched wings, these were bridges to be thrown over the intrenchments. The tops of the towers were enveloped in smoke from the discharges from small cannon and muskets. They rolled on amid the swarm of heads like gigantic commanders, now blazing with the fire of guns, now disappearing in smoke and darkness. The soldiers pointed them out to each other from the distance, whispering:

"Those are Tartar moving towers. Khmyelnitski wants to grind us in those wind mills. See how they roll with a noise like thunder."

"Fire at them with cannon!" shouted others.

The prince's artillerymen fired ball after ball, grenade after grenade, at the terrible towers. But as they could only be seen when the flashes lighted the darkness, the balls for the most part missed their mark.

Nearer and nearer drew the dense throng of Cossacks, like a dark wave rolling along at night on the expanse of the sea.

"Ugh!" exclaimed Zagloba, who was with Skshetuski's cavalry, "I feel hotter than ever before in my life. The night is so close that everything on me is wringing wet. The devil invented these machines. May the earth swallow them up. These rascals stick like a bone in my throat, amen! There is neither time to eat nor sleep,—the very dogs live better than we! Ugh! how hot it is!"

The air was indeed oppressive and sultry, and besides it was pregnant with the exhalations of corpses which for days had been putrifying on the battle-field. The sky was shrouded with heavy black clouds. A storm was threatening Zbaraj. Perspiration trickled over the bodies of the soldiers and their breathing was heavy.

At that moment drums began to rumble in the darkness.

"They will open attack at once," said Skshetuski, "do you hear the drums?"

"I hear, I wish the devil were drumming on them. It is sheer desperation."

"Kill! kill!" shouted the onward-rushing mass.

Along the entire length of the rampart the battle raged. Vishnyovyetski, Lantskoronski, Firley, and Ostrorvga were attacked simultaneously, so that one could not assist the other. The Cossacks, drunk with gorzalka, attacked more fiercely than ever, but were met also with braver resistance. The heroic spirit of their leader reanimated the soldiers. The fierce regular infantry composed of Mazovian peasants, fought the Cossacks with such fury that they got mixed up with their lines. They clubbed with their muskets and fought also with fists and teeth. Beneath the blows of the terrible Mazovians several hundred of the splendid Zaporojian infantry succombed, but fresh bodies immediately took their places. Along the whole line the battle grew more furious. The musket barrels burned the hands of the soldiers; they became short of breath; the commanders could scarcely speak through hoarseness. The Starosta of Krasnostavsk and Skshetuski rushed with the cavalry upon the enemies flank, and bathed in the blood of entire divisions as they trampled them down.

Hour after hour passed, but the attack abated not, for the gaps in the ranks of Khmyelnitski's Cossacks were instantly filled with fresh men. The Tartars filled the air with shouts and sent clouds of arrows at the defending soldiers. Men from behind urged the "blacks" on with clubs and scourges. Rage fought with rage, breast struck breast, and man embraced man in the struggle of death.

Thus they dashed like breakers upon rocky islands.

Suddenly the earth trembled beneath the feet of the warriors, the whole sky was enveloped in bluish flames, as if God could no longer look upon the atrocious deeds of men. An awful crash drowned the shouting of the men and the thunder of cannon: The artillery of heaven began a still more terrible cannonade. From east and west the tempest raged. It seemed as though the vault of heaven burst, together with the clouds, and was about to fall on the heads of the combatants. At moments all the world seemed like one vast flame, and then all were blind in the darkness, and again, the red zigzag streaks of lightning rent the black veil. A whirlwind swept away thousands of caps, streamers, and flags, and scattered them over the battle field in the twinkling of an eye. A chaos of thunder clasps, tempest, lightning, fire, and darkness followed,—the heavens raged like the men.

Over the town and castle, the intrenchments and the camp burst the unprecedented tempest. The battle was discontinued. Finally the floodgates of heaven opened and not streams, but cataracts, poured down upon the earth. The storm enveloped the earth so that one could not see a step in advance; bodies floated in the ditch. The Cossack regiments abandoned the assault and fled precipitately to their camp. Hurrying along blindly, they ran into each other, and thinking that the enemy was in pursuit, they scattered in the darkness. Right behind them plowed artillery and ammunition wagons, sinking in the mire and overturning. The water washed away the Cossacks' earth-works, roared in the winding trenches, flowed over the covered places, though provided with ditches, and rushed roaring over the plain as if in pursuit of the fleeing Cossacks.

The downpour grew heavier and heavier. The infantry in the trenches left the ramparts and fled to their tents. But the cavalry of the Chief of Krasnostavsk and Skshetuski received no order to retreat. They stood close to each other as if in a sea, shaking the water from themselves. Gradually the storm abated. At midnight the rain finally ceased. Between rifts in the clouds here and there a star shone. Another hour passed, and the water had fallen a little. Then suddenly the prince himself appeared before Skshetuski's squadron.

"Gentlemen," he inquired, "are your powder-pouches dry?"

"They are, Most Serene Prince," answered Skshetuski.

"Good! Dismount, wade through the water to those war machines, put powder under them, and blast them; but go quietly. The Chief of Krasnostavsk will go with you."

"Your order wil be executed, Sir," answered Skshetuski.

Then the prince caught sight of Zagloba, who was drenched to the skin.

"You asked to go on a sally, now go with these," he said.

"The deuce take it," murmured Zagloba, "this completes my misery."

A half hour later two divisions of knights, two hundred and fifty men in each, hurried along wading through water that reached to their armpits. They held their swords in their hands. They were making for those terrible towers of the Cossacks, which stood about half a furlong from the intrenchments.

One division was led by that lion of lions, the Chief of Krasnostavsk, Marek, Sobieski, who would not hear of staying within the trenches; the other by Skshetuski. Attendants carried after them pails of tar, dry wood for torches, and powder. Thep proceeded without noise, like wolves creeping towards a sheepfold on a dark night.

The little knight joined Skshetuski as a volunteer, for Pan Michael loved such undertakings more than life. He trod along in the water with joy in his heart and his sword in his hand. Beside him went Pan Bodbipyenta with his unsheathed "Cowl cutter" sword towering above all, for he was two heads taller than the tallest of the others. Among them Zagloba hastened to keep pace, panting, grumbling, and mimicking the words of the prince, "You asked to go on a sally, go now with these. A dog wouldn't go to its wedding through water like this. If ever I advise a sally in such weather may I drink nothing but water all my life! Why, I am not a duck and my belly is not a boat. I have always abominated water, and all the more do I despise this water in which peasant carcasses are soaking."

"O keep quiet," said Pan Michael.

"Keep quiet yourself, you are no bigger than a gudgeon and know how to swim, so it is easy for you. I must say that it is ungrateful on the part of the prince to begrudge my enjoying a rest after my victory over Burlay. Zagloba has done enough, may everybody do as much, but let Zagloba alone, for you will be badly off when he is no more. For God's sake, if I fall into a hole, pull me out by the ears, for I should drown at once."

"Keep quiet," said Skshetuski, "behind those dark shadows Cossacks are lurking, they might hear you."

"Where? what did you say?"

"Why there, in those mounds in the grass."

"As though that too was wanting. May the bright thunder strike them. . . . "

But the remaining words were choked off by Pan Michael, who put his hand on Zagloba's mouth, for the earthworks were scarce fifty steps away. The men kept as quiet as possible, but the water splashed beneath their feet: fortunately it began to rain again and the noise drowned that of their footsteps.

There were no sentries stationed at the coverings. Who in the world could have expected a sally in such a tempest, which divided the contending armies as with a lake.

Pan Michael and Longin pushed ahead and reached the earthworks first. The little knight let his sabre drop by his side, and putting both hands to his mouth cried out "Hello! there."

"Hey! Men!"

"What is it?" answered from within the voices of the Cossacks who evidently thought that some one had come over from the Cossack wagon camp.

"God be praised," said Volodiyovski, "let us in."

"Don't you know how to get in?"

"Yes, I know," answered Volodiyovski, and having found the entrance he jumped in. Longin and others followed him.

Then from the interior of the mound arose terrified cries. At the same time the knights shouted and rushed together into other mounds. Groans and the clash of steel mingled in the darkness. Here and there dark figures rushed past, others fell to the ground, now and then shots were heard; all that scrimmage did not last long, not even a quarter of an hour. The Cossacks for the most part, in deep sleep, were surprised and even offered no resistance, and were killed before they could reach their arms.

"To the infernal machines!" cried the voice of the Starosta of Krasnostavsk.

The knights rushed to the towers.

"Fire them from the inside, for the outside is wet," thundered Skshetuski.

But the order was not easy to carry out; for in these towers built of pine beams, no door or any sort of inlet could be found. The Cossack gunners mounted them on ladders, and the guns, of small calibre, as only for such was there room, were drawn up with ropes. The knights for some time ran round the towers, striking the walls with their swords and puliIng with their hands at the corners.

Fortunately the attendants had brought axes, and they began to hack at the towers. Pan Marek Sobieski ordered casks of powder that had been prepared for the purpose to be laid beneath. The casks of tar and torches were lighted, and the flames began to lick the wet wood.

Before it ignited and the powder had exploded, Longin bent down and lifted up an enormous stone which the Cossacks had dug from the ground.

Four of the strongest men could not move it from its place, but he raised it with his mighty hands, and in the light of the burning tar the blood could be seen rushing to his face. The knights gazed upon him with amazement.

"It is Hercules himself! May bullets strike him!" they exclaimed, raising their hands with astonishment.

Meanwhile Longin went up to one of the machines under which no fire had been set yet, bent backward, and hurled the stone at the centre of the wall. Those present bent their heads, the stone whizzed in its course and burst open the mortices; a crash was heard, the tower opened as if broken in two, then tumbled down with a crash.

Tar was poured over the masses of timber and it was set on fire at once.

Shortly afterwards several tens of the towers were ablaze, like gigantic torches they illumined the plain. Rain was still falling, but the fire prevailed and the towers were ablaze to the astonishment of both àrmies, since the night was so wet.

From the Cossack camp Stepka, Kulak and Mrozovitski, each at the head of some thousands of Cossacks, rushed to the rescue. They attempted to extinguish the flames, but in vain,

The pillars of flame and the red clouds of smoke rose higher and higher towards the sky and were reflected in the lakes and ponds that had been formed by the tempest on the battle field.

Meanwhile the knights hurried in close lines towards the entrenchments, and were greeted from afar with shouts of joy. Suddenly Skshetuski looked about, glanced through the lines, and thundered out, "Halt."

Longin and the little knight were missing. Probably in their zeal they had remained too long in the last tower, or perhaps they had found Cossacks in hiding. Anyway they had not noticed the returning knights.

"Return," commanded Skshetuski.

The Starosta of Krasnostavsk did not know what was the matter. He hurried up to inquire, and just at that moment the two lost men appeared, as if they had emerged from the earth half way between the towers and the knights.

Longin with his shining "Cowl cutter" in his hand, took giant strides, and beside him Pan Michael trotted along. Both of them had their heads turned towards the Cossacks, who were pursuing them like a pack of unleashed hounds. By the red gleam of the fires the pursuit was clearly visible. It looked as if an enormous elk with its young one was fleeing before a crowd of hunters, ready at any moment to stand at bay against the pursuers.

"They will be slaughtered; for heaven's sake, onward!" shouted Zagloba in a heartrending voice. "They will slay them with arrows or musket shots. For Christ's sake, be quick!"

Without considering that a new battle might begin the next moment, he rushed sword in hand, together with Skshetuski and others, to the rescue. He slipped, stumbled, got up again, snorted, shouted, and shaking all over, rushed onward with the last remnant of his legs and breath.

But the Cossacks did not shoot, their guns were wet as were also the strings of their bows. They pressed on, however, and some running ahead had almost overtaken the fugitives, when the knights suddenly turned like bears at bay, and giving a great shout they raised their swords on high. Longin with his enormous sword appeared to them like a supernatural being.

As two tawny wolves turn about when the hounds press too closely upon them and show their white teeth, thus keeping the panting pack at a distance, so these two repeatedly turned, and each time the pursuers halted. Once a man, bolder than the rest, ran up to them with a scythe in his hand, but Pan Michael jumped at him like a wild-cat and wounded him to death. The rest paused to wait for their comrades, who came bounding on in a dense mass.

But the lines of knights also came nearer and nearer, and Zagloba rushed along swinging his sword above his head and roaring out with an unearthly voice:

"Strike! kill!"

Now the ramparts thundered, and a bomb, screaming like an owl, described a red arc in the sky and fell amid the dense Cossack crowd. Soon there followed another, a third, and a tenth. It seemed as if the battle was to begin anew.

Before the siege of Zbaraj, this kind of missile was unknown to the Cossacks, and when sober, they stood in great terror of them, seeing in them evidences of Yeremy's sorcery The pursuers therefore stopped for a moment, and scattered in every direction when the bombs burst among them, causing terror, death, and destruction.

"Save yourselves!" they yelled, in panic-stricken voices.

All scattered, and Pan Longin and the little knight hurried up to the ranks of the hussars. Zagloba embraced now one. now the other, kissing them on the cheeks and brows. Joy overpowered him. But he attempted to restrain it lest he should show his soft heart, therefore he cried:

"Hey! you blockheads! I won't say that I love you, but I feared for you. Suppose they had killed you! Is that the way you understand military discipline, to lag behind? You deserve to have your feet tied to the tails of horses and to be dragged through the square. I shall be the first to tell the prince to punish you. Let us go to sleep now. Praise be to God for that! Those dog-brothers were in luck that the grenades dispersed them, for I should have cut them up like cabbages. How could I see my friends in danger and not fly to their aid? We must have a drink on this to-night. Praise be to God for that! I almost thought that we should have to sing a requiem to-morrow. Still I am sorry that no encounter took place, for my hand is itching terribly, though I made those fellows in the shelters taste horse-beans and onions."

CHAPTER IV.

It became necessary to build new ramparts and to concentrate the camp in order to render the entrenchments of the Cossacks useless, and to make defence easier for their own reduced forces. They worked therefore all through the night after the storm. But meantime the Cossacks did not remain idle. On the night between Tuesday and Wednesday they approached silently and threw up a second and much higher wall around the camp, from which at early dawn they opened fire amid loud shouts. For four days and four nights they continued an uninterrupted fire. Great destruction was wrought on both sides, for the best gunners of both armies were pitted against each other.

From time to time crowds of Cossacks and of detached hordes rushed to the assault, but they did not reach the ramparts, for the fire was too hot. The enemy possessing strong forces changed the divisions in action, allowing some to rest and sending others to the fight. In the opposite camp, however, there were no reserve troops. The same men had to keep firing, rush to the defense at any moment whenever assaults threatened, bury the dead, dig wells, and raise the ramparts higher for better protection. They slept, or rather dozed, on the ramparts under fire, while balls were flying so thickly that every morning they could be swept from the square. For four days no one removed his clothing, which when wet from rain was dried by the sun; during the day the bodies of the men were scorched, at night they were chilled. For four long days no one had a warm mouthful of food; they drank gorzalka, mixing powder with it to give it more substance; they munched biscuits and tore with their teeth dried-up bits of smoked meat; and all this in the midst of continued firing, smoke, of the whizzing of bullets, and the thunder of cannon.

To be struck on the head or about the body was nothing; the soldier tied a dirty rag about his bloody head and fought on. They were wonderful men. In ragged coats, with rusty

733

weapons, shattered muskets in their hands, and eyes red with sleeplessness, they were ever watchful, and ever ready, and eager day and night, in rain or in sunshine, to do battle.

The soldiers loved their leader in danger, in storms, in wounds, and in death. Their souls were the exalted souls of heroes, their hearts became hard as steel, their senses were dulled. Horror became a delight to them. Different squadrons vied with each other in enduring hunger, sleeplessness, toil, and in bravery and fury. It came to such a point that it was difficult to keep the soldiers on the ramparts; mere defense was not enough, they delighted in rushing upon the enemy like ravenous wolves upon a flock of sheep. In all the regiments a wild joy reigned. Had any one hinted at surrender he would have been torn to pieces on the spot. "Here we shall die," repeated every mouth.

Every command of the leader was executed with lightning-like rapidity. Once it happened that the prince, as he went at evening around the ramparts, noticing that the fire of the quarter regiment of Leschynski was growing weaker, rode up to the soldiers and asked:

"Why are you not firing?"

"We are out of powder, we have sent to the castle for some."

"There is some much nearer," said the prince, pointing to the enemy's entrenchment.

Hardly had he spoken when the entire regiment rushed from the ramparts, threw itself upon the enemy, and broke like a cyclone upon the entrenchments. With muskets clubbed, with swords and pikes, they slaughtered the Cossacks; four cannon were spiked; after half an hour they returned decimated, but victorious, and laden with stores of powder. Day followed day. The Cossack entrenchments formed an ever-closer ring around the Polish barricade and pushed into it as a wedge into wood. The firing was now at such close range that, not counting the assaults, about ten men a day fell in each squadron. The priests could not come to them with the sacrament. The besieged sheltered themselves with wagons, tents, skins, and suspended garments. The dead were buried at night on the spot on which they fell; but the living fought all the more fiercely over the graves of their comrades. Khmyelnitski let the blood of his men flow without stint, but every assault brought upon him greater losses. He was astounded at the resistance; he counted upon time to shatter the courage and strength of the besieged, but time passed and they only showed an increasing contempt for death.

The leaders set an example to the soldiers. Prince Yeremy slept on the bare ground on the ramparts, drank gorzalka, ate smoked horse-meat, and endured the greatest hardships. The royal standard bearer Konyetspolski, and the Starosta of Krasnostavsk led divisions to the attack in person. During the assaults they exposed themselves without armor in the densest rain of bullets. Even leaders like Ostrorog who possessed no military knowledge and upon whom the soldiers looked with suspicion, seemed now to be changed into new men by Yeremy. Old Firley and Lantskronski slept also on the ramparts, and Pan Pshiyemski pointed cannon during the day time, and at night dug under ground like a mole, putting countermines beneath the mines of the Cossacks and blowing them into the air; or he built underground tunnels through which the soldiers stole like ghosts and surprised the Cossacks in their sleep.

Khmyelnitski finally decided to enter into negotiations, with the idea of accomplishing something by strategy. On the 24th of July, towards the evening, the Cossacks began to cry out to the Polish soldiers to cease firing. A Zaporojian envoy announced that the hetman wished to see old Zatsvilikhovski. After a short consultation the commanders accepted the proposition and the old man left the entrenchments.

The knights saw from the distance the respect with which Zatsvilikhovski was treated by the Cossacks; for during the short time he was a commissioner, he had gained the regard of the wild Zaporojians, and Khmyelnitski himself held him in high respect. The firing ceased. The Cossacks came from their entrenchments close to the ramparts, and the knights went down to meet them. Both sides were on their guard, but there was nothing unfriendly in this meeting. The nobles had always liked the Cossacks more than the "blacks," because of their valor and endurance in battle. Now they met them on equal terms, as knights with knights. The Cossacks looked with wonder upon that impregnable den of lions which held in check their might and that of the Khan. They mingled more freely and began to deplore that so much Christian blood was being shed. Finally, they treated one another to tobacco and gorzalka.

"Hah! noble knights!" said some of the veteran Zaporo-jians, "if you had always fought in this way there would have been a different outcome at Zolta Woda, Korsun and Pilavyets. Why you are devils, and not men; we never have seen the like of you."

"Come to-morrow and the day afterwards; you will always find us the same."

"Yes, we shall come, but thank God now for a brief rest. Much Christian blood is being shed, but hunger will conquer you in the end."

"The king will come before hunger; we have just risen from a hearty meal."

"And should provisions became scarce we will look for them in your wagon-trains," said Zagloba, with his arms akimbo.

"God grant that our brother, Zatsvilikhovski, is successful in making terms with our hetman. If not, we shall attack again this evening."

"We are waiting for you."

"The Khan has promised that you shall all die."

"And our prince has resolved to honor the Khan by drag-ging him by the beard at his horse's tail."

"He is a wizard, but he cannot accomplish that."

"It were better for you to fight with our prince against the heathens, than to rise in arms against your sovereign."

"With your prince? H'm! that would be nice."

"Why do you rebel? the king is coming; fear the king. Prince Yeremy was also a father to you—"

"He is a father as death is a mother. The plague has not swept away so many warriors as he."

"He will do worse; you don't know him yet."

"Nor do we wish to know him. Our chiefs say that the Cossack whom he looks upon is lost."

"It will be so with Khmyelnitski."

"God knows what will happen. This is certain, that both cannot live together on this earth. Our father says that if you will surrender Yeremy to him, he will let you all go free, and that he with all of us will do homage to the king."

At this the soldiers began to gasp and grind their teeth.

"Keep quiet, or we will draw our swords."

"You Poles are faithful," said the Cossacks, "but you shall die."

And thus they conversed, sometimes in a friendly manner,

sometimes angrily threatening each other. In the afternoon Zatsvilikhovski returned to the camp. Negotiations had not been agreed upon, and a truce had not been obtained. Khmyelnitski demanded the surrender of the prince and of the royal standard bearer Konyetspolski. Finally, he enumerated the wrongs that had been inflicted upon the Zaporojians, and sought to persuade Zatsvilikhovski to remain with him; this had angered the old knight and he sprang up and rode away. In the evening an assault took place which was repulsed with great slaughter. The whole camp was afire for two hours. Not only were the Cossacks repulsed from the ramparts, but the infantry captured the first entrenchment, destroyed the embrazures, and burned fourteen moving towers. Khmyelnitski had vowed to the Khan that on this night he would not withdraw as long as a man remained alive within the entrenchments.

At early dawn the firing and the undermining of the ramparts was begun afresh. The whole day long the battle raged, and flails, scythes, swords, stones, and clods of earth, were used in the combat. The friendly feeling of the day before, that regretted shedding Christian blood, had given place to a wild exasperation. Rain fell off and on in the morning. The soldiers received only half rations on this day, at which Pan Zagloba grumbled greatly but empty stomachs doubled the rage of the knights. They swore that they would not surrender, but would fight to the last breath. In the evening the Cossacks, disguised as Turks, made a fresh assault, but this lasted but a short time. A noisy and restless night followed. The firing did not cease for a moment. The combatants challenged each other and they fought singly and in groups.

Pan Longin rushed out on a sally, but no one dared to oppose him, they only shot at him from a distance. But Skshetuski and Volodiyovski gained great glory, and the latter in single combat killed the famous warrior Dudar.

Even Zagloba sallied out, but only to indulge his tongue: "Since I defeated Burlay," said he, "I cannot fight any common rascal." In a battle of words he found not his equal among the Cossacks; when in safety behind an embankment he drove them desperate by shouting out, in a stentorian voice, which seemed to issue from the depths of the earth:

"You sit here, you peasants, before Zbaraj, but the Lithuanian army is marching up from the lowlands of the Dnieper.

They are enjoying themselves with your wives and daughters. Next spring you beet-soup-swillers will find in your homes, provided you find any homes, whole crowds of little beet-soup-swillers."

This was true. The Lithuanina army under Radzivil was really traversing the lowlands of the Dnieper, burning and destroying everything, and leaving only land and water behind them. The Cossacks knowing this, became enraged, and rained bullets on Zagloba, which fell about like pears from a tree that has been shaken. He dusked his head, however, behind the embankment, and called out again:

"You dog-souls have missed me, but I did not miss Burlay. Come on, I will fight you in single combat. You know me, come on. Pepper away, you peasants, as long as you can; next winter you will be nursing young Tartars in the Crimea laboring along the Dnieper. Come on! I'll give you a mite for the head of your Khmyelnitski. Give him a slap on the snout from me, from Zagloba, do you hear? You dirt! Is there not enough of your carrion lying about on the field smelling like dead dogs? The plague sends her regards to you; to your plows and scows and pitchforks, you dirty scoundrels; you should be rowing loads of salt and cherries against the stream, instead of disgusting us with your presence here."

The Cossacks laughed in their turn at the gentleman who shared a single biscuit among three. They asked why the gentlemen did not make their vassals pay their rents and tithes. But Zagloba always got the best of this kind of badinage. These interchanges of compliments, interrupted by curses and wild laughter, lasted through whole nights while firing and great and small combats raged. Then Pan Yanitski rode off to negotiate with the Khan, but the latter only repeated that they must die; whereupon the envoy, growing impatient, said:

"You prophesied this long ago but nothing has happened to us yet, he who comes for our heads brings his own."

The Khan asked that Prince Yeremy should confer with his Grand Vizir on the field, but this was discovered to be a treacherous trap, and the negotiations were broken off. The fighting went on unceasingly, in the evening assaults, during the day, cannonading and musketry-fire, flying shells and grenades, attacks, skirmishes, desperate sallies by the cavalry, defeats, and ever-increasing bloodshed.

A wild desire for danger and bloodshed possessed the soldiers. They went into battle with songs and laughter as if to a wedding. They had become so accustomed to the thunder of cannon, that the divisions that were detailed to sleep, slept peacefully under fire amid showers of bullets. Provisions grew scarcer; the commanders had not stocked the camp sufficiently before the arrival of the prince. The price of food rose very high, but those who had money for bread and gorzalka gladly shared their purchases with the others. No one took thought of the morrow, for everyone knew that one of two things was inevitable; either relief by the king or death. They were prepared for either, but more ready for battle. Ten resisted thousands with a valor unequalled in history, and with a fury that rendered every assault a defeat for the Cossacks. Besides, not a day passed without several sallies being made and attacks upon the enemy's own entrenchments. On the evenings when Khmyelnitski thought that fatigue had overcome the besieged, and he was preparing for an assault, joyful songs would reach his ears. He was lost in amazement and admiration, and the thought came to him that Yeremy was a mightier wizard than all the Cossacks put together. Then he would become furious with rage and throw himself into the battle. He shed oceans of blood, for he comprehended that his star was beginning to pale before that of the terrible prince.

In the camp of the Cossacks they sang songs about Yeremy and told stories about him at which the hair of the warriors stood on end. They said that at times when he appeared by night on the ramparts, he would visibly grow until he was taller by a head than the towers of Zbaraj, that his eyes then looked like two moons and that the sword in his hand shone like that star of ill omen that God sets at times in the sky for the destruction of men. They also related that at his call dead heroes arose with clank of armor, to join his living warriors. Yeremy was in the mouth of all; beggar minstrels sang of him; the old Zaporojians "blacks" and Tartars spoke of him. And in these stories and in the superstitious terror, there was evidenced a certain wild love, which these children of the steppes bore for their bloody destroyer. So it was; Khmyelnitski paled before him, not only in the eyes of the Khan and the Tartars, but even in the eyes of his own men. He saw that he must take Zbaraj, or his authority would vanish like mist before the dawn, he must trample this lion under foot or die.

But the lion not only defended himself but every day rushed with greater rage and fury from his lair. Neither superior force, nor treachery, nor stratagem, prevailed against him. The Cossacks and the "blacks" began to murmur. It was difficult for the latter to stand the smoke, fire, shower of bullets, smell of corpses, rain, and heat, in the face of death; but the brave Cossacks did not fear battle, labor, storms, fire, blood, death—they feared "Yeremy."

CHAPTER V.

In this memorable siege of Zbaraj many an obscure knight made himself a name of undying fame, but the greatest praise was due to Pan Longin Podbipyenta, whose great merits were only surpassed by his modesty.

The night was dreary, and dark, and wet; the soldiers weary from watching at the ramparts, dozed, leaning upon their weapons. After ten days of continuous battle, this was the first moment of peace and rest. In the new trench of the enemy scarce thirty paces distant, one could hear no shouts nor curses, nor the usual tumult. It appeared as if the enemy, who had desired to tire out the besieged, were themselves tired out. Here and there gleamed the faint light of a fire behind a mound. From somewhere there arose sweet, soft notes of a lute, played by some Cossack. In the distance the Tartar horses neighed, and on the embankments from time to time one could hear the calls of the sentinels.

The prince's cuirrassiers were that night on infantry-service in the camp. Skshetuski, Podbipyenta, the little knight, and Zagloba, conversed in low tones upon the rampart, and in the intervals of their discourse they listened to the splashing of the rain in the trench. Skshetuski remarked:

"This quiet seems strange to me, my ears are so accustomed to noise and uproar that they ring in the stillness. But I hope no treachery lies hidden in this silence."

"Since I receive but half rations it is all the same to me," Zagloba murmured sadly. "My courage requires three things: Sufficient to eat, plenty to drink, and plenty of sleep. The best strap drys and cracks if it is not oiled, and especially if it be soaked in water like hemp. The rain soaks us, the Cossacks hack us up, is it any wonder if we fall to pieces in strips? It is a pretty mess all round; the price of a loaf has risen to a florin and a quart of gorzalka to five. The water is not fit for a dog, for the wells are infected by the corpses, and I am as thirsty as my boots, which open their mouths like a fish."

"But your boots drink water without making any fuss over it," said Volodiyovski.

"Keep quiet, Pan Michael, why you are no larger than a titmouse, a grain of millet is sufficient for you, and you can't drink more than a thimbleful. But I, thank God, am not so delicate, and was not scratched up by a hen, but was born of a woman; therefore I need food and drink adequate for a man, and not for a bug. As I have had nothing in my mouth but saliva since noon-time, I can't relish your jokes."

Zagloba snorted with anger, and Pan Michael, feeling with his hand, said:

"I have in one of my pockets a flask that I snatched from a Cossack to-day; but since I was scratched up by a hen, I think the gorzalka of such an insignificant creature would not be to your relish either. Here's to you, Yan," said he, addressing Skshetuski.

"Give it to me, for I feel cold," said Skshetuski.

"Drink to the health of Pan Longin."

"You are a rascal, Pan Michael," said Zagloba. "Blessed be the hens that could scratch up warriors like you; unfortunately such hens do not exist. I did not have you in mind when I made the remark."

"Take it from Pan Podbipyenta," said Pan Michael. "I do not wish to offend you."

"What are you doing, man? Leave some for me," cried Zagloba, in alarm, as he watched the Lithuanian drinking. "You throw your head too far back, I wish to God it would remain so; the trouble with you is that your inside is too big, you don't fill up soon enough. Just look at him pouring the gorzalka down, as if into a decayed tree-trunk. May you be killed!"

"What's the matter, I drank but a few drops," said Longin, passing the flask.

Zagloba put it too his lips and drained the contents, then he puffed and said:

"The only consolation is, that when our misery is over, and God allows us to carry our heads out of these dangers, we will make up for it all. I think some feasts will surely be prepared for us. The Bernardine Jabkovski is a fine feeder but I can drive him away even with a goat's horn."

"And what news did you and the priest Jabkovski hear to-day from Mukhovietski,' said Pan Michael.

"Hush!" said Skshetuski, "someone is coming from the square."

They all grew dumb and a dark figure appeared and asked in a low voice:

"Are you watching?"

"We are, Your Highness," said Skshetuski, rising.

"Be on your guard. This quiet threatens evil."

The prince then passed on to see if sleep had overcome the tired soldiers anywhere. Pan Longin clasped his hands:

"What a leader! What a warrior!"

"He rests less than we do," said Skshetuski, "he examines all the ramparts from here to the second lake in this manner every night."

"God give him health!"

"Amen!"

Silence followed. All looked with straining eyes into the darkness, but they could see nothing; silence reigned over the Cossack entrenchments, every fire was extinguished.

"We could devour them now like susliks," murmured Volodiyovski.

"Who can tell," replied Skshetuski.

"I am so sleepy," muttered Zagloba, "that I can scarcely keep my eyes open, and yet sleep is forbidden. I should like to know when it will be allowed. Whether there is firing going on or not, one must remain under arms and keep watch, nodding from weariness, like a Jew on his Sabbath. It is fit service for dogs! I don't know what excites me so, whether it is the gorzalka or the confusion that overtook the priest Jabkovski and myself this morning on account of an undeserved lecture that we got."

"How did that happen?" asked Pan Longin, "you began to tell us, but did not finish."

"Then I'll tell you now; it may help to keep us awake. Well, I went with Father Jabkovski to the castle, hoping to find something to munch there. We looked about everywhere, but could find nothing, and we came back in a bad humor. In the Court we met a Calvinist priest who had been giving the last consolation to Captain Shenberk of Firley's squadron, who was wounded yesterday. I asked him: 'Why are you prowling about here and angering God? You will bring a curse upon us yet!' Then he, evidently relying upon the protection of the Castellan of Belsk, replied: 'Our faith is as good as yours, and better, perhaps." When he said this we were petrified with horror. But I held my tongue. I thought to myself, Father Jabkovski is here, let him carry on the argument. Jabkovski immediately came out with a great argument, for he punched him under his ribs. The Calvinist made no reply, but tottered till he fell against the wall. At this moment the Prince and Mukhovietski passed by, and then we caught it. We should not argue nor make an uproar, for this was neither the time nor place for it. They scolded us as if we were two schoolboys; and hardly with right, for unless I am a false prophet, these ministers of Pan Firley will bring misfortune upon us."

"And what about Captain Shenberk, was he converted?" asked Pan Michael.

"No, he died in error, as he had lived."

"Oh, that men should renounce their salvation rather than their stubbornness," sighed Pan Longin.

"God protects us in the face of the overwhelming forces of the Cossacks," Zagloba continued, "and yet men continue to insult him. Is it known to you, gentlemen, that balls of thread were shot into the square from yonder trench, and the soldiers say that where the balls fell the ground was covered with leprosy?"

"It is known that devils are employed by Khmyelnitski to do such things," said the Lithuanian, crossing himself.

"I saw the witches myself," added Skshetuski, "and I tell you, gentlemen——"

He was interrupted by Volodiyovski, who suddenly pressed his arm and whispered:

"Silence!"

Then he sprang to the edge of the ramparts and listened attentively.

"I don't hear anything," said Zagloba.

"Sh! the rain drowns everything," said Skshetuski.

Pan Michael waved with his hand for silence and continued to listen carefully for some time. At last he approached his comrades, "they are coming," he whispered. "Inform the prince, he has gone towards Ostrorog's quarters," said Skshetuski softly, "meantime we will warn the soldiers."

Instantly they hurried along the ramparts, stopping every moment and whispering to the sentinels:

"They are coming! they are coming!"

The words flew from mouth to mouth like lightning. About a quarter of an hour later the prince arrived on horseback and gave instructions to the officers. Since the enemy evidently purposed to surprise the camp while asleep, and the

prince wished him to remain in this illusion, the soldiers were
to keep as quiet as possible and to let the assailants come
right up to the ramparts, and then, when a cannon was fired as
a signal, they were to attack them at once and take them by
surprise.

The soldiers were ready; their muskets in their hands they
waited in silence. Skshetuski, Volodiyovski and Longin stood
next to each other. Zagloba remained near them also, for he
knew from experience that most of the balls fell on the square,
and that he was safest on the rampart near these three warriors. He posted himself a little behind the knights, so as to
escape the first onset. Longin knelt a little to one side, and
Volodiyovski pressed close to Skshetuski and whispered in
his ear.

"They are coming, surely."

"With measured tread."

"These are no 'blacks,' nor Tartars."

"Zaporojian infantry?"

"Or janissaries, for they march well. We could attack them
best with cavalry."

"It is too dark for cavalry to-night."

"Do you hear them now?"

"Sh!"

The camp seemed sunk in sleep; the deepest silence prevailed, broken only by the patter of the rain. Another sound,
like a pattering, might be heard, ever increasing and growing
more and more distinct; at last a long, dense mass, but a few
steps from the trench, made itself visible, inasmuch as it was
darker and blacker than the darkest of nights.

The soldiers held their breath, and the little knight jogged
Skshetuski's elbow as if thus to express his satisfaction.

The assailants reached the fosse and lowering ladders into
it, they descended, and then leaned them against the rampart
on the opposite side. The rampart was wrapped in a silence
as if all were dead upon and behind it.

In spite of all the caution of the assailants, a step creaked
and shook on the ladder-rounds now and then.

"You'll get your dish of horse-beans all right," said Zagloba
to himself.

Volodiyovski had ceased jogging Skshetuski, Pan Longin
grasped firmly his "Cowl-cutter" and prepared to give the
first blow, for he was nearest to the edge of the rampart.
Three pair of hands showed on the edge of the rampart, then

three helmet crests gradually and cautiously mounted higher and higher.

"These are Turks," thought Pan Longin.

In an instant a terrible roar of thousands of muskets resounded; it became as light as day. Ere the light vanished Longin swung his arm and landed such a mighty stroke with his terrible sword, that the air whistled about it.

Three bodies fell into the trench; three helmeted heads rolled before the kneeling knight.

Though hell was raging upon earth, heaven opened before Pan Longin. Wings seemed to sprout from his shoulders; choirs of angels sang in his breast, as if he were rising up to heaven; he fought as in a dream and every blow of his sword was like a prayer of thanks.

All his ancestors from Stoveyko down were rejoicing in heaven at this last holder of the Podbipyenta Cowl-Cutter, was such a man.

This assault, in which on the enemies' side the auxiliary forces of the Rumelian and Silistrian Turks, together with the Khan's guards, took the main part, was repulsed with more bloodshed than any preceding attack, and drew down a terrible tempest of wrath upon the head of Khmyelnitski. He had assured the Khan that the Poles would fight with less rage against the Turks, and that if these troops were given to him, he would certainly capture the camp. He was, therefore, now obliged to mollify the Khan and the enraged murzas, and to win them with presents. He presented the Khan with ten thousand dollars and Tukhay Bey, Korz Adze, Subagazi, Nuv-ed-Din Galzi, with two thousand each.

In the meantime the camp-followers dragged the bodies from the trench. The soldiers rested until morning, for they were convinced that the assault would not be repeated. All slept soundly, except Longin Podbipyenta, who lay in the form of a cross all night upon his sword, and thanked God that he had permitted him to accomplish his vow and to have gained such glory that his name was repeated from mouth to mouth in camp and town. Next morning he was summoned to the presence of Prince Vishnyovyetski, who praised him highly, while the soldiers came in crowds all day to congratulate him and to look at the three heads which had been placed by a servant before his tent and which were already blackening the air. There was no little amazement and envy, and some could scarce believe their own eyes for the heads and

PAN LONGIN SLASHED TERRIBLY.

linked cowls were cut off from the helmets as evenly as if they had been done with shears.

"You are a terrible cutter," exclaimed the nobles. "We knew well enough that you were an excellent knight, but the heroes of the ancient times might well envy you such a stroke, for the best executioner could not land a better."

"The wind does not take off caps from heads as easily as these heads were taken off," said others. All shook hands with Longin. He stood with downcast eyes, gentle and bashful as a bride at her wedding, and modestly said as though explaining it: "They were conveniently situated."

The crowd then examined the sword, but since it had extraordinary width and length, none could handle it freely, not even Father Jabkovski, though he could break a horse shoe like a reed.

Around the tent the babel of voices increased. Volodiyovski and Zagloba and Skshetuski received the visitors and entertained them with stories, for the last biscuit in the camp had been consumed and for a long time they had eaten no other meat but horse-flesh. Wit, however, made up for food and drink. At length when the others had commenced to disperse, Marek, Sobieski, the Starosta of Krasnostavsk and his lieutenant Stempovski approached. Pan Longin hurried out to welcome him. Sobieski greeted him warmly, and said:

"So you are having a holiday to-day?"

"It is indeed a holiday," said Zagloba, "for our friend has accomplished his vow."

"Praise be to God!" answered the chief, "then it will not be long before we congratulate you, little brother, on your marriage. Have you any one in view?"

Longin blushed with shame and confusion, but the chief continued:

"I see by your embarrassment that it is so. It is your sacred duty to keep in mind that such a stock should not die out. God grant that on stones should be born such soldiers as are you four gentlemen."

Then he shook hands with Longin, Skshetuski, Zagloba, and the little knight. They were rejoiced to hear praise from such lips, for Pan Krasnostavsk was a model of bravery, honor, and all knightly virtues, he was a personified Mars. All the gifts of God had been showered upon him, and in beauty he surpassed even his younger brother, who later became king. In nobility of birth, and in fortune he was equal to the first in the land, and his military acquirements were even praised by the great Yeremy himself. In him would have arisen a star of the first magnitude in the firmament of the Commonwealth, but that by God's decree, the younger brother Yan absorbed the glory, while he himself was dimmed before his time in a day of disaster. The knights therefore were greatly delighted at being praised by this hero. But he had not ended yet, and continued:

"Prince Vishnyovyetski has spoken much of you to me, for he loves you beyond all the others, and hence I do not wonder that you serve him without seeking promotion, which comes more readily in the service of the king."

Skshetuski replied to this:

"We are all enrolled in the hussar regiment of the king, with the exception of Zagloba, who from natural valor, serves as a volunteer. That we serve under the prince is due to our love for his person, and our desire to participate in as many battles as possible."

"If you love fighting, then you have done well. Pan Longin would have hardly found his three heads under any other command," said the chief. "But as far as war in concerned we all have had enough of it."

"More than of anything else," retorted Zagloba. "From early morning the soldiers have been coming hither with praises, but if any one had brought us a bit of bread and a drink of gorzalka, he would have pleased us best."

Then Zagloba looked meaningly into the eyes of the chief, and blinked at him. The chief smiled and said:

"Since yesterday noon nothing has passed my lips; but a swallow of gorzalka could, I think, be procured somewhere. Will you gentlemen come with me?"

But Skshetuski, Longin and the little knight protested, and began to scold Zagloba, who excused himself as well as he was able.

"I did not intend to drop a hint," he said, "for I prefer to give away something of my own, than to accept from another, but when such an exalted person gives an invitation it would be boorish to refuse."

"Come with me," said the chief, "for I like to be in pleasant company, and as no firing is going on, we can seize the occasion. I cannot invite you to lunch, for even horse-meat is scarce now, but I have still two bottles of gorzalka, which I do not intend to keep for myself."

The others still hesitated, but after being repeatedly urged, they consented and went along. Pan Stempovski hurried before them and managed to find a few biscuits and some bits of horse-meat. Zagloba cheered up wonderfully and said:

"May it please God that His Majesty the King, may come to our aid, then we will at once make an attack upon the wagon-loads of provisions that his militia bring with them. They always carry a great number of delicacies, and all of them care more for their stomachs than for the Commonwealth. I would rather eat with them than have their assistance in battle, but perhaps they may show greater valor under the eyes of the king."

The chief grew serious.

"We have vowed," said he, "to fall one after the other, rather than to surrender, and so it must be; we must prepare for still harder times. The provisions are giving out, and what it still worse, the powder is also. I would not say this to others, but to you I can speak freely. Soon nothing will be left to us but grim determination in our hearts, swords in our hands, and the readiness to die. May it please God to send us the king soon, for this is our last hope. The king is a soldier, and to deliver us he would spare neither comfort nor life, but his army is small, and you gentlemen know how slowly the general militia move. And how should the king know in what straits we are and that we are living upon crumbs."

"We have resolved to sacrifice ourselves," said Skshetuski.

"But cannot we send word to the king?" asked Zagloba.

"If we could find a man of such virtue as to undertake to make his way to the king by stealing through the enemy's camp," said the chief, "he would achieve immortal fame; he would become the savior of the whole army, and would avert grave disaster from our country. Even if all the forces have not assembled yet, the mere knowledge that the king was near might disperse the rebels. But who will go, who will undertake it in face of the fact that Khmyelnitski has every road so well guarded that not the smallest mouse could slip through? An undertaking of this sort means certain death."

"But what have we wits for?" said Zagloba. "A good idea strikes me already."

"What is it, what is it?" asked the chief.

"Every day we are taking a number of prisoners, what about bribing one of them? He could say that he had escaped from us, and he could hurry on to the king."

"I will bring the idea before the prince," said the chief.

Longin was deep in thought; his forehead was covered with wrinkles; he sat silent. Suddenly he raised his head and said, in his usual mild tone:

"I will undertake to steal through the Cossacks."

The knights sprang up in astonishment as they heard this. Zagloba stood with his mouth open, Volodiyovski twirled his little moustache, Skshetuski grew pale, and Krasnostavsk, striking his velvet vest, exclaimed: "You will undertake this?"

"Have you considered well what you say?" asked Skshetuski.

"I have thought over it for some time," replied the Lithuanian, "for this is not the first time that the knights have said 'if the king only knew of our condition!' And hearing this, I said to myself, 'If God permits me to fulfill my vow I will go at once!' I am but of small worth anyway, what would it signify even should I perish on the way."

"But you will certainly perish," said Zagloba. "Do you hear that the chief says it is sure death?"

"What does that matter, little brother?" said Longin, "if it please God He will guide me through in safety, if not, He will reward me in Heaven."

"Man alive, have you lost your senses?" said Zagloba. "First they will torture you and then put you to a horrible death."

"Even so I will go, little brother," replied the Lithuanian gently.

"A bird could not fly through without being pierced by an arrow. They have surrounded us like a badger in a hole."

"Nevertheless, I will go," repeated the Lithuanian. "I owe God thanks for allowing me to fulfill my vow."

"Look at him! examine him closely!" Zagloba cried in desperation, "you might as well have your head cut off at once and have it shot from a cannon over the camp, for this is the only way you can get past them."

"Permit me, my friends, I pray you," said the Lithuanian, clasping his hands.

"Oh, no! you shall not go by yourself, for I will go with you," said Skshetuski.

"And I, too," added Volodiyovski, striking his sword.

"The bullets strike you!" cried Zagloba, placing his hands to his head, "may the bullets strike you for your 'I too, I too,' for your audacity. They haven't seen enough blood yet, nor of destruction, nor bullets! Is it not enough what is happening here? No, they want to be more certain of losing their heads. Go to the deuce and let me alone! May the enemy kill you." . . . .

Then he rushed around the tent as if mad.

"God is punishing me," he cried, "for associating with whirlwinds, instead of living in the company of sensible men. Well, it serves me right."

He paced the tent for some time in feverish excitement, finally he stopped near Skshetuski, clasped his hands, and looking into his eyes, began to snort with anger:

"Have I done you any wrong, that you are planning my ruin?"

"God forbid!" answered the knight, "what do you mean?"

"I am not surprised that Longin gets such notions. He has always had his wit in his fist instead of his head, and since he chopped off the heads of the three biggest fools among the Turks, he has become the fourth one——"

"That is not a nice thing to say," interrupted the Lithuanian.

"And I am not surprised at that fellow, either," said Zagloba, pointing at Volodiyovski; "he can jump on a Cossack's boot or cling to his breeches like a burr to a dog's tail; he can get through easier than any of us. Neither of them have been enlightened by the Holy Spirit. But that you, instead of restraining their madness, spur them on by being willing to go yourself; that you should desire to deliver all four of us over to certain martyrdom; that is the worst blow of all. Fie! the deuce take it, I did not expect such madness from an officer whom the prince himself esteems as a sensible cavalier."

"How is that! all four?" asked Skshetuski, astonished, "will you go, too?"

"Yes," cried Zagloba, thumping himself on his chest. "If one of you go, or all go together, I will go too. My blood be on your heads, next time I shall know with whom to associate. This knowledge I have paid dearly for."

"O that you would . . . . " said Skshetuski. The three knights embraced him; but he was really angry and pushed them from him with his elbows, saying:

"Go to the devil, I don't want your Judas kisses."

The thunder of cannons and muskets resounded from the ramparts, Zagloba started and cried, "there you have it, there you have it, now go."

"It is only ordinary firing, the testing of the guns," remarked Skshetuski.

"Ordinary firing," repeated Zagloba, mimicking him; "pray is not this enough for you, half the army has melted away under this ordinary firing, and these fellows now turn up their noses at it."

"Be calm!" said Longin.

"Keep qiet, beet-soup-swiller!" roared Zagloba, "you are the most guilty, you concocted the whole scheme, if no one is mad, I am mad."

"But I shall go nevertheless, little brother," answered Longin.

"You'll go, you'll go, and I know why, don't pretend to be a hero, you are too well known for that; you are tired of virtue, and you want to take it outside the ramparts and sell it. You are nothing but a wench who takes her virtue to the market. Fie on you! that's what you are, you do not really desire to hasten to the king, you desire to roam through the villages like a horse through the pasture, behold! a nice knight, who offers his virtue for sale! Sheer bitterness! sheer bitterness! as I love God."

"It is shameful to listen to him," cried Longin, clapping his hands over his ears.

"Stop this quarreling," said Skshetuski, earnestly. "Let us speak about the business."

"In God's name!" said the chief, who had listened in astonishment to Zagloba, "this is a matter of great importance, but without the prince you cannot decide anything. There is no need of further discussion. You gentlemen are in service and obliged to obey orders. The prince is, I presume, in his quarters, let us see what he thinks of your offer."

"Exactly what I think," remarked Zagloba, and hope brightened his face. "Let us make haste."

They went on and passed through the square, where the enemy's bullets were falling. The soldiers were on the ramparts, which, from a distance, looked like booths at a fair, over them hung clothes of various colors and sheepskins, and they were packed with wagons, portions of tents, and all sorts of other articles that might serve as a protection against the continuous volleys which for weeks had ceased neither by night nor by day. Above these odds and ends appeared a bluish line of smoke and behind them rows of soldiers in red and yellow uniforms, working hard against the nearest entrenchments of the enemy. The square looked like a heap of ruins; the level space had been dug up with spades, trampled by horses, and not a green blade of grass was showing. Here and there were mounds of earth freshly turned over about newly-made wells, remains of broken wagons, cannon, barrels, or heaps of bones whitening in the sun. No dead horses could be seen, for these were immediately removed to serve as food for the soldiers, but everywhere were heaps of rusty iron balls, which fell every day upon this small bit of ground. At every step the horror and misery of war was betrayed. On their way the knights met small groups of soldiers, some carrying wounded or dead, others hurrying to the ramparts to relieve their weary comrades. The faces of all were blackened, sunken, unshaven; their eyes were red and inflamed, their uniforms faded and torn, their heads were covered with dirty rags instead of helmets. and caps, their weapons were broken. The thought forced itself upon one, "when one or two weeks have passed what will become of this little handful of victims?"

"You see, gentlemen," said the chief, "it is high time that the king should know our condition."

"Famine is showing its teeth already like a dog," said the little knight.

"What will happen when we have eaten up the horses?" asked Skshetuski.

Conversing thus they reached the tent of the prince on the right side of the ramparts, in front of which stood a few aides on horseback, whose duty it was to take the prince's orders through the camp. The poor beasts, fed on dried and chopped-up horse-flesh, and tortured by an incessant, internal burning, reared continually and were unable to remain on one spot. This was the case with the horses of the entire cavalry, which, when they went out against the enemy, looked like a herd of griffins or hippo-centaurs, seeming to be more in the air, than chasing along the ground.

"Is the prince within," asked the chief of one of the orderlies.

"He is closeted with Pan Pshiyemski," answered the orderly.

The chief entered without announcing himself, but the four knights remained outside. After awhile the flap of the tent was pushed aside and Pan Pshiyemski stuck his head through the opening. "The prince wishes to see you at once," he said.

48

Zagloba entered the tent in good spirits, for he hoped that the Prince would not consent to let his best knights go to certain destruction; but he was mistaken, for ere they could bow to him he said:

"Pan Krasnostavsk has told me of your readiness to go from the camp and I accept your service. There is no sacrifice too great for the country."

"We merely came to ask for your permission," said Skshetuski, "for your Highness is master of our lives."

"I understand that all four of you wish to go."

"Your Highness," said Zagloba, "they want to go, but not I. God is my witness that I have not come here to praise myself or to recall my services, and if I do so it is merely to save me from the suspicion of being thought a coward. Skshetuski, Volodiyovski, and Pan Longin Myshykishki are great knights, but Burlay, who fell beneath my hand (not to mention other deeds)was also a great warrior, equal to Burdabut, Bohun, and the three heads of the janissaries. Therefore, as regards valor I do not stand behind the others, but valor and madness are not to be confounded. We have no wings and we can't get through on land that is certain."

"You will not go then?" asked the prince.

"I said that I did not wish to go, not that I will not go. Since God has punished me by making me their comrade, I must remain with them while I live. If things go badly the sword of Zagloba will be of some service. But I fail to comprehend how the death of the four of us can be of any benefit, and I confide in your Highness to save us from it by refusing to allow this insane expedition."

"You are a good comrade," replied the prince, "and it proves your faithfulness that you do not wish to part with your friends, but your confidence in me is misplaced, for I accept the offer."

"The dog is dead," muttered Zagloba, letting his hands drop.

Firley the Castellan of Belsk now entered the tent. "Your Highness," said he, "my men have just captured a Cossack who says that there will be an assault to-night."

"I have already been informed of it," replied the prince, "everything is ready, but let the work be hastened on the ramparts."

"They are nearly finished."

"Very well," said the prince, "before evening we will occupy them."

Then he turned to the four knights:

"After the assault, if the night is dark, will be the best time to start out."

"Why," said the castellan of Belsk, "is your Grace preparing a sally?"

"The sally is another matter," said the prince. "I myself shall lead it, but now we are speaking of something else. These gentlemen undertake to steal their way through the enemy's camp and to notify the king about the condition of affairs."

The castellan was dumbfounded, he opened wide his eyes and stared at the knights in turn. The prince smiled with pleasure. It was his weakness, he liked to have his soldiers admired.

"In God's name," said the castellan, "are there such brave hearts in the world? God knows, gentlemen, I shall not attempt to dissuade you from so brave a deed."

Zagloba grew purple with rage, but he said nothing he merely growled like a bear. The prince thought for a while and said: "However, gentlemen, I do not want to waste your blood in vain, and I will not consent to have all four of you go together. First one shall go; should he be killed, the enemy will not be backward in boasting about it, as they had boasted about the death of my servant, whom they caught near Lemberg. Should the first one be killed, the second shall go, and then, in case of necessity, the third and fourth. It may be that the first one will be fortunate enough to get through, in such a case I do not wish to risk the lives of the others."

"Your Highness," interrupted Skshetuski.

"This is my will and my command," said Yeremy, with emphasis. "And that there may be no disagreement, I declare that he shall go first who offered himself first."

"It was I," said Pan Longin, with a face beaming with happiness.

"Then to-night after the assault, if the night be dark," added the prince. "I shall send no letters to the king. Tell what you have seen; take my signet ring as a credential."

Podbipyenta took the signet and bowed low before the prince, who, placing his hands upon his head, kissed him repeatedly upon the forehead, saying in a voice broken with emotion:

"You are as close to my heart as a brother. May the God of Hosts and our Queen of Angels guide and protect you through the enemy's lines, soldier of God, Amen."

"Amen," repeated the Starosta of Krasnostavsk, Pan Pshi-Yemski, and the Castellan of Belsk.

The prince's eyes were swimming in tears, for he was a true father to the knights. The others wept, and Podbipyenta shivered as of a fever, and a flame passed through his bones; this pure, humble, heroic soul was greatly rejoiced by the hope of the coming sacrifice.

"You will go down in history," cried the Castellan of Belsk.

"Not to us, not to us, but to Thy name O Lord, let the glory be given," repeated the prince.

The knights left the tent.

"Whew! Something seized me by the throat and chokes me, and in my mouth is a taste as bitter as wormwood," said Zagloba. "And over there (pointing to the smoking earthworks of the Cossacks) they still keep on firing. . . . Oh, that the lightning might strike you! Oh, it is a hard life in this world! Longin, must you really go? May the Holy Angels protect you! O, that a plague might choke those peasants!"

"I must leave you now," said Longin.

"Why, where are you going?" asked Zagloba.

"To the priest Mukhovietski, to confession, my dear friend. I must cleanse my sinful soul."

Then Podbipyenta hurried to the castle; the others turned towards the ramparts. Skshetuski and Pan Michael were silent, but Zagloba said:

"Something holds me by the throat. I did not think that I should feel such sorrow for him, but he is the most virtuous man in the world. If ever any one disputes this I'll slap his snout for him. My God! my God! I thought the castellan of Belsk would advise against this folly, but no, he assisted the prince with his drum. The devil brought us that heretic. 'You will go down in history,' he said. 'History will write of you.' Let it write of him, but not on the skin of Longin. Why in the world does he not go himself? He has six toes on his feet like every Calvinist, and therefore can run all the better. I tell you, gentlemen, that it is getting worse and worse in this world, and no doubt the priest Jabkovski prophecies correctly when he says that the end of the world is near. Let us sit down awhile at the ramparts, and then go to the castle in order to enjoy the company of our friend, at least until evening."

But Longin spent the whole time after confession and communion, in prayer. He did not make his appearance until evening, when the assault had begun. This was a terrible assault, for the Cossacks attacked just when the troops were transporting their artillery and wagons to the newly made ramparts. It seemed for a time that the little Polish army must succumb before the fierce onset of two hundred thousand of the enemy. The Polish forces had become so mixed up with their foes that they could not distinguish their own and three times they closed in. Khmyelnitski put forth all his power, for the Khan and his own captains had told him that this must be the last assault, and that henceforward they would content themselves with starving the besieged. But within three hours all attacks were repulsed with such losses that later a report spread that forty thousand of the enemy had fallen. So much is certain, that after the battle, a great bundle of flags were brought to the prince, and that this in reality was the last assault. But harder times followed for the besieged, continuous firing, undermining of their ramparts, loss of their wagons, suffering and famine.

Immediately after the assault the untiring Yeremy led his weary troops to a sally, which completed the defeat of the enemy. Quiet now reigned in the tabor and the camp.

The night was warm but cloudy. In the darkness four men made their way carefully and quietly to the eastern end of the ramparts. They were Longin, Zagloba, Skshetuski and Pan Michael.

"Take good care of the pistols," whispered Skshetuski, "lest they should get wet. Two squadrons will be in readiness all night. If you fire we shall rush to the rescue."

"It is confoundedly dark, nothing can be seen even by straining the eyes," whispered Zagloba.

"So much the better," answered Longin.

"Keep still," interrupted Pan Michael. "I hear something."

"It is nothing, the rattle of a dying man."

"I would you were already near the oaks."

"O God! my God!" sighed Zagloba, trembling as if in a fever, "in three hours it will begin to dawn."

"Then it is time now," said Longin.

"Yes, the time has come," repeated Skshetuski, with a choking voice. "God be with you!"

"God be with you! God be with you!"

"Farewell, brothers, and forgive me if I have offended any of you."

"You offend! O God!" exclaimed Zagloba, throwing himself into his arms.

Then Skshetuski and Pan Michael embraced him. For a moment suppressed sobs shook the breasts of the knights. Only Longin was calm although he was deeply affected.

"Farewell," he repeated once more, and going to the edge of the rampart, he dropped into the ditch and after awhile appeared on the opposite bank. Once more he waved a farewell to his friends, and disappeared into the darkness.

Between the road to Zaloshtsits and the highway leading from Vishnyovyets there was an oak grove, interspersed by narrow meadows. Near by was an old and dense pine forest which extended beyond Zaloshtsits It was towards this that Longin attempted to make his way.

The way was very dangerous, for in order to reach the grove, he was obliged to pass all along the Cossack entrenchments. Longin, however, had purposely chosen this way, for it was just around the camp, where people were continually passing to and fro throughout the night, that the guards paid least attention to the passers by. All other roads, ravines, thickets, and paths, were beset with guards who were patrolled continually by sergeants, setniks, colonels, and even by Khmyelnitski himself. A passage across the meadows, along the Gniezna could not be thought of, for there the Tartar herders kept guard over the horses from evening until dawn.

It was a cloudy night, and so dark that nothing, neither man nor tree, could be seen at a distance of ten steps. This circumstance was favorable to Longin; though on the other hand he was obliged to walk very slowly and carefully, lest he should fall into one of the ditches or pits that covered the entire battle-field and had been dug by Polish and Cossack hands. In this manner he reached the second Polish rampart that had been evacuated just before evening, and after he had crossed the ditch, he crawled towards the entrenchments of the Cossacks. He stopped and listened, the entrenchments were empty. The sortie made by Yeremy had driven the enemy out, and they had either fallen, or had fled to the wagon-train. A number of corpses lay upon the slopes and tops of the mounds. Longin stumbled every moment over bodies as he picked his way over them. From time to time a groan or a sigh indicated that life in some of them was not extinct.

Beyond the ramparts was a spacious tract, extending to the second trench, and this was also full of bodies. Here there were still more holes and ditches, besides at a small distance from each other, were earth shelters looking like hayricks in the darkness. These were also deserted, and everywhere the most profound silence reigned. Nowhere a fire or a man were visible, no one on the entire plain except the fallen.

Pan Longin started to pray for the souls of the deceased and continued his journey. The sounds of the Polish camp, which followed him to the second rampart, grew fainter and fainter until they were lost in the distance. Pan Longin stopped and looked back for the last time.

He could scarcely see anything for no light was burning in the camp, only one little window of the castle twinkled faintly like a star, or like a glow worm which gleams out and darkens in turn.

"My brethren, shall I see you again in this life?" thought Longin.

Sadness pressed upon him like a heavy stone, he could hardly breathe. There where that little light was shining, there were his friends, his brother hearts, Prince Yeremy, Skshetuski, Pan Michael, Zagloba, the priest Mukhovietski— he was loved, there he would be gladly defended. But here— night, desolation, darkness, corpses about his feet, looming apparitions, before him the entrenchments of the blood thirsty, accursed and pitiless enemy.

The weight of sadness pressed so heavily upon the shoulders of this giant that his courage began to fail.

Dreadful alarm haunted him and whispered in his ear "You can't get through, it isn't possible. Return now, while there is still time! discharge your pistol, an entire squadron will hasten to your aid! Through those defenses, through those savages, nothing can pass."

That starving camp hourly sprinkled with balls, filled with death, and the stench of corpses, appeared to Longin now as a quiet, safe retreat. His friends there would not upbraid him if he returned. He would tell them that the deed was beyond human power, they themselves should not go, nor should they send another, they would await further for the mercy of God and the coming of the king.

But if Skshetuski should go nevertheless, and perish:

"In the name of the Father, Son, and Holy Ghost! these are temptations of the devil," thought Longin. "I am prepared to die and nothing worse can happen to me. Thus Satan frightens the weak soul with desolation, darkness, and corpses, for he makes use of everything. Should a knight heap shame upon himself, lose his fame, disgrace his name, not save the army, renounce a celestial crown? Never!"

And he went on with his hands extended forward.

Now he again heard a noise, but not from the Polish camp, but from the opposite side. It was still indistinct, but deep and threatening like the growling of a bear who suddenly awakens in a dark forest. But unrest had now left the soul of the knight, sadness had ceased to oppress him and was transformed into a sweet remembrance of his dearest friends. At length, as if in answer to the threatening murmur that came from the entrenchments, he repeated once more to himself:

"But still I will go."

After some time he reached that part of the battle-field, where on the day of the first assault, the prince's cavalry had put the Cossacks and janissaries to flight. Here the way was more even, there being fewer ditches, earth shelters, and but few corpses, for the Cossacks had removed the dead that had fallen in earlier struggles. It was clearer here too, the ground was not so covered with obstacles. The land sloped towards the south, but Longin at once turned towards the flank, in order to creep through between the western lake and the wagon train.

He could get over the ground now much faster, for there were less impediments, and he had almost reached the line of the wagon train, when a new noise attracted his attention.

He halted at once and after waiting for a quarter of an hour he could distinguish the tramp and the breathing of horses. "Cossack patrols," thought he. Now the voices of men reached his ear. He sprang aside and as soon as he felt a depression in the ground with his foot, he threw himself upon the earth and lay there motionless, holding his pistol in one hand and his sword in the other.

The horsemen came still nearer and soon were right upon

him. It was so dark he could not count them, but he could hear every word of their conversation.

"It is hard for them, but it is hard for us also," said one, in a sleepy voice, "and how many good warriors have bitten the dust."

"Queen of Heaven," said another voice. "They say the king is not far away. . . . what will happen to us then?"

"The Khan is angered at our leader, and the Tartars are threatening to put chains upon us."

"On the pastures they fight with our men. Our father has forbidden us to enter the horse enclosures, for whoever enters is lost."

"They say that among the market men are disguised Poles, I wish that this war had never broken out."

"We are worse off now than before."

"The king is in the vicinity with the Polish army, that is the worst of it."

"Hey! in Sich you would be sleeping at this hour, but here you have to knock about in the darkness like a vampire."

"There must be vampires about, for the horses are snorting."

The voices grew fainter and fainter in the distance until they could be heard no more. Longin rose and went on.

A drizzling rain, fine as mist, came on; it grew still darker. To the left of Longin at some distance off, there gleamed a small light, then a second, a third, a tenth, and so on. Now he was sure that he was on the line of the wagon train. The little lights were set far apart and emitted but a feeble glimmer. Probably everybody was asleep, or perhaps here and there some might be drinking or preparing food for the morrow.

"Thank God that I came out after the assault and the sally. They are no doubt tired unto death," said Longin to himself.

Scarcely had he said this, when he heard anew the trampling of horses. It was another patrol. The ground about had been torn up a good deal, so that it offered good hiding places. The patrol passed by so near that he was almost run over. Fortunately the horses were used to prostrate bodies and did not become frightened. Longin went on.

Within a distance of about a thousand steps, he met two more patrols. Evidently the whole entire circle about was guarded like the apple of the eye, but Longin was only glad that he did not meet any of the infantry sentries, who are generally stationed before the wagon trains, in order to give notice to the patrols.

His joy, however, was of short duration. He had hardly gone ahead one furlong, when scarce ten steps in front of him, a dark figure emerged. Longin, though of undaunted courage, felt a slight chill pass through his body. It was too late to retreat and to skirt around the sentinel. The figure approached, he must have been noticed, a moment of hesitation followed, then a husky voice asked:

"Vasil, is that you?"

"It is I," replied Longin.

"Have you the gorzalka?"

"Yes, I have it."

"Give it to me."

Longin approached him.

"Why are you so big?" asked the voice, in terror stricken tones.

Something staggered in the darkness. A cry of "God——" instantly smothered, issued from the mouth of the guard. Then a crunching was heard like that of breaking bones, a rattling from the throat, and a figure fell noiselessly to the ground.

Longin went on.

But he skirted about, as he had evidently struck a line of patrol; he approached closer to the wagon train in order to pass between the pickets and the line of wagons. If there was no line of pickets here Longin could meet none but pickets going out to relieve others, for there were no mounted patrols here.

It was soon apparent that there was not a second line, the line of wagons, however, was not further away than a couple of bow shots. Strangely he seemed to be getting nearer to it, although he attempted always to remain at an equal distance. It was evident also that all were not asleep about here. He could see groups sitting around smouldering fires. In one place the fire was brighter, so bright that its gleam almost discovered Longin, and he was obliged to retreat back towards the pickets so as not to get into the belt of light. From a distance he could distinguish oxen suspended from posts near the fire, which were being skinned by butchers. Groups of men watched this proceeding; some were playing upon pipes; it was evident that this was the part of the camp occupied by the drovers. The other rows of wagons were hidden by the darkness.

The line of the bulwark which was faintly illuminated again appeared to get nearer to him. At first he had only had it on his right, now he suddenly found it just in front of him.

He stopped and considered what was best to be done. The bulwark and the camps of the Tartars and the "blacks" surrounded Zbaraj, like a ring, within this ring sentries were posted and patrols were moving about to see that no one should pass.

Longin was in a terrible position. He would either have to creep through between the wagons or seek another way between the Cossacks and the Tartars. Otherwise he would have to roam about the outer circle until dawn, or return to Zbaraj. But even in the latter case he might fall into the hands of the enemies. He understood, however, that one wagon could not be crowded up closely to another because of the nature of the ground. There ought to be considerable openings; besides such openings were necessary for intercourse and exit. . . Longin determined to look for such a passage and so again approached the row of wagons. The light of fires burning here and there might betray him, but on the other hand they were useful, for without them, he could see neither the wagons nor the passage ways between them.

After searching carefully for about a quarter of an hour, he found such a passage-way and readily recognized it, for it looked like a black belt. There were no fires on it and there could be no Cossacks, for this was a road that must be left for the horsemen. Longin got on all fours and commenced to creep along that dark opening like a snake into its hole.

A quarter of an hour; a half hour passed, and he was still creeping, praying, and commending his body and soul to the protection of heaven. He called to mind that the fate of Zbaraj depended on his passing through this gully. He prayed not only for himself, but also for those who at the moment were praying within the ramparts for him. All was quiet on both sides of him. No one stirred, not a horse snorted, not a dog barked, and Longin luckily crept through. Before him he already saw dark bushes, behind which was the oak grove, and beyond that the forest continued as far as Toporova; beyond the forest was the king, safety, glory, and merit, in the eyes of God and man. What was the stroke by which he cut off three heads in comparison to this deed which required something else than an iron hand.

Longin felt the difference, but his clean heart was not

swelled by pride, like that of a child it melted in tears of thankfulness.

Then he arose from the ground and walked on, beyond the wagons there were but few pickets; if any, those could be easily avoided. It began to rain harder and the rain pattering upon the bushes, drowned his footsteps. He let his long legs out and went on like a giant, trampling everything in his way; each step was equal to five of an ordinary man. The wagons were left further in the distance, the oak grove drew ever nearer, and in it was salvation.

The oaks were at hand, beneath them it was as dark as under the earth; but so much the better. A light breeze sprang up. The oaks rustled as if breathing a prayer, "Almighty God! Gracious God! preserve this knight! for he is Thy servant and a faithful son of the land on which we have grown with Thy glory."

One mile and a half separated Longin from the Polish camp. Perspiration covered his brow, for the air was peculiarly sultry, as if a storm were gathering; but he hurried on regardless of the storm, for the angels were singing in his heart. The grove became thinner, and this meant the first meadow was close by. The oaks rustled louder, as if they wished to say, "Wait awhile yet, you are safe with us." But the knight has no time and steps out into the open meadow. A solitary oak, taller than the rest, stands in the centre, towards this Longin moves.

Suddenly, when he was but a few steps away from the giant oak, about twenty dark figures rushed out from beneath its branches, and sped like wolves towards the knight.

"Who are you, who are you?"

Their language was unintelligible. The covering of their heads were pointed.

These were Tartar herders, who had sought shelter here from the rain.

At that moment red lightning illumined the field, revealing the oak, the wild figures, and the gigantic knight. A terrible cry rent the air, in a moment the battle began.

The Tartars threw themselves at Longin like wolves at a deer, and clutched him with their sinewy hands; but he only shook himself, and his assailants fell from him as ripe fruit from a tree. Then his terrible sword, "Cowl-cutter," flew from its sheath, and soon resounded groans, howls, shouts for help, the whistling of the sword, the cries of the wounded,

PAN LONGIN'S LAST FIGHT.

the neighing of horses, and the crash of broken Tartar sabres. The quiet field echoed with all the wild sounds that can be uttered by the human throat.

The Tartars hurled themselves in packs at the knight, but he leaned his back against the oak, and defended himself in front with his whirling sword, which cut and slashed in a terrible manner. Bodies lay stretched at the feet of the knight, the others fell back panic stricken.

"A div! a div!" they howled out in terror.

The howling was not in vain. Scarce a half hour passed before the whole meadow was filled with people afoot and on horseback. Cossacks an l Tartars flocked with scythes, clubs, bows, poles, and burning pitch pine. Excited questions began to fly from mouth to mouth. "What is the matter, what has happened?" "A div!" answered the herders. "A div!" repeated the crowd, "a Pole, a monster, beat him, take him alive, alive."

Longin fired two shots from his pistol, but the distance was too great for them to be heard from the Polish camp. Now the crowd approached him in a semi-circle, he stood in the shadow of the tree, looming like a giant, with his back against its trunk, and waited, his sword in his hand. The crowd came nearer and nearer. Finally a voice of command called out:

"Seize him!"

All who had not bitten the dust rushed at him; the shouting ceased; those who could not get at him held lights for the assailants. A confused crowd of men struggled beneath the tree, groans arose and for a time it was impossible to distinguish anything. Finally a cry of terror arose from the assailants. The crowd dispersed in a moment.

Beneath the tree stood Pan Longin alone, and at his feet a crowd of bodies quivering in their death throes.

"Ropes, ropes!" shouted a voice.

Several horsemen flew away and in a moment brought back ropes. Then a number of strong men seized a long rope by both ends and tried to tie Longin to the tree; but he slashed with his sword and the men on both sides fell to the ground. A second attempt was followed by the same result.

Perceiving that too many men in a crowd only get in each other's way, a number of the boldest Nogais tried again to capture the giant alive; but he rent them like a wild boar rends the attacking dogs. The oak, which consisted of two mighty trees that had grown together, protected the knight in its central depression; whoever in front got within ranage of his sword died without uttering a groan. The superhuman strength of Longin seemed to increase with each moment. Seeing this the maddened hordes drove away the Cossacks and all round resounded a wild cry:

"Bows, bows!"

When he saw the bows, and the arrows poured out from their quivers at the feet of his assailants, Longin recognized that the hour of his death had arrived, and he began to say the litany of the most Holy Virgin.

Silence fell, the crowd held its breath in expectation of what would happen. The first arrow whizzed forth just as Longin repeated "Mother of the Redeemer," and it grazed his temple, another arrow flew forth as Longin said "O Blessed Virgin," and it stuck fast in his shoulder. The words of the litany mingled with the whizzing of the arrows and when Longin had said "Star of the morning" arrows were sticking in his shoulders, in his sides, and legs. Blood oozing from a wound in his temple flowed over his eyes; he saw as through a mist, the meadow, and the Tartars. Presently he heard no longer the whizzing of arrows; he felt that his strength was forsaking him, that his legs were bending beneath him: his head dropped on his breast. For the last time he fell on his knees. Then he said in a half groan, "Queen of the Angels," and these were his last words on earth.

The hosts in heaven received his soul and placed it as a translucent pearl at the feet of the Queen of the Angels.

THIS IS THE SECOND.

CHAPTER VI.

On the next morning Pan Volodiyovski and Zagloba were standing on the ramparts among the soldiers, looking attentively towards the hostile camp, from whence a dense mass was approaching. Skshetuski was in consultation with the prince; but they took advantage of this moment of peace to speak about the events of the preceding day and about the present movements in the enemy's camp.

"That is not a good omen," said Zagloba, pointing at the black mass that moved along like a gigantic cloud. "They surely come to the assault again and here the hands are stiff."

"They will scarce think of making an assault in broad daylight and at this time," said the little knight, "all they will do will be to take possession of our rampart of yesterday, undermine the new one, and fire upon us from morning until evening."

"We could easily decimate them with the cannon."

Pan Michael lowered his voice and answered: "The powder is getting scarce. I have heard it will not suffice for six days if we use as much as we have lately. But the king will surely be here before that."

"I care not what happens, if only our poor Longin gets through all right. I could not sleep all night for thinking of him; and whenever I fell into a doze I saw him in danger and was so alarmed that I perspired all over. He is the best man that can be found in the Commonwealth, even if you looked all over the land with a lantern for three years and six Sundays."

"But why did you always turn him into ridicule?"

"Because my mouth is dirtier than my heart. Don't make my heart bleed with recollections, dear Michael, for I have reproached myself enough already, and God forbid that any disaster befall Pan Longin, for I would find no peace till the day of my death."

"You must not grieve so long. He never was angered at

you and I often heard him say 'an evil mouth, but a golden heart.'"

"God give health to this good friend! He never knew how to talk, but his great virtue made up a hundredfold for this deficiency. What do you think, Pan Michael, will he get through all right?"

"The night was dark and the peasants were tired and worn out after the defeat. Our sentinels were not in good condition, theirs must have been much less so."

"Praise be to God! I asked Longin to find out whether our poor princess had been seen anywhere, for I think Jendzian must have escaped with her to the royal army. Longin will hardly take a rest, and will surely come here with the king. In that case we shall soon hear of her."

"I put faith in the wit of that fellow Jendzian, and I trust that in some manner he has saved her. Should she have perished I could never be happy again in this life. I only knew her for a short time, but had I one I could not love a sister more."

"She was a sister to you, but to me a daughter. These cares will doubtless make my beard as white as snow, and break my heart. Hardly do you learn to love anybody, when, one, two, three, and that one is gone. And all that is left for you is to sit and worry, and grieve, and torment yourself, and brood, going about with an empty stomach and a cap full of holes, through which water falls upon your bald pate as through a poorly-thatched roof. Dogs are better off in the Commonwealth nowadays than the nobles, and we four are the worst off of all. It is time to go to a better world, Pan Michael. What do you think?"

"More than once I have wondered whether it would not be better to tell Skshetuski everything. But I am restrained from doing so because he never mentions her name, and if any one happens to mention it he starts as if his heart had been pierced."

"Tell him all about it now; open the wounds that have healed in this fire of war, leaving but a scar behind, while now, perhaps, some Tartar is dragging her by the hair over the Perekop. I see wax-tapers (funeral) when I think of such an end. It is about time to die; it cannot be otherwise; for there is nothing on earth but affliction. If only Pan Longin has a happy escape!"

"Heaven must favor him more than others, for he is virtuous. But look! what is the rabble doing over yonder? The sun is so dazzling to-day that I can't see."

"They are digging under our newly made rampart of yesterday."

"I said that there would be an assault. Let us depart, Pan Michael, we have stood here long enough."

"They are not digging in order to make an assault at all events; they must make an open road for retreat, and they will probably bring up their engines on which their gunners are stationed; just see how their spades are flying; already they have leveled the ground for about forty paces."

"Now I see, though the glare is dazzling to-day."

Zagloba covered his eyes with his hand and looked attentively. The blacks rushed through the cut dug into the rampart and immediately spread over the bare space between the ramparts. Some began to fire at once, others, digging up the ground, began to heap up a new rampart to enclose the Polish camp with a third ring.

"Oh, ho!" exclaimed Pan Michael, "did I not say so? They are rolling up the engines already."

"Well then, the assault will be very lively. Let us go," said Zagloba.

"No, these are another kind of engines," said the little knight.

Indeed the machines that had appeared in the opening were built upon a different plan from the usual kind. Their walls consisted of ladders fastened with hasps and covered with cloths and skins; behind these from the middle of the machine up to the top the best marksmen were ensconced.

"Let us go, let those dogs worry on," exclaimed Zagloba.

"Wait awhile," replied Volodiyovski.

He began to count the engines in order, noting each new one as it appeared in the opening.

"One, two, three . . . . it is evident that they have quite a number . . . . four, five, six . . . . they are still coming . . . . seven, eight . . . . they will kill every dog on the square, for those must be their best marksmen . . . . nine, ten . . . . each one stands out distinctly for the sun shines upon them . . . . eleven . . . . "

Suddenly Pan Michael ceased counting.

"What is that?" he asked in a voice of astonishment.

"Where?"

"There upon the highest one . . . . a man is hanging."

49

Zagloba strained his eyes. Indeed the sun was shining upon the body of a man dangling by a rope from the highest engine, and swaying to and fro with its motion.

"True," said Zagloba.

Pan Michael suddenly became as pale as linen and cried out in accents of terror:

"Almighty God! It is Podbipyenta!"

A murmur rose on the ramparts as when a wind blows through a forest. Zagloba bent his head, covered his eyes with his hand, and with blue lips groaned out:

"Jesus Maria! Jesus Maria!"

Now the murmur changed into a babel of confused words, and then into a roar like storming waves. The soldiers on the ramparts saw that on that rope of infamy was hanging Pan Longin Podbipyenta, the sharer of their misfortune, the spotless knight. And anger, terrible anger, caused the hair of the soldiers to stand on end.

Zagloba at last took his hands from his eyes. He was fearful to look upon. His face was blue, his eyes were protruding and he foamed at the mouth.

"Blood! blood!" he roared, with so terrible a voice, that a shiver passed through the bystanders.

He sprang into the ditch. Everything alive upon the ramparts plunged after him. No power on earth, not even the command of the prince could have restrained this outburst of fury. They climbed out of the ditch, scrambling over each other, seizing with their hands and teeth the bank of the ditch, and when one was over he rushed off blindly, not looking to see if others followed.

The infernal engines were smoking like pitch-ovens, and shook with the thunder of discharges. But this did not deter the assailants. Zagloba rushed ahead, swinging his sword over his head and raging like a mad bull. The Cossacks sprang against the assailants with flails and scythes. It seemed as if two walls were tumbling over each other with a tremendous crash. But the well-fed pack of hounds could not defend themselves long against the hungry and maddened wolves. Thrust from their places, cut with swords, torn with teeth, crushed and beaten, the Cossacks could not withstand the furious onslaught. Confusion set in and they fled to the openings. Zagloba, raging, rushed into the densest crowd like a lioness whose cubs have been stolen. He was snorting with rage and he struck down and trampled upon those that opposed him; he cleared a way about himself, and nearby like another destroying flame came Volodiyovski, wild as a wounded leopard.

The marksmen, entrenched in the engines, were cut to pieces; the others were driven to the opening in the ramparts. Then the soldiers mounted the engine and untying the body of Pan Longin, they lowered it carefully to the ground.

Zagloba threw himself upon the corpse. . . Volodiyovski's heart was also bleeding, and he wept bitterly at the sight of his dead friend. It was easy to see in what manner Pan Longin had perished, for his whole body was covered with little holes made by the points of arrows. But the face was not disfigured, save for the wound on the temple, that an arrow had made. The few drops of blood had dried up on his cheeks, his eyes were closed, and on his pale face was a peaceful smile. Had it not been for the bluish tint on his face and the rigor of death upon his features, it might have seemed that Pan Longin was sleeping peacefully. His comrades bore him to the ramparts and thence into the chapel of the castle.

By evening a coffin was made, and the funeral took place at night in the churchyard of Zbaraj. All the clergy of Zbaraj were present, except the priest Jabkovski, who had been shot in the back during the last assault and was at the point of death. The prince came also, having for the time being transferred the command to the Chief of Krasnostavsk. There were present also the commanders, the crown ensign, the ensign of Novogorad, Pshiyemski, Skshetuski, Volodiyovski, Zagloba, and all the companions-in-arms of the squadron in which the dead man had served. The coffin was placed by the newly-made grave, and the ceremony began.

The night was calm and starlit. The torches threw their light upon the yellow boards of the hastily-made coffin, upon the figure of the priest, and upon the set faces of the knights standing about.

The smoke rising from the censors filled the air with the odor of myrrh and juniper. The silence was broken only by the stifled sobs of Zagloba. The deep sighs that issued from the strong breasts of the knights, and the distant thunder of cannon on the ramparts.

Now the priest Mukhovietski raised his hand to indicate his desire to speak, the knights therefore held their breath. He was silent for a moment, then he fixed his eyes upon the star-studded firmament and spoke as follows:

" 'What knocking do I hear at night on the gate of Heaven?'
asks the hoary warden of Christ's kingdom, awakened from
sweet slumber. 'Open, Holy Peter, open, it is I, Podbipyenta.' "

"But what rank, what deeds, what merits, can O Podbipyenta bolden thee to trouble the venerable door-keeper? By
what right dost thou wish to enter there when neither birth,
though even as high as thine, nor senatorial dignity, nor royal
offices, nor majesty, nor ever royal purple, is allowed free
entrance; where one cannot drive on the broad road in a
chariot and six, surrounded by haiduks, but must clamber by
the narrow and thorny path of virtue?"

"Ah, open, Holy Peter, open quickly, for by just such a
narrow path wandered our mess-mate and dear brother Pan
Podbipyenta till he at last appeared before you; came naked
like Lazarus, pierced by Pagan arrows like the holy Sebastian,
poor like Job, pure as a virgin who has never known a man,
pure as a lamb, patient and silent, without a blemish of sin,
with the sacrifice of his blood, shed gladly for his earthly
fatherland. Admit him, Holy Peter, for if not him then
whom wilt thou admit, in these times of corruption and god-
lessness? Admit him, Holy Peter, admit this innocent lamb
and let him graze on the heavenly pasture; let him crop its
grass, for he has come hungry from Zbaraj. . . . "

In this manner the priest Mukhovietski commenced his discourse, and then he depicted the whole life of Longin with
such eloquence that everyone felt wicked in the presence of
the silent coffin that bore the spotless knight, who had surpassed the lowliest in modesty and the greatest in virtue. All
struck their breasts and a constantly-growing sorrow oppressed
them, as they recognized more clearly what a paroxysm had
seized the Fatherland and how irretrievably Zbaraj had lost.
The priest continued in inspired words, and when he described how Longin had left the camp and died the death of
a martyr, he forgot his rhetoric and quotations, and when he
addressed farewell words to the remains of the hero, in the
name of the clergy, the commanders, and the army, he burst
into tears, and sobbing like Zagloba, continued:

"Farewell, brother! farewell, comrade! not to an earthly,
but a celestial King, to the surest tribunal, dost thou bear our
lamentations, our hunger, our misery, our suffering and oppression. Thou wilt there more surely effect our deliverance,
but thou wilt return no more; therefore do we weep, therefore

do we wet thy coffin with tears, for we loved thee, dearest brother."

All shed tears with the worthy priest, the prince, the commanders, the soldiers, and, most of all, the friends of the deceased. But when the priest began to intone *"requiem aeternam dona ei Domine!"* there arose a general chorus of sobs, though all were strong and accustomed to the sight of death.

When the coffin was placed upon the ropes it was hard to tear Zagloba away, he clung to it as if a brother, or his father, lay dead within it. At last Skshetuski and Volodiyovski succeeded in dragging him away. The prince stepped up to the coffin and took up a handful of earth; the priest began to say "Anima ejus . . . " the ropes were let down, the earth began to fall upon the coffin, being thrown down from the hands and helmets of the bystanders; soon above the remains of Pan Longinus Podbipyenta there arose a high mound, upon which the moon shed its pale, sad light.

The three friends returned from the town to the square, from whence came the incessant noise of battle. They walked in silence which none of them wished to break. Other groups discussed the dead hero and gave him unstinted praise.

"Even the funeral of Sierakovski was not more imposing than this," said an officer passing near Skshetuski.

"Well, he deserved it," answered another officer, "who else would have undertaken to get through to the king?"

"I heard that among the soldiers of Vishnyovyetski some volunteers offered their services," added a third officer, "but after such an awful example they will probably change their minds."

"The thing is impossible, a snake could hardly creep through."

"As true as I live it would be sheer madness."

The officers passed on. Silence reigned again, then suddenly Pan Michael spoke.

"Did you hear what they said, dear Yan?"

"I did," answered Skshetuski, "it is my turn to-day."

"Yan," said Pan Michael, earnestly, "you have known me for a long time and know that danger does not frighten me. But danger is one thing and suicide quite another!"

"And you say this, Michael?"

"I do, for I am your friend."

"And I am your friend also—give me your word of honor that you will not go as a third if I should fall."

"No, I cannot do that," exclaimed Pan Volodiyovski.

"See then, Michael! how can you ask something of me that you would not do yourself? God's will be done!"

"Then let me go with you."

"The prince has prohibited that, not I. You are a soldier and therefore must obey."

Pan Michael was silenced, for in fact he was above everything a soldier. He twisted his moustaches excitedly. Finally he said "the night is very bright, don't go to-night."

"I wish that it was darker," answered Skshetuski, "but delay cannot be thought of. As you see, the weather has become clear and is liable to remain so. We are in the direst need of powder and provisions. The soldiers are digging in the square for roots, the gums of some of them are already rotting from the rubbish they are eating. I go to-night, at once, I have already bidden farewell to the prince."

"You are a desperate man, I see."

Skshetuski smiled sadly, "enough of this, Pan Michael, I pray. I am not indeed swimming in delight, but I shall not seek death voluntarily, for that is a sin. Anyway it is not a question of dying, but of getting to the king and saving the camp."

A violent desire suddenly seized Volodiyovski to tell Skshetuski all about the princess; he had already opened his lips when he thought: "The news would turn his head and he would fall an easier prey to the enemy." He therefore bit his tongue and checked himself and said instead, "which way are you going to choose?"

"I told the prince that I should go over the pond and then along the river until I got beyond the enemy's camp. The prince thought also that this was the best way."

"I see that there is nothing else to be done," Pan Michael replied. "We can only die once and it is more honorable to die on the battle-field than in bed. God guide you! God guide you, Yani, if we do not meet again in this world we shall meet above and I shall always keep my friendship for you."

"So shall I mine for you, may God reward you for all your good deeds. And listen, Michael; if I perish they will hardly exhibit me as they did Longin, for they received too severe a lesson, but they will be sure to make it known, and in that case let old Zatvilikhovski go to Khmyelnitski for my body, for I would not have it dragged by dogs about the enemy's camp."

"Rest assured of that," answered Pan Michael.

Zagloba who at first had not listened attentively to the conversation, now realized what is was about, but he did not have the strength to dissuade Skshetuski from the hazardous enterprise, he only groaned in sorrow:

"Yesterday one, to-day another, my God! my God! . . . "

"Trust in God!" said Volodiyovski.

"Yani . . . " began Zagloba.

But he could say nothing further. He merely leaned his hoary, careworn head upon the breast of the knight and clung to him like a helpless child.

An hour later Skshetuski entered the water of the western pond.

The night was very bright and the middle of the lake gleamed like a silver shield. Skshetuski was soon lost to sight owing to a dense growth of bullrushes and reeds upon the shore; further in, where the reeds were scarcer, there was a luxuriant growth of pond-lilies and other water-plants. This mixture of wide and narrow leaves, slimy stalks, and snake-like stems, winding themselves about Skshetuski's legs and body to the waist, made it exceedingly difficult for him to advance, but nevertheless it concealed him from the sentries. To swim across the pond's bright centre could not be thought of, for any dark object would have been easily seen. Skshetuski therefore determined to skirt around the shore of the pond to the swamp at the other side, through which the river flowed into the pond. Sentries of the Cossacks and Tartars were likely to be there, but on the other hand a whole forest of weeds grew there, only the edge of which had been cut down to make huts for the "blacks." It was possible to creep through this marsh even in daytime, unless some places should be too shallow. But it was a dreadful way. Beneath the stagnant water not more than a yard from the shore, the mud was deep, and with every step that Skshetuski took, bubbles rose to the surface of the water, the noise of which could be distinctly heard in the stillness; besides, in spite of the slowness of his movements ripples formed about him and spread to the open water where the moonlight was reflected. Had it been raining Skshetuski could have swam straight across the pond and reached the swamp within half an hour at the utmost, but there was not a cloud in the sky. Broad streams of greenish light fell upon the pond transforming the leaves of the water-plants into shields of silver, and the tufts of reeds to silvery spears. No breeze was stirring. Fortunately the gurgling of the bubbles was drowned by the uproar of the guns. Skshetuski, observing this, moved forward only when the discharges on the ramparts and in the trenches were at their liveliest. But this calm, clear night had another difficulty in store; swarms of mosquitoes rose from the reeds, formed a cloud about his head, lighting on his face, and eyes, stinging him, buzzing about him, and humming their melancholy vespers. Skshetuski was not unaware of the difficulties of his way when he selected this road, but he had not foreseen all of them. He did not foresee its terrors. Any depth of water, however familiar, has at night something mysterious and terrifying about it and invites the unwelcome question: "What is concealed at the bottom?" This pond of Zbaraj was positively terrible. The water in it seemed thicker than ordinary water. The stench of corpses emanated from it, which came from the hundreds of Cossacks and Tartars whose bodies were decomposing in the water. Though on both sides dead bodies had been pulled ashore, yet who could tell how many had been left hidden among the reeds and thick bulrushes? Though Skshetuski was embraced by the cool water, perpiration rolled down his forehead. What if suddenly a pair of slippery wet arms should embrace him, or a pair of greenish eyes should gaze at him from under the water-plants? The long stalks of the water-lilies wound about his knees and his hair stood on end, for he thought that he felt the embrace of a drowned man who grasped him so as not to let him loose again. "Jesus Maria! Jesus Maria!" he murmured continually, pushing himself forward. From time to time he lifted his eyes heavenward and felt comforted at the sight of the moon, the stars, and the serene sky. "There is a God," he repeated to himself in an undertone, so that he could hear himself. At times he looked at the shore and then it seemed to him as if he were looking out from some cursed, infernal world full of mud, swamps, black depths, pale moonlight, ghosts, corpses and night upon God's earth. A yearning seized him to flee at once from that network of reeds to the shore.

But he pushed on further and further along the shore

and was already so far away from the camp, that upon God's world several paces from the shore, he saw a Tartar on horseback. He stopped and looked at him observingly and, judging from the way that the figure nodded with a uniform motion towards the neck of the horse, he presumed that he was asleep. It was a strange sight, the Tartar nodding continually as if silently bowing to Skshetuski, who kept his eyes glued upon him. There was something awful in this, but Skshetuski breathed more freely, for in the presence of this manifest danger, imaginary ones that were a hundred times harder to bear, disappeared. The world of ghosts vanished, the knight at once regained his sang. froid; ana such thoughts as these crowded into his head: "Is he asleep or not, shall I go on or shall I wait?"

Finally he went on, making his way even more carefully than at the beginning of his journey. He had gone half way to the swamp in the river, when the first breath of a light wind arose. Soon the reeds were swaying and striking against one another, and giving forth a rustling sound. Skshetuski was relieved, for in spite of all precaution, in spite of the fact that sometimes he spent several minutes in advancing a single step, an involuntary movement, a stumble, or a splash might betray him. Now, aided by the loud rustling of the leaves, which swept over all the pond, he pushed ahead more boldly. Everything seemed to be beginning to stir, the rocking waves of water began to splash on the shore.

This movement was not confined to the reeds along the shore, for suddenly a dark object appeared before Skshetuski, and began to move towards him as if preparing for a spring. At the first moment Skshetuski almost cried aloud; but fear and a feeling of nausea restrained his voice, and at the same time a horrible stench almost suffocated him.

After a time when the first fancy of having his way barred by a drowned man was gone, only the feeling of nausea remained, and the knight pushed on. The rustling of the reeds contiued and grew louder. Through the waving tops Skshetuski saw a second and a third Tartar sentry. He passed these and a fourth one also.

"I must have gone round half the pond already," thought he, and he rose slightly to ascertain his position. Something struck his legs, he looked down and at his knees saw a human face.

"This is the second one," thought he. This time he was not frightened, for this second corpse lay on its back, still and motionless, and gave no suggestion of life or action.

Skshetuski made haste lest his head should turn. The reeds were getting denser and denser, this on the one hand afforded more cover, but on the other it made his progress more difficult. Another half hour, another hour passed, he pushed right on, but grew more and more fatigued; in some places the water was so shallow that it hardly came above his ankles; in other places again, he went in almost to his belt. Dragging his feet out of the bog, slow and tedious labor, fatigued him more than anything else. His forehead was covered with perspiration, and from time to time cold shivers passed from head to foot.

"What is the matter," he anxiously thought, "am I getting delirious? The swamp has not appeared yet. Suppose I do not recognize the place amid the thick reeds and pass it by?"

It was a fearful danger, for in that way he might circle around the pond all night and find himself in the morning in the same place whence he started, or fall into the hands of the Cossacks.

"I have chosen a bad way," thought he, and became dispirited. "I cannot get through the lake, I will return and to-morrow I will go the way Longin did. Till to-morrow I could rest."

But he went on, for he realized that he was tempting himself by letting his thoughts run on going back to rest. It also occurred to him that as he was going so slowly and had stopped every moment, he could not yet have reached the swamp. But thoughts of rest tempted him more and more. He fought against his thoughts and prayed at the same time. The cold chills passed through him more often; he drew his feet out of the mud with ever-increasing weaknesss. The sight of the Tartar sentries had stirred him, but he felt that his mind was growing numb as well as his body and that the flush of fever was coming upon him.

Another half-hour passed, but the swamp was not yet in sight.

But more often now he stumbled against the corpses of drowned men. Night, dread, the rustling of the reeds, labor, and sleeplessness, confuse his senses. He began to have visions. He sees as from afar, Helena in Kudak, and he with Jendzian is sailing down the stream of the Dnieper. The

reeds rustle, he hears the song. "Do you hear the thunder-
storms and tempest yonder." . . . The priest Mukhovietski is waiting in his stole, and see, Kryshtof Grodzitski
takes the place of the father. . . . The girl is looking
day after day down from the walls upon the river. Suddenly she claps her hands and exclaims "He is coming! he
is coming!"

"My Lord," says Jendzian, pulling him by the coat sleeve,
"the lady is here . . . "

Skshetuski awakens, the tangled reeds stop him. The
vision disappears, consciousness returns. Now he does not
feel such weariness any longer, for the fever gives him
strength.

"Oh, is not this the swamp yet!"

But around him were the same reeds as if he had not
advanced at all. Near the river there must be open water,
this consequently cannot be the swamp.

The knight goes on, but his thoughts obstinately return
to the beautiful vision. Skshetuski resisted in vain, in vain
begins to pray "O Blessed Virgin," in vain struggles to re-
gain full consciousness. Again he beholds the Dnieper, the
boats, Kudak, Sich—but now the vision is more confused,
there are a number of persons. Besides Helena are the
prince and Khmyelnitski, Longin, Zagloba, Bohun, Volodiyovski, all in festival attire for his wedding. But where is
the wedding? They are in some strange place, it is not
Lubni, nor Rozloga, nor Sich, nor Kudak. . . . water
is all about in which corpses are floating. . . .

Skshetuski awakens a second time, or rather he is aroused
by a noise coming from the direction in which he desires
to go. He stops therefore and listens.

The noise is coming nearer, rustling and splashing can
be heard; it is a boat.

Now it is clearly visible through the reeds. Two Cossacks
are sitting in it. One of them is rowing. The other holds
in his hand a long pole which gleams like silver in the
distance, and with it he pushes the water-plants aside.

Skshetuski sank into the water up to his neck, so that only
his head stuck out above the rushes, and watched. "Is it
an ordinary patrol, or are they upon my track?" wondered
he. But soon he concluded by the quiet, careless movements
of the Cossacks, that it must be an ordinary patrol, there
must be more than one boat on the pond, and if the Cossacks

were on his track doubtless several boats would have been together and a crowd of men besides.

Meantime the boat passed by. The rustling of the reeds had drowned their words, but Skshetuski distinguished this fragment of their conversation:

"The devil take them for ordering us to guard this foul water."

The boat disappeared in the thicket of reeds. But the Cossack in the front of the boat struck with regular strokes at the water-plants as if he wished to frighten the fish.

Skshetuski pushed on. After awhile he saw another Tartar picket close to the bank. The moonlight fell upon the face of the Nogai which resembled a dog's snout, but Skshetuski feared these pickets less than the loss of consciousness. He therefore exerted all his will power in order to call to mind clearly where he was and where he was going to. But the struggle only increased his fatigue, and soon he noticed that everything appeared double and threefold, and that at moments the lake seemed to him to be a camp and the bunches of reeds, tents. Then he wished to call Volodiyovski to go with him, but he had sufficient consciousness to restrain himself.

"Don't call, don't call," he repeated to himself incessantly, "that would mean ruin."

But the struggle with himself grew harder and harder. He had left Zbaraj weak with hunger and loss of sleep, from which soldiers there were already dying. This nocturnal wandering, the cold bath, the stench of corpses, the roaming about in the mud and the tearing apart of the roots of the water-plants had greatly weakened him. Added to this was the excitement, the fear, and the pain of mosquito-bites that had covered his face with blood. He felt that unless he soon reached the swamp, he would have to go ashore let come what would, or he would collapse among the reeds and drown.

The swamp and the mouth of the river seemed to him a harbor of salvation, though new difficulties and dangers were in store there for him.

He fought against the fever and proceeded, diregarding caution more and more. In the heat of the fever Skshetuski heard human voices, conversation, as if the pond were talking about him. "Would he reach the swamp or not, would he work himself through or not?" The mosquitoes about him, with their thin voices, hummed a more melancholy tune every moment, the water was getting deeper, now it reached his belt, now his breast. He thought if he should have to swim, he would get tangled in this muddle of plants, and drown. Again an irresistible and unconquerable desire to call Pan Michael seized him. He already had put his hands to his mouth to cry:

"Michael! Michael!"

But fortunately a merciful reed struck him in the face with its wet brush. He regained his senses and saw before him, somewhat to the right, a feeble glimmer. He kept the light steadily in view and advanced towards it for some time.

Suddenly he stopped. He saw a sheet of clear water before him. He breathed more freely. It was the river with a swamp along either bank.

"Now I shall stop circling along the shore and enter that wedge."

On either side of the wedge a narrow fringe of reeds extended. The knight proceeded along the one which he had reached, and soon realized that he was upon the right track. He looked about. The pond was already behind him, he passed along by the narrow strip of water which could be nothing else but the river. The water here was colder too. After awhile a dreadful weariness oppressed him. His knees shook beneath him and before his eyes the black cloud hovered. "I can stand it no longer," thought he, "I must go ashore and lie down. I can go no further, I must rest."

He fell upon his knees, his hands grasped a dry tuft covered with moss, like a little island among the rushes.

He sat down upon it and began to wipe his bleeding face with his hands and to draw deep breaths.

After a time the smell of smoke came to his nostrils, and when he looked towards the shore, he saw about a hundred paces away, a fire, and around it a small group of men. He was exactly in line with the fire, and when the wind bent the reeds apart he could see everything plainly. At the first glance he recognized Tartar herders, who were sitting about the fire engaged in eating. A ravenous hunger seized him, the past morning he had eaten a bite of horse-meat, scarce enough to have satisfied a wolf's cub, two months old; since then he had eaten nothing. He began to tear up the stalks of the water-lilies about him and to suck them greedily;

thereby he allayed his hunger and quenched the thirst that
was tormenting him. At the same time he did not take his
eyes from the fire which was growing paler and fainter. The
people round it became enveloped in a fog and seemed to
be fading away.

"Oh, sleep is overcoming me, I shall sleep on this island
throughout the night."

Suddenly a commotion arose around the fire. The herders
rose up. Then a shout "Horse! Horse!" struck Skshetuski's
ears. A short neigh was the response. The fire smouldered
away and died. After a time the knight neard a whistling
and the dull thump of horses' hoofs from the wet meadow.

Skshetuski could not understand why the herders had
scattered. Then he observed that the reeds and the leaves
of the lilies were growing paler, and the water took on a
different glimmer than that of moonlight, and that the air
was veiled with a light fog.

He looked around: it was dawning.

He had spent the whole night in skirting the pond ere
he reached the swamp and the river. He was barely beyond
the beginning of the journey. Now he must go along the
river and attempt to pass the camp during the day. The
air was pentrated more and more with the light of dawn,
In the east the horizon was soon a pale green color.

Skshetuski slipped from the island into the swamp again,
and pushing towards the bank he bent the reeds apart and
looked out.

At a distance of about five hundred paces was a Tartar
patrol. Otherwise the meadow was empty, only the dying
fire spluttered on a dry spot near. The knight made up his
mind to creep to it through the tall grass, which in places
was interspersed with rushes. Having reached the fire he
looked greedily for some remains of food. He found indeed
some freshly-picked mutton-bones with bits of tendon and
fat, besides some roasted turnips left in the ashes. He fell
upon the food with the greediness of a wild beast until
he noticed that the patrols on the road that he had passed
were coming towards him across the meadow on their way
to the camp.

He then retreated and in a few minutes disappeared among
the reeds. He found his island again and lay down on it
noiselessly. The patrol passed by. Skshetuski began to gnaw
some bones again which he had brought along with him, and

soon they cracked beneath his strong jaws as if between the teeth of a wolf. He gnawed off the tendons and fat, sucked out the marrow, and partly allayed his hunger. Such a breakfast he had not had for a long time in Zbaraj.

Now he felt invigorated. The food as well as the dawning day, braced him. It grew brighter and brighter. The eastern horizon was transformed from a greenish into a rose-red and golden color. Although the rawness of the morning chilled the knight, he found consolation in the thought that the sun would soon warm his tired body. He carefully examined his surroundings. The island was fairly large, somewhat short, but broad enough to allow two men to lie upon it comfortably, the reeds surrounded it like a wall upon all sides, thus concealing it from sight. "They cannot find me here," thought Skshetuski, "unless they fish in the reeds. But there are now no fishes for they have all died on account of decomposition. Here I will rest and think what is best to be done."

He turned over in his mind whether he should continue to go on by the river or not. At length he determined to go on if the wind should rise and cause the reeds to sway; otherwise his movements and the noise would betray him, especially as he probably would have to pass close to the camp.

"I thank Thee, God, that I am still alive," he whispered.

He gazed up at the sky and then his thoughts flew over to the Polish camp. He could see the castle plainly at the moment it was gilded by the first rays of the rising sun. Perhaps some one was looking from the tower at the pond and at the reeds through a field-glass. Pan Michael, Zagloba, and Vododiyovski would no doubt watch all day long from the ramparts to see if he were hanging from some of the war-towers.

"They will not see me," thought Skshetuski, and his breast swelled with a pleasant feeling of safety. "They will not see me," he repeated several times. "I have only gone a small part of the way, but it was no trifle. God will aid me further."

Now he looked with the eyes of imagination beyond the camp, beyond the forest, behind which was the royal army, the general militia of the country, hussars, infantry, foreign regiments. The earth groaned beneath the burden of men, horses, and cannon, and in the midst of this crowd of people was the king himself. . . . Then he saw a great battle, broken camps,—the prince with all his cavalry rushing over heaps of corpses, the salutations of the armies. . . .

His aching and swollen eyes closed upon the dazzling light; his head sank beneath the weight of thoughts; a pleasant weakness overcame him; he stretched himself at full length and fell fast asleep.

The reeds rustled. The sun rose high in the sky and warmed with kindly rays the knight and dried his clothes. He lay motionless and sound asleep. Had anyone seen him thus, lying on the island, with bloody, upturned face, he would surely have thought that this was a corpse that had been washed ashore. Hours went by but he still slept. The sun reached its zenith and began to descend in the vault of heaven, but he still slept. The piercing crys of horses biting each other and the loud shouts of the herders as they lashed the stallions, awoke him.

He rubbed his eyes, looked about, and tried to remember where he was. He looked up in the sky, still red with the last rays of the setting sun; stars were twinkling. He had slept through the whole day.

Skshetuski however, felt neither rested nor refreshed; on the contrary all his limbs were aching. But he thought that new toil would brace his body, and putting his feet into the water he continued his journey.

He now proceeded in clear water skirting the reeds, lest he should by the noise of his steps excite the attention of the herders who were guarding the banks. The last gleam had died away and it was quite dark, for the moon had not yet risen from behind the woods. The water was so deep that Skshetuski in some places found himself over his head and was obliged to swim. This was difficult on account of his clothes and because he had to swim against the current. But not the keenest Tartar eye could have seen the head which was moving along the dark wall of reeds. He therefore pushed forward rather boldly, sometimes swimming, but mostly wading in water up to his belt or beneath his arms, until he finally reached a spot where his eyes beheld thousands and thousands of lights on either side of the river.

"Those are the camps," thought he, "now God help me."

And he listened.

A murmur of many voices reached his ears. Those indeed were the camps. On the left bank of the river, following its bend, lay the Cossack camp with its thousands of tents and wagons—on the right side the Tartar camp—both resounding with noise and tumult, full of the babel of human voices, wild rolling of drums and shrill whistling of fifes, bellowing of cattle, neighing of horses, and shouts. The river divided them and kept them from quarreling and fighting with each other, for the Tartars could never exist in peace beside the Cossacks. The river was widest here, perhaps widened purposely. Judging by the fires the tents and carts were on one side and reed-huts upon the other, but a few steps from the river. Close to the water, no doubt, pickets were stationed.

The reeds and bulrushes became thinner; evidently the banks along the two camps were bare. Skshetuski sneaked on for some tens of steps and then stopped. The shadow of a mighty force seemed to fall upon him from those multitudes.

He felt at the moment as if the entire vigilance, the entire wrath of these thousands of human beings were concentrated upon him, and against them he felt powerless and defenceless. He was all alone.

"No one can ever pass here," thought he.

But he crept on still, for a painful, irresistible curiosity dragged him forward. He wished to have a nearer view of this terrible force.

Suddenly he stopped. The thicket of reeds came to an end, as if it had been mowed down with knives. Perhaps the reeds had been cut for the building of huts. Further on the clear water was red from the fires reflected in it.

Two great bright fires were burning close to the banks. By one was a Tartar on horseback, by the other a Cossack with a long lance in his hand. They turned their faces toward each other and the water. In the distance several such pickets were to be seen.

The flames cast their light on the river, and formed what looked like a bridge of fire. Along the banks were two rows of small boats used by the guard on the lake.

" 'Tis impossible," murmured Skshetuski.

Sudden despair seized him. He could go neither forward nor backward. A day and a night had passed since he had been roaming through the mud and reeds. And he breathed the foul air and waded the water of the lake only to realize here, after having reached the camps of the enemy through which he desired to pass, that it was impossible?

50

But to return was also impossible. The knight knew that he might find strength enough to drag himself forward, but not to go backward. A dull rage mingled with his despair. At first it urged him to step out of the water, choke the guard, and then throw himself among the crowd and die.

The breeze with a mysterious whisper began to rustle again the reeds, bringing with it sounds of the bells of Zbaraj. Skshetuski began to pray fervently. He beat his breast and with all the strength and desperate faith of a drowning man he besought Heaven to aid him. He prayed, while from the two camps arose ominous noises, as if in response to his prayer. Black figures flitted about in the glare of the fire, looking like a herd of devils in hell. The pickets stood motionless. The river flowed on with blood-tinted waves.

"The fires will burn out when the night comes on," said Skshetuski to himself, and waited.

An hour passed, and another. The noise decreased. The fires began to smoulder, except the two watch-fires which flared up brighter and brighter. The pickets were relieved; it was evident that guard would be kept until morning.

It came to Skshetuski's mind that perhaps he might slip through more easily in the day-time, but he abandoned the thought at once. In the day-time they drew water, brought their cattle down to drink and bathed; the river would be full of people. Suddenly Skshetuski glanced at the boats. On either side were about ten boats in a row and on the side of the Tartar camp the rushes reached to the first one. Skshetuski sank in the water to his neck and slowly moved towards the boats, at the same time fixing his eyes on the Tartar picket. At the end of half an hour he was close to the first boat. His plan was simple. The sterns of the boats which were raised above the water, formed a sort of arch, beneath which a man's head might pass with ease When all the boats lay closely side by side, the Tartar picket could not see a head pushing along under them. There was more danger from the Cossack picket, but he might not see the head either, for in spite of the fire opposite the boats, it was dark beneath them. There was indeed no other way.

Skshetuski hesitated no longer and was soon beneath the sterns of the boats. He crept, or rather dragged himself along, for the water was very shallow. He was so near the Tartar standing on the bank, that he could hear the breathing of his horse. For a moment he stopped and listened. Fortunately the boats lay closely side by side. Now he fixed his eyes upon the Cossack picket whom he could see quite plainly. He was looking at the Tartar camp. The knight had passed about fifteen boats when he suddenly heard steps on the shore and the voices of men. He ducked at once and listened. During his journeys in the Crimea he had learned the Tartar language. A cold shiver ran through his body as he heard the words of command:

"Embark, and put off."

Although in the water the knight felt fever burning him; if the Tartars should take the boat beneath which he was concealed he would be lost; should they step into the one in front of him, he was lost also, for this would leave an open lighted space.

Every second seeemed an hour to him. Steps sounded on the planks—the Tartars took the fifth boat right behind him and put out, rowing in the direction of the pond. This proceeding attracted the attention of the Cossack picket to the boats. Skshetuski lay motionless for a good half-hour. Not until the sentry was relieved did he begin to crawl ahead again.

In this way he reached the end of the row of boats. Beyond the last one the rushes grew again and a little further on reeds. When he reached shelter the knight fell on his knees, breathless and covered with sweat, and thanked God with all his heart.

He went onward more boldly, taking advantage of every faint breeze that stirred the reeds. From time to time he looked backward. The watchfires appeared more and more distant; they twinkled faintly and began to fade away. The lines of reeds and rushes were getting denser and darker, for the banks were more swampy. The pickets could not be posted so closely to each other now, the noise of the camps grew fainter. Supernatural strength seemed to flow into the limbs of the knight. He forced his way through the reeds, over islands, sinking in the mud, falling into deep water, swimming and getting out again. He did not dare to go on shore yet, but he almost felt that he was saved. He did not know how long he thus waded on, but when he again looked back the watchfires appeared like little points of light in the distance; a few hundred steps more and they disappeared altogether. The moon went down; all about was

still. Then arose a stronger, mightier rustling than that
of the reeds. Skshetuski almost cried aloud from joy—on
both banks of the river he saw the wood before him.

He made for the bank and emerged from the reeds. He
breathed the fragrance of pine. The pine-forest joined the
reeds and rushes, and here and there gleamed the silvery
leaves of ferns in the black depths.

The knight fell upon his knees for the second time and
kissed the earth as he prayed.

He was saved.

Then he plunged into the darkness of the forest, asking
himself whither he should go? Whither would these forests
lead him? Where was the king and the army?

The journey was not over yet, nor was it now safe nor easy.
But when he considered that he had emerged from Zbaraj,
that he had stolen through pickets, swamps, mud, camps, and
nearly a half million of enemies—then it seemed to him that
all danger was over and that this forest was a clear road leading directly to His Majesty the king.

And so this hungry and shivering wreck, smeared with his
own blood and with red and black mud, walked on in gladness and with hope in his heart that he would soon return
to Zbaraj in different circumstances and in greater power.

"You shall not remain much longer a prey to hopeless-
ness and starvation," said he, thinking about his friends in
Zbaraj, "for I will bring the king."

His heroic heart was rejoiced at the near rescue of the
prince, the commanders, Volodiyovski, Zagloba, and all the
heroes enclosed within the ramparts of Zbaraj. The depth
of the forest received him and embraced him with shelter-
ing darkness.

CHAPTER VII.

In the reception room of the court at Toporov there sat three gentlemen in secret conference. It was evening; several wax-candles stood on the table, which was covered with maps of the surrounding country. There also lay upon the table a tall hat with a black feather; a field glass, a sword with the hilt set with pearls, a lace handkerchief embroidered with a crown, and a pair of deerskin gloves. At the table in a high armchair sat a man rather small and slender, but strongly built, and about forty years of age. His face was swarthy and sallow and bore a weary expression; his eyes were black and so was his Swedish wig, the long locks of which fell over his neck and shoulders; a thin, black moustache curled up at the ends, adorned his upper lip, but the under lip and beard protruded, imparting to his physiognomy a characteristic mark of lion-like courage, pride, and stubbornness. It was not a handsome face, but there was dignity in it. A sensuous expression betraying inclination to enjoyment of life was strangely blended with a certain sleepy torpor and frigidity. The eyes seemed dull, but one could easily imagine that in moments of enthusiasm, rapture, or scorn, they could flash like lightning; they at the same time betrayed both mildness and affability.

The black dress composed of a satin kaftan with a lace ruff, beneath which a gold chain glittered, increased the distinction of this remarkable figure. There was something majestic about it, despite the sorrow and care which expressed themselves in the features and attitude. This in truth was the king, Yan Kazimier Vaza, who nearly a year since had succeeded his brother Vladislav.

Seated a little behind him was Hieronom Radzieyovski the chief of Lomza, a short, thick-set, ruddy man with the face of a courtier; and opposite to him a third man who was leaning upon his elbows, attentively studying the maps before him, and from time to time raising his eyes to the king.

His countenance was less majestic, but expressed more

789

official dignity, than that of the king. It was a face furrowed by care and thought, cold and intelligent, with a stern
look which did not mar its uncommon beauty. His eyes were
blue and penetrating, his complexion delicate in spite of his
age. His gorgeous Polish dress, his beard trimmed in the
Swedish style, and the tuft of hair on his forehead imparted
to his regular classical features, something of senatorial
dignity.

This was Yerzy Ossolinski chancellor of the Crown and
prince of the Roman nobility, a diplomat and orator, who was
admired throughout all the courts of Europe; the famous
opponent of Yeremy Vishnyovyetski. His extraordinary
ability had long before attracted the attention of former
rulers and had procured for him the most important offices,
by virtue of which he guided the ship of state, at the present
hour so near to ruin.

The chancellor was fit to be the pilot of such a ship; in-
dustrious, patient, intelligent, and farseeing, he would have
directed with a steady hand any other State except the Commonwealth to a safe harbor, and could have secured domestic
strength and many years of power to any other State—if he
could have been the absolute minister of a monarch, for example, such as the King of France, or the King of Spain.

Educated beyond the boundaries of his own countries, following foreign models, in spite of his innate intelligence and
quickness, in spite of his long experience, he could not ac-
custom himself to the powerless rule in the Commonwealth,
and all his life he did not learn not to take this circumstance
into account, although this was the rock upon which all his
plans and endeavors were shattered—though he now saw
the ruin that was pending, and later he died with despair in
his heart.

He was an ingenious theorist who, however, did not understand how to be ingenious in practice, and he fell into a
maze of errors from which he could not escape. If he once
hit upon an idea that promised to bear good fruit he clung
to it with the stubbornness of a fanatic, not recognizing that
this idea though salutary in theory, might in practice, because of actual circumstances, be followed by terrible disasters.

Wishing to strengthen the country and the government he
let loose the terrible Cossack element, not forseeing that
the storm would turn not only against the nobility, the mag-

nates, the great estates, the abuses and arrogance of the nobles, but also against the most vital interests of the State.

Khmyelnitski rose up in the steppes and had grown to be a giant. The defeats of Zolta Woda, Korsun, and Pilavyets fell heavily on the Commonwealth. At the outset this Khmyelnitski entered into a confederacy with the Crimean power, the enemy of the country. One blow followed another—there remained war and nothing else. The terrible element should have been crushed first of all, so as to make it of use in the future; but the chancellor, instead of doing this, occupied with his own thoughts, was still negotiating a delay and still trusting even Khmyelnitski.

The force of circumstances shattered all his theories. Every day it became clearer that the results of the chancellor's efforts were entirely different from what he had expected, till at last the days of Zbaraj had sadly confirmed all.

The chancellor was almost crushed by worry, exasperation, and general unpopularity.

He did what, in times of misfortune and adversity, all do whose self-confidence is stronger than all disaster; he looked for people whom he could hold responsible.

The entire Commonwealth was to blame, and all classes, the past, and the form of government. But he, who in fear lest a rock lying on the slope of a mountain might fall and crush everything in his way, wishes to roll it to the top without considering the strength that is at his command, will only cause the rock to roll down all the sooner. The chancellor did worse, for he called to his aid the terrible rushing torrent of the Cossacks, and had not taken into consideration that this force was bound to undermine the very ground on which the rock was resting.

While therefore he sought for people upon whom to lay the blame, all eyes were turned towards him as the cause of the war, the disasters, and misery.

But the king still believed in the judgment of the chancellor, all the more because public opinion did not spare His Majesty and accused him equally with the chancellor. So they sat, careworn and weary, at Toporov not knowing what to do, for the king had only twenty-five thousand men at his command. The conscript summons had been issued too late, and recruits therefore were gathering very slowly. As to who was the cause of this, and whether this delay was not a new blunder of the stubborn policy of the chancellor, that secret was known only to the king and his minister; it suffices that both felt at that moment helpless against the power of Khmyelnitski.

What was more serious still was that they had no accurate information about him. In the camp of the king it was not known whether the Khan with all his forces was with Khmyelnitski, or if only Tukhay Bey with a few thousands of his hordes was accompanying the Cossacks. This was a question of life or death. With Khmyelnitski alone the king might, in case of necessity, try his fortune, though a force ten times greater was under the command of the rebel hetman. The magic of the royal name had great influence with the Cossacks; greater perhaps than with the crowds of general milita, and the rude and untrained nobility. If, however, the Khan were with the Cossacks, it was hopeless to battle against them.

Widely varying reports were floating about, but no one knew the true state of affairs. The cautious Khmyelnitski held all his forces together and did not let a single party of Cossacks or Tartars go from camp so that the king might not get information.

The rebel chieftain had a design to seal up the starving Zbaraj entirely with a part of his troops, while he with the rest of his Cossacks, and the entire Tartar forces, would surround the king unexpectedly and deliver him over to the Khan.

It was not without reason therefore that the brow of the king was clouded, for there is no greater pain to majesty than a feeling of helplessness. Yan Kazimier lay helpless in his armchair with his hand resting on the table and pointing to the maps, he said:

"These lead to nothing, nothing! I need informants."

"That is what I am longing for too," answered Ossolinski.

"Have the scouts come back?"

"They have, but they bring no news."

"Not even a captive?"

"Only peasants from the neighborhood who know nothing."

"And is Pan Pelka back? he is a famous scout."

"Your Majesty," interrupted the Chief of Lomza from behind the arm-chair, "Pan Pelka is not here, nor will he return, for he is dead."

A deep silence fell. The king gazed upon the flickering candles and drummed with his fingers on the table.

"Have you no counsel?" he asked at length.

"We must wait," said the chancellor, earnestly.

A frown wrinkled Yan Kazimier's forehead. "Wait?" he repeated, "and in Zbaraj, Vishnyovyetski and the commanders are dying of hunger."

"They can hold out for some time yet," remarked Radzie-yovskı.

"You had better hold your peace, chief, if you have no good plan to offer."

"I have a plan, Your Majesty."

"What?"

"Let us send sone one to Khmyelnitski as if going to nego-tiate; the envoy will discover if the Khan be with him, and will bring us information."

"That is not possible," said the king, "after having de-clared Khmyelnitski a rebel, set a price upon his head, and bestowed the baton of the Zaporojians upon Pan Zabuski, it would be beneath our dignity to enter into negotiations with Khmyelnitski."

"Then let us send an envoy to the camp," replied the chief.

The king looked inquiringly at the chancellor, who in turn looked at the king with his severe blue eyes, and after some reflection said:

"The advice would be good, but Khmyelnitski would no doubt seize the envoy; therefore it would not work."

Yan Kazimier waved his hand.

"I see," said he, slowly, "that you have no plan and now I will give you mine. I will go with the whole army to Zbaraj. Let God's will be done! There we shall find out if the Khan be present or not."

The chancellor knew the indomitable courage of the king and did not doubt that he would do what he said. Besides he knew from experience that when the king had once made up his mind to do a thing all persuasion was useless. He did not offer any opposition therefore at once; he even praised the idea, but deprecated too great haste. He explained to the king that a delay of one or two days would make no difference, and in the meantime direct news might arrive. Every day must increase the dissension and insubordination among the mob because of the constant defeats and the news of the king's proximity. The rebellion might melt before the pres-ence of Majesty, as snow beneath sunbeams, but it required time. "The king," he went on to say, "bears a responsibility before God and posterity of saving the whole Commonwealth; he should not expose himself to danger especially as in case of misfortune the army in Zbaraj would be hopelessly lost."

"Do what you please, but I must have an informant to-morrow."

Again silence fell. A golden, full moon shone in through the windows, but in the chamber it grew darker for the candles were flickering.

"What time is it?" asked the king.

"It is near midnight," answered Radzieyovski.

"I shall not sleep to-night. I will ride around the camp, and you come with me. Where are Ubald and Artishevski?"

"In the camp. I will go and order the horses," answered the chief.

He went towards the door. There arose a noise in the hall, a lively conversation was audible, then the sound of hurried steps; the door was opened and Tyzenhauz, the king's chamberlain, rushed in breathless.

"Your Majesty," he cried, "an officer from Zbaraj has arrived."

The king sprang up, the chancellor rose also, and both cried out, "impossible!"

"It is so, he is standing in the antechamber."

"Let him come in," exclaimed the king, clapping his hands, "let him allay our anxiety; show him in at once, do you hear?"

Tyzenhauz disappeared, and a moment later there appeared in his stead, a tall, strange figure.

"Step nearer, sir," said the king, "nearer, we are glad to see you."

The newcomer walked slowly to the table and at sight of him the king, the chancellor, and the chief of Lomza, fell back in astonishment. Before them stood a man, or rather a spectre, fearful to look upon. Tattered rags covered his emaciated body; his face was pale and stained with blood and filth; his eyes glittered feverishly, his black, tangled beard fell over his breast; the stench of corpses emanated from him, and his legs shook so that he had to lean upon the table.

The king and the two officials gazed at him with wide, staring eyes. Now the doors opened and a number of dignitaries, military and civil, entered; among them Generals Ubald and Artishevsi, Sapieha, the Lithuanian Vice-Chancellor,

the Chief of Jechyts and Pan Sandomierski.   All took places
behind the king and looked at the newcomer.   Then the king
asked:

"Who are you?"

The unfortunate man opened his mouth, attempted to
speak, but the words would not come, his beard quivered and
he was barely able to whisper:

"From . . . . Zbaraj."

"Give him some wine," said a voice from the crowd.

In a moment a goblet of wine was brought; the newcomer
emptied it with great difficulty.   Meanwhile the chancellor
had thrown off his cloak and covered the stranger's shoulders
with it.

"Can you speak now?" asked the king, after a time.

"I can," replied the knight, with a somewhat firmer voice.

"Who are you?"

"Yan Skshetuski, Lieutenant of Hussars." . . . .

"In whose service?"

"In the service of the Voyevoda of Russia."

A murmur spread through the chamber.

"What news do you bring with you?" asked the king, in
a feverish tone.

"Distress . . . famine . . . one grave."

The king covered his eyes with his hands.

"Jesus of Nazareth! Jesus of Nazareth!" he murmured.

Then he asked again:

"Can they hold out for a time yet?"

"Powder is scarce, the enemy is on the ramparts."

"Is the enemy strong?"

"Khmyelnitski . . . . and the Khan with all his hordes."

"The Khan is there?"

"He is."

Deep silence followed.   Those present looked at one another, . . . anxiety was expressed on every face.

"How have you been able to hold out?" asked the chancellor, with a doubtful accent.

Then Skshetuski raised his head, as if new strength had
come to him.   A flash of pride glowed in his face and in a
voice unexpectedly strong, he said:

"Twenty assaults repulsed, sixteen battles won in the open
field, seventy-five sorties—" . . .

Silence fell again.

Then the king straightened up, shook his wig as a lion his

mane, while a flush crimsoned his sallow face and his eyes flashed.

"By God!" he exclaimed, "enough of listening to advice, of this paltering and hesitation! if the Khan be there or not, if the general militia be gathered or not, by God! I have had enough of this; to-day we shall march to Zbaraj."

"To Zbaraj, to Zbaraj!" shouted a number of powerful voices.

The face of the newcomer brightened like the dawn.

"Gracious King and Ruler," he said, "we will live and die with you." . . .

These words touched the noble heart of the king, and regardless of the knight's repugnant appearance, he pressed his head with his hands and said:

"I prefer you to others, dressed in satin. By the Most Holy Mother, men who have done less have been rewarded with governorships. But what you have done shall not pass unrewarded. Do not thank me, I am your debtor."

Then the others cried in chorus:

"There has been no greater knight, this one is the greatest of those in Zbaraj. He has achieved immortal glory."

"How did you penetrate the Cossacks and Tartars?"

"I hid in swamps . . . crept through reeds . . . wandered through woods, . . . roamed about, . . . was without food."

"Give him food," exclaimed the king.

"Food," repeated the others, "give him clothes also."

"To-morrow you shall have a horse and clothing," said the king, "you shall not want for anything."

All, following the king's example, rivalled one another in bestowing praises. Again they put questions to him which he answered with difficulty, for increasing weakness overcame him, and he was scarce conscious. Food and drink was brought to him. Then there entered the priest Tsietsishovski, the royal chaplain.

The dignitaries stepped aside to make room for him, for he was a very learned man and much respected. His word had almost as much weight with the king as the chancellor's, and it often happened that he openly spoke from the pulpit about matters that few hinted at even in the Diet. He was immediately surrounded and they began to tell him that an officer had arrived from Zbaraj; that the prince, in spite of famine and suffering, was still holding out against the Khan, who together with Khmyelnitski was laying siege to Zbaraj;

that the latter had not lost during the past year so many men as had fallen before Zbaraj; and finally that the king intended to hasten to the prince's aid, even though he and his army should perish.

The priest listened attentively, moving his lips and gazing constantly upon the emaciated knight who was refreshing himself, the king having commanded him not to regard his presence, and even waiting on him himself, and from time to time pledging him in a little silver goblet.

"And what is the name of this officer," asked the priest.

"Skshetuski."

"Yan Skshetuski?"

"Yes, Father."

"Lieutenant with the Voyevoda of Russia?"

"So it is!"

The priest raised his wrinkled face, murmured a prayer, and said:

"Let us praise the name of the Lord, for through hidden paths he leads man to bliss and peace. Amen. I know this officer."

Skshetuski heard these words and involuntarily his eyes sought the face of the priest, but his face, form, and voice seemed entirely strange to him.

"So you alone undertook to get through the enemy's camp?" asked the priest.

"A worthy comrade made the attempt before me, but he fell," answered Skshetuski.

"So much greater is your service. I see by your appearance that it must have been a terrible undertaking. God beheld your sacrifice, your virtue, your youth, and was with you."

Then the priest turned to Yan Kazimier.

"Gracious King," said he, "have you then irrevocably made up your mind to hasten to the rescue of the Voyevoda of Russia?"

"To your prayers, Father," replied the king, "I commend the country, the army, and myself, for I know that it is a terrible undertaking; but I cannot allow the prince to perish before my eyes with such knights as our comrade here, on those unfortunate ramparts."

"God will give us victory," exclaimed several voices.

The priest raised his hands and a deep silence fell.

"I bless you in the name of the Father, and of the Son, and of the Holy Ghost."

"Amen!" said the king.

"Amen!" repeated all.

A peaceful expression settled upon the sorrowing countenance of Yan Kazimier, but in his eyes there shone an unusual light. A conversation in low tones was carried on by those present concerning the intended expedition, for many doubted yet if the king could really march out at once; he, however, took his sword from the table, and made a sign to Tyzenhauz to gird it on him.

"When does Your Majesty intend to begin the march?" inquired the chancellor.

"God has given us a pleasant night," answered the king, "the horses will not get overheated." Then turning to the dignitaries, he added, "let the signal to mount be given."

The commander of the camp immediately disappeared. Chancellor Ossolinski remarked in a low tone that all were not ready, and that the wagons could not leave before morning. But the king replied:

"Let him remain behind who prefers the wagons to his country and his king."

The room became empty. All hurried to their regiments to get them in order and join the march. Only the king, the chancellor, the priest, Skshetuski, and Tyzenhauz remained.

"Gracious Lord," said the priest, "from this officer you know now what you wish to learn, he must have rest now, for he can hardly stand on his feet. Permit me, Your Majesty, to take him to my quarters over night?"

"Very well, Father," replied the king, "your request is granted. Let Tyzenhauz and some one else escort him, for he could hardly get there alone. Go, go, dear officer, nobody here deserves rest so much as you. And bear in mind that I am your debtor. I would rather forget myself, than forget you."

Tyzenhauz took Skshetuski by the arm and led him out. In the antechamber they met the Chief of Jechyts, who supported the tottering knight on the other side. The priest went ahead and before him a servant with a lantern. But the night was bright, calm, and warm. The golden moon sailed like a boat above Toporov. A confusion of voices arose from the square, and creaking of wagons and noise of trumpets sounding the reveille. At a distance, before the church, illumined by the light of the moon, numbers of soldiers, infantry, and cavalry, could be seen. Horses were neighing in the village. The creaking of wagons mingled with the rattle of chains, and the noise of moving cannon;—the din increased every moment.

"They are marching out already," said the priest.

"To Zbaraj, ... to the rescue," . . . . whispered Skshetuski. Was it joy, or the hardships that he had gone through, or both together, that made him so weak that Tyzenhauz and the Chief of Jetchyts had almost to carry him?

On their way to the priest's house, they passed through the soldiers assembled before the church. These were the cavalry of Sapieha and the infantry of Artsishevski. They were not yet in ranks and stood about without order, massed in places and obstructing the passage.

"Make way, make way," cried the priest.

"Who passes here?"

"An officer from Zbaraj." . . . .

"Bow to him! Bow to him!" exclaimed many voices.

And they immediately made way, but others crowded round to look upon the hero. They gazed in astonishment upon that emaciated, disfigured face, bathed in the moon's light and whispered to each other: "From Zbaraj . . . from Zbaraj!" . . .

With difficulty they arrived at last at the priest's house. There, after he had been bathed and washed from the blood and filth, he was placed in the bed of the priest, who went immediately to join the expedition.

Though Skshetuski was scarcely conscious he could not sleep at once because of the fever; he did not know where he was or what had happened. He heard only a humming noise, the clatter of hoofs, the rumble of wagons, the thundering tread of infantry, shouts, and sounds of trumpets; all this was mingled in his ears with one great roar. "The army is departing," he murmured to himself repeatedly.

Meanwhile the roar gradually grew fainter and died away, till at last deep silence fell upon Toporov.

Now it seemed to Skshetuski as if he were sinking with his bed deeper and deeper into a bottomless abyss.

CHAPTER VIII.

Skshetuski slept for several days, and even when he awoke, the fever had not left him, and he was delirious for a long time; he talked of Zbaraj, the prince, the chief of Krasnostavsk; he conversed with Pan Michael and Zagloba, he shouted to Longin, "not that way;" but the name of the princess was not mentioned by him. It was clear that the great power with which he had enclosed her memory in his innermost heart, did not forsake him even in his state of weakness and sickness. He seemed to see the chubby face of Jendzian bending over him, just as he saw it when the prince, after the battle of Konstantinov, had sent him with some squadrons to Zaslav to disperse the crowds of rebels, and Jendzian had appeared to him unexpectedly in his quarters. The sight of this face confused his mind for he felt as if time had stood still and that nothing had changed since that period. He thought he was again on the Khomora and sleeping in the hut, then he thought that he awoke and was marching with the troops to Tarnopol . . . . Kshyvonos, beaten at Konstantinov and flying to Khmyelnitski. Jendzian had come from Hushch and was sitting by him. . . . Skshetuski wishes to speak to him, to order the lad to saddle the horses, but he cannot. . . . . Again he thinks that he is not on the Khomora, that since then Bar has been taken,—at this he grinds his teeth in pain, and his unhappy thoughts are lost in the void that follows. He knows nothing, sees nothing, then out of the chaos there arises Zbaraj: . . . the siege. . . . He is not then on the Khomora. Yet Jendzian is by him, bending over him. Through an opening in the window shutter there came a ray of daylight, lighting the face of the lad, full of anxiety and sympathy.

"Jendzian!" exclaimed Skshetuski, suddenly.

"Oh, my master, do you at last recognize me?" cried the lad, and fell upon his knees. "I thought that my master would never wake any more." . . .

A period of silence followed, naught could be heard save the sobbing of the lad, who embraced the feet of his master.

800

"Where am I?" asked Skshetuski.

"In Toporov . . . . my master came from Zbaraj to the king." . . .

"God be praised, God be praised!"

"And where is the king?"

"He has gone with the army to rescue the prince."

Again silence followed. Tears of joy ran down Jendzian's face, and after a time he began to repeat:

"God be praised that I look upon your face again." . . .

Then he arose and opened the window and the shutters. The brisk morning air entered the chamber and with it the bright light of day. With the light Skshetuski fully regained his senses. . . .

Jendzian sat down at the foot of the bed.

"Then I came from Zbaraj?" asked the knight.

"You did, my master. Nobody else could have done what you have done, and it was you that incited the king to go to the rescue."

"Pan Podbipyenta attempted to get through before me, but he perished." . . . .

"Oh! for God's sake! Pan Podbipyenta dead! such a generous and virtuous gentleman! It has nearly taken my breath away. How did they vanquish such a giant?"

"They shot him to death with arrows."

"And Pan Volodiyovski, and Pan Zagloba?"

"They were well when I came away."

"Thanks be to God! they are my master's dear friends . . . . but the priest has forbidden me to talk." . . .

Jendzian grew dumb and seemed to be turning over something in his mind. His chubby face gave evidence that he was lost in reflection. After a time he said:

"My master!"

"What is it?"

"I wonder what will be done with the fortune of Pan Podbipyenta? He is said to have owned villages and boundless wealth. Did he leave anything to his friends? for I hear that he had no relatives."

Skshetuski did not answer; Jendzian noticed that the question did not please his master, and he began again as follows:

"God be praised that Pan Zagloba and Pan Volodiyovski are well. I feared that they had fallen into the hands of the Tartars . . . . we went through a lot of suffering together . . . . but the priest has forbidden me to talk. . . . Oh, my

51

master, I thought that I should never see them again, for the Tartar horde pressed so closely upon us that we knew not what to do."

"Then you were with Pan Volodiyovski and Zagloba? They did not say anything to me about it."

"For they did not know whether I was saved or not."

"Then where did the horde press so closely upon you?"

"Beyond Ploskir, on the way to Zbaraj. We had made our way far beyond Yampol, my master, . . . but the priest has forbidden me to talk."

Silence intervened again.

"God reward you for your good will and trouble," said Skshetuski, "for I know why you went there; I was there before you . . . . but in vain."

"Oh, my master, if it were not for the priest. . . . . But this is what he said: 'I must go with the king to Zbaraj and you (he said) look after the noble, but tell him nothing lest his soul should leave his body.'"

Skshetuski had so long since given up all hope, that these words of Jendzian's did not excite him in any way. . . . He lay motionless for awhile and then he asked:

"How did you come to be here with the priest and the army?"

"The wife of the castellan of Sandomir, Pani Vitovska, sent me from Zamost to inform the castellan that she would join him at Toporov. . . . She is a brave woman, sir, and desires above all to be with the army so as not to be separated from the Castellan. Thus I arrived here a day before my master; by this time she ought to be here also; . . . but this will be useless if the castellan has gone away with the king."

"I can't understand how you could be in Zamost if you were beyond Yampol with Volodiyovski and Zagloba. Why did you not come with them to Zbaraj?"

"You see, my master, when the horde pressed so closely upon us, there was no other way; they were obliged to check the horde while I fled on and did not draw rein until I reached Zamost."

"It is lucky that they did not perish," said Skshetuski, "for I thought that you were a better man. Was it right to leave them in such a strait?"

"I, my master, had we been only three, I would surely not have left them, ... my heart cuts me . . . . but there were four of us; . . they threw themselves against the horde and ordered me . . . . to escape . . . . if I were sure that joy that would not kill you . . . . for we found beyond Yampol . . . . but the priest . . . . "

Skshetuski stared at the lad and rubbed his eyes as one who awakens from sleep; suddenly he felt as if something had broken within him, he grew pale as a corpse, sat up in bed and cried in a voice of thunder:

"Sir, oh sir," exclaimed the lad, frightened by the change that had taken place in the face of the knight.

"Who was with you?" cried Skshetuski, seizing the boy by the shoulder, shaking him, holding him with a clutch like iron, while he himself shook as if taken with a chill.

"I will tell," cried Jendzian, "let the priest do what he pleases. The lady was with us and she is now with Pani Vitovska."

Skshetuski grew rigid, he closed his eyes and fell back upon the pillows.

"Help!" cried Jendzian, "my master has breathed his last. Help! what have I done! Oh, that I had kept my mouth shut! My God! my most dear master, speak but one word . . . .for God's sake! the priest was right to forbid. My master! Oh, ... my master!" . . . .

"It's nothing," said Skshetuski, "where is she?"

"Praise be to God that you have regained your senses . . . . my master. It is better that I speak no more. She is with the wife of the Castellan of Sandomierz, you will see them soon . . . . any moment. . . . . Thanks be to God! . . . . only do not die, sir; they must be here. We fled to Zamost, there the Priest gave her to Pani Vitovska for property. . . . for there are insubordinate men in the army. Bohun honored her; . . . . I had much trouble on the way . . . . but I told the soldiers 'that she was a relative of Prince Yeremy,' and they respected her as such. . . . I also had to spend considerable money on the way." . . . .

Skshetuski lay motionless again, but his open eyes were directed towards the ceiling, his face was very serious and one could see that he was praying. When he had finished he rose and said:

"Give me my clothes and have the horse ready."

"Where do you intend to go?"

"Give me my clothes, quickly."

"If my master only knew, there are plenty of clothes for him, for the king ordered some before he went away, and other gentlemen also. And there are three fine horses in the stable. . . . if I only had one like them. . . . but it were better that my master should lay down and rest for awhile longer, for there is none whatever strength left in you."

"Nothing ails me, I can sit on my horse, by the living God! make haste!"

"I know well that my master's body is of iron, let it be as he commands. I only ask, my master, that you will protect me from the priest, Tsietsiskovski . . . Here are some clothes, better ones cannot be procured from the Armenian merchants. Dress yourself while I get some food for you, for I ordered the priest's servant to prepare some."

Jendzian busied himself with the food, while Skshetuski dressed himself hastily in the clothes that the king had ordered for him. From time to time he seized the lad and pressed him to his breast, and the boy told him everything from beginning. How he had met Bohun in Voldava, who was then convalescing from wounds inflicted upon him by Volodiyovski; how he had learned from him the whereabouts of the princess and how he had acquired the safe conduct; how he had gone with Volodiyovski and Zagloba to the ravines at Valadynka and how, after killing Cheremis and the witch, they had rescued the princess; and finally what danger they were in while fleeing before the soldiers of Burlay.

"That Burlay was killed by Pan Zagloba," interrupted Skshetuski, feverishly.

"He is a brave man," answered Jendzian; "I have never seen the like of him. for one is brave, another eloquent, a third frolicsome, but Pan Zagloba unites all these qualities in one person. But the worst experience we had, dear sir, was in the woods about Ploskirov when the horde pursued us. Pan Michael and Pan Zagloba remained behind in order to draw the attack upon themselves and thus delay the pursuers. I, however, rode towards Konstantinov, avoiding Zbaraj; for I thought that after they had killed the little gentleman and Pan Zagloba, they would surely pursue us in the direction of Zbaraj. I can't understand how God saved the two gentlemen. . . . I thought that they must have been killed. I and the princess slipped through between Khmyelnitski's forces who were approaching from Konstantinov, and Zbaraj, under whom the Tartars were marching."

"They did not go there immediately, for Pan Kushel beat them back. But speak faster."

"If I had only known that; but as I did not know it I pushed on with the princess between the Tartars and Cossacks, as through a defile. Fortunately the region was desolate, and nowhere did we find a living being, neither in villages nor towns, for all had fled. But I was half dead from fear that the Tartars would catch me, nor did I escape this fate either."

Skshetuski stopped dressing himself and asked: "How was that?"

"It was this way, my master. I met a division of Cossacks under Donyets, the brother of that Horpyna with whom the princess was lodged in the retreat. Fortunately I knew him well, for he had seen me with Bohun. I brought him messages from his sister, showed him the baton from Bohun, and told him all, how Bohun had sent me for the princess, and that he was waiting for me beyond Vlodava and he believed me, for he was Bohun's friend and knew that his sister was guarding the princess; I thought that he would let me pass but he said: 'Over there the general militia is gathering; you will surely fall into the hands of the Poles; stay with me; we will go to Khmyelnitski, the lady will be safest in his camp, for Khmyelnitski himself will watch over her for Bohun.' When he spoke thus I was dumbfounded for what could I answer? but I told him that Bohun was waiting for me and that my head was at stake if I did not bring the princess at once. Then he said: 'we will inform Bohun, but over there are the Poles.' I argued with him until he finally said 'I wonder why you are so afraid to go to the Cossacks— are you a traitor?' Then I saw that nothing remained but to flee during the night, for he had already begun to suspect me. I had everything in readiness for the road when Pan Pelka with some royal troops, fell upon Donyets that night."

"Pan Pelka?" cried Skshetuski, holding his breath.

"Yes, my master, he was a great soldier, too bad that he is fallen—the Lord have mercy on his soul! I do not know if anyone could lead an attacking party better than he— perhaps only Pan Volodiyovski. But Pan Pelka came and made such a weep that not a man got away and even Donyets himself was captured. A few weeks ago he was drawn by oxen to the stake—and it served him right. But even with Pan Pelka I had plenty of trouble, for he was a man who had no respect for virtue. . . . . God rest his soul! I feared that the princess, who had just been rescued from

the Cossacks, would meet a worse fate among our own men.
. . . But when I told him that she was a relative of the
Prince, it checked his designs. I must tell you, my master,
that whenever I mentioned the name of our prince, he took
off his cap and spoke of entering his service, therefore he
respected the princess and led us to the king in Zamost.
There, the priest Tsietsishovski (a very holy man) took us
under his protection and placed the princess under the guard-
ianship of Pani Vitovska."

Skshetuski took a deep breath and embraced Jendzian
heartily. "You shall be my friend, my brother, and not my
servant. But now let us get away. When ought Pani
Vitovski to arrive here?"

"She should have come a week after me. . . . it is
now ten days. . . . for eight days my master lay without
consciousness."

"Let us depart, let us depart," repeated Skshetuski, "for
my heart is bursting with joy."

But ere he had finished speaking the clatter of horses was
heard in the yard and the window was suddenly darkened
by the forms of horses and men. Through the glass Skshetuski saw first the old priest Tsietsishovski, then beside him
the emaciated faces of Zagloba, Volodiyovski, Kushel, and
other acquaintances among the red dragoons of the prince.
A shout of joy resounded, and the next moment a number
of knights headed by the priest, crowded into the room.

"Peace has been concluded at Zborov, and the siege has
been raised," exclaimed the priest.

Skshetuski had guessed this on seeing his comrades from
Zbaraj; soon he was in the arms of Zagloba, and Volodiyovski,
who embraced him in turn.

"We were informed that you were alive," exclaimed Zagloba, "but our joy is all the greater that we find you looking
so well. We have come here on purpose to see you. . . .
Yan! You have no idea what glory you have achieved and
what reward awaits you."

"The king has rewarded you," said the priest, "but the
King of Kings has still more in store for you."

"I know it already," replied Skshetuski. "God reward
you for it! Jendzian has told me all."

"And the joy did not suffocate you? that's good. Long
live Skshetuski! long live the princess!" cried Zagloba. "We
did not say a word to you, Yani, because we did not know

whether she lived. But the lad has rescued her bravely; what a clever fox! The prince awaits you both. Oh, we went for her beyond Yahorlik. I killed that infernal monster that guarded her. Those twelve boys ran away but you will overtake them. I shall have grandchildren, gentlemen. Jendzian, speak, what difficulties did you overcome? Just imagine, we two, including Pan Michael, held back the entire horde. I was the first to throw myself against the whole force. They hid in caves, but it was of no avail. Pan Michael too, stood by bravely. . . . Where is my little daughter? Give me my little daughter."

"God give you happiness, Yani, God give you happiness," said the little knight, embracing Skshetuski once more.

"God reward you for all you have done for me! I cannot thank you with words. My life and blood could not repay you," answered Skshetuski.

"That's not worth speaking of," exclaimed Zagloba. Peace is established! A miserable peace, but what could be done? we ought to rejoice that we are out of that pestilent Zbaraj. But we are delivered now, gentlemen. That was our work, and mine, for if Burlay were living yet all negotiations would be in vain. We shall go to the wedding. Then, Yani, keep your eyes open. You cannot guess what a wedding-present the prince has prepared for you? I'll tell you about it at another time. But where is my little daughter? The devil! Give me my little daughter. Bohun cannot take her away from us again; he would first have to break the fetters that bind him. Where is my dearest little daughter?"

"I was just about to mount to go to meet Pani Sandomierska," said Skshetuski. "Let us go, let us go! or I shall lose my senses."

"Hayda, gentlemen, let us ride with him, let us lose no time, Hayda!"

"Pani Sandomierska cannot be far away," said the priest.

"To horse!" cried Pan Michael.

But already Skshetuski was outside the door and threw himself upon his horse in a manner that gave no evidence of his recent illness.

Jendzian kept close to his side; he preferred not to be left alone with the priest. Pan Michael and Zagloba joined them and thus they galloped at the head of a party of nobles and red dragoons, who flew along the Toporov road like poppy leaves driven by the wind.

"Hayda!" shouted Zagloba, digging his heels into his horse.

Thus they rushed along for about ten furlongs when they beheld at a turn of the road a line of wagons and carriages escorted by a few dozens of attendants. Some of these rode ahead when they saw a body of armed men, in order to inquire who they were.

"Soldiers of the royal army," shouted Zagloba, "and whom do you escort?"

"The lady of the Pani Castellanova Sandomierska," was shouted in reply.

Skshetuski was so overcome by agitation that, not knowing what he was doing, he slid from his horse and stood tottering by the roadside. He took off his cap, perspiration ran over his temples, and the knight who had bravely faced all danger, now trembled in every limb, in sight of his happiness. Pan Michael also sprang from his saddle and supported the feeble knight in his arms.

Following their example all stood with bared heads by the roadside, while the line of wagons and carriages began to pass by them. Pani Vitovska was accompanied by a number of ladies who looked with wonder at the row of knights and soldiers, and asked each other what it all meant.

At length in the midst of the train a carriage appeared, more richly decorated than the others. Through its open window the knights beheld the dignified counteance of an elderly lady and beside her the sweet, beautiful face of the princess Kurtsevich.

"My little daughter," cried out Zagloba, throwing himself blindly against the carriage, "my little daughter, Skshetuski is here! . . . Little daughter!"

Shouts of "Halt! halt!" were heard, confusion arose, then Kushel and Volodiyovski led or rather dragged Skshetuski to the carriage. He had grown weaker and weaker, and hung with ever-increasing weight in their arms. His head sank upon his breast, he could go no further and collapsed by the step of the carriage.

A moment later the strong and beautiful arms of princess Kurtsevich raised up the weak, emaciated head of the knight.

Zagloba, observing the amazement of Pani Sandomierska cried out:

"This is Skshetuski, the hero of Zbaraj. He stole through the enemy, he saved the army, the prince, the entire Commonwealth. God bless them both! long may they live!"

"Long may they live!" shouted the nobles.

"Long may they live!" roared the dragoons, in tones of thunder that echoed over the fields of Toporov. . . .

"To Tarnopol! to the prince! to the wedding!" cried Zagloba. "Now my little daughter, your sorrows are over! . . . for Bohun there remains the executioner and the sword."

The priest had raised his eyes towards the heavens and his lips repeated the inspired utterance "They that sow in tears shall reap in joy. . . "

Skshetuski was placed in the carriage beside the princess and the retinue moved on. The day was beautiful, the oak groves and field swere bathed in sunshine. Low down on the stubble fields, on the fallow lands and higher above them, and still higher in the blue air, there waved here and there the silvery threads of spider's webs, which late in the fall cover the fields in that country as if with snow. And peace reigned all about, only the snorting of the horses in the train disturbed the general quiet.

"Pan Michael!" said Zagloba, pushing his stirrup against that of Volodiyovski, "somethng has seized me by the throat again, and holds me fast, as when Pan Podbipyenta—God grant him eternal rest!—departed from Zbaraj. But when I think that these two have found each other at last, I feel as light-hearted as if I had drunk a quart of Petertsiment wine at a draught. If married life does not become your lot, you shall in your old age educate their children. Everyone is born for some special object, Pan Michael; we two are better fitted for war than for married life."

The little knight did not answer but twirled his moustaches vigorously.

They were bound to Toporov and thence to Tarnopol where they were to join Prince Yeremy, and proceed with him to Lemberg for the wedding. On the way Zagloba told the Pani Sandomierska all that had happened recently. She learned that the king after a bloody but indecisive battle, near Zborov had made a treaty with the Khan, not a very favorable one, but which secured peace for a time to the Commonwealth. K'hmyelnitski, by virtue of the treaty, remained Hetman of the Zaporojians and had the right to select and organize a standing army of forty thousand men, from the mass of common people, after swearing an oath of fealty to the king and State.

"It is beyond doubt," said Zagloba, "that war with Khmy-elnitski will break out anew, but if our prince only receives the supreme command, then all will be right. . . . "

"Why do you not tell Skshetuski the most important news?" said the little knight, bringing his horse nearer.

"That's true," said Zagloba. "I wished to tell him at the outset, but could hardly catch my breath until now. You of course know nothing, Yani, of what happened after your departure. The prince has captured Bohun."

Skshetuski and Panna Kurtsevich were so much aston-ished at these words that they could not speak, they only raised their hands; then after a few moments Skshetuski asked:

"How, by what means?"

"The finger of God is evidenced," replied Zagloba, "noth-ing else but the finger of God. The treaty already had been concluded and we were just marching out from that pestilent Zbaraj, when the prince hastened with the cavalry to the left wing lest some horde should make an attack. . . . for the Tartars often disregard treaties. . . . Suddenly a band of three hundred horsemen attacked the entire cavalry of the prince."

"Bohun alone would dare that," exclaimed Skshetuski.

"It was he. But Cossacks cannot cope with the soldiers of Zbaraj. Pan Michael soon completely surrounded them and cut them down to the last man; Bohun was captured after being again wounded. He has no luck with Pan Michael; he himself must be convinced of that now, for this was the third encounter. Probably he was seeking death."

"It appeared," interrupted Pan Michael, "that Bohun had hastened from Valadynka to Zbaraj. It was a long journey, however, and when he learned that a treaty had already been concluded, he lost his senses from rage and disregarded every-thing."

"He who draws the sword will perish by the sword, for such is the nature of things," said Zagloba, "he is a mad Cossack, but boldest when most in danger. A quarrel arose between us and that gang of robbers on his account. We thought that war would break out anew, for the prince cried out that the treaty had been broken. Khymelnitski wanted to save Bohun, but the Khan was very much enraged at him, for he, according to the Khan's own words, 'has brought my word and my oath into contempt.' The Khan threatened

to make war upon Khmyelnitski and sent a messenger to
our prince saying that Bohun was a common robber and requesting that he be treated accordingly. It is said that it
was also the Khan's aim that the Tartars should lead away
in quiet their captives, of which they had taken so many
that they would be sold in Stambul for two hobnails a man."

"What did the prince do with Bohun?" asked Skshetuski,
impatiently.

"The prince had alreay ordered a stake to be pointed for
him when he changed his mind and said 'I will present him
to Skshetuski, he may do as he pleases with him.' Now the
Cossack is in a dungeon at Tarnopol, the barber-surgeon is
bandaging his head. My God! how often his soul tried to
run away from him! No dogs ever worried the skin of a
wolf as we have his. Pan Michael alone bit him three times.
But he's a hard nut to crack, and to tell the truth an unfortunate man. May the hangman help him! I bear him
no ill-will, though he was furiously incensed against me and
for no cause. Why, I drank with him and took his part
as if he were my equal, till he raised his hand against you,
my little daughter. I could easily have done for him at
Rozloga. But there are very few who pay good for good,
and there is little gratitude in this world. May the——"

Here Zagloba began to nod his head. "And what will
you do with him, Pan Yan?" he asked, "the soldiers say
that you will certainly make an outrider of him, for he has
a fine appearance; but I cannot believe that you will deal
with him in such a fashion."

"Certainly I shall not," answered Skshetuski, "he is a soldier and a valiant knight, and because he is unfortunate is
no reason for disgracing him with menial service."

"May God forgive him everything," said the princess.

"Amen!" said Zagloba. "He prays for death to rescue
him, and he could have found it had he not come late to
Zbaraj."

All grew silent and occupied themselves with their own
thoughts until in the distance appeared Grabova, where they
made their first halt for refreshments. There they found a
number of soldiers returning from Zborov. Pan Vitovski,
the Castellan Sandomierski, had also come there with his
regiment to meet his wife, and with him was the Chief of
Krasnostavsk Pan Pshiyemski, a number of nobles of the
general militia, who were on their way home. The court

at Grabova had been burned down as well as all the other
buildings, but the day was warm and bright; so that no
shelter was necessary, so they disposed themselves in an oak-
grove under the open sky. Ample stores of food and drink
had been brought along and the servants immediately set
about preparing supper. Pan Sandomierski ordered tents
to be pitched for the ladies and dignitaries, and soon a regular
camp was arranged. The knights crowded before the tents
to get a look at Skshetuski and the princess. Others discussed the late war; those who were not at Zbaraj, but at
Zborov, asked the prince's men for the particulars of the
siege. Everyone was joyous and gay, especially as the day
was so beautiful.

Zagloba of course, did most of the talking among the
nobles, telling for the thousandth time how he had killed
Burlay; and Jendzian among the servants who were preparing the meal. But the clever lad found a fit opportunity
to draw Skshetuski aside and humbly embracing his knees,
he said:

"My Lord! I should like to ask a favor of you."

"I could hardly refuse you anything," answered Skshetuski, "since through you I have regained what is dearest
to me."

"I thought at once," said the lad, "that your lordship
would grant me the favor."

"Speak, what is your wish?"

Jendzian's chubby face grew dark, and hatred and revenge
were reflected in his eyes.

"I ask but one favor, nothing more," said he, "and that
is that your Lordship give Bohun to me."

"Bohun?" asked Skshetuski, in great astonishment. "What
do you want to do with him?"

"It is ever in my mind, my Lord, that I get my revenge,
and that I pay him back, with compound interest, for the
disgrace he inflicted upon me in Chigrin. I knew also that
your Lordship will put him to death, and therefore I wish
to settle with him first."

Skshetuski frowned.

"It cannot be," he said with decision.

"Oh, my God! would that I had died," said Jendzian, in
piteous tones. "Have I lived only to be disgraced?"

"Ask anything else," said Skshetuski, "and I will not refuse
it, but I cannot grant this request. Go home and ask your

parents if it is not more sinful to fulfill such a vow than to give it up. Do not thrust your own revengeful hand before God's lest it fall also upon you. You should be ashamed of yourself, Jendzian! That man is praying for death and is wounded and in bondage. Do you wish to be his executioner, to torment him? do you wish to put shame upon a prisoner, or to butcher a wounded man? Why, are you a Tartar or a Cossack butcher! as I live I cannot allow this! Don't mention it to me again!"

So much power and firmness of will was evidenced in Pan Yan's voice that the lad lost all hope of gaining his request; he only said, in a sorrowful voice:

"Were he well, he could vanquish two of my size with ease, and now that he is ill, I am not permitted to have my revenge—when can I pay him back?"

"Leave vengeance to God," said Skshetuski.

The lad opened his mouth; he evidently wanted to say something more, to ask something, but Pan Yan had already turned towards the tents, before which a numerous company had assembled. Pani Vitovska sat in the centre with the princess at her side, and around them the knights. In front of them stood Zagloba, bareheaded, and engaged in telling those who had been only at Zborov all about the siege of Zbaraj. All listened to him with breathless attention; emotion was portrayed on their faces and those who had not been at Zbaraj regretted their absence. Pan Yan took a seat beside the princess and grasping her hand, pressed it to his lips; then they leaned against each other arm in arm and sat quietly. The sun was setting and gradually evening was coming on. Skshetuski listened as attentively as if something new to him was being related. Zagloba mopped his forehead and his voice grew louder. Memory or imagination pictured those terrible scenes to the knights. They beheld the ramparts surrounded by a turbulent sea of men, and the mad assaults; they heard the tumult, the howls, the thunder of cannon, the rattle of musketry; they beheld the prince in his silver armor, standing upon the ramparts amidst a shower of bullets. . . . then the suffering, the famine, those blood-red nights during which death circled like a huge spectral bird above the camp. . . . the departure of Pan Longin Podbipyenta and of Skshetuski . . . . All listened with rapt attention, at times raising their eyes to heaven, or grasping their swords, and Zagloba ended as follows:

"It is now but one grave, one great tomb, and that under it do not lie buried the honor of the Commonwealth, the flower of its knighthood, the prince, and I, and all of us, whom even the Cossacks called Zbaraj lions, is due to this man here!"

Then he pointed at Skshetuski.

"As I live, that is true!" exclaimed in one voice Marek, Sobieski and Pan Pshiyemski.

"Glory to him! honor and thanks!" shouted the assembled knights in thundering tones. "Vivat Sksehtuski! Vivat the young couple! long live the hero!" Each time they shouted more loudly.

A wave of enthusiasm spread through the assemblage. Some ran for goblets, others threw their caps in the air. The soldiers began to rattle their sabres and there arose a general shout.

"Glory! glory! long may he live! long may he live!"

Skshetuski, like a true Christian knight, bowed his head in humility; but the princess rose, shook her tresses, her cheeks aflame, and her eyes gleaming with pride, for this knight was to become her husband, and the glory of the husband falls upon the wife like the sun's light upon the earth. Late that night the assembly broke up and started away in two directions. The Vitovskis, Pan Pshiyemski and the Chief of Krasnostavsk marched with their regiments towards Toporov, while Skshetuski, with the princess and Pan Michael's squadron, went on to Tarnopol. The night was as bright as day. Myriads of stars gleamed in the heavens; the moon rose and silvered the cob-web covered fields. The soldiers began to sing; later, light mists arose from the meadows and made the whole region look like a great lake gleaming in the moonlight.

On such a night Skshetuski had gone forth from Zbaraj, and now on such another night he felt the heart of the princess beating against his own.

EPILOGUE.

This historic tragedy, however, did not end either at Zbaraj or at Zborov. Even the first act was not concluded. Two years later the Cossacks rose again in rebellion against the Commonwealth. Khymelnitski took the field mightier than ever before, and with him marched the Khan with all his hordes, and the same leaders who before surrounded Zbaraj—the wild Tukhay Bey, Urum Murza, and Artim, Girey, Nur-ed-Din, and Galgi, and Amurad, and Subagazi. Mighty pillars of flame and lamentations of people marked their path. Thousands of warriors covered the fields, filled the forests; from half a million throats there issued war-cries, and it seemed to the people that the last hour of the Commonwealth had come.

But the Commonwealth too, had shaken off its lethargy. The chancellor's former policy of establishing peace by means of treaties had been abandoned. It was now clear that the sword alone could insure peace of long duration. So, when the king advanced against the inundating enemy, an army of one hundred thousand soldiers and nobles marched with him, besides swarms of irregulars and camp-servants.

Not one of the characters of our story was missing. There was Prince Visnyovyetski with his entire division, in which, as formerly, served Skshetuski and Volodiyovski; there were the two hetmans Pototski and Kalinovski, who then had been ransomed from the Tartars. There was also Colonel Stefan Charmyetski, subsequently the scourge of King Charles Gustavus of Sweden, and Pshiyemski commander of the whole artillery; and general Ubald, Pan Artsishevski, and the Chief of Krasnostavsk; and his brother, the Chief of Yavrov, afterwards King Yan III, and Ludvig Veyher, the voyevoda of Pomerania, and Jacob voyevoda of Marburg, and the standard bearer Konetspolski; and Prince Dominik Z slavski, the bishops and dignitaries of the Crown—senators—the whole Commonwealth with the chief leader, the King.

On the fields of Berestechka at last myriads of the hostile armies met, and one of the greatest battles in the history of

the world was fought. Throughout Europe its echoes resounded.

It lasted for three days. During the first two days fortune hung in the balance, on the third a general engagement
decided the battle. Prince Yeremy began that engagement.
At the head of the entire left wing, bareheaded and without
arms, he swept like a cyclone against enormous masses formed
of mounted Zaporojians, from all the Crimea, Tartars,
Nogoais, Byalogorods and Silistrian and Rumelian Turks,
Urumbalis, janıssaries, Serbs, Wallachians, Peryerovs, and
other wild warriors gathered from the Ural the Caspian Sea
and the marshes of Moeotis as far as the Danube.

As a river loses itself in the foaming waves of the sea, so
the squadrons of the prince were lost in that ocean of enemies. A cloud of dust rolled over the plain like a whirlwind and enveloped the combatants.

The rest of the army and the king looked on upon this
superhuman struggle, and the vice chancellor Leshchynski
raised aloft the wood of the Holy Cross and blessed with it
the vanished squadrons.

Meanwhile on the other side the entire Cossack camp, consisting of about two hundred thousand men, moved slowly
against the royal army, issuing from the woods like a dragon,
and vomiting fire from their cannon.

But ere the bulk of the enemy had issued from the clouds
of dust in which Yeremy's squadrons had disappeared, horsemen began one by one to drop away from their ranks, then
hundreds, thousands, and tens of thousands, and these all
rushed to the hill held by the Khan and his chosen guards.
The wild masses fled in mad terror and disorder—the Polish
squadrons chasing them. Thousands of Cassacks and Tartars covered the battle-field; among them, pierced through
by a double-handled sword, lay the mortal enemy of the Poles
and the faithful ally of the Cossacks, the wild, brave Tukhay
Bey.

The terrible prince had triumphed.

The king looked upon the prince's victory with the eve
of a leader and determined to crush the hordes before the
Cossacks could arrive. The entire army was set in motion,
all the cannon roared, spreading death and destruction. Soon
the brother of the Khan, the splendid Amurad fell with a
bulllet in his breast. The hordes broke out in a howl of
terror. The Khan, who had been wounded at the very out-

set of the battle, looked with dismay upon the field. From the distance amid the thunder of cannon came Pshiyemski and the king himself; the earth groaned beneath the weight of the onrushing cavalry.

Islam-Girey stricken with terror did not await the attack, but fled, and after him all the hordes, the Volosha, the Urumbalo, the Zaporojian Cossack cavalry, the Silistrian Turks, and the Turkish converts fled like a cloud before the tempest.

Khymelnitski in desperation overtook the fugitives, and begged and implored the Khan to return to the battle, but the Khan, bellowing with rage at the sight of him ordered the Tartars to seize him and bind him to a horse, and thus he was borne along.

The Cossack camp alone was left, the commander of that, Colonel of Kropivenski, Dziedzial, did not know what had happened to Khmyelnitski; seeing however the defeat and shameful flight of all the hordes, he stopped the advance, and then retreating, he took up a position upon the swampy banks of the Pleshov.

A terrible storm arose, immense torrents of water poured down from the heavens; "God was washing the land after a just battle."

A drizzling rain lasted for several days and the royal army rested after the battle of the previous day. The Cossacks seized the occasion to surround their camp with ramparts and thus transform it into a gigantic, moveable fortress.

When fair weather returned a siege began: the strangest ever seen.

One hundred thousand royal troops besieged the army of Dziedzial which numbered two hundred thousand men.

The king was short of cannon, provisions and ammunition. Dziedzial had an inexhaustible supply of powder and provisions, besides seventy cannon of heavier and lighter calibre.

But at the head of the royal army was the king. The Cossacks had not Khmyelnitski.

The royal army was flushed with recent victory; the Cossacks were in despair.

Several days passed. All hope of the return of Khmyelnitski and the Khan vanished.

Then negotiations were entered into. The Cossack leaders came and bowed their heads humbly before the king, pleaded for mercy, haunted the tents of the Senators, clung to their garments, and promised to find Khmyelnitski, wherever he was even under the ground and deliver him to the king.

52

The heart of Yan Kazimier was not obdurate. He was willing to let the "blacks" and soldiers return to their homes, provided they would surrender all the chiefs, for these he intended to detain until Khmyelnitski should be given up. But such a compact was not agreeable to the officers, who did not look for forgiveness in view of their many offences. Hence the struggle continued even while the negotiations were going on; desperate attacks were made, and Polish and Cossack blood flowed in torrents.

The Cossacks fought during the day, bravely and with the courage of despair, but at night swarms of them stood before the royal camp and howled for mercy.

Dziedzial was inclined to give in to the royal demands, and was willing to sacrifice his own head if he could save the people and soldiers. But dissensions arose in the Cossack camp. Some wished to surrender, others wished to defend themselves to the death; but all of them were planning how to escape from the camp. But this seemed an impossibility even to the boldest. The camp was enclosed by the forks of the river and by great swamps. They might defend themselves for years, but to leave the camp there was only one road, the road through the royal army. But no one thought of that road.

The negotiations dragged on interrupted by battles. The dissensions among the Cossacks grew apace. As the outcome of one these Dziedzial was deposed from his office and a new leader was chosen.

His name gave new courage to the despairing Cossacks; the echo of it in the royal camp stirred in the hearts of several knights half-forgotten memories of past sufferings and misfortunes.

Bohun was the new leader's name. He had previously won high distinction among the Cossacks both in the council and in battle. The public sentiment had always indicated him as the successor of Khmyelnitski. Bohun was the first of the Cossack commanders to appear with the Tartars on the field of Berestechka at the head of fifty thousand men. He took part in the three-days cavalry combat, and though defeated with the Khan and his hordes, by Yeremy, he had managed to keep the greater part of his army together and to bring it safely into camp. Now the party opposed to the negotiations made him commander-in-chief in place of Dziedzial hoping that he might be able to save the camp and the army.

Indeed the young commander would not hear of negotiations, he only wanted battle and bloodshed, even though he should drown in the blood. But soon he was convinced that with the troops under him it would be impossible to cut a way through the army of the king. He therefore hit upon another plan. History has preserved the memory of his unparalled efforts, considered by contemporaries worthy of a hero, and which might have saved the army and the "blacks."

Bohun determined to bridge the swamps of Plesov and thus enable the besieged to retreat over them.

Entire forests fell beneath the axes of the Cossacks and sank into the swamp. Wagons, tents, skins, coats, were thrown into the swamp, the bridge grew longer day by day. Nothing seemed impossible to this commander.

The king delayed the assault in order to avoid bloodshed. But when he saw this gigantic work he recognized that delay was dangerous and issued an order that the army be in readiness at evening for the final assault.

No one in the Cossack camp knew of this intention. The bridge had been pushed onward during the night, and in the morning, Bohun, with the chiefs, rode out to examine the work.

It was Monday, July 7th, 1651. The morning was misty, dawn in the east was blood red, the sun rose looking sickly and bronze-colored; a peculiar bloody glow was in the woods and over the water.

From the Polish camp they were driving the horses to pasture; the Cossack camp was astir and resounded with the voices of men. Fires were burning, the morning meal was being prepared. All saw the departure of Bohun with his suite and the cavalry following them, with whom the commander intended to fall upon the Voyevoda of Bratslav, who harassed the rear of the camp and was injuring the Cossack works with cannon.

The "blacks" viewed this marching forth with calmness and even with confidence. The eyes of thousands followed the young warrior and the lips of thousands sent after him their benediction:

"God bless you, Falcon!"

The commander, the suite, and the cavalry had reached the edge of the forest; for a moment they gleamed in the morning sun and then began to disappear in the forest.

All at once a terrified voice shouted at the entrance to the camp:

"Men save yourselves!"

"The chiefs are fleeing!" shouted others. "The chiefs are fleeing!" repeated hundreds and thousands of voices.

A murmur ran through the crowds as a wind rushes through the woods, and suddenly a terrible, unearthly cry burst from two hundred thousand throats.

"Fly! fly! the Poles! The chiefs have fled!"

Masses of men rushed along like a roaring torrent. Fires were trodden out, wagons upset, tents torn to pieces. All were crowding, pushing, squeezing, and trampling. A terrible panic bereft all of their senses. Heaps of corpses soon obstructed the way; these had been trampled to death amid roars, and shouts, and groans. Crowds rushed towards the bridge and swamp and pushed one another from the bridge. The drowning ones, locked in deadly embraces and howling to heaven for mercy, sank in the cold, slimy mud. On the bridge a battle for place was fought. The waters of the Pleshov were filled with corpses. The Nemesis of history now took terrible payment for Pilavyets and Berestechka.

The fearful clamor reached the ears of the youthful commander, and he knew at once what it meant, but in vain did he return at once to the camp, in vain did he confront the crowds with hands raised to heaven. His voice was lost in the roar of thousands, the frightful torrent of the fleeing crowds carried him away with his horse, his suite, and the cavalry, to destruction.

The royal army was astonished at the commotion, which at first was mistaken for a desperate attack; one scarcely could believe the evidence of his own eyes.

But when the astonishment had passed a few moments later the squadrons did not even wait for an order to attack, but rushed towards the masses of the enemy. In front of all swept the dragoons like a whirlwind and at the head the little colonel swung his sabre above him.

It was a day of rage, of vengeance, and judmgent. . . Whoever was not crushed to death, or drowned, perished by the sword. The forks of the river were so filled with blood that one could not tell whether water or blood was flowing. The panic-stricken crowds pushed one another into the water and drowned. The ravages of death in the woods were all the more terrible, for some of the rabble commenced to defend themselves furiously. Battles raged in the swamp, on the field, in the forest. The Voyevoda of Bratslav cut off the retreat of the fugitives. In vain did the king issue orders that the soldiers be restrained. Compassion was dead; the slaughter, the like of which the oldest veterans had not seen, and at the memory of which the hair stood on their heads in later times, lasted until night.

When at last darkness fell upon the earth, the victors themselves were shocked by their bloody work; they sang no Te Deum; and no tears of joy, but tears of regret and sorrow flowed from the eyes of the worthy king.

Thus ended the first act of the bloody drama, whose author was Khmyelnitski.

But Bohun did not lose his life with others on that dreadful day. Some say that seeing the defeat he saved himself by flight, others say that a well-known knight protected him, but no one could get at the truth.

This much is certain that in the wars that followed, his name was often mentioned among those of the most famous Cossack leaders. A shot fired by some enemy, struck him a few years later, but even this did not put an end to his existence.

After the death of Prince Yeremy Vishnyovyetski, brought on by military hardships, Bohun came to rule over the greater part of Lubni, which fell away from the Commonwealth. It was said that afterwards he would not recognize the authority of Khmyelnitski. The latter, cursed by his own people, and broken sought foreign aid, but the proud Bohun refused all protection and was ready to defend his Cossack independence with his sword.

It was said that a smile never lighted the countenance of this extraordinary man. He did not live in Lubni but in a village which he rebuilt from its ashes, and was called Rosloga. There also he is supposed to have died.

Civil wars survived him and continued for a long time. Later came the plague, and the Swedes; the Tartars made constant incursions in the Ukraine, and bore numbers of the people into slavery. The Commonwealth was devastated, so also was the Ukraine. Wolves howled about the cinders of former cities, and the once blooming land became one vast cemetery. Hatred grew in the men's hearts and poisoned kindred blood.

Printed in the United States
215017BV00001B/7/A